LONELY ALPHA

THE POISONVERSE

OLIVIA LEWIN

Copyright © 2023 by Olivia Lewin

All rights reserved.

No part of this book may be reproduced in any form or by any electronic or mechanical means, including information storage and retrieval systems, without written permission from the author, except for the use of brief quotations in a book review.

This is a work of fiction intended for adults aged 18+. Names, characters, places, and incidents described within are either the product of the author's imagination, or are used fictitiously. Any resemblance to actual persons is entirely coincidental.

Published by Reber Media Company

Cover design by Marie Mackay

❀ Created with Vellum

CONTENT

HOLD UP! Is there anything I should know as a reader?

> Lonely Alpha is an omegaverse with 18+ content, including both FF and MM spice. MMFFM, with AAAOA pack dynamic.

> It's in Canadian English! Expect colour instead of color and some other regional differences!

What about content warnings?

> Violence, knife and gun violence, attempted sexual assault, attempted strangulation, violence between love interests due to flashback/trauma (resolved quickly)

> Via flashbacks: depictions of emotional, physical, psychological abuse, torture, house fire

> Minor depictions of: drinking and drunkenness, drug use and detox, rude comments on weight

And for spicy sexual content, there's: nesting, knotting, heat, light knife play, BDSM, breeding kink (no pregnancy), pegging

If you need more clarification, feel free to email me!

olivia@lewinauthor.com

Warnings for all my books also live at: www.olivialewin.com/contentwarnings

ONE

LEIGHTON

"Why the hell did you let her into my apartment?"

I could hardly take my eyes off the omega sitting on my couch, not even to hiss my question at Liberty.

Liberty was focused on my uninvited guest as well, her candy apple red bag of cleaning supplies sitting on my small dining table.

"Look, you haven't been up close and personal with her yet," Liberty said defensively.

"What is *that* supposed to mean?"

We were both keeping our voices hushed, although a glass door separated the breakfast nook from the living room where the omega sat. Her gaze was focused down, her posture prim and proper as she perched on the edge of my black leather couch. Liberty hadn't even thought to get her name before she'd let her in.

"You know that feeling you get when you look at someone and realize they would do anything to get their way?"

Heaving a sigh, I turned to her. "Libby, the woman on my

couch is a five-foot-tall omega who can't be more than twenty-one years old. What was she going to do to you?"

Liberty still had one eye on the omega when she answered me, her weight shifting nervously from foot to foot. "Talk to me again when you've tried to stand in her damn way."

Admittedly, it was concerning that my housekeeper, best friend, and assistant was this freaked out. She wasn't unfamiliar with dangerous men and women—if she was easily unnerved, she wouldn't have done well working for me. However, I was having trouble seeing what she saw.

"Fine. Let anyone in my apartment without permission again, and I fire you."

She snorted, grabbing her cleaning supplies and heading through the kitchen toward the condo's front door. Her spine was straight, watching my guest until she couldn't anymore. "Who would replace me? Toss out these empty threats all you want, Leigh. You know I'm irreplaceable," she teased.

Liberty fled like the hounds of hell were nipping at her heels before I could respond, my front door slamming behind her.

When I looked back at the omega, she was looking at me.

Blue eyes caught and held mine, her eyelashes thick and dark. Honey brown hair fell in waves around her face, the strands so long they brushed the couch cushion she sat on. A dark dress hugged her curves before flowing out from her waist, the style ultra-feminine with ruffles and lace. She wore dark flats adorned with bows.

Paying closer attention, I tried to pinpoint what had unnerved Liberty.

The way she held herself was poised but tense, her hands on the couch like she was ready to push to her feet and run. A bandage wrapped around one hand, giving no sign of what the injury was. Her dress was discoloured in places, the stains barely visible on the dark fabric and hidden by ruffles. Those flats were caked in dirt and sand, bits falling off and dirtying my shag rug.

And her eyes...

I blinked first.

She *was* surprisingly unnerving to look at, after all.

Pushing through the glass doors and into the living room, I strode across the open-concept space until I was standing in front of her. We were separated by my glass coffee table, adorned with a display of fake florals in whites and blacks. I took only shallow breaths, not wanting my impression of her to be influenced by the siren call of her omega scent.

The less I inhaled, the less it would affect me. I had a bad feeling about the hints of chocolate and coconut I caught from her.

"Who are you?" I asked, crossing my arms over my chest.

Closer, I could see a thick scar slashing through her left eyebrow. Whatever gave it to her had almost taken out her eye.

"Kiara," she said.

Short fingers tucked a strand of hair behind her ear. The movement of her hair wafted her scent toward me, making it impossible to avoid. That coconut and chocolate scent was heavy and sweet. It called to me, admittedly, and tempted me to see if it smelled even sweeter between her legs.

I raised an eyebrow, used to keeping my reactions off my face. "I'm going to need more information than that, after you barged into my home."

"There was no barging," she denied. "The housekeeper let me in."

I couldn't respond to that because it was technically correct. It wasn't as if I could accuse her of intimidating Libby into doing what she wanted.

"Give me something else, or get out," I said.

"It's a long story, but you need to dark bond me."

What?

For a second, I thought I'd gotten lost in her soft, lilting voice and hadn't heard correctly. Then I caught a flash of something in her eyes—desperation was the closest descriptor I could come up with. Her teeth sank into her bottom lip.

What had her so desperate she would ask for a dark bond?

They weren't a bond omegas *wanted*. Fuck, it was illegal for me to dark bond an omega like her. That kind of connection gave the alpha complete control. Kiara would have to listen to every command I gave her, and she'd never met me before.

"You need to leave," I said.

Rounding the coffee table and reaching for her shoulder, I froze before we could touch. This close, I spotted things I hadn't noticed from afar.

The dark spots on her dress were definitely blood. Faint scents were on her, lessened with chemicals like she'd tried to use dampener on her clothing. That wasn't what was most telling, though.

Just above the neckline of her dress, above one of those stains, was a smear of dark red upon her ample cleavage. It was flaking off, falling down into her clothes.

She stared between my outstretched hand and my face until she glanced down at her chest. Horror grew in her expression and she jumped up, scrambling back toward the glass windows.

"I can explain that," she said, her voice wobbling.

Could she? Or would it all be lies? I doubted I had a truthful, law-abiding omega in my house if she was half-drenched in blood and asking for a dark bond.

What were my options here? Calling the police was the most reasonable thing to do. They were the ones who could test that blood and figure out what had happened to cause it.

Going against my better judgement, I didn't pull my phone from my pocket.

"Go ahead, then," I demanded. "Explain."

She flinched at my tone, and a flash of regret stabbed me.

"I didn't mean to do it," she said. "I promise, I didn't."

As a corporate fixer—one who dealt with plenty of under the table business—I'd heard that more than once. That gleam of panic in her baby blues was familiar.

"Tell me what you did, Kiara."

One of her hands pressed to her sternum, the other stroking through her hair. Fidgeting, like she was about to lie. She didn't look away from me as she spoke, trying to sell her words as truth.

"A man in my apartment building attacked me, so I hit him with the fire extinguisher. I didn't think he'd bleed so much or get so... hurt."

That was when she glanced away, and I saw what Liberty had.

She did have the look of someone who was dangerous when you stood in her way.

I wonder what the man did to her? He must have been standing between her and something she wanted desperately.

Even though I didn't quite believe it was as simple as that, a quiet rage boiled in my stomach on her behalf. No one should dare rough up an omega.

"And then I ran," she continued, "and just kept running. That was how Soren found me."

Of course. *Soren.*

"Fuck," I growled.

Running a hand through my straight black hair, I fumbled in my pocket for my phone. No missed calls. Trust Soren to send a crazy omega to my house and not even give me a fucking heads up.

He was what you could call... eccentric. Meddling. Annoying as fuck. I was unfortunately stuck with him because of my in-depth knowledge of some of his many crimes. He never let me forget my place as his well-paid and well-connected dog.

"Why did Soren send you here?" I asked.

She shrugged. The midafternoon sun shone through the window around her, beginning to peek around the neighbouring high-rise buildings. It gave her a halo, making her ample curves seem pillowy and innocent.

Kiara was *not* innocent. I knew that much.

"He said you'd be able to help me. With the dark bond." She tacked on the clarification.

"I will not be dark bonding anyone."

Her plush lips parted and she looked like she was about to plead, but I tapped Soren's contact info and brought my phone to my ear.

He made me wait until the fifth ring before picking up.

"Leigh-Leigh, darling, to what do I owe the pleasure?" he asked.

His voice was silky smooth, a tool he used to con the world into believing he was a songbird and not a snake.

"You know what. Why did you send her here, Soren?"

"Oh, Kiara? She needs an alpha. You're available. Since you're not in a pack and not registered as silver status, a dark bond is the only kind you can experience, after all. I thought you would appreciate it."

As a packless alpha, I couldn't bond an omega to me with a normal bond. I'd also never find a scent match omega—something I was more than happy with.

If I'd opted in to silver status, I would have been able to experience either, but it was always too much hassle for me. The process was irritating. The Institute tried to talk you out of it, preferring alphas and omegas to be opted into pack dynamics and not the one-on-one bonds of silver status. It was never worth it when I didn't plan to bond an omega anyway.

Dark bonds were different.

I could bite her right here and now, and the bond would stick.

It would be illegal to do it against her will, but if she gave me permission that was a nonissue.

"You're a nuisance," I muttered before I could stop myself.

My spine stiffened, and I internally cursed for talking back to Soren. I could almost see his feral grin in front of me right now. He was carefree and smirking right until the second you tried to disobey him.

Then he showed you the reason he was a billionaire who had dirt on everyone in New Oxford.

"At the end of the day, Leigh-Leigh, who you bond isn't my business," he said nonchalantly. "However, you're expected to keep Kiara safe and in your vicinity. She's useful to me. Is that clear?"

"Crystal," I grit out.

"I expect to be showered with gifts the next time we see each other, darling. You know how delicate my feelings are. Being called a nuisance is like a stake to the heart."

Soren wanted for nothing, but if gifts would appease him, I would find something to match the horrendous decor of his Citrine Hills mansion. I would hate every minute of catering to him, but working for him was one of the many things in my life I had no choice but to do.

"Of cour—"

He cut me off with the beep of the line going dead.

My gaze rose to Kiara again. She had watched the interaction with interest, that hand still oddly placed on her sternum while the other hung by her side. With a few taps of my phone, the front door deadbolt was locking with a loud buzz and the alarm system was engaged.

"Looks like you're staying," I said.

Her expression brightened, hand finally dropping from her torso. She'd taken one step toward me when I held up a hand.

"Not to get dark bonded. You're staying because Soren wants you safe, and I've been saddled with that responsibility."

"No, you need to—"

I cut off her objection. "If you try to leave, the alarm is going to go off. I'll promise you this—being in here is going to be far more comfortable than trying to escape, dark bond or not."

Her jaw set, teeth grinding together. Kiara didn't seem pleased with this compromise.

Well, she could join the fucking club.

I wasn't going to do anything that would put my job with Soren in jeopardy, not when so much was riding on it. What the criminal billionaire wants, he gets. "I'll show you to the room you'll be staying in and find you some clothes. We're going to need to do something about the bloody dress."

If only Liberty were still here. Collecting samples and eliminating blood stains was her specialty.

I didn't wait for Kiara to follow as I strode into my office, where I would pull the couch out into a bed for her to stay.

Indefinitely.

Fuck me.

TWO

KIARA

Soren had said her name was Leighton Winston.

She hadn't bothered to introduce herself, too busy reaming me out for arriving here in the first place. The name I'd been told suited her, though. It was regal and uptight, hinting at old money. It was the kind of name I'd expect to find in a Gossip Girl novel.

Leighton herself wouldn't be out of place in Gossip Girl either.

Her black hair was pin straight, the cut perfectly angled to highlight her features. The clothes she wore were ironed crisp—a bright white blazer and slim leg trousers with a fashionable belt. A green blouse beneath the blazer coordinated with the vibrant green of her eyes and made her light smattering of freckles stand out.

She'd removed her shoes, wearing only a pair of socks, and I was trying not to be self-conscious about keeping mine on. My family wore shoes throughout the house, only taking them off in our bedrooms. It was the only way I'd ever known to do it. It seemed my family's habits might not be the most common.

I tailed after her slowly, brushing my hands nervously down

my dress. The fabric was stiff from the dried blood, my skin pulling tight where it was flaking off me. I didn't want to take it off. This dress was a reminder of why I was here, and I didn't know where she was going to find clothes that fit me anyway.

Leighton was slim with narrow hips and shoulders, and I was not.

"There's an attached bathroom where you can shower and I'll set up the pull-out couch for you to sleep on," Leighton said.

She was brusque and business-like. Her lips were turned down into a scowl, each movement sharp as she grabbed a towel from a small linen closet. When she tried to hand it to me, I stared at it.

This predicament wasn't going to work for me.

I'd come here for one reason. To get a life-saving bond. A dark bond. I should have known I'd be better off asking for one on the street, but Soren had been convincing.

He must be like that with everyone. Leighton had been seconds away from tossing me out on my ass and was now holding me captive because of what he'd said on the phone.

I ignored the tightness in my stomach over the thought of asking anyone other than this woman for a bond.

"Take the towel, Kiara. Wash off the blood and muse over your situation in the shower. I don't know what you did to get to this point, but I doubt it was as simple as a neighbour attacking you."

Irritation raced through me and I did my best to keep my expression demure, the kind of sad smile that would fit the frilly dress I wore.

Sure, I'd lied about the neighbour.

What I'd escaped was way worse.

Pressing my hand to my sternum, I took comfort in the stiff knife I had tucked between my breasts. Its sharp edges sliced and poked my skin if I shifted wrong. Some of the blood on the dress was mine, but it was a small price to pay for the safety of a weapon.

I grabbed the towel.

Her scent was on it, and I would have to pretend I was unaffected by the vanilla cream aroma. This entire apartment smelled like her, no one else's scent present except hints of the housekeeper's. I would have to make sure I erased all those hints, scent marking this house as mine. I felt a primal need to do so immediately.

"Is there soap?" I asked, peering into the bathroom.

"Yes."

"Is it scent free?"

She scoffed. "No. I don't keep scent free soap."

My nose crinkled. It was like I could already smell the artificial berries and florals of normal soaps. They'd drown my scent and make it impossible to claim her like I wanted to.

I didn't know why the idea of not being able to rub my scent all over her was so offensive. My instincts raged, though, throwing a fit that culminated in me releasing a low whine.

Leighton's gaze snapped to mine and I froze.

My heart rate increased until it thudded in my ears. I waited for the spike of her aura, accompanied by a command that I not be so brazen. My father had put me in contact with a few alphas —all interactions supervised and followed by discipline if I did anything wrong.

Any time I'd reacted with a whine or whimper, I'd been intimidated and berated.

I had a flash of memory of an alpha bodyguard with a scent of overpowering cedar. He'd gotten close to me on the cusp of my heat, hours before I was due to take the drugs that put me to sleep. A single touch of his hand on my shoulder had been enough to have me whimpering, unbidden lust rushing through me.

His aura had flared so strongly I'd fought to keep down the tears in my eyes. If I cried in the presence of an alpha, my father's discipline after the fact was far worse.

"Don't be so needy," the alpha had growled. *"Alphas don't want an omega who needs to be attended to like a fucking child."*

I waited for a similar sentiment from Leighton.

As seconds wore on, I chewed on my bottom lip and clutched the folded towel closer to my chest. I itched to touch the firm edge of the knife's handle but settled for focusing on the feel of it against my skin.

There was no flare of aura to keep me cowed.

In fact, her aura was different in general. The weight of it was like a soft blanket over me, her essence all-encompassing. Her aura was out more than any male alphas I'd met, allowing me to feel her and how she didn't mean any harm.

"Fine," she muttered finally. "I'll get the scent free soap from the master bathroom."

She spun on her heel and left me reeling.

She was... giving me what I wanted.

No one had ever done that before.

Leighton didn't know me at all, and she'd listened to my involuntary complaint and took it to heart.

My body had a visceral reaction as I waited for her to return. Every inch of my skin prickled in anticipation of touch. Arousal pooled in my core. That had happened before, yes. But I'd always been scared of that reaction.

I was a needy omega.

Alphas didn't want that.

This time, I wasn't scared and there was no sour tinge of fear marring my arousal. I fidgeted with anticipation of Leighton's return, and I wasn't disappointed when she did.

Her nostrils flared, sucking in a breath of my heightened

scent. She wasn't furious or disgusted. The bright green of her irises grew smaller and smaller as her pupils expanded.

I loved the heavy dose of vanilla cream I got from her.

It made me almost weak in my desire.

"Here's the soap."

She refused to hand anything to me directly. Leighton looked me over from head to toe, left the body wash and hair products on the couch, and closed the office door tightly behind her.

She was reacting to me the same way as I was to her. We would end up with more than a bond of convenience—this could *be* something.

All I had to do was make her see it.

Hot water slid down my curves, but I trembled. Red-tinted liquid circled the drain, and I clutched my decorative knife in my hand.

Adrenaline was wearing off.

Reality was crashing in, stripping me of my false bravado.

"What do I do?" I whispered to the knife, turning it over as the shower purged blood from the curls and indents of the design.

There was no answer the inanimate object could give, despite it being my only companion.

My body ached and wounds stung as the events of the day were rinsed off, leaving only the aftermath. A couple of bruises on my arms. Scraped knees. Minor knife wounds on my abdomen where I'd been hiding the weapon. An achy wrist, vaguely throbbing shoulder, and a gash through the palm of my left hand.

I struggled to process the physical effects, and the mental ones were completely out of my league. I'd gone from Jonathan to Soren to Leighton in less than twelve hours, passed around like a little omega toy. My father had always said that's what I would be.

But Leighton didn't want me.

It shouldn't make my heart clench and stomach tighten, but it did. She was the only one I'd ever wanted, an alpha above any of the few I'd met. Her aura soothed instead of intimidated. Her presence felt comforting and there was nothing I wanted more than her claiming mark on my neck.

She could save me with it.

"I need the bond," I murmured.

The sharp knife slipped from my fingers, dropping to clatter on the porcelain tub. I leaned to pick it up, my muscles protesting, when I heard a sharp knock on the door.

Freezing, I waited for her to barge in.

She didn't. "I left clothes for you on the couch. If they don't fit, let me know. We'll get you some of your own tomorrow."

She's leaving?

All alphas I'd met would have jumped at the chance to intimidate me when I was extra vulnerable.

Her footsteps receded but I stayed still until my half-bent position left blood rushing to my head. Reaching for the knife, I hissed when the edge pierced my skin once again. More tainted water circled the drain, and I grabbed the weapon properly the second time around.

"I thought we were friends," I said. "But I guess friends do hurt each other occasionally, don't they? This feels kind of one-sided. What have I done to hurt you?"

My fingers brushed the hilt until I caught on a piece of paint that was threatening to flake. I was sure my knife would agree this tit for tat was warranted.

Besides, if the blade ever got back to my father, I wanted him furious at its condition.

Picking paint off with my nail, I continued until a small portion of the hilt was silver again, metal bare.

"We're even."

I placed the knife down on the edge of the tub and washed

myself, the shivers finally subsided. The water was cooling rapidly, but my skin never prickled from the cold. My blood ran hot as I thought of Leighton.

She was everything.

Another level of perfection. Terse but kind. Attractive in a way none of the other alphas I'd met had been.

She'd be the second friend I ever had—the first being this knife. Then, she would become so much more than that.

My alpha.

Soren must have sent me here because he thought I could convince her, and I could.

When I was dried off, I found a pair of sweatpants and a t-shirt on the couch. They would be about four sizes too big for Leighton, but they were almost too tight on me.

I didn't put my bra back on, the fabric soaked, so I thought at first there was nowhere to put my weapon. Leaving it behind made dread creep into the edges of my vision, greying it out.

Palming the handle, I slid it down the side of my thigh, sliding the blade under the waistband of my panties. The thickness of the handle kept it from falling, combined with how tight the pants were on me. With the shirt pulled down, you could hardly see the bulge where it sat.

With my safety assured, I steeled myself to step into the living room once again.

She was out there, waiting to learn how much she could gain from dark bonding me.

And I planned to show her.

THREE

LEIGHTON

The only clothes I had to fit Kiara were sweatpants and a t-shirt.

There was something deep in my core that curled pleasantly when I saw her first come out in the outfit. The shirt tightened around her breasts, the ample flesh bouncing in a way that mine didn't. My sweatpants fit her like a glove, and I made every possible effort to avoid looking at her ass.

I still had a bad feeling about her.

Being tempted by her body and coconut chocolate scent was asking for trouble when I already had enough of that on my doorstep. I'd been hoping she would use the gardenia scented body wash in the second bathroom, but when that little whine had pulled from her in complaint...

I had to give her the scent free soap.

Now she was getting her natural perfume all over my couch. I had a feeling it would be best if I spritzed it down with scent eliminating cleaner before I sat on the furniture again.

I tossed my phone back and forth between my hands as I mused over what to do about her.

Soren had told me to keep her, so I kept her.

It sounded fucked up, but at the same time, she hadn't tried to leave. Was I holding her hostage if I'd never physically stopped her from escaping? I bet she was still going to try and convince me to dark bond her, so my most pressing concern was finding out why she'd made that request.

Oh, and figuring out how I was going to sleep, because I sure as fuck wasn't letting my guard down around her.

"Are we going to sit here in silence all night? Could you at least get me a book?" she asked.

I punched a button on the TV remote, tossing it to her. She caught it, staring at the device. "Watch something. I'm going to go make a call."

Kiara's fingers brushed reverently over the remote as she nodded. I watched as she fumbled for which button to press, clearly not used to using one. I guess where she lived didn't have cable or movie streaming.

Heading into my master suite, I closed and locked the door behind me.

There was one person I could call, but I despised asking for help. Especially from him. He already saw me at my most vulnerable, though, so he might be the only one I could ask about this. Ambrose knew secrets about me no one else did.

Like the secret that we were sleeping together.

My world would implode if it became common knowledge. Leighton Winston, fucking an alpha in her brother's rejected scent match pack.

My brother wouldn't care—he was happily mated to a completely different pack, so he'd only get pouty that he hadn't been told—but the world would. Tabloids would play it as a family drama, and mother would rain fiery fury down on me.

Ambrose's pack wouldn't be pleased to learn about it either, but it wouldn't have quite the same consequences as it would for me.

Despite my hesitance, I called Ambrose. His heavy voice spoke almost before the phone had rung, picking up immediately. "Hello, Leighton."

I fought the shiver of arousal he sent down my spine. Most of my memories of him saying my name involved compromising positions and rope bondage.

"I need a favour."

"Anything."

He agreed so readily. I had to sit down on the bed because I was bouncing, the careful composure I showed the world shattering under his attention.

Ambrose represented what I could have had, if I didn't spend my life at the beck and call of two narcissists. If I'd put myself first instead of caring about appearances and my job above everything else.

"Come over. I have a... guest."

There was a low rumbling growl from his end of the line. "Are you safe?"

"Perfectly. I'm not going to explain over the phone."

If Soren didn't have my phone bugged, I was sure my mother did. Maybe both of them. Some of my clients may have even tried to get their grubby hands on my technology, and I was no wizard with it. Liberty tried her best to implement protections, but she also was not an expert.

"I'll be there in ten minutes."

Ambrose hung up. He'd never been to my condo, and yet he didn't ask for my address. I wasn't going to question how he knew things about me he shouldn't.

And still nobody knew the things that truly mattered. I sighed.

I left my bedroom to find Kiara in the living room again, aggressively punching buttons on the remote. A violent movie played, some kind of thriller, and the screen was so dark I couldn't tell you who the actor in it was. It was a miracle they hadn't reshot the scene after firing the lighting techs.

"Um, can you turn on the subtitles?"

She held the remote out to me with a limp wrist.

As I pressed the correct combo of buttons to get subtitles on, she watched my fingers. It was like she was absorbing the knowledge of how it worked. Her stare was intense.

When I handed it back to her, she brushed her fingers across mine and I hissed, glaring.

"Don't try anything with me, Kiara. Seduction isn't going to work."

It already felt like a lie because of how her touch had lit me up from the inside out. I twitched with the urge to push her back on the couch, plunge my fingers inside her pretty cunt, and taste how aroused I made her. She was unable to hide the effect I had. Her arousal was clear in her scent.

"That was an accident," she said.

I didn't try to argue. It wasn't worth it.

Crossing my arms over my chest, I stood behind the couch and watched the movie. Kiara was certifiably terrible at keeping still. She shifted and fidgeted, grabbing pillows and clutching them before tossing them away again.

When she let out a needy little moan, I clenched my teeth and tried to keep a handle on my aura. Female alpha auras were different than male alphas—we had more of a soft intimidating effect, as opposed to the aggressive flares of a male. My aura was always out, but right now it was threatening to expand until she felt nothing but me, both soothing and arousing her.

Which was exactly what she wanted, of course.

"Leighton, can you—?"

I didn't get to hear whatever ridiculous thing she planned to ask for in that sweet, innocent voice. A knock sounded on the door and I turned on my heel.

He crowded through the door the second I turned off the alarm and opened it, his aura flaring as he looked around the entryway. Before I could explain a single thing, he was storming past the kitchen and into the living room, leaving his strong scent of hot iron and smoke in his wake.

Ambrose stopped short when he spotted her.

Kiara was wide-eyed, a strand of damp hair stuck to her cheek.

"Ambrose, meet Kiara," I said dryly.

Walking past him and into the room, I sat on an armchair Kiara had yet to touch.

The other alpha was still staring with an unreadable expression on his face. He had never been especially expressive. Heavy scarring on his left side inhibited his facial muscles significantly, so I got all my clues about his emotions from his eyes and lips.

Ambrose had dark brown eyes that looked soulless at first glance but became warm and soulful the longer you looked into them. Genuine smiles rarely turned his lips, only little smirks when I did something that pleased him. He was handsome in a rugged way that I'd admired for far longer than we'd been sleeping together.

"Nice to meet you, Kiara," he said after a pause. "What is going on, Leighton?"

"She wants me to dark bond her."

That had his lips turning down into a fierce scowl. With his hands in fists, he moved to a chair and sat down in it. The leather creaked under his form. He was big, even for an alpha. "Why is she still here, then?"

"As it turns out, I have to keep her."

"And what do you need me to do?"

We were talking about Kiara like she didn't exist, and she

fought not to react but failed epically. Her hands clenched into fists against her thighs, and she tried to ignore us in turn. The gaze she turned to the TV screen was blank, though. She wasn't watching.

"Can we sleep in shifts?" I asked.

"What are you expecting me to do?" Kiara burst out, shooting me a pouty glare and giving up on the movie.

I shrugged. "Don't know."

I didn't want to find out, though.

"It's not like I'm going to attack you in your sleep."

"Why should I trust that you won't?" I asked.

"You could kill me if I did that," she said.

"Probably, but you're a little desperate. Desperation makes you dangerous."

Ambrose watched her keenly, his foot tapping against the floor. He'd barged in without bothering to take off his shoes. Liberty was going to have a stellar time scrubbing dirt out of my rug when she came back. If she came back. I got the sense she was uncomfortable being in the same space as Kiara.

Ambrose didn't appear to have that same immediate discomfort. Maybe Libby's reaction had been overblown?

"You'll sleep. I'll stay awake," Ambrose said, responding to my question after Kiara's outburst.

"No, you need—"

"I never sleep. Don't worry."

He said that like it was normal, but I wouldn't question him. We kept our distance for a reason. I didn't ask about him, and he didn't ask about me. Although, he knew things he shouldn't and gave me gifts that crossed the line when he thought he could get away with it.

"OK. I appreciate you coming over."

Abruptly, he stood. "We need to talk privately."

I lifted an eyebrow at him, glancing to Kiara. She was back to angrily *not* watching the movie. It felt rude to eliminate her from a conversation that was very clearly going to be about her.

Then again, it had been rude of her to come in here and demand I dark bond her.

She had to know it would make me a social pariah. No one would want to employ me anymore, no matter how good I was at my job. Dark bonding a gold pack omega was bad enough—it was legal. But to dark bond a normal omega? Even though aura-seeing seers could tell she'd given permission for that type of bond, everyone would assume I'd somehow tricked the system and coerced her into it.

Standing, I nodded toward my master suite. "Help yourself to any food in the fridge," I said to Kiara.

She held a pillow to her chest and nodded stiffly, not having any more complaints as we left the room.

FOUR

LEIGHTON

With the bedroom door closed and locked behind us, I relaxed. I wasn't scared of Kiara. Not... really. But it was obvious she was upset by our guest derailing her plans, and I didn't know what she was going to do with that anger.

It could be anything or nothing. She could pettily rip pillows to shreds or come at me with a kitchen knife the next time I walked into my living room. I just didn't know.

"Why is she still in your condo?" Ambrose asked.

He shed his coat and shoes and made himself comfortable on my bed. I tried to swallow past my arousal. This was dangerous. We'd only ever fucked at The Pointe Lounge, the BDSM and sex club where Ambrose worked. There, neither of our scents were prominent. To have him here, in my space, was a temptation I'd always known I would have trouble resisting.

"Extenuating circumstances."

He patted his thick thighs, wanting me to come sit on his lap. I hesitated. The level of submission I gave Ambrose was exclusive to sex only. I wouldn't have him telling me what to do in my life.

Instead of on his thighs, I sat beside him on the bed.

"Tell me what they are."

"I can't," I said.

His hand trailed across the duvet to land on my thigh and I stiffened. "You know I would rather burn alive than reveal your secrets to anyone."

My gaze slid to the scars. He didn't talk about them much, but everyone knew what happened. House fire in Citrine Hills. He'd been in college, home with his parents on summer break. The scars were from the flames, but rumour had it he'd had more than burn scars. Some had been from knives.

I'd never asked him.

It was one of those things that would make us far too close and personal.

Saying he would rather burn alive than sell me out was probably the most serious promise he could give me. He'd come so close to that being his reality, and the incident left far more than just the physical scars.

"Give me your phone."

He did in an instant, and I tossed both of ours into a signal blocking box I kept in my nightstand. When it was secure, I sighed. "We better hope Liberty did a good job of scanning this place for spyware, because if Soren finds out I'm telling you about this, it won't be pretty."

Ambrose lifted an eyebrow. "Soren Rosania?"

"How many Sorens do you know who would have resources to bug my house?"

"Point taken. Go on."

"I work for him. Not just on a temporary basis when he needs something covered up. I'm in his fucking pocket, and I can't escape it."

Ambrose clenched his jaw, the scarred muscles in his face twitching rapidly as they sometimes did when he was agitated.

"You can't help me," I said before he could offer. "Soren knows some family secrets that go way beyond me, so I won't risk pissing him off. I don't know how Kiara found him, or who the fuck she really is, but he sent her to me. I called him to tell him I wouldn't be dark bonding her, and he told me to keep her safe and close. So here we are. There's an omega in my house who is desperate for a dark bond, and whether I bond her or not she's valuable to an unhinged billionaire."

His thick fingers stroked my thigh. I would never admit out loud how much his touch soothed me.

"I can do some digging. Dash could—"

I shook my head. "Don't tell Dash about any of this. I'll dig on my own."

"He needs a task anyway."

"And you think giving him a task that relates to me is a good idea?" I asked.

Dash was the lead of Ambrose's pack. He took it the hardest when my brother rejected them. I couldn't tell you what was going through his head, but he became more of an asshole every year. More erratic, too. Some of the tabloid articles on him read like they should be fake, but they weren't.

Any reminder of my brother was a trigger for him, and I may be the biggest reminder of them all.

"I wouldn't tell him it's for you."

"No. If he's looking into it, he could easily find out about me. I won't be responsible for whatever he does next."

Sighing, Ambrose wrapped his arm around me and pulled me close. I let him. I even swung my feet over his thighs and leaned on his chest.

Damn it.

Was it sad that a top-secret tryst was the part of my week I most looked forward to? Skin to skin contact and the ability to not be in charge for two hours was the only thing keeping me sane.

"You don't have to do everything by yourself, you know," he murmured.

"I called you, didn't I?"

It wasn't enough to take even half the burden off my shoulders, and he was aware of that. His huge, scarred hands trailed down my lithe form without purpose, not pushing me for more.

I pushed into him instead, arching my back when he grazed his palm across my clothed stomach.

His fingers brushed the underside of my breasts, but he didn't cup them. His touches were chaste, meant to bring comfort until I took his hand and shoved it to the apex of my thighs. My core waited for him, wet and throbbing. I wasn't ready to admit that Kiara played a part in why I was aroused tonight. I would pretend it was all for him.

"Ask for it, doll. I don't respond to demands," he said.

Ambrose's voice was gruff, his hard cock creating a bulge in his jeans that rubbed against my thighs. I glanced at the closed door, wondering if Kiara would hear if we did anything. We probably shouldn't. This situation didn't warrant sex.

He caught my chin with his hand, fingers digging into my cheeks. "I won't be ignored. Pay attention to me, or go ask her for what you want. Think she can give it to you?"

Is that jealousy? My eyes widened.

"Touch me, Sir." I had to say something to get my mind out of those dangerous places.

"Just touch you? Or do you want me to do more than that?"

He dropped his hand from my face and undid my blazer, letting me shrug it off. My blouse was next, then my pants until I was sitting half on his lap in only a plain underwear set. His sharp inhale through his nose had me pressing my thighs together, a hint embarrassed by how much of my scent he was basking in right now.

Teasingly he touched my breasts and thighs, but didn't give me enough pressure to take me out of my head.

"Tell me what my pretty little doll needs from me today," he purred.

I exhaled shakily, meeting his eyes. "I need to forget."

It wasn't an uncommon request.

Ambrose was my safety, the place I went when I needed to escape the lonely reality of my life. He was always there, and always gave me everything.

Even though I gave him nothing in return.

I'd bleed him dry at this rate. He was letting me, and I was too selfish to stop.

"Then I'll make you forget everything except pleasure."

He shoved me onto my back on the bed, his rough grip enough to make me yelp. I felt myself sinking into the space where I needed to be. Reality became hazy as he tore his shirt over his head, taking off his jeans.

I whimpered at the sight of him nude. It wasn't something I could get used to. His hairy thighs flexed with every motion, reminding me of how they helped him drive into me hard enough I saw heaven. Scars peeked around the side of his legs, but most of his scarring was on his back side. He didn't often face his back toward me. I wasn't sure if it was because he was ashamed, he thought I wouldn't find him sexy if I saw, or something else entirely. I'd only caught accidental glimpses of the mangled, healed skin.

Knowing he had a vulnerability helped me feel safe around him. We shared our burdens with each other in the few stolen hours we spent together each week.

Ambrose dragged me down the bed by my ankles until he had me where he wanted me. Then he straddled my face. His balls hung over my mouth and I surged up, groaning as I sucked on them. His cock was a sight to behold, just like the rest of him.

Thick, uncircumcised and with a knot at the base, sometimes I felt more familiar with it than I did with my own body.

Dragging his balls from my mouth, he leaned back and smeared precum across my lips. I parted my lips, letting my tongue slide around the head. Even his cock tasted smoky to me, matching his scent.

"Good, doll. You want me to fuck your throat, don't you?"

"Yes, please."

He smacked his cock against my cheek and I groaned. "Is that how you ask?"

"Please, Sir."

Instead of showering me with praise, he rewarded me with his cock in my mouth. Ambrose wasn't gentle with me, and I didn't want him to be. He fucked my mouth in a way that had me coughing and choking on him.

My eyes rolled back in my head, and I squirmed but was utterly helpless to touch myself. His body blocked my arms from reaching my pussy, so I clutched his thighs.

"There we go," he groaned above me. He slid my hair between his fingers before using a tight grip to pin my head down to the bed. "My perfect fuck doll. Relax your throat and let me come down it."

The urge to do as I was told was immense. I did what I could, and he knew what I could handle. When I gagged, he pulled back, only to press back in a second later. By the time he'd worked his cock down my throat, his knot pressing against my lips, my pussy was dripping arousal down onto the bed.

"One more time," he promised as I gasped for air. "You can do it."

I nodded shakily. There was no part of me that was even considering saying no to him.

His cock spread my lips again and he pressed in until my throat flexed around it. He fisted his knot and groaned, barely pulling out before he was coming. I swallowed him down as my eyes fluttered shut, back arching. My body wordlessly begged for more of him.

When he moved away, I whined, reaching out only to have him bat my hand away. "Your turn, doll."

My legs fell apart when he moved between them, ripping my panties off me in one motion. He growled, his chest vibrating as the sound sent tingles through my entire body. One finger swiped across me, gathering my wetness so he could suck it into his mouth.

I fought the urge to wrap my legs around him and pull him closer. It would only make him deny me. Usually I had ropes burning my flesh and preventing me from doing it. Resisting without being forced was difficult.

"Always so wet for me. Do you want to come?"

My head bobbed. I ran my hands down my torso and across the lacy fabric of my bra. I had to find something to do with them—otherwise I'd end up with a demanding grip in his hair. Demanding didn't work. He didn't listen.

"Words," he barked.

"I want to come, Sir."

"How do you want to come?"

He leaned down, hot breath washing over my pulsing pussy. My thighs clenched as I moaned, threatening to jolt up and wrap around him.

"Hold me down," I said. "Keep me still and make me come with your tongue please, Sir."

Ambrose smirked up at me, pressing his hands into my thighs to pin them to the mattress. "Does my doll miss her restraints?"

I flushed, a flash of shame rolling through me at how desperately I needed the restraints to truly let go. He responded immediately, kissing my clit softly.

"You've got a tie somewhere, don't you?" he asked.

"In the walk-in closet."

The air from his movement brushed my naked skin. He was gone and back before I could really feel his loss. Silky fabric circled my wrists, pinning them together as he tied a knot. When I tried to pull them apart there was no give and my body slumped into the bed in relief.

"There we go, doll. That's better, yeah?"

His voice soothed me, and he pressed my thighs into the mattress again. Having less range of movement made me sink further into that fuzzy space where my brain turned off and I just existed. Where I could be Ambrose's doll without worries.

"Yes, Sir," I said breathily.

He leaned down, tongue brushing my clit this time instead of that teasing press of his lips. I moaned, my thighs fighting to close and his strength stopping them from moving.

Ambrose teased me until I was struggling for real, desperate to get close to his mouth. "I love the way you need me," he murmured. "I love how you want to be restrained but are always frantic and straining by the end."

His sweet nothings lit me up, causing me to ache in a spot dangerously close to my heart. They were words I couldn't stomach hearing except under these circumstances, and he made sure to give them to me every time.

When he finally dove in with the intent of making me come, I arched and shouted at the ceiling. He was better than anyone else at eating pussy, and I never could last long. Each stroke of his tongue shot me closer to the ultimate pleasure until I reached it.

My body writhed through the orgasm, my breath coming in quick pants. He didn't give me time to come down. Ambrose ripped the tie from my wrists, flipped me to my knees, and re-tied the silk with my hands behind my back. When he pushed me over I yelped, but he was careful to catch me before I face planted into the bed. My cheek came to rest gently on the blanket.

His cock rubbed against my pussy and his fingers dug into the globes of my ass as he let out a strangled groan. "Tell me how badly you want me."

I always had to tell him everything with my words and not my body. With how much I was dripping for him, he knew the answer. But, like being restrained, I loved being forced into words I never would have otherwise said.

"I'm desperate for your cock," I whimpered.

I saw the way he looked down at me, reverent affection filling his gaze. I always pretended it was my pussy that gave him that look—it was easier to swallow than the reality.

"Yeah, doll? Tell me more."

He pressed his tip to my entrance, teasing me with the possibility of him slamming home.

"You know I love being your fuck doll, Sir," I moaned. Words spilled out that would have made me red with shame if I'd been in the company of anyone else. "I need you to fuck me until I forget my name. Until I'm only your needy doll."

This time his growl vibrated all the way down to his cock and I pushed my hips back. His hands stopped me from moving, but he didn't keep me waiting any longer.

I moaned as he speared me with his length. He was thick enough around that it was borderline uncomfortable when he first pushed inside. Then the discomfort always melted to arousal as my pussy adjusted to letting him fuck me.

"Always so fucking tight," he hissed. "I know you don't let anyone else fuck this pussy, do you doll? You're only mine. You were made to take my cock."

My only response was another moan. For this, he didn't expect words. He was under no illusions of exclusivity, no matter how he liked to add it to his dirty talk in bed.

I would never admit he was the only one I fucked and had been since we started years ago. There was no one else I trusted enough, but telling him that would only complicate an already delicate situation.

Those thoughts flitted away when he bottomed out, the stretch blanking my mind once again. I tried to separate my arms, pussy gushing when I couldn't. His fingers dug into my ass, bruising me as he stopped me from controlling anything. Ambrose fucked me on his own terms, slow at first with a gradual increase of speed.

"More," I begged.

He wasn't fucking me with full strokes. Only half of his length was inside, and it wasn't hitting deep enough to make me see stars. There wasn't the pleasant feeling of his knot bumping against my clit with every motion.

Ambrose grunted, smacking my ass with the rough palm of his hand. "If I give you more, I'll be filling your pussy up with cum."

"Please, Sir."

His hand slid across my hip and down to the apex of my thighs, finding my clit with unerring accuracy.

"You need to come for me first, doll."

"I will," I said. "Fuck me and I will, *please*."

The next thrust was full of everything that had been missing. Rough domination, his cock plunging deep enough inside me it almost made me fight to get away. I didn't, trying to match his thrusts and frustratingly being held in place.

It didn't matter. Even without my help, we were both going to explode.

Pressure built in the pit of my stomach until the world evaporated and I screamed with pleasure. I trembled, pulsing beneath him as he groaned and stuttered to a stop. Ambrose cursed as he filled me, his release combined with mine making my thighs slick and messy.

He took a while to stop panting, his cock going soft and slipping out of me. When he let me go I slumped to the bed on my stomach, unable to hold myself up. He undid the tie around my wrists, placing it on my side table and kissing the reddened spots where the fabric had trapped me.

"I'll clean you up, doll. Be right back."

I hazily realized that he went to my bathroom, but it felt like I was trudging through heavy fog. It always did after being tied up and fucked by Ambrose. Sub space. I'd looked it up once.

As much as I normally hated being vulnerable, this was the one exception.

A warm cloth rubbed against my skin, fixing the mess we'd made. It slowly brought me back to reality, that familiar sense of loss seeping into my consciousness.

That was followed by a feeling of horror.

"Fuck," I cursed. "Kiara is in the living room. There's no way she didn't hear."

Sitting up, I shoved at Ambrose's hands when he tried to keep stroking me. My stomach turned at the thought of her—a stranger—hearing me beg for more and revel in being tied up.

Although, my panic was quickly tempered by curiosity.

What did the little omega think about this? She'd been angry to see Ambrose. Was she possessive over me? Why did that give me a sense of pride?

"She must have heard," Ambrose agreed.

His lips pressed together, rolling inward like he was physically stopping himself from saying more. He wasn't anywhere near as upset as I was about it, though.

"I need to go check on her. She might be trashing the place."

I was half up when Ambrose pressed back on my chest to force me down again. My breath hitched and my body was instantly ready for another round, which he could tell. His nostrils flared, gaze flicking down to my pussy.

"I'll do it. There's no need for her to see you freshly fucked. Let me bring you something to eat, too. It's dinner time."

It was impossible to say no to him when I was still recovering from the haze. Biting my lip, I nodded. "Fine. There should be leftovers in the fridge."

"Got it."

He pressed a kiss to my temple and was gone, leaving me to stare at the ceiling and wonder if I'd made a huge mistake by bringing him here.

FIVE

KIARA

My stomach turned with violent discomfort, but I couldn't turn up the movie.

The sounds of her pleasure were too sweet of a melody. Her scent was sweet too, vanilla cream, but regrettably mixed with the abrasive hot iron and smoke scent of the other alpha.

Ambrose.

The one she'd called because she thought I was going to do something to her. I would never hurt her. Not when I wanted her so badly. It was worse with every second—the need growing in my core.

Ultimately, I needed a dark bond—or even a normal bond, but I'd never convince a pack to bond me without knowing each other unless I offered them total control.

Any alpha or pack would do.

But I didn't want any alpha anymore. I only wanted her.

That was a problem when my life depended on being bonded and protected before I was found. I needed a plan to convince her to do it—and I doubted seduction was going to work fast enough now that Ambrose was here, standing in my way.

Any sexual frustration I caused her, she could work out with him.

I growled, tugging my hands through my damp, tangled hair. This wasn't going according to plan. Not even a little.

When Leighton screamed loud enough to shake the TV screen, I shoved my face into a pillow and screamed too. Hers was pleasure, mine was pure frustration. And rage. Maybe a little bit of rage.

My anger was still calming when Ambrose wandered into the kitchen. I stiffened. We couldn't see each other from here, but I knew it was him. His footfalls were heavier, reminding me of how my brother always stomped around the house without a care in the world. Ambrose's scent was heavier in the air now too, Leighton's vanilla cream fading fast as his smothered it.

Confronting him was a terrible idea. I had to be smart about my next steps, but I didn't feel very smart.

I was on my feet and pushing through the glass door before I could second guess. Ambrose acknowledged me with a head tilt while he made up three plates of food.

"Where's Leighton?" I asked.

My hand pressed to the hard steel of the knife hidden in my pants. Ambrose's presence was intimidating, but I could stab him if I had to. I'd done it before, the fresh memory smacking me in the face. I bit my bottom lip, trying and failing to ignore it.

Jonathan's bony fingers dug into my arm, his nails pricking me and threatening to break the skin. I yanked myself back, using my weight to make him let go. It had me landing on my ass with a cry that echoed in the high-ceilinged lounge.

He cussed, glaring down at me with his beady little eyes that were always squinting. "Bitch," Jonathan hissed. "Tobias knew you'd need more taming before heading off to your new pack. Get the fuck up."

I didn't listen, pushing myself back across the carpet on my ass. It was difficult to think past the pounding of my heart. In my panic, my long dress got stuck underneath me and I stalled.

That was all the pause Jonathan needed to catch up. I hadn't been moving fast enough anyway. Panic was filling my brain, all my senses working on overdrive. He was aroused, his beta scent heavier than normal. He grabbed my arm again and pulled, ignoring when I cried out.

My shoulder bloomed with fiery pain, almost yanked out of the socket by his efforts to get me up. I resisted, knowing what would happen.

He'd already tried to remove my dress.

Next time, he would succeed.

I pushed him back one more time, this time scrambling to my feet. I tripped over the dark hem on my way up, catching myself on the mantle of the fireplace.

And there, right in my sight line, was my salvation.

A decorative knife. One of the small ones in my father's collection, but sharp. He kept them all sharp.

The sharp end pointed to me but I grabbed it, adrenaline preventing me from registering the pain in my hand. This was my one chance. Jonathan was wide-eyed by the time I turned back to him—he'd seen the knife, but he took too long to react.

I stabbed him in the neck.

Blood spurted from the wound, and he screamed as loud as I had. The thick liquid coated me, drenching me in his scent and warming me from the outside in.

I should feel horrified or panicked. He was going to die—that much was obvious from the light fading in his squinty eyes. I'd killed a man.

Except instead of any of that, I only felt... euphoric.

Elated enough that I followed him down to the floor and punctured his neck all over again, a laugh bubbling up in my throat.

Swallowing a lump of emotion, I shifted uncomfortably from foot to foot. My hand stung, the wound fresh but covered in a wrap bandage Soren gave me. Ambrose was taking too long to respond, studying me with an irritating amount of indifference.

"Answer me."

Fuck.

My demand came out as a whine, my gaze flitting toward Leighton's bedroom.

She might not discipline me for whining, but he might. I fought back the urge to cower. That's not what I was going to do out here—I wouldn't let my existence away from my father be a copy of how I lived when I was with him.

I stood tall.

"She's resting. You won't see her again tonight."

My eyes narrowed. I hated how my body slumped in relief when he didn't react to the whine. "I need to see her."

"Why's that, little omega?" Ambrose abandoned his perusal of me in favour of putting plates in the microwave, letting it whir to life.

I opened my mouth, then closed it again. There was no reason I could give him that was... Well, reasonable. My deep-seated desire to see Leighton was so I could claim her the same way he had, by bathing her in my scent.

Why did he get to have her, but I couldn't?

I'd offered her a dark bond. Handed her the ultimate submission on a silver platter, and she wasn't interested. Father said every alpha wanted a dark bond, but it was yet another thing he'd been wrong about. I was getting a crash course in all the lies he'd told as he'd kept me locked away from the world.

"Please let me see her," I said instead of telling him a reason.

He sighed. "If you plan on telling her your story—your real one, not what you've already said—I'm sure she'd be happy to come out here. Otherwise, we're going to spend the evening in her room."

My teeth clamped down on my lower lip and I fought not to tremble. Was it panic rushing through me right now? Anger? Fear? Annoyance? I'd never had much of a grasp on my own emotions. My brother Tobias said it was because I was a fickle omega, and they didn't know how to control themselves.

His harsh words were an echo I couldn't escape from. *"All omegas are brainless sluts who will throw themselves at any alpha that breathes."*

Was I doing that? Was I proving him right?

No. Leighton was different. I'd never wanted an alpha before her. I couldn't deny that Ambrose appealed to me in an annoying way, but he was mainly just an obstacle in my path to what I wanted.

"I'm going to take that as a no." He yanked me from my thoughts by pushing a plate toward me. "Dinner. We'll be in Leighton's room."

There was an unspoken threat not to bother them unless I was going to give them the information they wanted. I stared down at my plate as he turned and walked off with the other two meals, leaving me alone again.

He couldn't stay here, but I got the sinking feeling he was going to.

Leaving the plate on the counter, I went back into the living room and paced. There had to be some way to convince her. I needed her... to want me.

I snatched a pillow from the couch, rubbing it to my neck. A primal purr rumbled in my chest. The sensation was foreign but satisfying, instinct telling me this was what I had to do. Mix my scent with my alpha's all over the condo.

When every pillow was done I rolled on the cushions. It wasn't enough. There was more to do.

In the fixation, I barely registered what I was doing. My scent was left on every soft surface that would hold it—and plenty of solid things that wouldn't. I didn't know if it was going to last when I scent marked the kitchen counters, but I wanted Leighton to come out here tomorrow and realize that I was it for her.

Me.

Then she'd claim me.

I marked the bar stools and the benches in the breakfast nook. The shower curtain in the office bathroom. Some of her clothes that I'd found in the dryer. I even rolled around on the dirty shag rug in the living room.

If I was everywhere, she couldn't ignore me like she was right now.

By the time the urges faded, I was panting. My core clenched uncomfortably, my body aroused by how much of her scent I'd inhaled in the process of doing that. She was everywhere in here, and I was too.

"Soren knew I could do it," I muttered under my breath. "And I can. She'll *have* to dark bond me."

He'd been my saviour last night. I'd run onto a golf course in my frantic escape from my father's house, and nearly been hit by a flying golf ball. Soren had followed it, tailed by a single security guard as he—for whatever odd reason—played a game against no one under a dark, moonless sky.

His honey brown eyes had been unnaturally bright as he'd scanned me from head to toe.

My dishevelled dress, the fabric and my skin both streaked with dark red. Blood dripping from the knife clutched in my right hand. More sliding down my left palm onto the manicured grass. I'd had to wander through a field full of stagnant puddles to get there, and my shoes were filthy.

Instead of calling the police, he'd gestured to his guard. The man was an alpha with curly dark hair, the light aroma of green tea and honey swirling through the crisp night air. Soren himself had been drenched in scent dampeners.

The guard had come forward and handed me a golf club.

I'd stared at it.

"Come on, then. We've got to finish out this game," Soren said.

There were no sounds behind me, nor any sign that I was yet being followed. Everyone listened to Tobias, and he had given me to Jonathan for the night and told no one to disturb us in the lounge. That meant I had until morning to get as far away from the house as possible, and I had nothing to lose.

Holding the club in one hand and my knife in the other, I'd whispered my admittance to Soren. "I don't know how to play."

And he'd taught me.

His guard had wrapped my hand, I'd tucked my knife safely in my bra, and we'd played until we got to the final hole. Then Soren had informed me he knew the perfect place for me to go—speaking as if he knew the situation I was coming from, though I'd never told him of my life or who I was.

A long nap and quick tidy up later, and his car had dropped me off here.

With Leighton.

I had a lot to thank Soren for, but there was no point in thanking him until I'd gotten my dark bond.

Ambrose's scent tickled my nose again and I growled. Shovelling down a couple mouthfuls of food, I grabbed the pillows, starting all over in my quest to make Leighton forget anyone other than me existed.

SIX

AMBROSE

Leighton called, and I answered.

That was how this one-sided infatuation worked. She was convinced we could never have anything more than our backroom trysts at The Pointe Lounge, but I was continuously hoping to convince her otherwise.

All the barriers were superficial, really.

Her brother would understand. He was the sweetest omega on the planet and would want his sister to stop pretending she enjoyed being alone in this empty apartment. Her mother could be dealt with. A few weeks of media attention was nothing in the grand scheme of things.

My pack was a different matter, but Dash was on a downward spiral anyway. He was circling the drain despite everything Mercury and I had done to help. Maybe a shakeup was what he needed.

But now there was this.

How did the fidgety omega fit into my romance with Leighton?

She'd scent marked every inch of the condo overnight, and I got the sense she was trying to deter me. I wouldn't be deterred, especially not when her scent was annoyingly... pleasant.

Besides, when Leighton had wandered into the coconut scented hallway, she'd immediately turned back around and pounced on me. I'd made her come riding my cock. While Leighton had denied her horniness had anything to do with the omega, it was obvious.

Kiara hadn't been pleased to see me after I'd reaped the benefits, and Leighton had fled straight from her bedroom to go to work. It left me alone with Kiara, and I relished the chance to assess her.

"So, little omega," I said. I lounged on the armchair, placing both hands behind my head leisurely. "Tell me why you want a dark bond."

She peered at me out of the corner of her eye.

The young woman was nervous around me in a way she wasn't around Leighton. I couldn't tell if it was because I was a male alpha, because I was big, or because of my scarring. I'd kept my aura pulled in so I didn't scare her, but she was intimidated nonetheless.

Yet, also fiery.

Each glare would be followed by her shrinking in on herself. I never reacted, and she was growing bolder with time. I saw a little bit of what Leighton did.

Kiara was plotting something, for sure. It was there in the way she furtively glanced around the room and fidgeted. I'd noticed her pressing her hand flat against the side of her left thigh like she was holding something precious. I bet she was hiding some kind of memento there.

However, I had yet to be convinced she was dangerous.

Though I was happy to assuage Leighton's concerns by guarding the bedroom door and watching her sleep last night.

"I'm not going to tell you that," she said.

I lifted an eyebrow. "Why not?"

"It's none of your business. The dark bond is between me and Leighton."

Her scent spiked and I couldn't deny it threatened to make my cock hard. She was wearing Leighton's favourite loungewear, and their mixed scents were heady.

"I think you know that it's my business," I said.

Kiara's plump lips pursed and she tried not to show her displeasure. It was too late. First thing this morning, she'd pinned me with a feral glare fitting of a possessive omega. She'd claimed Leighton as hers, and she wasn't pleased with me touching.

How unfortunate for her that I had Leighton first, and my alpha lover wasn't anywhere close to letting Kiara touch her.

"She's not in a pack with you. Therefore, not your business."

"Oh, but she's in bed with me. Tell me why you want that dark bond, little omega. Maybe I can help you get one. Just not from her."

Growling low in her throat, Kiara's fingers dug into her cushy thighs. Her gorgeous blue eyes were narrowed with irritation.

I'd been around plenty of omegas, considering my job at The Pointe, and I knew which mannerisms were pure instinct. Kiara wasn't reacting with rational thought right now.

"I will *not* be telling you anything."

"Do you think you're going to be able to convince Leighton to do it?" I asked. "I've been pushing for her to admit she loves me for years now, and nothing's come of it. She's bull-headed. Do you have years to wait?"

She huffed and turned away.

It did cross my mind that, maybe, Leighton was better off with Kiara. Things with my pack were complicated in more ways than one, and I worried I'd blow it up for all of us by continuing this clandestine relationship.

But I couldn't let her go.

I wouldn't let anyone go, not after I'd had my family ripped away from me by force.

In my opinion, I had the right to be a bit selfish after that.

We sat in silence for a while. It was something I was comfortable in, but she clearly was not. Kiara became increasingly agitated, her aura pulsing around her. I doubted more than ten minutes had passed when she pushed to her feet and stormed for the kitchen.

I could see her from my seat, but the glass double doors separated us. Pulling out my phone, I took the opportunity to call back Mercury. My packmate, and... more.

"Where are you?" Mercury asked, his tone both cold and breathless. "You're not at the club and not at the house."

"I'm aware I'm at neither of those places," I confirmed. "I'm out."

Mercury's heavy breathing came through the line for a second as he processed that.

I didn't go out.

I knew how suspicious this was, but I couldn't betray Leighton's trust when she'd finally called me for something that wasn't a hookup. He would understand when he found out. Probably. My packmate knew there was a woman, he just didn't know who she was.

"You're at her place, aren't you?"

"I am."

"Jesus, Ambrose. You're going out, staying at this woman's house, and not telling us? We haven't even met her. I didn't think it was that serious."

Kiara was cutting an apple, the knife coming down violently onto the cutting board. I watched the sharp implement, partly to ensure she didn't chop off one of her fingers and partly so I could catch her if she tried to steal it. An angry, unstable omega with a knife didn't sound like a good time.

Especially not when the glint of a blade could send my mind in dark directions.

"There was a bit of an emergency," I said.

"You didn't even text me."

"Didn't know you'd realize."

"You're an asshole, you know that?"

"I know, baby," I murmured.

Kiara didn't try to steal the knife, putting it on the counter and shoving an apple slice into her mouth. Why was the way she chewed sexy? I'd been around too many omegas to be having these potent reactions to her.

"And now you're calling me baby, great," Mercury muttered. "I thought we agreed you wouldn't do that at around the same time we agreed it was best not to sleep together."

I sighed, laying my head back and closing my eyes. Neither of us had *wanted* that. Mercury had put a pause on our years-long relationship because he thought it would be better for Dash. Our devolving pack lead was the most bitter about being rejected by our scent match, and Mercury thought it would help if he didn't have to see us being affectionate all the time.

At least until Dash had someone to be romantic with, too.

I doubted that was happening anytime soon.

"You're saying we agreed as if it was a mutual thing. It was a slip of the tongue, Mercury. Won't happen again."

He went silent. I could picture the look on his face, his teeth chewing nervously on his bottom lip and his brown eyes wide.

"Please just don't—"

I snapped my eyes open when I heard the door to the kitchen opening. Kiara stepped through with her last piece of apple. A glance confirmed the gleam of silver still on the countertop. No weapon. The only daggers she had were in her glare as she went back over to the couch.

"—you need to tell me where you're going."

The tail end of Mercury's words made it clear what he had said. "I won't leave you hanging again. I've got to go."

I choked back the 'love you' that wanted to come out, slamming my thumb on the end call button instead.

"Did you get in trouble with your pack lead?" Kiara asked slyly.

I bet she hoped I had. She wanted me to be forced to run home with my tail between my legs, leaving her alone to manipulate Leighton into giving her that dark bond. Didn't she realize what a negative impact that would have on Leighton's life?

"No," I said. "He's happy I'm here to keep Leighton company."

The lie made her eye twitch, jaw clenching. Mercury wasn't pack lead—Dash was, and he wouldn't be keen to hear Leighton Winston's name. Kiara didn't know that, and I didn't plan on enlightening her.

"So, you'll be staying then?" Her hand pressed to her thigh.

"Yes. I'll stay for as long as you do."

She crossed one leg over the other and huffed, falling back into the couch cushions. Every brush of those pillows wafted more of her scent into the air.

Chocolate, coconut, and Leighton's vanilla cream were everywhere.

Why did the omega's scent have to be so delectable, and such a perfect match to my lover's?

"That's unfortunate," Kiara said.

Her voice was quiet, and I took it for resignation. Maybe she would tell us how she'd ended up here now I'd made it clear she wouldn't get what she wanted. I wasn't opposed to helping her. Anyone Soren deemed useful had to have some shit going on.

We wouldn't be helping her at the expense of Leighton's professional or personal reputation, that was all.

She watched TV until her anxiousness forced her up to pace. Leighton had said she would be back around lunchtime with food and clothes for Kiara, and it was drawing close to that time. I would be grateful for a moment with her, considering Kiara's company wasn't exactly thrilling.

"Is there something you would rather do than pace?" I asked. "We could play a game. Leighton has to have a pack of cards around here somewhere."

She spun to glare at me. "A game?"

"Well, you've proven you can't watch television. Cards are a little more active, and maybe I won't have to watch you wear a hole in the rug."

Her arms crossed over her chest, and it took a monumental amount of effort to avoid glancing down at her cleavage. The shirt was so tight her nipples poked prominently against the fabric.

OK, I'd avoided the glance this time, but that wasn't to say I'd never caught myself looking.

Internally cursing, I pushed to stand. "I'm finding some cards. Take it or leave it. I'll play some solitaire if you'd rather not."

I left her in the living room and wandered into the kitchen, pulling open drawers to find the designated junk drawer. Everyone had one. Leighton must. I'd gotten halfway around the kitchen when the front door lock buzzed.

I turned, but before I'd gotten the 'hello' out, I choked.

My lower back exploded in pain, tearing long-buried memories out of their carefully constructed box. Warm blood dripped from the wound, soaking my jeans as I turned around slowly.

Kiara stood behind me, clutching the handle of a small knife.

Her form blurred, my attention focusing on the gleam of metal.

She'd stabbed me, and I tried desperately to ground myself in that reality. It was no fucking use. The coppery scent of my blood hit the air, and I couldn't see Kiara anymore.

There was only *them*.

The men and the violence and the fucking pain.

"Hey look, the kid's awake. Wonder if we can get Mommy to talk now."

"You should have stayed asleep, son."

"Wouldn't it be better for your parents if you died right now? But I'm not going to kill you. No way. You'd have to figure out how to do it yourself."

"This was the only way." Her whispered words were enough to make me lose myself.

My hand grabbing and tightening around her throat cut off the tail end of the last word.

"...The only way your mom lives is if you do as I say..."

I could feel the lick of flames against my skin again, smoke clinging to my throat and making every inhale agony. The steady drip of blood down my back was dried by the fire.

I sighed in relief. No more pain. None. Only heat and an orange glow.

My grip tightened around the neck of my attacker. If I was going down, they were going down with me.

They deserved it. Burning alive.

But I couldn't quite keep my fingers from clenching and squeezing, the gasp bringing me sick satisfaction.

Did their throat burn like mine?

Were the flames eating their skin? *It wouldn't hurt me like it hurt them.* Half the skin on my back had been flayed off, so the fire was sweet oblivion, killing flesh they'd been so eager to harm.

"Ambrose?"

A voice and sweet vanilla scent invaded my consciousness.

Something was off. I blinked rapidly, trying to dispel the

smoky grey haze in front of my eyes. It didn't work, and then hands grasped my arm.

No. They need to die.

I choked them with more force, vaguely registering their skin was smooth and delicate. It didn't feel right. There weren't remnants of stubble scratching at me. They weren't strong enough to fight back.

Why weren't they strong enough to fight back?

Nails dug into my wrist, stopping me from causing the harm I wanted. Every second my agitation grew, the pain coming back in waves that washed over me. There wasn't time. I needed to... I needed... death.

Theirs and mine.

It had been a long time coming.

SEVEN

LEIGHTON

"Ambrose!"

I shouted his name again, trying desperately to push back at his aura. It was flaring, the entire condo drenched in hot iron and smoke.

I hadn't expected to walk into my home to find Ambrose bleeding from his back, his hand around Kiara's neck. There was an unfamiliar knife abandoned on the floor. I'd fucking known she was dangerous, but I couldn't comprehend *this*.

She was paying for her deceit now.

Ambrose was lost in memories, his eyes unseeing while he clutched her throat.

Kiara was going blue, gasping for breath as she struggled against his hold. Her feet dangled from the ground, and with her short legs her kicks weren't landing on him.

"Kiara, your aura," I urged. "Fucking calm him. You can do that. Calm him down."

She only struggled some more, her consciousness almost gone. Rational thought wasn't there anymore. An omega aura may be able to calm a raging alpha but she wasn't going to be useful.

I tried to use mine instead, making myself as big as possible and delivering a command I hoped would break through. "Ambrose, let her go."

His fingers loosened enough she could suck in a breath. Tears began to stream down her cheeks. I released Ambrose's hand where I'd been trying to pry it away from her. My torso pressed to his side instead and I purred, hoping it would do some good even though I wasn't an omega.

"Good. Drop your hand and listen to me, OK?"

It took a second, but he was coming back. The unseeing sheen on his eyes was dropping, the dark orbs looking lighter by the second. He didn't lower her gently, releasing her so abruptly she dropped to the floor. Kiara cried out and the sound had me clamping down on sudden anger.

She was hurt. He'd hurt her.

But *he* was the one with a seeping knife wound in his lower back.

Shit.

I stepped between them, hustling Ambrose back until he could lean against the counter. His expression twisted with pain as he brought a hand to the wound. His fingers came back sticky with blood. "Fuck," he groaned. "Leighton, I need…"

My tea towel was draped across the counter, and I grabbed it. Reaching around, I pressed it to his back and plastered myself to his front. His arms came around me, holding me limply.

"It'll stop bleeding soon," I said, more confident than I felt.

The knife was small. It can't have hit an organ. Not possible. Kiara wouldn't have done that.

His gaze flicked to the knife on the floor and then landed on Kiara. His jaw went slack, body slumping. "*Fuck*," he said again.

She was coughing, holding her bruised throat as tears

streamed from her eyes. She was avoiding eye contact, looking at the floor as she recovered her breath. Ambrose grabbed the tea towel from me, pressing it to the wound. "Check on her."

"Your wound is more serious."

He shook his head sharply. "I'll heal. I could have crushed her windpipe, and omegas are fragile."

Ambrose had a point, but I hesitated.

What was running through her fucking head when she decided to stab him? Was she going to try to hurt me next? This was why I'd called Ambrose in the first place—I just hadn't expected he would be the one to get hurt.

I didn't want to help her, but my instincts were screaming at me. I was irrationally angry at Ambrose for the harm he'd caused her. Seeing the extent of the damage would only heighten that instinctual alpha rage.

He had to push me toward Kiara to get me to move. I was thinking too hard about it until he forced the matter.

Crouching beside her, I reached out.

Through her coughing she let out a little whimper, leaning in close with her throat exposed. The skin was turning purple, tiny red spots marring her neck and face. When she peered up at me with desperate, tear-filled eyes, they were bloodshot.

I wasn't a goddamn doctor. How badly was she hurt?

"Can you breathe?"

She nodded, flinching at how the movement strained her neck.

"Can you talk?"

"You're going to dark bond me, right? Please do it." Her voice was hoarse and quiet, sounding nothing like her usual lilting tone.

I reared back at the question. "What the fuck? No. I told you no, why would I change my mind now?"

A little wrinkle appeared between her eyes, her lips turning down. "I'm dangerous," she said.

Ambrose groaned and I snapped my gaze to him. The tea towel was soaked, his blood still dripping. *Had* she hit a fucking organ? I didn't have time to deal with her insistence on a dark bond. Whipping out my phone, I made the first rational decision since walking into the high-tension situation.

I called Liberty.

"How did it go with the omega?" she asked in place of a greeting.

"I need you and Jasper here, now. Tell him to bring his kit."

She hung up halfway through a curse. Jasper was my multi-talented doctor on staff. He was also my lawyer, but when I told him to bring his kit it meant I needed him in a medical capacity.

They were on their way, which was good, because I was out of my depth here. Feeling this total loss of control was something I really did not enjoy.

Then, there were the conflicting feelings tightening my chest.

Kiara had stabbed Ambrose, so I wasn't pleased with her. If it had been as simple as that, I would know which side to be on, but it wasn't. He'd almost killed her. Would have, if I hadn't stopped him. There was a small part of myself that had already claimed the omega as mine—or at the very least, my responsibility—despite not wanting to bond her.

She should be safe with me.

"Can you please dark bond me?" Kiara's voice was slowly getting stronger, her hacking coughs lessening to an occasional clearing of her throat. That was a good sign.

"No."

"But I'm dangerous. It's better if I'm controlled, right?"

"Where the fuck are you from, Kiara? No one I've ever met thinks that. A dark bond isn't the answer to a dangerous omega. Dangerous omegas get arrested," I said.

Her blue eyes blew wide and she scrambled back. "I can't go to jail."

She wouldn't. Omegas never did. There weren't enough of them to go around as it was—they either got off with probation or were offered special jobs that only omegas could do.

Most people knew that, too. Why didn't she?

I narrowed my eyes at her. "Why not? You've refused to tell me anything true. You stabbed Ambrose. Tell me why I shouldn't call to have you taken into custody right now?"

Her scent spiked with fear. She was running from something, and whatever it was would catch up to her if she ended up with the authorities. Maybe she'd killed someone with that knife before she'd shown up here covered in blood. They would punish her for that.

She could have had a reason for the violence. A neighbour attacking her, or an abusive family member. The thought had crossed my mind that she might have been protecting herself.

But stabbing Ambrose hadn't been protecting herself, so why was I making up excuses for her?

"I thought..." She trailed off.

Ambrose slumped against the counter and I rushed to him, leaving her. He was more injured than her after all. His eyelids were drooping shut. "Hey, stay conscious. Jasper is on his way. He's a doctor. We'll get you patched up."

He didn't answer, his breathing heavy. I helped him lower down to the tile floor and he laid down, pressing his cheek to it. "Everything's burning," he mumbled.

It wasn't. There was a chill in the air, even. I kept the air conditioning to a crisp temperature, fighting off the mid summer heat. When I pressed my hand to his forehead he was hot though, his body struggling to close the wound and fix whatever it had nicked.

"Nothing is burning," I soothed. "You're going to be fine. We'll cool you down when the doctor gets here."

My fingers stroked his dark hair back from his forehead, giving me a clear look into his eyes. His gaze was flitting around, unfocused. He was disoriented, his jaw tight and eyebrows pulled together.

"No, it's burning," he said.

I was about to correct him again when a breeze brushed past me, footsteps clapping against the tile. Kiara sprinted for the door barefoot. Her breaths came in laboured wheezes, and she'd snatched up her knife on the way past.

The front door was still open, leaving her with the perfect escape.

I froze, glancing between the spot where she'd just been, and Ambrose's delirious form. The urge to follow her was almost unbearable, and it wasn't because Soren had told me to keep her here. He could get fucked for all I cared in this moment.

I just didn't want her wandering around New Oxford barefoot without getting her injuries checked over. Ambrose's wound had turned out more serious than we'd thought at first glance, and hers could be too.

Reaching down I put pressure on his wound again, the towel squelching from the amount of blood he'd lost. My heart stuttered as I watched the door. There was no good answer—following her would leave Ambrose alone. Staying with Ambrose would have her running around the city alone and vulnerable.

What the fuck was I supposed to do?

Ambrose mumbled something unintelligible beneath me and I yanked open a nearby drawer, putting a fresh towel on his wound. The flow was staunching. Slowly. Pressing down, I cursed and prayed that Liberty and Jasper would get here soon.

EIGHT

KIARA

It hadn't worked.

More than not working, it had backfired severely.

My life had flashed before my eyes when Ambrose's hand had tightened around my throat. Black had teased the edges of my vision as Tobias's taunts invaded my final moments of consciousness.

"You're going to die young, sis. Young and alone. I'll make sure of it."

"No one could ever love you. Omegas are toys, not people."

"Remember me when the life is bleeding out of you, sis. Remember how I helped you out and warned you about how it was going to happen."

That first gasping breath had me sobbing with relief, but that wasn't the end of it. I needed the dark bond. Father always said dangerous omegas got dark bonded, so I'd made sure I was dangerous.

And didn't alphas *want* dark bonds? Weren't they more

appealing? They were the only kind of bond a lone alpha like Leighton could give.

Leighton had still said no.

I was so sure—so absolutely certain—that Father hadn't lied about that. It made so much sense. Control erratic omegas with commands they can't deny. The dark bond was a perfect solution.

But apparently they didn't use dark bonds as a form of control in the real world. Without her bond, I was too vulnerable to be taken into custody.

Father would find me in an instant. I'd be back in his hands.

Then I would get a dark bond from his business associates. Old men who smelled like dust and spiderwebs, who looked at me like I was a piece of meat. Well, I didn't know for sure. I'd never met them, but my father and Tobias had been setting up my arranged mating for months.

I was making a solid assumption based on the alphas and business associates Father had brought around the house in the past. The pack they wanted to gift me to wouldn't be any different.

They would treat me like I was nothing and try to force me to do what they said. I couldn't take it anymore.

I *was* a piece of meat as long as I was with my father and Tobias.

So, I had run. Tobias giving me to Jonathan had been a wrench in a plan that had already been in motion—or maybe it was a gift. My brother had unwittingly given me a head start I'd desperately needed.

Despite Soren's trust in me, I'd ruined any chance I'd had at seducing Leighton. I knew that the second I caught the look of horror on her face. With no dark bond on the horizon and police probably on their way, I had no choice but to run again.

Someone else would bond me. I had to find someone, right?

They couldn't be as perfect as Leighton—no one could—but I didn't have a choice.

I tore out the door in a sprint that made my entire body heavy with fatigue, the knife clutched in my hand. The stairwell door was the only barrier to my freedom, and I shoved it easily. Down the stairs I went, flight after flight until I had to pause.

Every breath was painful and tears streamed down my cheeks. My neck throbbed, but it was the price I had to pay for knowing nothing about the world. Pain, but nothing to show for it.

I made it down the rest of the stairs with my fading adrenaline. I'd been running on so much of it for the past forty-eight hours, I had to be low on it.

Is that how adrenaline works?

It didn't matter.

I rushed through the lobby after shoving my knife into the waistband of my pants, getting an odd look from the building manager perched behind a desk.

Sun blinded me as I stumbled out onto the sidewalk. Pavement burned my bare feet but it was a fine distraction from the other aches and pains of my body. With no possible destination in mind, I picked a direction and walked in it.

I couldn't tell how long passed as I walked down dirty sidewalks, rocks and twigs poking my scorching feet. The high-rise buildings were behind me now, and I found myself in a residential area of family homes on small lots. It felt peaceful, with trees lining the edge of the road. There was soft grass for me to walk on, soothing my aching soles.

Was I ever going to see Leighton again?

Had I... *killed* Ambrose?

The idea of killing him didn't give me the same thrill I'd gotten from stabbing Jonathan. Nothing about causing Ambrose harm thrilled me. A part of me shattered when I'd pierced through his shirt and into his skin, but I'd tried not to let the knife go too deep.

Only deep enough to make me a flight risk.

"Are you alright, Miss?"

A woman with a small dog paused on her walk, looking me up and down in concern.

I had smears of blood on me, bare feet, and a ring of bruises around my neck. 'Alright' was not how I'd describe myself right now. Giving her what I could muster of a smile, I nodded. "Yes, perfectly."

She didn't believe me. I palmed the hilt of my knife, hidden beneath my shirt, and tried to calm myself. Would she call the cops? Police meant my father would find me. Would he? How would he know the report was made on me specifically?

Who am I kidding?

Since I'd killed Jonathan and fled the house, I bet he'd had someone checking up on every report about every woman in the city. They'd realize this was me.

Tobias would come for me.

He'd slick his golden brown hair back with gel and put on a suit before coming out to find me. He'd sweet talk the police. *"Oh no, Sir. This is my younger sister. She's always been a little... off, you see. We've got to get her home to her medicine."* They'd let him take me because he was convincing and because they knew who he was. A low-level cop wasn't going to be the one to challenge a crime family pretty boy.

Then I'd be back there.

I shuddered.

"I could call someone for you," the woman offered, bringing out her cell phone.

I wanted Leighton.

Maybe if I told her everything, about my family and my brother... Maybe she wouldn't let him take me back. Leighton was kind. Would she give me a dark bond to save me? Even if she hated me? I almost opened my mouth and asked if it was possible, but an arm draped across my shoulders.

"That's so kind of you, ma'am," Tobias' smooth voice washed over me. "My sister isn't having a good day, but I managed to catch up with her."

I froze.

For a second, I couldn't move an inch, not even a twitch.

Then I began to tremble, shudders wracking me as I glanced to my side, confirming what I already knew.

My brother had found me, and he was doing exactly what I'd expected him to.

The woman's eyes widened as she looked at him. I imagined he got that reaction a lot. Tobias was handsome in a dangerous businessman kind of way. He carried himself with cocky confidence and no one doubted his competence. She was clearly doubting mine, though.

"Oh, that's wonderful. I'm glad you're safe then, dear."

His fingers dug into my shoulder in silent warning. I wasn't going to say anything. The woman wouldn't get out one word before Tobias brought out his gun and shot her between the eyes.

My escape had been short-lived, after all. If I couldn't get out of his grasp, I was going back to a bond that I didn't want—that I didn't *choose*.

I nodded, failing to force a passable smile. She continued on her way, her dog yipping at birds. Tobias dragged me in the opposite direction, forcing my injured feet onto the pavement.

"You've done some very bad things, sis," he muttered. "Jonathan was a friend of mine."

He was. It made me all the more happy that I'd killed him.

"If you weren't so valuable, I'd do to you what you did to him. Father would never have to know I caught you. I'd hide your body somewhere it would never be found, and he could believe you escaped us, even though you never fucking could."

I walked with him, flicking my eyes around. We were in public, but the residential area was quiet. There had to be a way for me to escape.

Even if he shot me in the back, it would be better than going with him.

"But you've got that magical omega pussy, sweet sister. You're the key ingredient in a business alliance that's going to make us a lot of fucking money. You knew that, and you just don't want to do your part for the family, even when everyone else is."

It took everything in me to curb my disgusted reaction.

His part in the family was working for Father. Mine was apparently gifting myself, body and mind, to whomever they told to bond me.

"I hope you didn't go off and fuck some alpha. Did you, Kiara? There's blood on you. Did some big alpha force himself on you? Actually, I hope that did happen. It'll fucking teach you to run from us again."

Ambrose would never. He'd been horrified when he realized he'd harmed me at all. I couldn't imagine him doing anything sexual without my consent. The two alphas I'd met had changed everything I thought I knew about alphas.

We drew closer to a black van every second, and when the door slid open my heart jumped. If I got in that van, I'd never be seen again.

No dark bond would save me.

Nothing would.

I couldn't go back.

I palmed my knife. It was the only friend I had and the only thing I could trust to help me out of this situation. Tobias didn't know I had it. The blade wasn't obvious and he underestimated me. He was cocky. The asshole should fear me, considering I'd stabbed his friend's throat to shreds with this blade.

Inhaling shakily, I steeled myself and waited until the last possible second. I wouldn't vanish behind the bulky body of the van and be gone forever. I yanked out the knife, tearing my shirt in the process, and sliced at Tobias.

He cursed and jumped back, my attempt at slitting his throat only leaving a small red line on his arm.

I took off, knife clutched in my fist. Every breath hurt as I wove around cars and crossed the street. There would be somewhere for me to veer off, somewhere I could escape where he wouldn't be able to shoot at me.

Tobias might go for the kill shot if he decided to pull out that gun.

But he also might not. It was worse if I ended up with a hole in my leg, stopping me from running again but leaving me perfectly usable to sell off.

My lungs burned with the effort, my feet getting more torn up with every step. I was tempted to glance back, but I might trip over myself if I did. And maybe it was better not to know how close I was to being captured.

A park came up beside me and I spotted an exit on the other side, a narrow pathway hemmed in by trees. The grass of the field was cool against my feet, and I didn't look back as I crossed the wide-open space. I kept my eyes forward until an arm wrapped around me, pulling me to a stop.

I thrashed and cried out until my next breath caught the aroma of vanilla cream.

My body drooped with a whimper, and I tilted my head to the side. I met her eyes, trying to determine how furious she was about Ambrose. Even if she was here to punish me for that, I needed her to save me anyway.

"Please," I whispered. "Leighton, please."

She inhaled sharply, my fear probably potent enough she tasted it.

"Who are you running from, dove? You don't need me to dark bond you. I can keep you safe without it."

I shook my head. More tears dripped down my cheeks. There weren't footsteps pounding against the gravel of this pathway yet, but there would be. People would come. Tobias would follow me.

"You can't," I whispered. "My family... You can't. My brother is already here. Bonding me is the only way. I give you permission. Dark bond me."

Someone shouted from behind us, back the way I'd come down the path. She cursed, her hold on me tightening as she glanced over her shoulder. There was only a second to choose.

Would she be my salvation, or would I go back to Tobias for the final time?

I clutched at her, pressing closer in desperation. My skin was tacky with sweat, and she was warm too, like she'd been running. Had she been running after me?

Her lips on my neck had me letting out a little moan of relief. "This is going to hurt."

It couldn't hurt more than anything else I'd been through.

Her teeth punctured the skin, forging a bond that tore through me like fire. My nerve endings lit up and I couldn't be sure if it was pleasure or pain. Maybe I'd been through so much pain I found it pleasurable now—at least coming from Leighton.

I felt her there too, our consciousness linked. Every part of her was open like a book for me to read, from her anger to her concern.

"Let her go." My brother's voice was deadly.

We were no longer alone, each end of the narrow path filled with my brother's men. He stood at the front, glaring at Leighton and I, all tied together.

Her tongue brushed over the wound in my neck, and she

stood to her full height once again. One arm held me, but her other hand was shoved into her purse. "Why would I let my omega go?" Leighton asked.

It was the coldest tone I'd heard from her. Her aura expanded outward, larger-than-life. It would feel oppressive to them—but not to me. For me the heavy weight and the vanilla cream created a layer of comfort across my skin, stopping my trembling.

"She's not yours."

"My mark on her neck says different."

Tobias looked at the mark, baring his teeth. "You can't dark bond a normal omega. It's illegal."

Leighton tugged me closer to her side. Her phone was now in her hand. "She gave me permission."

"No, she fucking didn't," he hissed.

"Look, why don't we ask a seer?" Leighton said sweetly. "Kiara gave me permission to claim her, so she's my omega. Fuck off."

"We're taking her home," Tobias said.

He was losing his cool. It wasn't often a problem for him, especially not in the company of others. It made me even more obsessed with Leighton. She effortlessly riled him up.

Unfortunately we weren't out of the woods, because we were on a darkened path alone. My brother could have his men do anything to us. No one would come fast enough. Did Leighton have a plan, or had I just brought her down with me?

NINE

LEIGHTON

Kiara trembled against me. Now that we were bonded, I felt her panic and fear leeching into me, almost making me scared myself.

I couldn't be, though.

I knew who the man in front of me was. He was the kind that fed on fear, but I doubted he would know what to do when put up against a female with far more power than him.

Someone like me.

"You're not touching her with even one of your disgusting little fingers. Do you know why?" I glanced back at the men on our opposite side.

It would have been better if I'd caught her before she'd made it down here, but I'd been so far behind. Jasper and Liberty had gotten to my condo to treat Ambrose, and I'd no longer been able to push down the panicked feeling in my chest. I'd known she would be in trouble. How could she not be, covered in injuries with no fucking shoes?

She'd been caught by her other pursuers first—the ones she'd begged me to save her from.

And while I'd been confused about why she needed to be bonded to be saved, I understood now.

I made sure my phone was in position, held down by my side with the camera trained on Tobias. It had only taken a few taps to start the video stream to one of my contacts.

"Because you're Tobias Connolly, of the Connolly crime family," I said, cutting off his attempt at cursing me out. "I'm live streaming this entire encounter to a friend of mine, who is going to put it online and send it to the police the second you touch a hair on either of our heads. Kiara is my omega, and the Institute's seers will prove that. Since your sister is now mine, you're going to fuck off. Do you understand me, Toby?"

His eyes were the same colour as hers, but there was nothing but hatred in them. They narrowed at me, scanning me up and down. Was he going to call my bluff? I got the sense he had more brains than that. Plus, he was a beta. They weren't ruled by instincts like most male alphas were when they got into a high stress situation like this.

"Kiara wants to come home with me, doesn't she?" Tobias softened his voice to ask.

He thought his sister was a fucking fool. She wasn't going to fall for sweet talking from a man she'd been running from.

"No," she mumbled, pressing closer to me like she wished she could be absorbed into my body and disappear. "I don't."

"You heard her. My omega comes home with me. Are you going to let us leave, or will this be the headline story on the five o'clock news?"

He stared between me and her until discomfort slithered down my spine, but then he waved his hand. He'd schooled his face into a mask of nonchalance, but it was impossible to hide the fury boiling in the depths of his eyes.

"Fine. Let them go."

His men parted, standing on either side of the path so we

could pass through the middle of them. I pushed Kiara in front of me as we walked. If anyone dared to touch her, I wasn't above hunting them down and cutting off their hands, but no one did.

"Have a good life, little sis," Tobias said as we rushed away from them.

It was a promise, telling her that if he had anything to do with it, she wouldn't.

I didn't respond no matter how much I wanted to, because it was better for me to get her out of here without pissing him off. He could change his mind. There would be consequences to it, but the Connolly crime family had money, leverage, and plenty of lackeys who would be willing to take the fall.

"My car is around the corner," I said to Kiara when we were out of hearing range. "Dark green sedan."

I was parked illegally beside a fire hydrant because I couldn't be fucked to find a proper spot once I got news about her whereabouts. Someone had called in a tip about a barefoot omega woman walking through the area. The same tip, I knew, her brother must have tracked. It was pure luck Tobias had found her first. If I'd started looking one street over, it would have been me.

She didn't speak until I'd helped her into the passenger seat and revved the engine.

"Thank you," she whispered, following it up by clearing her raspy throat.

I sighed. "Don't thank me yet. We've got to get you cleaned up first."

Her teeth sunk into her bottom lip and she looked down at her hands. She was holding her knife. More fresh blood was on it, and her brother had a small gash on his forearm. Pride filled me for a second before I remembered what else she'd used that knife for.

And how it had ended with her getting exactly what she wanted.

Did she at least feel guilty?

Fuck, I could tell. We were in each other's heads, to an extent, feeling all the emotions. Guilt was at the forefront of hers.

"Is Ambrose...?"

"He'll live."

She clenched her hands into fists, likely to stop another question from rolling off her tongue. I was grateful for the quiet because it gave me a chance to process.

Not only did I have an omega now, but she was dark bonded and was going to bring a whole shit storm down onto my head.

I had to get back into a position of control, or I was going to crack. I already had the ultimate control over Kiara, but that wasn't going to be enough. Telling her what to do wouldn't fix the situation.

"You're not allowed to use that knife on me or Ambrose," I said, unsure of what I had to do to give her a command. I put the weight of my aura behind it, and felt the command settle over me like a light blanket.

She'd put herself under my control, so I thought it was fair that I made sure I didn't get fucking stabbed. Her back stiffened and she nodded, the motion mechanical. "I won't."

We stayed quiet for the rest of the drive and while I pulled into my parking garage. Kiara didn't say a word even as we got in the elevator, luckily alone so no one saw how dishevelled she was. The next sound I heard from her was a soft gasp when she followed me into the condo, spotting Ambrose groaning on the couch.

Jasper knelt beside him, stitching up the knife wound on the small of his back. With Ambrose's shirt ripped halfway up his torso, I could see more of his scars than I'd ever been able to before. The skin was uneven, unable to heal completely, and around the edges of the burning were knife wounds.

Much like the one Kiara had given him today.

"She looks like shit," Liberty said, blowing a bubble with her chewing gum.

She sat on an armchair across the room, laptop resting on her folded legs.

"Things happened," I muttered.

"You know, I told you she was trouble."

A growl rumbled up without my consent. Something about Liberty talking about her that way irritated me to no end. My friend's eyes widened, and she popped to her feet. "Oh, fuck. Leigh, did you dark bond her?"

"*Things* happened. I'm going to get her cleaned up and then we can have a big old conversation about how everything is imploding. Kiara, come."

She began walking immediately. I cursed. It was hard *not* to put my aura behind my words—I was so used to it. My bark wasn't like a male alpha's and was actually far more natural. In this situation that was a downside.

"That wasn't a command. Sorry."

Her feet stuttered to a stop and a breath whooshed out of her. The tension in our bond dissolved too, telling me the order was no longer affecting her. Taking the commands back was as easy as doling them out in the first place, luckily.

I led her through the house to my bedroom, grabbing a bag from beside the front door on the way. They were the clothes I'd bought her, and it was a good thing she had them now. She was a mess and Tobias' scent clung to her like a bad odour clung to an old pair of shoes.

"Sit on the bed." I had to soften my tone, being very careful to avoid making it a command. It would take some getting used to.

She hesitated, glancing down at herself. "I'm dirty."

"Doesn't matter. You could take your clothes off first, if you wanted to."

Her knife was placed gently on the bed when she reached for the hem of the t-shirt, and I immediately regretted everything.

She definitely should keep that on, but I hadn't been thinking about how aroused she made me even when clothed from head to toe. I couldn't look away as the fabric slid up her torso, freeing her tits with a generous bounce. Biting back my groan, I almost swallowed my tongue when she pushed the sweatpants down her hips. Her underwear were cheeky, showing off a lot of her ass. I wanted to fucking lick it.

No, Leighton. Absolutely no licking your dark bonded omega.

Kiara sat her ass down on the bed tentatively, like she was still worried about getting it messy. She was covered in far more bruises and cuts than I was comfortable with her having, but none were actively bleeding except for her torn up feet.

I grabbed alcohol wipes, bandages, and tweezers from my ensuite bathroom and came back to the bed to kneel in front of her.

Her eyes went wide and she reached a hand out for the supplies. "I'll do it," she said. "You should check on Ambrose."

Maybe that was what I *should* do, but she was my claimed omega now. Feeling her hurting was sending slivers through my soul, and I couldn't handle it. Ambrose was going to live—Jasper had assured me of that the second he stepped into the kitchen. There was nothing I could do for him while the doctor worked, but plenty I could do for her.

"Give me your foot."

That was a command, and she was forced to listen, leaning back so I could take her foot in my hand. The skin was dirty and burnt, blisters forming from when she'd walked for blocks on the hot cement. A couple of rocks had sliced her and a couple slivers were embedded in the more sensitive parts of her foot.

I got to work.

Every time she flinched, I growled. It was pure instinct.

It was a long and painstaking process, but I cleaned her feet up and bandaged them, knowing she would be tender for a few days. Then I moved on to the other wounds littering her skin.

There was nothing I could do about her bruises and Jasper would be checking the damage to her throat, but there were cuts along her thigh and sternum, the places she'd been clutching desperately since she arrived. "Is this where you kept the knife?" I asked.

I wiped the wound with the alcohol, trying to ignore how close to her I was. The sweet scent of her core was calling to me, but that was off limits. Just like licking her was off limits.

"Yes," she said.

Her voice was raspy and I told myself it was because of the damage to her throat and not because of arousal. I was lying and I knew it. Her arousal was heavy in the coconut chocolate perfuming up my room and calling to me through the bond we now shared.

"Why did you hurt yourself to keep the knife with you?" I asked.

"It's... safety," she admitted.

"What will you do if I take it away?"

Her arousal soured and she stiffened. I knew she was holding the knife behind her back. She couldn't use it on me, so I wasn't worried despite her history of being erratic.

"Please don't," she said, her voice small.

I sighed. "You know, if you'd gone out and gotten a dark bond from some random alpha, they wouldn't give a shit about your requests. You wouldn't be able to stop them from taking your knife and whatever else they wanted from you."

Her body trembled as I moved up to her sternum. The way her breasts rested blocked most of my access to her injuries, unless I wanted to get handsy with her. I peered up at her. "I'm going to clean these wounds too."

She brought her hands up and lifted the squishy flesh that I was desperate to bury my face in. I tried to focus on my task, getting it done as fast as possible so we could separate. Some distance would be better for both of us.

"Are you going to take it?" she asked as I finished up.

"Not unless you stab someone else."

Her throat bobbed as she swallowed, then coughed. "I didn't want to. I thought it was the only choice and would work to get you to dark bond me."

I barked a laugh, standing up and going over to the bag of new clothes. "It was far from your only choice, dove. But I guess it did work in the end." I tossed her the bag and she caught it. "Get dressed and come out to the living room again. You can shower later. We've got a lot of things to talk about first."

She nodded, and I strode from the ensuite, trying to force myself to stop thinking about her as 'dove.'

TEN

KIARA

I should have been prepared for anything after being dark bonded, but the prospect of my knife being taken had my brain threatening to shut down.

She even had a name now. It was Nyla. In a roundabout way, I'd picked it because of Leighton. Nyla was close to 'nilla,' which was similar to vanilla… which was the scent I couldn't get out of my nose.

With the new clothes strewn out on the bed beside me, I flipped Nyla around in my hands.

She was so small but had done so much damage. Jonathan. Tobias. *Ambrose*.

God, I needed to apologize to him. I'd regretted using Nyla on him the second I'd done it, even more so when I saw him slump with the wound still dripping.

"Are you sorry too, or are you leaving me to take full responsibility for stabbing Ambrose?"

She didn't respond, meaning I was left with all the responsibility.

That was fine. Nyla may have made the wound, but I made the decision and I deserved to be punished for that.

Leighton had gotten me a lot of clothes in a couple of different sizes. Most were baggy and comfortable—I assumed there were no plans to take me out of this condo, especially now—but a few were cute trendy pieces. They were like the ones I'd seen in the fashion magazines my mom liked, or on television on one of the few occasions when I'd been allowed to sit with Mother and watch it.

I put on a pair of sweatpants and a t-shirt for now, but smiled over the prospect of having the other clothes for later.

I hesitated before going out to the living room. It was strange to be leaving this solitary existence after I'd done something so... wrong.

If my father had caught me, I would have been locked in the basement for weeks. Whenever I severely misbehaved, I ended up there. All alone, with nothing to do but stare at the wall and hum to myself. No one ever visited until my confinement had ended.

Except Tobias.

He would visit and taunt me from the doorway. Sometimes he'd steal my food, leaving me with a grumbling stomach and overwhelming sense of sadness. The one person who could have helped me by keeping me company or sneaking in a treat wanted me to suffer, just like Father did.

I glanced around the room, holding Nyla in my fist and reminding myself that I would never go back. If I was stuck in this apartment forever, that would be fine. Leighton was far better company than my brother or the bugs.

By now, the doctor would be finished stitching up Ambrose. I had to go out there and face him—I'd have to see the contempt in his expression. At least it wouldn't be unfamiliar to me, and this time I actually deserved it.

Sure, I didn't like him with Leighton. It infuriated me. Stabbing him was going too far, though. He was just the only person around that wasn't her, and I'd needed to prove I was dangerous.

And he really had shoved my face in their relationship by making her scream like that last night. Did he maybe deserve it a little bit?

I tried my best not to pout.

Taking a deep breath and holstering Nyla in the waistband of my pants—visible to everyone in the room, because I didn't want to seem like I was hiding her—I stepped out of Leighton's bedroom. When I entered the living room everyone hushed, turning to look at me.

Jasper was the first to react, letting out a world-weary sigh. "Come here. Let's check out those strangulation bruises."

He shot a sidelong glance at Ambrose, who was sitting up on the couch, facing me, and letting Leighton take a peek at his back. I avoided eye contact with the alpha, scurrying over to Jasper and sitting on the coffee table where he pointed.

The doctor was a skinny beta with short dark hair and a pair of wire-rimmed glasses. I'd put him in his early thirties, with a youthful look about him. He was dressed casually, but there were a couple drops of blood on his button up shirt, and a small trash can sat full of disposable gloves. He snapped on another pair before leaning in close.

I held my breath, closing my eyes as he brushed his fingers up my neck. I whined deep in my throat when he got to the main bruising, even the slightest touch hurting. Breathing hurt too. So did speaking.

"Fuck," Ambrose cursed, standing abruptly only to groan from the pain.

Jasper drew my displaced attention back to him by probing a different area of my neck. "Open your mouth," he instructed.

He shone a light down my throat and then looked at both of

my eyes before sitting back with a sigh. "You didn't lose consciousness?"

I shook my head. I'd been woozy and lightheaded, but never passed out.

"I'm going to check your neuro vitals anyway, but you're probably fine. Look at me."

I listened, and he shone the light in my eye. He hummed in approval when I flinched away from the light. "You know your name?"

"Kiara."

"Where do you live, Kiara?"

My teeth sank into my bottom lip, unsure how to answer. "Here," I said after a long pause.

He glanced around with a slight wrinkle of his nose. "Sure smells like it," he muttered. "Wiggle your fingers and toes for me."

I did as he'd asked, not having trouble moving either set of limbs. He passed me a bottle of water and I gulped some down while he watched my throat contract and relax with keen medical interest. When I put the bottle down, half empty, he nodded.

"Those bruises are going to be a bitch to deal with, but you'll live. Put some ice packs on them to help with swelling, and pop an anti-inflammatory if you need to. Just don't do any of this bullshit again. Either of you, for fuck's sake."

His glare turned from me to Ambrose and back again, then settled on Leighton for good measure. She lifted an eyebrow at him. "What did I do?"

"It was your bright idea to bring the alpha you're fucking into a house with an omega who's obsessed with you."

I flushed. Obsessed... was a harsh word for it.

"I didn't know she had the knife," Leighton said.

Jasper shrugged. "You let her stay in your house. Everyone was suspicious of her. I'd say that one's on you."

Leighton cursed under her breath. "Fine. No one is free of

fault. Believe me, I won't be calling you back for more impromptu medical treatment."

"Better not. You know I hate practicing medicine. There's a reason I'll only do it for you."

"And I appreciate you doing it."

"Yeah, yeah. Appreciate me with a couple extra dollars on my next paycheque. I've got to go. My little cousin has a basketball game tonight. If Ambrose's wound starts seeping or anything call me. Or if she can't breathe. Christ, you people are a mess."

He gathered up his supplies, muttering some more about how much he regretted ever going to medical school. Then he waved behind him on the way out.

"So is this like a family conversation, or can I hang out and hear the story of how the unhinged omega came to be dark bonded?" Liberty asked, her laptop now half closed as she peered at the rest of us.

Leighton looked at me and I froze under the assessment. I still hadn't looked at Ambrose, but I felt his gaze burning into me. His scent burned the air too, the hot iron and smoke heavy with gently boiling anger. He must be furious at me for stabbing him. That was within his rights.

"Depends. Kiara? Can Liberty stay? She'll undoubtedly hear about some of it anyway since she's going to be running point on keeping us alive after that debacle."

Liberty sat up straighter in her seat, curiosity sparkling in her eyes. "Debacle?"

I waited for Leighton to get into it, but she didn't. Silence reigned in the living room until I looked up and caught Leighton's eyes. My cheeks flared with heat. She was pointedly waiting for an answer. "It's fine," I squeaked.

"You sure?"

I nodded, cringing at the movement. Neck movement hurt, but it was instinctual to communicate that way.

"When I went after Kiara, I ended up listening to police scanners while trying to follow her scent away from the house," Leighton said. "Someone called in a tip, but I wasn't the first person to get to her. Her brother was. Tobias Connolly tried to take her back home, which I'm assuming is exactly the reason she's been adamantly pushing for a dark bond since she got here."

Liberty released a soft 'ooo,' and I finally got the nerve to look at Ambrose. His jaw was clenched, the unscarred side of his face screwed up in anger. The scarred side twitched and pulsed, the muscles dancing. Oddly, when his eyes caught mine he softened, giving me a strained smile.

"She sliced him with that knife—it's been through a lot in the last twenty-four hours—before she got away. I caught her before they did, but we were left in a bit of a situation. It was dark bond her or let them take her."

"My knife's name is actually Nyla," I said absently. I was busy playing back the moments leading up to the dark bond.

"You should get her in to see a psychiatrist," Liberty said. "Whatever happened to her growing up with a crime family, she clearly didn't have many human friends."

I went pink, my hand going down to palm Nyla. I hadn't had *any* friends. Ever. I'd never gone to a public or private school, only ever having tutors who flitted in and out of my life by the whims of my parents. None stayed too long before being fired.

The only one who could have been my friend was Tobias.

And he'd been anything but.

"I'd appreciate if you stopped talking about her like she's crazy."

That was Ambrose coming to my defence, surprisingly. Leighton already had her mouth open though, her green eyes flashing with irritation.

"Oh, you lot are so fucked. On second thought, I don't want to be around for this shit show." Liberty snapped her laptop shut and stood with it under her arm. "How did you get away from Tobias Connolly unscathed after dark bonding his sister? That's all I want to know."

Leighton failed to hide her wince. "See, that's another minor complication."

"Weren't you sending a live stream of us somewhere?" I asked. "I thought it was here. To her."

Liberty was more than a housekeeper, if she was Leighton's emergency contact who could ferry a doctor in at the drop of a hat.

"About that." Leighton's attention swung to Ambrose, and she grimaced. "The only one who I could trust to record every second of a live streamed call was... Well..."

Ambrose cursed as she trailed off, grabbing his phone from his pocket. "Sixteen missed calls," he grumbled.

Liberty cackled, knowing exactly what was going on even as I didn't have a clue. "This is perfect. I'll start researching the Connollys and handling clients. Call me with updates, Leigh."

She strode out of the condo as Ambrose stared at his phone with increasingly sallow skin. Leighton pressed a hand to her temple, rubbing it. I was still in the dark. I was used to it—Father kept me in the dark about everything, all the time. But with Leighton and Ambrose, I really didn't like it.

"Who is it, and why is everyone freaking out?" I asked.

"Ambrose's pack lead. His name is Dash."

"Why is that bad?"

"That's... a long story." Leighton cringed. "And I'm not even sure where to fucking start."

ELEVEN

DASH

Having Leighton Winston in my fucking DMs was a perfect way to ruin a goddamn Thursday.

OK. The day had already been ruined by Ambrose's sudden anguish and Mercury's subsequent freakout as he tried to find our packmate. But 'Winston' popping up in my video calls was a surefire way to make everything worse.

The only Winston I wanted calling me was her brother, and that was never going to happen.

He was happy with his pack, as everyone said. Well, I sure as fuck wasn't happy and it was impossible to get over it when his older sister was everywhere all the time. For a corporate fixer, she definitely didn't stay in the shadows enough.

"Call me back, asshat. That's not a fucking request," I barked into the phone after Ambrose failed to answer for the fifth time in a row.

Pretty sure Mercury was out calling the cavalry to find him, at this point. Apparently, he was at the house of some woman he was seeing. I didn't know why Ambrose felt the need to keep a relationship a secret. We were an open pack.

Maybe I was the problem.

Maybe he thought my constant wallowing would chase her off before she got a chance to fall for him.

Fuck, he might be right.

It had chased off every woman I'd ever tried to date. Not that there were many. I clung to hope for my scent match for so long I didn't bother trying to find anyone else in a serious capacity.

Clicking a few buttons on my PC keyboard, I popped up the grainy feed from the recorded video call. To her credit, Leighton knew a lot of shit about me. She would have known I'd keep a recording, while a call to most people would end up lost to the ether, requiring a hack to retrieve. One she may not have had time for.

"Tobias Connolly has an omega sister," I murmured, tapping my pencil against the shitty desk I kept in the back room of the Dirt with Dash studio. "And Leighton dark bonded her. Did she want me to blackmail her? Why would I keep this to myself?"

She already owed me a favour—a fucking big one. Keeping this for her was going to add to the tally.

Humming, I grabbed my bag off the back of my chair and strode from the room, letting the door slam behind me. I avoided the staff by going out the back door and down the multiple flights of stairs. By the time I got to the bottom I'd worked up a sweat and was greeted by humidity out the ass when I stepped outside.

As much as I hated Leighton Winston, it was about time I paid her a visit to talk about repayment of favours.

The ride was smooth in my bright orange convertible, and I passed it off to the valet of a neighbouring building. When I went to wander off he tried to stop me, informing me parking was for patrons only, but I shrugged.

"I'll be a patron. Later."

I didn't even know what the fuck was in the building, but I wasn't parking my sports car on the street.

"Sir—"

Flipping my wallet open with a sigh, I slid a hundred dollar bill from the confines of it. I pushed it into the valet's hand. "Look, I'm busy. Take the tip and park the car."

I didn't wait to see if he listened. If someone towed my car they'd have hell to pay, but I could afford the tow truck's fees. I was too focused on Leighton to give a shit.

Sometimes, when I got something in my head I couldn't stop until I'd gotten it done. Like that one time I'd built a PC from top to bottom, including sourcing the parts, in twelve hours. Or when I'd personally installed a sophisticated security system at the Dirt with Dash studio. That part took a few days, but I'd gone off on a tangent and decided we needed cyber security too. I'd learned to code and hadn't slept for five days.

This time, my fixation was Leighton.

Couldn't say it was the first time, but the woman was so off limits it wasn't even funny. She was a constant reminder of the scent match mate that didn't want me, and female alphas didn't do it for me.

Except, she kind of did.

But I wasn't going to tell anyone that, not ever in my goddamn life.

I slid into her building behind an elderly couple with walkers, beaming widely at them as I helped them hold open doors. We made small talk in the elevator, and by the time I was on the right floor I was bouncing.

I knew which unit was hers, so I didn't knock. Just walked in, only to stop short at what I saw.

"Are you fucking kidding me?"

Leighton, Ambrose, and some pretty omega with honey brown hair all spun to face me.

Ambrose was barely clothed, his shirt ripped up the back and exposing those scars he was so self-conscious about. The omega had a ring of bruising around her throat and various other scrapes and bruises, her hand fisting what looked like the hilt of a knife at her hip.

And Leighton... she had a smear of blood on her top lip and her normally defiant, controlled expression was nowhere to be fucking found.

"How long have you been banging her?" I demanded, stomping into the condo. "What kind of goddamn betrayal is this? There are billions of people on the planet, Ambrose, and only her pussy was good enough? Or is it the omega you're fucking. I thought we decided as a pack that we weren't going to be with omegas."

The three of them were too stunned to speak, at least until I was nearly face to face with Leighton.

A perfect specimen of omega placed herself between me and the little snake, clogging my nose with coconut and chocolate. Her scent was spiking as her body trembled, and she clutched that hilt like it was the only thing keeping her stable.

"There's no need to talk to her like that," she said, putting on a show of confidence as her voice wavered.

I scoffed. "And what do you know, little omega?"

Reaching down I snatched the knife from her before she could stop me, whistling when I saw it wasn't in a case. Bare silver stared back at me. "You're prepped and ready to go, aren't you? Were you planning on stabbing me with this?"

No one had answered a single one of my questions, and I'd thrown out plenty of them. It was getting fucking old. She didn't answer me either, but when I looked down at her much shorter form I found her trembling like a leaf, tears dripping down her face.

Oh. *What the fuck?*

I didn't often feel remorse, but I had the urge to give the weapon right back to her and let her stab me with it.

Last time I'd gotten this tightness in my chest had been with our scent match, and look how that had gone. My life had been shit since he'd rejected us.

Before I could give in to the temptation, Ambrose plucked the knife from my hand and pressed it into the omega's palm. Her eyes blew wide as she stared at him, her plump lips parting a little. My packmate unnecessarily brushed his fingers across her wrist as he left the blade in her possession.

She was no longer trembling or panicking now that she had it back.

Emotional support knife. Got it.

"Dash, if you're done being a self-centered cunt, you should sit down," Ambrose grunted.

Leighton placed a palm on the small of her back, leading her to the couch and far away from me. As she turned, I caught sight of a bondmark on the omega's neck. It was as dark as a night sky. It blended into the bruises around her neck, but if it hadn't, it might have looked like it was... seeping. Bleeding darkness into the surrounding skin.

She was the Connolly daughter that I'd learned about on the video call. Kiara.

The woman was far less passive than I would have expected from someone of that upbringing.

"To answer the first question you barked at us, Leighton and I have been sleeping together for four years. No, I didn't tell you, and you know exactly why," Ambrose started.

Flexing my jaw, I turned my gaze from the omega to my packmate, who had none of the remorse he should have. We had one spoken rule—no omegas. The other rule was unspoken because it was *fucking obvious:*

No Leighton Winston.

"The omega's name is Kiara, and we're not sleeping together. However, she might have been planning on stabbing you with that knife and it would have been warranted, after you burst in like that."

I gave her another once over, annoyed at myself for being happy at the excuse to look at her again. Pointedly, I avoided looking at Leighton. Her vanilla cream scent being all over this place was bad enough. I didn't need to look at her cute goddamn freckles too.

The omega was holding the knife to her chest now, her legs pulled up onto the couch. She was broken and battered and dark bonded. There was no way she would have stabbed anything.

Then again, I had come in with my aura blazing and I was about a foot taller than her, and strong enough to toss her over my shoulder and—

Yeah, we were not going in *that* direction with my thoughts.

"Whether or not she would have stabbed you, I was about to," Leighton said. "What the fuck are you doing here, Dash?"

I lifted an eyebrow, reclining back in the chair until I could kick one leg over the other. "Why *wouldn't* I come check up on you after a video call like that?"

"Because you hate me." Leighton deadpanned.

Well, she wasn't wrong.

Or so I told myself.

"I can still blackmail people I hate."

Ambrose growled. My aura flared, instincts putting up a fight against being challenged. My packmate may have given me pack lead without a fight, but he wasn't strong enough to take it back now. In a battle of auras, mine won.

"You're not going to blackmail her," Ambrose bit out.

Rolling my eyes, I found my gaze drawn back to the omega again. I could have sworn she was watching me with interest. "Why not?" I asked.

The question was directed at Kiara—she stiffened, glaring at me. "She saved my life. Why would you blackmail her for that?" Kiara demanded.

"Because she saved your life by doing something that will ruin hers," I said slowly. "A dark bond isn't socially acceptable.'

Kiara's eyes widened. She flicked her gaze to Leighton, who was glaring me down. "You hate her enough to do that to her?"

Her question stunned me momentarily. I was expecting begging or acceptance, at least from the omega. Instead, she was going to call me out on the fact that I was being... Well, a self-centred cunt like Ambrose had said.

Fuck her for making me think about it. There was no reason to linger in my feelings about Leighton and her brother.

"Ambrose seems to want her life in one piece, so I suppose I can leave it," I said. My abrupt avoidance of the topic didn't go unnoticed. "I just want one small favour. No ongoing blackmail."

"Dash..." Ambrose said, going over to stand behind Leighton protectively.

"Oh, calm down. All I want is to know how she plans on keeping Kiara safe from the Connolly crime family all on her own."

Of all the ridiculous pieces of information to ask for.

My brain to mouth pathway was fucked up, because I *didn't care*. I didn't. I should have asked about her clients or their dirt or anything that could bring me some fun in this boring fucking existence. But, no. Instead, I ask about her omega.

The one that will be back with the Connollys within a week if Leighton doesn't have anyone to help her.

Leighton growled. "I've got it."

"If you had to live stream an interaction with Tobias Connolly to me, of all people, I don't think you've got it. And that doesn't answer my question, anyway."

"I don't need your help, Dash," Leighton said.

I hadn't offered her help. She'd jumped to the conclusion all on her own, and I smirked.

She crossed her arms over her chest and gave me that look—the one that always made me hard as stone. She looked down her nose at me with her eyes narrowed, lips tight with displeasure. Could I tell you why it was that look that made me want her desperately? No. But it was part of the reason I avoided her like the plague.

Being with my scent match mate's sister would be a constant reminder of the rejection that still tore my heart to shreds whenever I thought too hard about it.

It didn't matter how gorgeous she was, or how I'd always thought she would have been a great addition to our pack.

"Wasn't offering it," I said with a smirk. My crossed legs helped to hide the bulge in my pants, thank fuck. "But you do need help. Something clearly happened, and while you came out unscathed, neither of *them* did."

I nodded to Ambrose and Kiara, both injured. Kiara averted her eyes, staring down at her hands, and Leighton shifted in front of her. "The injuries have nothing to do with the Connollys."

I waited.

If it wasn't the Connollys, it was someone else.

"Kiara stabbed Ambrose," Leighton said.

My eyes widened. OK, I hadn't expected that. The little omega *could* stab someone with that knife she held so dear. I was impressed.

"And I... reacted," Ambrose grunted.

His expression filled with shame, posture drooping. Knowing his history—some of it, because he was too private to tell us everything that happened, the fucker—I figured his reaction was the reason behind those nasty bruises on her neck.

Losing his parents to that fire had messed him up, but the torture he'd endured before the flames consumed everything was what woke him up in cold sweats.

I used to fish for details until Mercury had threatened to kick me out of our apartment if I ever brought it up again. It was the only time Mercury had been so serious about calling me out, so I'd stopped.

"Damn. Well, knowing you got stabbed makes me feel a lot better. Thanks, little omega. You took the burden off my shoulders. If *I'd* stabbed him, he never would have let me forget it."

She peered up at me with wide eyes, so innocent I had to look away from the baby blues pre-emptively. I needed to get the fuck out of here, because between the two women I was about to lose my mind.

Abruptly, I stood. "I came to talk about the favour you owe me, but that can wait. Mercury is seconds away from calling the police to report Ambrose's absence, and I doubt that would go over well considering the state you're all in. You might want to wait on registering that dark bond until she doesn't look like she's been strangled half to death."

Leighton cursed. "Fuck. They'll think I coerced her."

A seer could tell if a dark bond was created with or without consent, but it wasn't foolproof. You could coerce an acceptance with threats of violence or blackmail. It was still illegal, just really hard to prove. The Institute did take shit like that seriously though, and there would be an in-depth investigation.

"They will," Ambrose muttered. "You're right that you've got to wait. They should fade within a couple of weeks. Until then, you're not safe from Tobias."

Even after the bond was registered, they weren't safe from

Tobias. None of us were stupid—a crime family wasn't going to stay above board and respect Leighton's claim.

"I'll stay with you," Ambrose declared.

I laughed. "No, you fucking won't. Don't you feel Mercury's panic through the bond? He needs you to show back up at our apartment, and then he needs to be tied down and fucked until he screams. It's the only way he's going to calm down and not give himself a heart attack."

A low growl rumbled from Ambrose, his hips shifting as if to relieve the pressure on his cock. "Mercury and I don't have that kind of relationship anymore, which you're aware of. I'll call him, but I can't leave Leighton and Kiara alone."

"And you only stopped fucking because of me. I'm fine, so go back to your lovebird shit. Leighton and Kiara won't be alone, anyway. I'll be staying."

Those were the most impulsive words to come out of my mouth all fucking day. Staying? No, I needed to haul ass out of here. That had been the plan, but not in the depths of my brain.

That impulsive part of me wanted to stay and see why Leighton was so tempting Ambrose hadn't been able to resist her —even though I already knew. And in the process I could see if Kiara was as chaotic as I was, because it would make me feel better about myself if I wasn't alone.

"No one is staying," Leighton said.

I grinned over at her.

If I'd been smart, that would be my out. I could flee with Ambrose and go back to finding betas to fuck at my favourite club.

I wasn't smart, and when I made an impulsive decision, I stuck with it.

"Really?" I asked. "Try and make me leave then, sweetheart."

TWELVE

LEIGHTON

Something about Dash Loranger had always pissed me off.

I think it started with how guilty he made my brother feel about rejecting him. The rejection hadn't been for no reason—my brother would have been miserable with them, not because of the pack but because of proximity to our mother.

Dash had never understood that.

He was one of those that believed a scent match was the be all, end all of omega bonds. It was fucking bullshit, in my opinion. Scent matches were compatible sexually and emotionally, but the universe couldn't account for lifestyle situations.

Besides his situation with my brother, Dash was pushy as fuck.

Case in point.

He was still in my goddamn apartment.

Ambrose had tried to drag him out, but Dash was the pack lead and his aura was strongest by far. I'd sensed Ambrose was about to challenge him for pack lead anyway, so I'd kicked Ambrose out.

It left Kiara and I sitting on the couch, staring down Dash like he was a cockroach that needed to be killed. Which was impossible. Cockroaches could survive the apocalypse, and so could Dash's willpower.

"Your help is not required, nor is it appreciated," I told him for about the fifth time.

As he had every time before, he smirked.

Cocky little shit.

"Don't worry, you'll need me eventually," he said.

The way he looked at Kiara had my hackles rising and I fought to stifle the growl. His gaze was appreciative, and he wasn't shy about looking at her tits. I wished it made her uncomfortable, but she was fighting arousal the same way I was fighting irritation.

To be fair, Dash was handsome in a way not many men were. If he hadn't started his stupid internet talk show, he could have been a successful model, or movie star, or any one of those professions that relied heavily on good looks. His scent was working in his favour too, the fresh aroma of spring rain and a sweet note of peaches.

"I doubt it," I muttered. "Kiara, you can take a shower now if you'd like. I think all the important conversations are over with."

She hopped to her feet so fast she swayed, holding a hand to her head. She was so fragile compared to what I was used to. Omegas couldn't take a beating the same way an alpha could, but this was the first time I'd seen it in action.

Dash stood, taking a step toward Kiara before my snarl ripped through the air. He held up his hands with a smirk.

"Calm down. I was only going to ask if she needed help in the shower."

Kiara let out the smallest whimper, her perfume heightening. I groaned and so did Dash, his hand going down to unashamedly readjust his pants.

"If she needed help in the shower, she'd be getting it from me.

Her bondmate," I snapped. "Don't even think about putting your hands on my omega, Dash."

His eyes narrowed, light green orbs darkening with mischief. I shouldn't have said that. Banning him would only antagonize him. If I'd learned anything from years of following Dash's antics on the tabloids, it was that as soon as he wasn't allowed to do something... he wanted it more.

A lot more.

It wasn't like I could sit back and watch him check out Kiara, though.

"Do you need help in the shower, dove?" I murmured, my hands resting on her hips.

She shook her head. "No. I think I'm fine."

"Let me know when you're done, and I'll help wrap your feet in fresh bandages."

Nodding, she hesitated for a beat, looking between the office where she'd been sleeping and my suite. She chose mine, scurrying off as a purr rumbled my chest.

I should *not* want her in my bed.

"Aren't you two the cutest couple in the world," Dash said in a sing-song voice.

The purr stuttered to a stop and I glared at him. "If you're going to insist on being here, enjoy sleeping on the couch," I said, gesturing to the leather.

It wasn't comfortable and wasn't meant to be, but I didn't want him on the pullout couch in the office. Kiara's scent was all over it and I couldn't scrub it off like I could with the leather. Her scent was already permeating my condo from everything she'd scent marked last night, and I wouldn't have him sleeping in a bed of it.

She was mine.

Not his.

"Such a gracious host. Shall I order us some food? It is that weird time between lunch and dinner, but I'm starved."

My stomach rumbled at the most inconvenient moment. "Whatever. Order the food. I have to go make some work calls."

I'd left right in the middle of my day, leaving any clients with urgent issues floundering. Then again, I wasn't often in my office anyway. They knew to call me.

And lo and behold, I had a series of missed calls from a series of clients and then one that stuck out like a sore thumb.

Mother.

What the fuck did she want?

I went into my office and closed the door, sucking in a deep breath of coconut and chocolate to calm myself down. Then I dialled her number, preferring to manage the more herculean task first.

"This is Edith Winston."

She always answered like she didn't have call display.

"Mother. You called?"

She heaved a long-suffering sigh from the other end of the line. "I expect you to answer your phone during work hours, Leighton."

I grit my teeth. "Something came up. My apologies."

"Ensure it doesn't happen again."

The woman spoke like she was my boss, but she wasn't. I was an independent corporate fixer—public relations specialist, on my business cards. She didn't control my work hours or my clients, but she did control my life due to circumstances far beyond my reach.

"Understood."

"A friend of mine needs your services. He's lost something precious to him."

"I'm not a private investigator. Does he know my rates?"

There was a pause so long I worried the connection had been lost. Mother would blame me for it, of course.

"You will do what I tell you, including finding what my friend has lost. And you will do it free of charge."

My growl volleyed down the line and I regretted it immediately. I hated being told what to do, but I didn't often lose control. This situation with Kiara had me on edge. I'd made a misstep with Soren yesterday too, and I could hardly believe how much my emotions were cracking my professionalism.

"If you ever do that again, you know what's going to happen," Mother said, a hard edge to her voice.

I did know.

It wasn't like I did her bidding willingly. I was being blackmailed by my own mother, for fuck's sake.

"Yes, I do."

"I'll text you the address of my friend. Go meet him immediately."

She hung up, the beeping of the line rattling around in my head. What was she going to do when she found out I dark bonded an omega? Would she decide I was more trouble than I was worth and release every secret she kept stowed away?

I ran my hands through my hair and slumped down into a desk chair, each breath heavy with stress. She'd been using me for years. I'd always been careful to keep people out of my life because of her, and now that I finally had someone to help my oppressive loneliness, everyone could be caught up in the crossfire.

Because it wasn't my secret she kept to blackmail me. I didn't have anything I fucking cared about.

It was my brother's.

The door creaked open and I lifted my head, eyes blowing wide when I saw Kiara there.

Her hair was dripping wet, the fluffy towel wrapped around her barely covering her ass. Thick thighs were on display, making it far too easy to imagine what was between them and how it would feel for me to be there.

She clutched at the towel and shifted from foot to foot, the knife held in her other hand. "Are you alright?" she asked, teeth biting down on her bottom lip. "I could feel… you."

My irritation.

Damn it.

This bond was hard to turn off. I hadn't realized I was projecting that.

I opened my mouth only to scowl when I caught the scent of Dash's arousal filtering into the room. Kiara had walked through the living room like this. Where *he* was.

He was irritatingly brazen in letting me know he was interested in what was mine, especially considering he'd walked in and claimed their pack never dated omegas.

"Come here." My command was potent in my words and Kiara immediately started forward.

She kept coming until she was standing between my legs. With how short she was, my legs ended up around the middle of her thighs.

"I'm fine, just have a minor problem to deal with," I said. "I appreciate you checking on me, but next time put some clothes on first."

Her throat bobbed as she swallowed. Seeing those bruises on her neck made it even harder not to touch her, but I was resisting. My hands were on my thighs, as much as I wanted them to be on hers.

"Why? I'm your omega now."

She tentatively dropped the grip on the towel. It stayed up on its own. Barely. Kiara reached that hand out and rested it on my shoulder. Warmth spread from the spot, arousal zinging through me. It was almost impossible to resist.

And why did I need to resist?

She was mine, like she'd said. If she ever fucked anyone else I'd have to kill them, but it wasn't fair to force her to stay celibate for the rest of her life.

"Dash," I muttered. Focusing on the conversation was hard when the towel was losing its grip on her breasts with every passing second. "He's not allowed to see you like this."

"Oh," she breathed.

Her thighs pressed together, but it didn't stop me from smelling her.

There were totally reasons why I shouldn't touch her right now.

I just couldn't think of a single one. My instincts were running wild in a way they never had around an omega before. Honestly, they had been since the moment I saw her, at home on my damn couch. Regardless of the situation, I would never have dark bonded an omega I wasn't inexplicably drawn to. The bond was for life. *She* was for life.

My hands came to rest on her outer thighs, just below the edge of the towel.

She stopped breathing, the knife hanging limp in her fingers.

"Do you want me to touch you, dove?"

Her whimper had me pulling her closer, my face level with her tits.

"Words," I commanded. "And tell me the truth."

Was it wrong to use the dark bond on her in a situation like this? Absolutely. But I didn't care. I wanted her to tell me.

She fought it for only a second before whining and giving in. "I want you to touch me so badly. Please make me come, Alpha."

My hands slid up under the towel, palming and squishing her ass. Being called 'Alpha' made me feral. It had never been a kink of mine before. I was in charge with every sexual encounter except Ambrose, but I'd never taken to names. Madame or

Mistress or Queen didn't do it for me, but Alpha? It worked far too well.

"Put your knife down," I murmured.

This one I didn't make a command. She needed to do it on her own. If she didn't put it down, we weren't in a position where we should be doing this.

Kiara hesitated, holding her knife up and inspecting it for a moment.

Then she placed it on the desk behind me, keeping it in her line of sight.

"Good. Now take the towel off."

She removed her hand from my shoulder, but I didn't have time to feel the loss. The towel came free, exposing her body beneath. I'd already seen most of it, but I'd been trying not to look. This time, I had no such restrictions.

Kiara's tits were the most perfect set I'd seen in my life. I brought my hands up from her ass to cup them instead, groaning when my delicate fingers couldn't contain them. Her nipples were a dusky pink, peaking against my palms as I caressed them.

I didn't focus on them for long, dragging my nails gently down her side and across her stomach. It was only enough pressure to leave little white lines in my wake, but Kiara pressed forward like she wanted more. Grabbing her ample hips, I tried not to go too fast.

All I wanted right now was to bury my fingers in her tight cunt. A patch of fine honey brown hair decorated the apex of her thighs, but with her tucked between my legs I couldn't see anything else.

"You're so gorgeous," I murmured, trying to tame my alpha impulses and focus on her before I went overboard.

"Th-thank you," she stuttered.

Both her hands were clenched in fists at her sides and she was shifting on her heels. Nervousness? Or regret over having asked for this?

"Do you want me to stop, dove?"

She shook her head so fast she winced, the movement agitating her injuries. "No, please don't. I just... um... this is... new."

My eyebrows drew together, puzzling through the words for a second before it hit me.

Fuck.

That should have been obvious.

I hadn't learned much about her life yet, but considering her family, it made sense for her to be a virgin. That knowledge had me almost as nervous as her.

Standing up, my movement forced her to take a step back. My lips were even with her forehead and I ran my hands through her wet strands of hair. She whined, her body responding to mine in ways I never could have imagined.

I moved her toward the pullout couch, careful to grab her knife before we were out of sight of the desk. I put it beside the couch instead. "Lay back. If it's new, I'd better make it special."

"It already is," she said.

"Extra special, then. Go on."

THIRTEEN

KIARA

My pulse was between my legs.

Was that normal? I'd never had a pulse there before, throbbing in time with the beating of my heart. Slick made my thighs slide together with ease as I laid myself back on the couch, trying to pay attention to the arousal and not the nerves.

I'd never been touched before, or touched anyone else. There was no one I wanted to try it with. Even if there had been, having sex with someone would have been the equivalent of killing them. My father would find out. He always knew everything going on in his home.

"You're going to have to spread your legs if you want me to touch you, dove." Leighton's voice was soft, urging me without demanding.

She wanted this as much as I did, and there was something thrilling about that.

Hesitantly, I parted my thighs the slightest bit, fighting the urge to look down. How did I look in this position?

"*Spread* your legs," Leighton said again. "How am I supposed to fit between them like that?"

I flushed, gaze flitting to my knife. She was my security blanket, bringing me comfort even though I couldn't use her on Leighton and would never dream to. "Why do you need to be between them?"

She grabbed the back of my knees and moved me on her own, shoving my legs apart just roughly enough that I moaned. Then she laid between my thighs, inhaling deeply. "This is why," she said. "God, you smell good, and I bet you taste even better."

"Taste?"

Leighton hummed, flicking her tongue out to swipe across my folds. "Yeah, you taste better than I could have imagined."

The foreign sensation made my core tighten, but she'd taken it away so fast I didn't know how to feel about it. I wanted her to do it again, but I wasn't going to ask. It wasn't like I knew the protocol.

"Have you ever come before, Kiara?"

I shook my head.

It had always seemed too risky. I'd had urges, been tempted to touch myself, especially in recent years. I never had. If Tobias had found me doing something like that...

He would have made fun of me for sure—he made jabs about everything from the colour of my hair, to my weight, to the way I walked. I got the sick sense he would have sent Jonathan to 'tame' me immediately if he'd caught me. That was a far bigger consequence than just being teased.

"You have no idea how much primal satisfaction it gives me to be your first."

If it was on par with how much rage I'd felt over her having sex with Ambrose, I did understand.

Her tongue grazed my core again before I could tell her my theory, which was all the better.

There was more time to revel in it because she didn't pull away. She kept lapping at me, practically drinking the slick I was producing. When her hands slid up my thighs, I moaned. Somehow even the twin sensations of her hands and her tongue were overwhelming. How did omegas have whole packs tending to them?

Leighton groaned against me, bringing her tongue up and swirling it around the little bud there.

I arched my back, shouting as my thighs threatened to squeeze Leighton to death. Despite her hands being right there, she didn't stop me from clenching them around her ears, and I tried to release my legs. It was impossible with the tension building in my core. That part of me was a pleasure centre I hadn't known existed.

My sexual education had been lacking, so I wasn't surprised I didn't know.

"What are you doing to me?" I asked breathlessly, eager to know how I could ask her to do it again.

She moved back enough to kiss my pussy, her warm breath tickling it. "I'm going to suck on your clit until you see stars, dove."

Clit. OK.

I was never going to forget that word.

"You should hold my thighs," I said. "I'm going to squish you with them if you keep doing that."

Her growl had me stiffening, fear slicing through me for a second. Leighton's expression immediately softened, turning her head to kiss my thigh.

"If you're not clenching your thighs in pleasure, I'm not doing a good enough job," she said. "Don't worry. I'm an alpha, and you're an omega. The only way you're going to hurt me is if I let you."

She had a point, but it couldn't be comfortable wearing my

thighs as earmuffs. I nodded, but decided I would try my best not to squeeze them shut.

"Touch yourself for me. I want to enjoy the view while I'm down here."

It was a command again. My eyes widened, only fighting the need to obey for a second. Pain echoed across my body if I tried to resist a direct order. My hands went down to my hips, trailing up my torso until they cupped my breasts and bounced them.

Leighton groaned, swirling her tongue around my clit again.

"If you need me to release the command, tell me," she said.

I barely nodded before suction made me cry out again, trying desperately to grind down on her face. She sucked and licked and dipped her tongue down into my entrance as slick drenched the blankets beneath us. I couldn't stop touching myself—physically couldn't, which was thrilling in its own way. My hands almost had a mind of their own as they caressed my body, showing off for my alpha.

Pleasure built, and I was getting to the point where I felt like I was going to see stars soon, but I didn't really know how to tell. When was the orgasm going to hit? It had to be soon, right? I was practically sobbing, my legs wrapped around her head and shoulders without a sliver of hesitation anymore. I was shoving myself against her face and she was accepting it with a series of groans, her tongue working me.

"You can't over think it, dove," she murmured. "Let your body do what it wants to do. Don't think. You can stop touching yourself if you'd like."

I moaned and tried to wipe my mind of everyone but her.

Leighton biting me to save my life. Her aggressive posture that made me wet even the first time I saw it. The way she'd delicately treated every wound on my body, showing a level of care I hadn't known an alpha could have.

I hadn't seen her without any clothes, but I could imagine

what she looked like under them. Freckled skin, matching the light smattering on her cheeks. Slim shoulders and hips.

Would she let me try this on her? I wouldn't be very good at it, but I wanted to know if she tasted like vanilla cream.

The pleasure reached a peak, and I figured out how I was supposed to know I was coming.

It was unfathomably good, my body convulsing as it rocked through me. I cried out her name, the fantasy of her still dancing in my head while the woman herself was between my legs, doing exactly what she'd promised.

Sucking my clit until I saw stars.

I might have even seen God.

By the time I could see straight again, my body heaving to suck in each breath, Leighton had taken her mouth off me. Her swollen, slick lips were kissing my inner thigh instead, and I hastily released the hold my thighs had on her.

"Now that you've had an orgasm, how many do you think you want a day?" she asked casually, sitting up and smoothing down her suit jacket.

"How many am I allowed?" I asked eagerly.

She laughed, trailing her fingers down my shin before shaking herself and getting off the couch. "I'll do my best to keep you well-supplied."

That wasn't an answer and I was about to call her out on it when I inhaled a scent I'd completely forgotten about.

Fresh spring rain and a hint of peaches.

Dash.

I'd walked past him to get in here when I'd felt Leighton's distress, but I'd tried to ignore him. His behaviour made me nervous in a way Ambrose's didn't, and I didn't like how he looked at Leighton. He liked her. Ambrose was one too many people for her to be sleeping with, so I wasn't about to let Dash have her too.

Ambrose got a pass since I'd stabbed him.

"The door was open," I whispered.

Dash could probably hear me anyway, even though I was talking to Leighton. With how heavy his arousal was, I bet he'd heard every whisper out of my mouth since Leighton had started touching me.

My mate's eyes flashed with feral glee, a smirk tilting her lips. "Was it?" she asked, grabbing the door and readying to swing it closed. "What a shame."

She slammed it shut, the sound like a gunshot and the wall shaking.

"How horrible of me to taunt him with everything he'll never be able to have," she said under her breath.

I tried to temper my arousal, which was already rising again.

Leighton had known the whole time that Dash was privy to everything. She hadn't closed the door because this was a claim on me.

"He'll never have you either, right?" I asked.

She looked at me with a lifted eyebrow, handing me my knife. I sat up and clenched it close to my chest. "He doesn't want me, but no. Dash is the last person I'd ever sleep with."

There was a hint of hesitation, but she was confident enough that I relaxed.

Leighton was mine.

A vision flashed through my head—Leighton between my legs with Dash behind her, Ambrose holding me from behind—but I shoved it out so fast I almost gave myself whiplash.

She was mine alone, and I was hers. After all, we were bonded now.

"Can you sit there for a couple of minutes while I return some calls? Then I can wrap your feet again."

I nodded, moving to grab the towel that I'd dropped onto the floor. She growled and I froze, peering up at her.

"No, dove. I want you naked while I make my calls. You're too stunning to cover up. It would be like putting a burlap sack over a piece of art. Unacceptable."

Flushing, I sat back on my ass and fiddled with Nyla. Leighton's gaze burned into me and I tried to ignore it, but the longer she looked, her voice sharp with her clients, the hotter I got. From the way she smirked when I squirmed, I had to assume that was the entire point.

As long as I got another orgasm out of this, I couldn't argue.

FOURTEEN

MERCURY

There were very few things that could panic me, but Ambrose being unreachable and furious was one of them.

I knew more about his history than anyone. He'd told me things as we'd laid side by side in bed—back when we still did that, before we'd put a stop to it. The only thing that played with his emotions enough to cause an angry aura flare like that were the memories of that night.

"What do you fucking mean you haven't heard from him?" I snapped. "He practically lives at The Pointe Lounge. When was the last time he was there?"

"Sir, we can't disclose information like that about our guests."

The woman's voice trembled. I wished I was there in person. Maybe if I barked a command, she would forget their privacy policy long enough to just tell me what I needed to know.

"He's my packmate," I growled. "And he's missing. What do you not understand? Tell me when he was last there and tell me the names of any women he's had with him."

"I'm going to get a manager."

The line clicked, and hold music started playing. I thought *she* was a manager. That was what the first man had said. Apparently they needed the manager of the manager to deal with me, but I didn't have time to wait. If the lounge was a dead end, I needed a new lead.

I hung up, calling Ambrose again.

I expected it to ring all the way to voicemail, so when his husky voice answered my breath hitched. "I'm on the way home right now."

"Where the fuck were you?"

"You know where I was."

"The woman?"

I'd successfully kept the jealousy out of my tone until this very moment. Who was she, and why was he ignoring my calls and spending time with her? We were pack. We used to be *lovers*. I was still in love with him, a fact we both tried steadfastly to ignore.

"Don't use that tone," Ambrose growled. "If you're mad at anyone, be mad at me. I'll explain when I'm there."

I hung up before I could get any more worked up. My panic had calmed at the sound of his voice, but it had only morphed into rage.

I wanted what we had back.

Why did Dash have to be falling apart? Why did I have to worry about him so much? Letting Ambrose go—going back to being just packmates and nothing else—had been the hardest thing I'd ever done. I never would have done it if I hadn't cared too much about the bitter scowls Dash levelled us with every time he came home to us being affectionate with each other.

Pacing across our living room, I didn't stop even when I heard the door swing open and closed. He would come to me, and it was better if I didn't start this conversation. I could be mean when angry, just like my fathers had been.

"Mercury." His gruff voice saying my name brought me back to all the times he'd brought me breakfast in bed. The man treated me with the love and care usually reserved for a goddamn omega, and I'd revelled in it.

"You can't just—"

I whirled to face him, stopping short with a gasp.

Bandages wrapped around his torso, his shirt ripped and jeans covered in blood. My fury bled to concern and I raced to him, searching the bandages for the source of the injury. Most of the blood was at the back, and when I tore the bandage down, it revealed a stitched-up wound. Thin and short, it was clearly a single stab from a knife.

"Who stabbed you?" I asked.

He grabbed my shoulders and moved me in front of him. We were almost the same height, but he was bulkier. I was willowy, with narrow shoulders and hips and a severe lack of muscle definition.

"This is going to take some explaining," he said.

My eyes narrowed. "Clearly. You were with the woman and somehow you got stabbed. What kind of trouble is she into?"

"Sit on the couch, baby."

I backed up and sat, unwilling to call him out on his use of 'baby' in this instance.

He sat on the ottoman facing me, so close my knees were between his. "I told you about the woman I was seeing," he said.

I nodded. "Yes. You started seeing her back when we were still together, and I said it was fine to see other people as long as it wasn't a new one every week."

Maybe I would have preferred to have Ambrose to myself—or at the very least, shared in his sexual endeavours outside the pack—but with his work at the BDSM club I was used to him touching other people.

"I didn't tell you who she was."

"Obviously. What does that have to do with anything?"

"It's Leighton Winston."

I jolted upright, only to have him grab my hips and shove me back down to the couch. "What?" I hissed. "We stopped having sex because it was hurting Dash, and you thought it was acceptable to be fucking our scent match's older sister behind our backs?"

Ambrose sighed, his scars doing that twitching thing they did. Muscle spasms, the doctors said. The muscles got confused that they couldn't move the way they used to be able to.

"I've never cared about hurting Dash. No offense to him, but he needs reality to slap him in the face or he's never going to pick himself up."

"That's not the proper way to care for your pack members," I said.

"You may think that depriving yourself of what you want is necessary for the good of the pack, but I don't. I want what I want, Mercury. And there are only two people I've ever wanted. You, and Leighton." He paused, then muttered, "Maybe three."

I wasn't going to go down that rabbit hole right now. My heart was wrenching apart as I tried to figure out what to feel. I was angry he didn't have the same opinion as I did—should I be? He was allowed to be different. I loved that he was different. He wasn't an anxious caretaker like I was.

More than anger, I was upset he'd let me put a stop to our relationship while he was still actively engaging in a relationship that would hurt Dash just as much—no. More.

"You need to move on and tell me the rest, or I'm going to start yelling at you," I said.

He sighed, his hands coming down to rest on my knees. Knees were about the least sexual place ever, but in my touch-starved state it was making me hard. I hadn't touched anyone since we broke it off.

Was I a little bitter that he had someone else the whole time? Absolutely. No matter how irrational it was.

It had been my choice to break things off for Dash's benefit. Ambrose never would have suggested it, and as much as I took shots at him for not caring about our pack lead's feelings, it made me happy.

I came before Dash in Ambrose's mind.

I was the only one struggling with my inability to keep both of them happy and mentally intact at the same time.

"Leighton called me last night and asked me to come over and help her with something, so I did. She had an omega on her couch, one who had turned up on her doorstep and begged her for a bond."

"She can't bond an omega. A bond wouldn't stick. She's not silver status, is she?"

Had I been keeping tabs on the Winston family? Yes. Sue me. Being scent matched to Leighton's brother drove our pack to the ground. While I could admit it wasn't his fault, I still wasn't keen on any of them. Especially since we'd had to deal with them a few months ago. Seeing them again had been hard on Dash.

"Dark bond," Ambrose said.

I stiffened. "Is the omega gold pack?"

A gold pack omega was one who hadn't gotten the injection the Institute recommended within a year of perfuming. That injection bound omegas and their children to our laws—things like not being able to kill your alpha. Gold pack omegas weren't forced to comply with rules like that, and neither were their children, rogue alphas.

Because of this danger they posed, they didn't get the kind of protections omegas who got the injection were given. It was legal to dark bond them, against their will or not.

"She's a normal omega."

"Why not just get a bond from a normal pack, then? Is she crazy?"

Ambrose growled and my eyes widened. He was protective of the omega. What kind of situation had he gotten us all into?

"Move on," I demanded. "Tell me the rest."

"The rest of the story is simple. I stayed the night, Kiara stabbed me because she thought it would force Leighton to dark bond her, and then she fled. Leighton called a doctor and went after Kiara once I was being treated."

I stared at him blankly, then down to the bandages. I needed to cover the wound again, because it was still exposed from when I'd looked at it.

"The omega *stabbed* you? And you're protective of her?" I asked coldly. "She needs to be put into goddamn custody."

This growl was loud enough that I returned it with a rumble of my own. "I almost choked her to fucking death, Mercury. She's been through enough."

That was the rage I'd felt from him. He'd been stabbed and he'd fucking lost it. The people who'd burned his house to the ground had used knives on him too before leaving him for dead.

"If she stabbed you, she had it coming," I said.

Ambrose glared, fighting to keep his aura under control. The intensity of his hot iron scent was almost cloying, the smokiness of it making me desperate to cough.

I was trying to keep myself together, too.

This omega had hurt what was mine. Why shouldn't she be punished for that?

"We are not turning her in for anything."

"Fine," I spat. If it came to a battle of auras, he would win. "But you're not going near her again, and Dash is never going to hear about this."

Dash would fall apart. I couldn't let him, not after I'd given so much of myself to keep him from doing that for the past six years.

Plus a tiny part of me worried what would happen to me if I let Leighton Winston and her new omega get under my skin.

His expression shuttered. Those eyes, usually holding so much warmth, went dark and cold, the depths still. "That's not up to you, Mercury, and Dash already knows. He's at Leighton's house with them right now."

He pushed to his feet and took a few steps away before sighing and turning back.

"You're trying to help and I fucking know that, but you've got to stop 'helping' everyone so much you take away their free will and yours. Let's continue this conversation later, once I've had a chance to cool down."

I bit my tongue to hold back my retort that he wasn't helping enough. Watching his retreating back until he vanished down the hallway to his bedroom, I slumped back onto the couch.

I needed a chance to cool down as much as he did.

It felt like the pack was falling to pieces around me, and I couldn't go through that. Not again.

FIFTEEN

LEIGHTON

My less-than-private claiming of Kiara hadn't gone unnoticed by Dash, but instead of the annoyance I'd hoped for, he was exuberant.

He grinned at me when I left my office to bring Kiara some clothes—after giving her another orgasm, of course. If I wasn't mistaken, she'd come faster the second time. She'd kept glancing at the closed door, and I wondered if thoughts of him listening in helped her get there.

The idea of her thinking of another alpha during sex wasn't as infuriating as it should be.

When she came out of the office, fully clothed but still a little flushed, he whistled low.

"You make such pretty sounds, little omega," he purred.

She avoided eye contact with him, looking at me instead. I wasn't sure what to tell her. He was going to be a flirt as long as he was here. We couldn't expect him to stop.

"I bet you wouldn't be able to get any of those sounds out of me," she said after a pause.

For that, she met his gaze head on, and I purred. She was fiery, and it hadn't been tamed by the dark bond. I liked that.

So did Dash, apparently. "Don't make a bet you can't win," he said.

"I can win."

"Really?"

"You can't touch her, so you'll never know," I said, going over to the couch and standing in front of Dash. "She's my omega, so you'd need my permission to touch her."

The asshole had the audacity to check me out, going from head to toe. My clothes were a little more rumpled than usual, but professional nonetheless. There wasn't much on display for him to enjoy.

"Oh, I'll make you both scream for me."

I scoffed. "I'd never let you touch me either. And why would you want to? I thought you were still hung up on my brother?"

Dash's expression soured so fast I might as well have dumped him in a vat of lemon juice. He glared at me with his lips pursed, letting Kiara and I leave the living room without another word.

In the kitchen, Kiara grabbed my arm and looked back at the closed glass doors blocking us from the living room. "Um, what happened with your brother to make him reject Dash and Ambrose?"

She was understandably confused. Most of New Oxford's rich people were just as confused about the rejection. My brother had met the Loranger pack at a gala, so it had been public knowledge they'd been scent matched... and subsequently never gotten together.

Rejecting a Loranger was unheard of. The family was one of those who'd helped build this city in their image, using their multiple billions of dollars.

"My mother isn't a nice person," I said carefully, "and being with someone like Dash would have put him too close to her for the rest of his life."

Kiara fidgeted. The woman never stopped moving, not even when she'd been pinned beneath my gaze while I'd been making calls.

"So what's he doing now?"

Kiara was shifty, and I had a feeling I knew why.

"He lives in the suburbs with his pack and has for years. I'm pretty sure they got a dog recently. It's all very domestic."

She relaxed, a smile sneaking onto her face.

She definitely wanted the Loranger pack and didn't want anyone else to be standing in her way. That was dangerous. I didn't want a pack. Never had. Especially not with everything going on.

With a curse, I pulled out my cell phone. No more missed calls, but my mother had done as she'd promised and texted me an address. It was across town in one of the more affluent neighbourhoods and would take some time to get there. So much for meeting him immediately. Having an omega was a bigger distraction than I'd anticipated.

Wrapping an arm around Kiara, I kissed her temple. "I've got to go. Work calls."

It was a good thing Dash hadn't left after all, as much as I despised admitting it. I wasn't going to leave Kiara alone, not even in the relative safety of my condo. Tobias might be able to get in. Plus, to be honest, I wasn't sure if I could trust her not to leave.

"Can't you do it tomorrow?" she asked.

I shook my head.

"Not this. It's urgent. Dash is here, though."

Her lips turned pouty, tempting me to kiss her, but I didn't. I'd kissed her pussy, but not yet her lips. When I did it for the first time, I wanted to have time to savour it.

I couldn't resist a quick squeeze of her ass, though. She gasped. "I'm going to have a quick shower, then I'll go."

Five minutes later I was in fresh clothes without the scent of Kiara anywhere on me. No one else deserved to catch her coconut chocolate scent, let alone whatever asshole my mother was forcing me to help. I hadn't had the time to wash my hair, but I had a scent dampening spray to eliminate those hints of her.

Kiara waited on my bed and I avoided kissing her for real once again, going for a chaste cheek kiss this time. She'd decided a nap was in order, and I couldn't blame her. Then I went out to tell Dash the situation, speaking as I stood in the mouth of the hallway.

"I have work. Don't touch Kiara, but don't leave," I said. "If you must leave, call me first. I think it's obvious why she shouldn't be alone."

He'd shaken off the anger and was back to nonchalant, a TV show playing as he made himself at home. "Demanding. This feels kinky to me."

"Are you going to listen?"

He smirked. "Will you tell me I'm a good boy after?"

Rolling my eyes, I took that as a yes. "Save me some of that food."

"Yes, Mistress."

"And never call me Mistress again."

I walked into the entryway and slid on my shoes before he could come up with a suitable response to that, letting the carpet of the hallway consume the sound of my heels meeting ground.

The house I pulled up in front of was large, but nothing like the extravagant mansion Soren lived in. There were neighbours on either side, visible if not truly close. A couple of expensive cars sat out in the driveway. They were showing off. No true car lover would leave a Bugatti exposed to the relentless mid-afternoon sun when they had a garage a hundred feet away.

I knocked on the front door after straightening myself in my car's tiny mirror, wishing I'd taken the time to fix my makeup properly. I'd only put on concealer and foundation after I'd washed off the evidence of Kiara's release.

An older woman opened the door, with blue eyes filled with worry, the shade eerily similar to Kiara's. "I'm Leighton Winston," I said. "I was sent to help out with something, though I'm not sure of the details."

I hated not having details. Soren and Mother were alike in the way they decided to toss things at me without any information. There was no way Soren didn't know who Kiara was, and he'd left me to figure it out on my own. In the same vein, Mother knew who she'd sent me to visit.

"Oh, perfect. My husband is waiting in his office."

She was the lady of the house, then. They weren't quite the level of rich where they had full-time staff to open their front door for them, though this house was clearly taken care of by a cleaning service, and I heard banging in the kitchen. A chef, possibly.

I followed her through the space and up a staircase that curved as it rose toward the second floor. On the second floor, the second door on the right was tightly shut and she gestured to it. I knocked once, the rap holding the force of my irritation without sounding overly aggressive.

"Come in."

The wife didn't follow me so I shut the door, spinning to face a man behind a desk.

My heart stuttered.

He had the same blue eyes as Kiara... and Tobias. How unlikely was it that a whole family had the same damn shade of blue? When I'd seen pictures of Noah Connolly, I hadn't focused too hard on the colour of his eyes.

While I hadn't recognized his wife, I knew enough about prominent New Oxford criminals to realize this was the leader of the Connolly crime family sitting in front of me.

Kiara's father.

My mother had said he'd lost something, and he sure as fuck wasn't getting it back.

Because Kiara wasn't a thing, she was a person. And she was *my* person.

I didn't growl, but I did grind my teeth together. "Noah Connolly. I didn't realize you were a friend of my mother's."

He observed me. I couldn't cower, nor could I show any aggression. The secrets my mother held against me were all at risk of being exposed.

"We go way back. She's spent some time in my casinos."

Underground casinos. They weren't legal.

I was a little surprised my mother had sent me here. She was adamantly against me knowing about her life. No one knew what she did other than attend galas. Not even my fathers knew. They'd all grown used to it years ago and basked in the perks of mating into the rich and prestigious Winston family while staying out of her way.

Had she been desperate? I'd never encountered her desperate before, but I'd be tucking this tidbit into my back pocket for when this undoubtedly blew up in my face.

"Interesting. What can I do for you today?"

"You fix things, yes?"

"Of course. That's my job."

"My daughter ran away. No one can know about it, and we need to bring her home."

Faking surprise, I took a small pad of paper and a pen out of my blazer pocket. "I wasn't aware you had a daughter."

"That's exactly why no one can know about it."

His jaw clenched, his wrinkles getting more prominent as his eyebrows drew together. Unlike Tobias and Kiara, he didn't have honey brown hair. His was wiry and dark grey, with some pure white strands sprinkled in. It was gelled into a combover.

"Of course." I spoke softly to placate him. "I'm very discreet, but I do need to know the details. I can't do my job without them."

"She's an omega, five feet and a couple inches tall, and quite chubby. Has my eyes."

I almost broke character and punched him in the fucking face.

Chubby?

He spoke like her weight was a bad thing, like it disgraced him. Had he ever said that to her directly? With a man like this, I bet he had. She'd grown up with those kinds of sentiments. No wonder she'd looked surprised when I'd called her gorgeous.

My aura lay thick over the room, intimidating him but without it being overt. A male alpha aura would be flaring by now, broadcasting their displeasure, but mine was easier to hide. Yes, it was out more than normal, but Noah Connolly didn't have to know that.

"Do you have a picture?" I asked through gritted teeth.

He opened a drawer in his desk and thumbed through some papers before pulling out a file. He tossed it onto the desk, and I picked it up. Inside was a series of pictures of her, taken from all angles. She had a big fake smile plastered on and was wearing a tight dress that left nothing to the imagination. Panic lived in the depths of her eyes.

It was a pamphlet describing her like she was a prize poodle being put up for auction.

My vision went red, nails piercing the file folder.

"May I keep this?" I asked.

"Yes. I have no need for it anymore."

"Do you have any idea where she might have run off to?"

He grunted and shrugged. "She doesn't know anyone. My son Tobias is out looking for her right now, and he knew her better. He may have some insight."

"Could I get his contact information?"

Keeping my tone pleasant was almost impossible. Every second in his presence my rage built, and I wanted to kill him. Fuck the consequences.

Noah gave me two business cards, one with his information and one with Tobias's.

"Is there anything else I should know?" I asked, itching to wrap this up and escape here.

"Nothing of note."

"Perfect. I'll keep you apprised of my findings."

I wouldn't be keeping him apprised of anything at all.

But I was going to have to do something about this, because all my worlds were colliding and it wasn't fucking looking good.

SIXTEEN

KIARA

Dash and I spent most of the time Leighton was gone eating in silence after my quick nap. I kept catching his gaze lingering on my lips as I slurped up pasta noodles, but he didn't make a move. That was good. I may have antagonized him on purpose, but I wasn't sure I was ready to tango with the consequences of that.

Leighton's frustration spiked through the bond multiple times while she was gone, but it felt muted because of the distance between us. Or maybe I just couldn't tune in properly when her aura was farther away.

When she came home, though, she was all smiles.

Well, OK. Leighton wasn't the grinning type, but she was as happy as I could expect her to be. She claimed the situation was taken care of and her client was no longer set to be on the evening news, so she could relax.

She was lying.

She wasn't good at hiding her anxiety when she spoke about the situation, and I knew what a liar looked like. I was always terrible at hiding my tells, but I could easily figure out other people's.

Leighton tapped her nails against things when she was lying or withholding. Sometimes it was her arm, sometimes it was a counter, but she always tapped. We weren't going to talk about how I'd been paying so much attention I figured that out within twenty-four hours of knowing her.

I let her maintain the lie, unsure if it was me she didn't want knowing, or Dash.

We went to sleep in the same bed with Dash taking the couch.

The next morning, I stretched out and groaned at the sheer comfort of the bed, before feeling around the opposite side and only meeting cold sheets. Leighton was gone.

Why was that so disappointing?

She may have touched me, but at the end of the day... I'd forced her to bond me. Begged her. She'd probably get sick of me eventually, and even though my heart would shatter it was still better than going back with my brother.

Rolling out of bed I used the toiletries she'd gotten me, brushing my teeth and splashing cold water on my face. I chose the nice clothes, maybe because I was feeling a little petty and wanted to show myself off in something a little more revealing than a t-shirt and sweats. The leggings were form-fitting and comfortable, and the top was low cut and emerald green, barely big enough to fit my boobs.

I was almost done brushing my hair when I heard a shout from the living room.

I rushed out to find Leighton hauling Dash out of her office with a grip on the back of his neck. He was shirtless, exposing a muscular torso and legitimate six pack abs, and wearing only a pair of boxer briefs with a prominent erection tenting them.

My throat was so dry I had to swallow four times to get the saliva flowing again. I was going to blame the bruises for that.

Definitely.

They did feel worse today, admittedly. Tilting my head in any direction hurt. I'd need to ice them soon.

"What are you doing?" I asked.

They both looked at me. Dash whistled again, strolling across the living room and blatantly disregarding Leighton's warning growl. He didn't stop until his erection was almost poking my stomach, my eyes about level with his collarbone.

"Leighton didn't like that I slept on the pullout couch," he said with a smirk. "She told me to sleep on the leather couch in the living room, but why would I listen? I got to drown myself in the scent of you and your slick all fucking night."

"You're a disgusting man," Leighton muttered. "All you did was sleep on dirty sheets."

"They weren't dirty before," he said, switching to a whisper and leaning in close to my ear. "But they sure as hell are now."

I shivered and Leighton stormed into the office to see if he was bluffing or telling the truth. I couldn't tell. Leighton's tell was obvious, but Dash... His mind worked different. Figuring him out was going to be harder.

"Go grab your knife, little omega. I think Leighton is about to come out and punch me in the face."

My hand went down to my thigh, patting the place I usually kept my knife. There was no comforting hardness there and blood drained from my cheeks as I rushed back to the bedroom, grabbing Nyla from the bathroom vanity with a sigh of relief.

I held her as I went back out to the living room, finding Leighton with her shoulder pinning Dash to the wall and one hand gripping his cock.

Not nicely. She was squeezing.

Through the wince in Dash's expression, it looked like he liked it.

"Don't you ever disrespect my house or my omega again," she hissed before letting him go.

I glanced down to his boxer briefs without thinking. He was still hard. That hadn't changed since the second I saw him.

"Did he actually...?" I averted my gaze and spoke to Leighton as she walked up to me.

"We're not going to talk about what he did or didn't do to your sheets."

But I want to know. Sneaking a glance toward the office, I decided I would have to go in there later to find out. Stealth might be my specialty, so I was pretty sure I could do it.

"I went out and got you something," Leighton said.

She placed her hand on my back and led me into the kitchen, where a couple pieces of faux leather and elastic laid on the counter. She daintily lifted one up, revealing a leather sheath attached to a belt, sized for my hips. Another one was elastic and smaller, more thigh sized. The third was black leather for the sheath with elastic that formed a harness for my chest.

I grabbed the waist one and placed Nyla carefully down on the counter as I fastened it around my hips. The style was kind of old-timey, like this was created as a prop for western movies. Surprisingly, it wasn't bulky though. It wouldn't fit under the outfit I was wearing, but a normal t-shirt would probably hide it unless someone patted me down.

Sliding Nyla into the holster, she fit perfectly. I pet the soft leather and ran my thumb over the hilt as a smile grew on my face.

"Thank you," I said, grinning up at her.

She quickly glanced away, crossing her arms over her chest. "Yes, well, I wasn't going to let you keep cutting yourself by sticking that knife anywhere and everywhere."

I'd grown used to the occasional slice when I moved wrong

and the blade caught my skin, but I was glad it was no longer a worry. Especially since I had all new clothes.

"Where did you go that was open so early?"

"The best place in New Oxford to get leather and faux leather products."

Dash snorted, coming into the kitchen and stealing a sausage from a pan on the stove. "Pointe Couture, yeah? Is that where you met Ambrose? He's a frequent customer."

Leighton smacked his hand when he tried to take another sausage, turning the heat on for another burner. "You're like a goddamn child. Ambrose and I met at The Pointe Lounge. We were looking for similar things, so the matchmaking service paired us without realizing the conflict."

Dash still wasn't clothed, retreating to the other side of the kitchen to lean against the fridge. His eyes sparkled with interest, and I got the sense Leighton had just revealed something he hadn't known.

Personally, I had no idea what was going on. The Pointe Lounge didn't sound like a place that would have a matchmaking service, at least not from the name alone.

"I know what Ambrose's interests are, sweetheart, and they don't involve being dommed by put together female alphas."

Leighton didn't respond, cracking an egg into the pan she'd placed on the burner.

He refused to leave it alone, poking and prodding in hopes of getting a reaction out of her. "Are you his little doll, then? I thought you were just fucking like normal, but if you met at the club…"

Her head rolled side to side, and she didn't look over her shoulder.

"Does Ambrose fu—"

I stepped in front of him and placed a hand over his mouth. He froze. "Don't talk to her like that," I said.

Ambrose did call her his doll, and he had fucked her like he owned her, but that wasn't Dash's business. I'd gathered that the lounge was some kind of... sex club, or something. I didn't have a complete understanding and didn't want one. The reminder of Leighton and Ambrose's sexual relationship being shoved in my face was altogether unpleasant.

His tongue flicked out and licked my palm, but I didn't pull it back. I kept it over his mouth until I got some kind of acknowledgment that he wasn't going to start talking again the second I removed it.

He didn't give me anything, but his tongue made a circle on my palm and then he reached up to gently grab my wrist. I was held in place as his tongue trailed from my palm up my fingers, and I gasped when he sucked two fingers into his mouth. He curled his tongue around the digits, showing me what he could do with it—they were the kind of moves that made slick pool in my core, because I wanted his tongue to lap it up.

"That's enough," Leighton said.

She banded her arm around my torso and pulled me away from him. Dash let me go with a smirk and my arm dropped to my side, those fingers wet with spit.

"What do you not understand about this being my omega?" she demanded. "Mine. If I wanted to share, I would be in a fucking pack, Dash. Keep your hands off her."

"So touchy. She put her hand there, and those cute fingers are begging to be sucked on."

There was nothing cute about my fingers. Fingers couldn't be cute. It wasn't even possible.

"It's probably been long enough that Ambrose can come back and you can leave," Leighton said. "Why don't you call him?"

She brought me with her to the stove, brushing her chin across my shoulder in a clear scent mark before planting a kiss on my cheek. "How do you like eggs?"

"They're fine," I said faintly.

There was the occasional cramp in my stomach that I was doing my absolute best to ignore, but maybe the food would help. Or maybe an orgasm would, after the tease Dash had just put me through. Or both.

Both sounded good.

SEVENTEEN

DASH

This was dangerous. Being in this condo was bringing up every single one of my red flags, but I couldn't leave.

Not when I could fucking tell that Kiara wanted me, and there was a part of Leighton that wanted me too. I was obsessed with getting them to admit it. I wouldn't leave until they did.

And if they admitted it... I wasn't sure I would want to leave then, either. All I'd want to do was show them all the reasons they were right to want me.

While Leighton cooked breakfast and rubbed against Kiara like it was going to put me off, I wandered back into the living room and snagged my phone from the coffee table. Mercury had called me, because of course he had. My packmate was worse than my dads had been when they were alive.

"Why haven't you come home?" Mercury asked the second he picked up.

"Didn't Ambrose fill you in? They need protection."

Leighton would deny that she needed protection, but she did. The Connollys weren't a family to fuck with unless you were well connected. She kind of was, but not on my level. Most of her connections started and ended with her mother—and Edith Winston was a bitch like no other. When she found out her daughter had dark bonded a normal omega, she wouldn't offer a lick of help.

"Hire them a goddamn security detail, then. What are you going to do? You host an internet talk show and go to kickboxing classes on occasion."

If I'd been anyone else, I would have been offended. *How harsh.*

"I've got my big strong alpha aura to scare people off."

"Leighton is an alpha and far scarier than you. Why are you really there? You've glared at Leighton every time we saw her at a gala, on TV, or in passing on the street for the past six years. What's with the sudden change of heart?"

He had a point, and I didn't have an answer. It was just the way my brain worked, maybe. I clung to things inexplicably until suddenly, it was like a switch flipped. And then I didn't cling.

My hatred for Leighton had flipped off the second she'd looped me in on that video call.

Instead I'd been... intrigued. That had only gotten worse when I realized she'd been fucking Ambrose all this time.

Except for the time she'd brought it up, I hadn't even thought about her brother.

"Come meet the omega. Maybe you'll get it then."

"You haven't been interested in an omega since—"

Mercury cut himself off before saying his name. It was a cursed name in our pack. The rejection had hit Mercury hard too, though not as hard as me. Ambrose hadn't really given a fuck.

That was the first time the mention of him didn't make me feel like I was cleaving in two.

How odd.

I glanced toward the kitchen, wondering if they had anything to do with it.

"You can't judge until you meet her," I said. "You seem tense, Merc. Did Ambrose not fuck you hard enough last night?"

I heard Kiara giggling in the kitchen, but nothing from Mercury. He would usually be quick to tell me off for being crass, so something was wrong with him.

"Had a fight, huh?" I asked casually.

My stomach twisted, but I was a pro at hiding my regret. They'd stopped their relationship a year ago because I'd been bitter and broken on the five-year anniversary of meeting our scent match for the first time. Five years since we'd been unceremoniously rejected.

Mercury had thought it would make me feel better—that it would help me get over the rejection if all of us were suffering the loneliness together.

It hadn't.

For a while I'd taken pleasure in them sharing in my misery, but I'd been drowned in guilt for most of the last year. They loved each other, but their affection for me was keeping them apart.

Well, Mercury's affection for me. Clearly, Ambrose hadn't given a shit about whether his lovers would hurt my feelings. I preferred that, in all honesty.

"That omega stabbed him, and you're all acting like that's somehow OK."

So his protective side had come out, and Ambrose had been defensive of Kiara. Definitely fight-worthy, especially since they'd been tiptoeing around each other for so long.

"She's enthralling. I might beg her to stab me," I teased.

Mercury took it far too seriously. "Don't you dare."

"If you don't come see her, I just might."

"You're lying to blackmail me," he said.

"Am I?"

"Yes."

"You know me better than that, Merc. It might have started as a tease, but I'm not above doing it."

He hung up.

That meant he was on his way. I texted him the address in case he didn't know it and wandered into the office to put yesterday's clothes on.

Mercury's pounding at the door startled Kiara. She jumped in her seat and yelped, hand going down to her knife. It was half out of the holster ready for use when Leighton got up from the table to answer the knock.

"Where is he?" Mercury demanded.

His aura flared, sharp cinnamon overshadowing the comforting aroma of old books that my packmate was known for. Kiara was wide-eyed and her coconut chocolate scent was sour until I leaned across the table.

"It's only my packmate," I murmured, my lips close to her ear.

That was what Mercury first saw when he walked in. Me, close enough to the dangerous little omega that she could take that teeny blade and shove it through my neck easily. Being so exposed got me hot and had the added benefit of making Mercury fucking panic.

"Do *not* stab him," he barked.

His order hung in the air before dissipating. The bark only lasted a few seconds, and if she'd wanted to, she could have ignored it with some effort. It wasn't like Leighton's orders that bound her in invisible chains.

I stayed in place as Kiara stared at him with her mouth hanging slightly open.

"Why would I stab him?" she asked, turning her eyes to me.

Her eyelashes looked so long and thick this close up.

"You stabbed Ambrose, unless there's another omega with a fucking knife," Mercury said.

The venom in his tone set Leighton off. "Sit down or get out of my fucking apartment."

If possible, my ass pressed further into my seat. While not a bark, it kind of felt like one. Except, more oppressive, and I wanted to do whatever she said. That last part might be because that was my kink, though.

My packmate grudgingly sat, glaring at Kiara. Leighton yanked me back so I wasn't leaning so close to her omega anymore, going to stand behind Kiara with her hands on her shoulders. "Why are you here?"

"Dash threatened me," Mercury muttered.

All eyes turned to me. I shrugged. "Threatened is a strong word."

"You told me you were going to beg her to stab you if I didn't come see her."

Kiara let out a little gasp, the kind I wanted to swallow down. Leighton sighed. "And you believed him? I thought you were supposed to know him well."

"I do," Mercury said, glaring at me. "That's exactly why I raced over here."

"He wouldn't have actually done it."

Leighton said it, but it sounded like a challenge. I grinned. She would push me back if I tried to lean across the table again, but that wasn't the only way to get close to the omega. My foot slid across the floor until it found hers, and then I ran the back of my socked foot up her leg until it was caught between her thick thighs.

"Kiara, would you please use your knife on me?" I murmured.

Her arousal perfumed the air. I glanced out the corner of my eye at Mercury—he was affected. He tugged at the tail end of one of his French braids.

"No," she said.

"Pretty please?"

Along with the words I pushed my foot further between her thighs until I could feel the heat of her against my sole. With those thin leggings, I could rub her easily. Her breath hitched, and Leighton was too busy glaring at me to look down and see what was happening.

I tilted my head to the side, raising an eyebrow questioningly.

"I'm not going to do it." Her voice wavered this time.

Then her legs spread, giving me the access I'd been prodding for. I wasn't sure if she was aware she was doing it, but with Leighton right there it would be easy for Kiara to stop me.

It was too fucking easy to rub against her now, and she was loving it. Leighton hadn't given her an orgasm so far this morning. I doubted she could come just from this friction, but it was making her desperate.

"Are you sure, little omega? Don't you want to? Stab me, just once. Please?"

"Dash, shut up." Leighton's fingers dug into Kiara's shoulders, away from the ugly bruising from Ambrose's freakout.

"Make me, sweetheart."

With a growl, she released her omega and stormed around the table. There was a cloth napkin shoved in my mouth before I could taunt her some more. My eyes went half lidded, arousal washing through me to match Kiara's.

I'd already won.

She was going to come from the friction. Kiara was panting. When she leaned forward and I felt the sharp pain of the blade sliding into my calf, I groaned.

She responded with a whimper, visibly grinding against me as she clutched the edge of the table with her free hand. Her pretty blue eyes rolled when she came with a soft gasp.

I dropped my foot when she stopped moving, the heel of my sock wet with her slick. She'd drenched three layers of clothing. How fucking sexy was that?

My cock was painfully hard, but there was nothing that was going to happen with it until I could jerk off. I didn't really care. My own pleasure was an afterthought when I'd given Kiara an orgasm and made Leighton pink with anger.

Mercury was here too, I guess. He was caught between awe and anger, his jaw slack as he stared at Kiara but with a bit of flint still lingering in his gaze.

Heavy silence descended over the breakfast table as Kiara went steadily pinker. My calf dripped blood onto the floor, but the wound wasn't deep. It would heal quickly.

The first one to speak was Kiara. She stood, that wet spot so fucking obvious on her leggings. "I'm going to change," she mumbled, avoiding eye contact with both Leighton and Mercury.

She looked at me, but only to glare.

It was adorable. Her soft features couldn't host a glare, not one that actually looked dangerous.

She was out of the kitchen a second later, and I was tempted to go and lick her slick off the wood chair. It would of course be disgusting, but tempting nonetheless.

For once, Leighton stayed speechless. She glared at me as she followed her omega, leaving only my packmate and I in the dining area.

His expression had settled on angry now that Kiara was out of the picture. "You're such an asshole. This is why everyone hates you."

I kept my grin in place, the napkin damp with saliva between my lips, but his words hit exactly where he wanted them to. My chest tightened, that pervasive feeling of loneliness rising again.

When your scent matched mate rejected you, you had to wonder if you were lovable at all.

If Mercury was the one picking at my well-known insecurities, it was a sign I may have really fucked up this time. He usually treated me like a piece of glass, liable to shatter at any moment.

In which case… Oh well.

This was the most alive I'd felt in years.

EIGHTEEN

LEIGHTON

Watching Kiara come was hot even when I wasn't the one making her.

I still couldn't believe Dash had fucking done that. It was too far.

She was peeling off her leggings when I came into the bedroom behind her, only leaving a soaked thong behind. I stroked my hand along the curve of her ass and she jumped, peering over her shoulder at me.

"Um..." She didn't know what to say.

"Did you want him doing that?" I asked.

"I didn't exactly... not want it?"

"Is that why you didn't tell me his foot was between your legs? I would have told him to fuck off, you know. Slicing him wasn't necessary, even though he asked for it."

Her cheeks were red and she sat on the edge of the bed, letting me take the pants off the rest of the way. This way I could make sure she didn't displace her bandages.

"I'm sorry," she whispered.

I sighed. "You don't need to apologize. He does. Dash can't just be doing things like that."

"But I liked it."

My eyebrow lifted. "The way he made you come?"

"The way I cut him."

She worried her lip between her teeth and I sighed, settling on the bed beside her. I'd never imagined having an omega would be like this. I kind of just wanted to care for her. Know everything about her, no matter how small or potentially fucked up.

Clearing her throat, she tentatively touched the bruises on her neck. The knife was in her holster, a little bloody and smelling of spring rain and peaches from Dash.

"I ran from my father because he was planning on giving me over in an arranged mating. I don't know to who. My father didn't give me any details. Tobias liked to drop hints—he said they were going to dark bond me and I'd be forced to give them permission. If I was going to be bonded to strangers anyway, I decided I would escape and find someone to bond me."

"Why a dark bond specifically?" I asked.

The question had been bothering me since the first time she'd asked me to bond her. A stunning omega like her could have gotten a normal bond. Not from me, because a lone alpha couldn't claim an omega like that, only a pack could. I wasn't Kiara's only option, though. Unless Soren had made it seem like I was, and I wouldn't put it past him.

"Getting a normal bond would have taken too long," she said. "A pack would be taking more of a risk by giving me a normal bond. It's for life, and they wouldn't know anything about me. The dark bond offers less risk and more control."

"You could have ended up with someone far worse than your arranged pack, dove. What if Soren hadn't found you and sent you to me?"

She shrugged helplessly. My hand landed on her thigh,

rubbing the bare skin in soothing circles. Her feelings were clear through the bond that neither of us knew how to turn off. A part of her was wallowing in a pit of despair over how shitty her options had been.

Thank fuck she'd ended up with me.

Even if I'd hated her, I would have rather had her safe as my bondmate.

And I certainly didn't hate her. Maybe I shouldn't have gotten soft with her so fast, but some combination of instincts and my own loneliness had pushed me to this point.

"At least it would have been my choice," she whispered. "I needed that." She cleared her throat. "But my point... My point was that I didn't get a chance to try and escape the way I meant to. Tobias decided I needed some lessons in..."

Her words stopped, but the meaning was clear nonetheless.

I could imagine what Tobias wanted for his sister.

"He sent his friend Jonathan to teach me. I fought back. He was only a beta, so I was able to get out of his grip for long enough to pick up Nyla. She was on the mantle. He didn't realize there was a knife there in time to stop me, so I stabbed him in the neck."

"And he died," I concluded.

"Oh, he did," she said. Kiara let out a laugh that was a little hysterical, her hand coming down to clutch at Nyla. "I followed him down when he fell and made sure of it. He wasn't coming back by the time I was done. Instead of feeling guilty or puking up my lunch or any of the normal things, I liked it. It made me really happy."

Her nose scrunched and she met my eyes, hers wide and set in flushed cheeks. "I didn't feel the same about stabbing Ambrose. I thought I would, but I didn't. Just now though, with Dash... it made me happy again. How fucked up am I?"

It was a rhetorical question that I answered anyway.

"You're not fucked up. Not at all, dove. You don't get a thrill out of stabbing innocent people, so there's nothing to worry about."

It was an odd compulsion, admittedly, but I couldn't judge.

"I absolutely don't. Jonathan deserved it, and Dash asked," she said.

"Dash also deserved it, for the record."

That made her laugh. I lived for that smile, those little crinkles in the corners of her eyes.

I'd figure out a way to keep her safe forever even if it fucking killed me. It might, considering who we were dealing with. The blackmail material my mom kept on me didn't help. I wasn't looking forward to when Tobias realized the woman his father 'hired' to help with the search and the woman who dark bonded his sister were one and the same.

"What do you think about Mercury?" she asked.

I shrugged. "Don't know him too well. He's uptight. A couple of months ago, my brother's pack needed help from Dash, and Mercury was furious. He reamed me out after it was all said and done, as if I had anything to do with it."

Rolling my eyes, I collapsed back on the bed. She peered down at me. "That was rude of him."

"He's protective of Dash. The man was broken after my brother rejected him. Until recently. The past day is the most playful I've ever seen him. Usually he's busy drinking whiskey and banging betas and stirring up trouble on his talk show."

She stiffened when I made the list. "Banging betas?"

"He's a bit of a man whore, according to the tabloids."

Her scent soured. "Oh."

"Do you not want him to do that anymore, dove?"

"I don't care. Of course. You're my alpha, not him."

Still laying down, I smirked. She'd let him get her off for a reason. Why was I having increasingly less of a problem with it?

Maybe it was because Dash had passively let me take his junk in my hand and squeeze. Plus, the napkin to shut him up. It was obvious I was the more dominant one.

"Liar," I murmured.

She brought her hand down to the knife, but didn't deny it. "Whatever. I should get dressed. I'm still hungry."

I watched her ass jiggle as she walked, enjoying the view. She put on new panties along with a pair of sweats. Had I only gotten her one pair of leggings? I was going to have to change that, pronto. I'd wanted to take a bite of her when she'd walked out wearing those. Would have if Dash hadn't been there.

"Are you coming?" she asked, pausing at the door when I wasn't following.

"Be out in five."

It was partly to make her suffer through the tension of being alone with Mercury and Dash after that, and partly because I really needed to relieve some tension. An orgasm was on my menu, or I wouldn't be able to deal with this circus.

She flushed but nodded, going out to finish her meal as I slid my hand down my stomach.

As it turned out, coming made it worse.

I'd imagined it was her tongue stroking me instead of my fingers, and that had morphed into Dash's tongue and Ambrose's cock. My thoughts were a damn mess, and the orgasm had left me unfulfilled to the extreme.

"Dash, you can't have her as your omega, and it's rude to talk about her like she's not there." Mercury's scolding tone was the first to come from the dining room.

"I know she's there. I'm speaking it into existence. She's going to be mine, and so is Leighton."

Leaning against the door jamb, I glared at him. "Is that so?"

He turned his attention to me. The man didn't have a lick of shame. "I do believe it is so."

"She's my omega."

"But she could be *our* omega."

"I would have to join your pack for that, and I don't plan to."

He pouted at me. "Why not? We're stellar."

"For one thing, I don't think Mercury wants me." The slim man didn't deny it. "And another, I don't want a pack. I never have."

"There are perks," Dash said.

"Like what?"

"So many tongues that would give way better orgasms than the one you just gave yourself."

I didn't react. I wasn't going to give him the goddamn satisfaction of informing him that I'd just imagined his tongue on me.

"I've got to work again today," I said. "Are you two both staying with Kiara?"

"No—"

"Of course we are." Dash beamed, cutting off Mercury's refusal.

"Perfect."

It wasn't perfect. This pack was getting way too entrenched into this, and they shouldn't. Dangerous people had me in their pocket. I wouldn't put it past my mother to start blackmailing them too. They had secrets, I was sure, and she was an expert at finding them.

"Ambrose will show up at some point when he wakes up and realizes Mercury is missing from our apartment," Dash said. "Then it'll be a full house."

Kiara shifted in her seat. She probably thought Ambrose was holding a grudge. He wasn't the type. One grudge was enough for him—the one he held against the people who set his house on fire and killed his parents. Besides, I'd seen the way he looked at her when we arrived back at home with her dark bonded to me.

He wanted a piece of both of us.

"Just don't overwhelm Kiara."

"There's nothing overwhelming about us," Dash said.

Mercury scoffed and I rolled my eyes. Walking across the kitchen to my mate, I kissed the top of her head and snagged some food from her plate. I didn't have time to sit down and eat with them, not if I planned on finding a solution to the whole situation.

"I'll be back as soon as I can," I murmured, and she nodded.

I was leaving her in the lion's den, but it was the best option because I was going to be walking into a snake pit.

NINETEEN

AMBROSE

Mercury was gone by the time I woke up in the morning.

Vanished. I had no fucking clue where he could have disappeared to. Mercury didn't work, currently. He'd taken on babysitting Dash as his full-time job. He helped on Dirt with Dash, our pack lead's famed internet talk show. Plus, he followed Dash around when he went out to clubs and made sure his image wasn't shattered to pieces.

He was the pack dad, despite not being the pack lead.

That was his nature—babying Dash to a level that was toxic to the man's healing. Maybe if he'd seen more consequences instead of Mercury sweeping up his mess, he would have pulled himself out of the funk by now. It was hard to know.

"He probably followed Dash," I muttered to myself as I threw on clothes.

The little knife wound in my back was almost healed already. My aura had worked to close the injury overnight, and it only twinged with a tiny bit of pain.

Kiara's bruises, on the other hand, would be worse today.

My entire pack was at Leighton's house, but even if they hadn't been I would have had to check on Kiara. It was only right when I'd nearly killed her.

It didn't take long to cab over, and her building was so busy someone was always going in or out the front doors. I slid in behind a young woman who took one look at me and decided not to question it.

The scars intimidated people. Sometimes I looked in the mirror and they intimidated me, even though they were mine and I'd sure as fuck gone through the wringer to get them.

When I knocked on Leighton's door, Dash answered with a grin. "Knew you were going to come join the party. Welcome back."

He was doused in Kiara's scent.

"What have you done?" I asked.

"Leighton made it very clear that her omega is hers last night. All I was doing was basking in the spoils of that claiming."

I had a feeling I knew what he meant, and I was shocked Leighton hadn't kicked him out the front door when she found out.

Shoving past him, I found the living room full of tense silence. Mercury and Kiara had a show playing on TV, but neither were watching it. Kiara was still incapable of sitting still and paying attention, and Mercury was watching her. Fully staring in a way that she could probably feel burning into her skin.

"Good morning," I said.

Kiara spun to face me, eyes wide.

"Why are you here?" she asked, looking me up and down.

Mercury snorted. I glared at him and he glared back, our fight from last night not wrapped up. He didn't understand why his actions were harming more than helping.

He also didn't understand why I wasn't mad at Kiara for pushing that knife into my back. It made sense that he'd have trouble with the concept, but now he'd met her I hoped he would come to realize how soft she really was. Desperation made people do stupid things—Dash was proof enough of that, though his 'stupid' had never turned violent.

"My entire pack is here, and I wanted to check on your bruises."

She turned her gaze to the floor, turning the remote control over in her hands. "They're fine."

Dash hovered at the edge of the room while I walked to the couch, crouching in front of her. She was wearing a pair of sweatpants and a shirt that showed off way too much cleavage. Or just enough cleavage, if I hadn't been trying to avoid looking.

"Let me check them," I commanded softly.

She looked up, giving me a better view of the ugly dark purple and green ringing her neck. There was a slight wince in every movement of her head. When I reached out to brush my knuckles across the bruises, she released a low whine from deep in her chest.

"Does it hurt, princess?"

"Not that much," she murmured.

"Don't lie to me."

"Fine. It hurts a lot."

I got lost in her eyes every time I looked in them, and right now was no different. Regret swirled in their depths, her thick eyelashes fluttering as her gaze flitted back and forth.

"I'm sorry," I said.

"I stabbed you."

"Yes, and I'm mostly healed."

She bit her lip. "Seriously?"

I turned around in response, lifting the back of my shirt so she could check under the bandage. Her warm fingers had me gritting my teeth against the arousal as she gently moved the bandage out of the way. One finger traced over the stitched-up wound, but there was no pain.

"It doesn't hurt?" she asked.

Shaking my head, I hissed when her palm skimmed up my back. My scars were there, on full display. I never showed them to anyone, let alone let anyone touch them. Only Mercury.

The second- and third-degree burns covered the more traumatic scarring that would have been present—the stab wounds. Sometimes my skin itched, but for the most part I had less sensation in the areas where I was burned.

It didn't feel that way right now, with her hands exploring my back.

"Don't touch him," Mercury barked.

Kiara's hand stopped moving, and I glanced back over my shoulder to find he was holding her wrist. He'd moved closer without me even noticing. I'd been lost in the gentle touch.

"Oh, um, sorry," Kiara whispered.

"It's fine," I said. "You can touch them."

Mercury's grip slipped on her wrist, his brown eyes wide. He was visibly ruffled, and I knew he felt it too. She was perfect. He just didn't want to admit it.

"No, I overstepped," she said.

Her hand didn't touch me again and I lamented the loss. Adjusting the bandages back over my nearly healed wound, I let my shirt drop down to cover me again.

"Have you iced your bruises yet this morning?" I asked.

She shook her head.

"I'll get it for you. We want to keep you as comfortable as possible."

A tiny smile twitched at the corners of her lips. She murmured a soft, "Thank you."

I looked at Mercury and he got the hint, following me into the kitchen. We closed the French doors behind us, blocking our conversation from Dash and Kiara. Hopefully, Dash could behave with her for five minutes. If he couldn't, he'd be feeling Leighton's wrath. I was pretty sure he wanted her furious, at this point.

"You left." I tried not to portray how it hurt me. I'd gotten heated last night, but we were usually great at coming back to conversations when we'd had a chance to calm down.

Mercury shuffled from foot to foot. The sour expression he'd been wearing out in the living room wasn't present anymore. He knew better than to put on that front with me. "Dash was playing with fire. Well, with Kiara's knife. I had to come here."

"No, you didn't."

"I wasn't going to just leave him."

"He's an adult. He can handle himself, baby."

"Don't call me that." His voice broke. His aura was tumultuous, old books and cinnamon spiking and softening in the air.

It was an impulse. One I had trouble suppressing, because I wanted him to be mine again—desperately. Finding solace in Leighton over the past year had been the only thing keeping me sane. I didn't know how he'd kept himself together. Pure willpower, I supposed. Mercury was stubborn.

"Sorry," I muttered. "But the point is that you don't have to watch his every move. If he's going to run himself into the ground, that's his prerogative. You've been watching over him for six fucking years."

Our scent match had rejected us so long ago that for me, it was a distant memory. I'd never cared much. Mercury had been hurt, but he would have left it in the past if not for Dash.

Dash was fixated on the idea of a scent match and how we couldn't have ours. He was bringing the whole pack down. I'd never tell him that to his face, but he was smart enough to know it. After so long, I imagined the guilt of the last six years was weighing him down as much as the pain of rejection. Maybe more.

It all compounded to make it harder for him to pull himself up.

Especially when Mercury was enabling him.

"The pack isn't going to fall apart under my watch," Mercury said.

I growled. "We *need* to. This isn't going to end up like your parents. We'll pick ourselves up again and be better."

I didn't want to watch the way his expression shuttered. Turning to the freezer, I pulled out a flexible freezer pack and grabbed a tea towel to wrap around it. There was a bottle of anti-inflammatories on the counter, so I picked them up too and poured a glass of cold water.

My lover didn't speak, but I hoped he was finally processing. I'd been saying this for years. Never so urgently—I'd assumed he would loosen the reins when it got to be too much for him. He never had, but it was time.

Dash could stand on his own.

He had something to pick himself up for. Kiara and Leighton. His obsession with them was clear, and while it wasn't necessarily a healthy coping mechanism, it would work for him.

The alpha and omega pair wouldn't be the tipping point that broke us. I believed they would be exactly what we all needed.

Including Mercury.

"Get away from her, Dash," I chastised when I swung open the French doors again.

He was far too close, her arousal sweet in the air. My pack-mate smirked, the nonchalance almost hiding the way he glanced back at the kitchen worriedly.

"I was only showing her all the clothes that I bought for her," he said.

His lean body flopped to the couch beside her, his thigh pressed against hers. Kiara blushed but didn't move away. I settled on her other side, placing everything on the coffee table.

"You don't have to wear anything he buys," I said. "I imagine some of his choices weren't exactly appropriate."

"Excuse you," Dash scoffed. "She'll have a full wardrobe by the time my personal shopper gets here, and everything is appropriate."

"I doubt it."

Handing her a pill from the bottle and the glass of water, I watched her wince as she swallowed it down. Maybe I needed to order her a smoothie, so she had something suitable to eat?

"She's got a smoothie and soup coming for lunch," Dash said, reading my mind. "My shopper is bringing it."

I nodded, then gently wrapped the covered ice pack around the front of her neck. She hissed at the abrasive cold, but then her eyelids fluttered shut and she leaned back. My fingers began to go numb as I held it in place for her, but it was the least I could do.

Giving her the bruises was probably the worst thing I'd done in my life.

It had been an accident driven by trauma, but it could have been avoided if I'd gone to more therapy like Mercury had always suggested. I hated to admit I was wrong, but I couldn't continue to tell my packmate that he was doing the wrong thing unless I could swallow my own pride.

"That feels good," she murmured, sighing.

"We can ice it whenever you like. I'll put everything away when it's been fifteen minutes, and we can do it again in a bit."

"Thank you."

"You don't have to thank me."

"He did give them to you," Dash said, shooting me a smirk. "Ambrose is a big fan of fixing what he's broken."

I glared.

Mercury stepped back out into the living room, and I tried to ignore the way his scent soothed me. He wasn't mine to take comfort in.

"People have given me bruises before, and they never took care of them. So I'm going to thank you."

Kiara didn't open her eyes to speak, stating that so matter of fact. I tried to stifle my growl and managed. Dash's instinct was to freeze, his eyes wide. A purr rumbled his chest and he reached for her to comfort, only to stall when a growl split the air.

Both of us turned to Mercury, who was gritting his teeth and looking at the floor. Trying to pretend it never happened and he wasn't protective of the omega.

Kiara's lips curved, but she didn't open her eyes.

It left her none the wiser to who that growl had come from, and maybe it was better that way. Mercury wasn't ready to acknowledge her yet. Hopefully, he would be soon.

TWENTY

LEIGHTON

This mansion never got less gaudy, no matter how many times I drove past the guarded front gate.

Soren Rosania lived in Citrine Hills, a neighbourhood on the outskirts of New Oxford where only the richest of the rich could afford to live. My family was rich, but we couldn't live here. This was a level above everyone else.

His mansion took advantage of the vast property, sprawling across an unreasonable amount of space. The rest of the area was filled with greenery maintained by his staff, including god-awful hedges shaped like cartoon characters and a small golf course.

I'd experienced it all before, so I ignored most of the finishings as I wandered up to the huge double front doors and knocked.

Soren's secretary Lyra answered, a prim smile on her face and her attire as insane as usual. "Good morning, Leighton," she said, gesturing me inside. "He's expecting you."

I hadn't called to warn him of my impending arrival, but I bet he knew about what was going on with Kiara. With him giving me a shitshow to deal with, it was only a matter of time before I showed up. Plus, the gate guards would have given him a three-minute warning while I came up the drive.

"Good morning," I greeted politely.

I followed her through the unorthodox house, noting that Soren was going through a Barbie phase. Lyra's pencil skirt and flowing blouse were both that shade of pink, and he'd put up some new decor around the place since I'd last been here.

She led me into his library and then exited with a smile, leaving me alone with the man of the hour.

Soren was the root of all my problems, including most of the ones that I had with my mother.

"Pleasure to have you visiting again, Leigh-Leigh," he said.

He was curled in a circle chair in the middle of the library, a book in his lap. It was all very domestic until you realized he was wearing bright pink latex pants, a pink leather harness over his chest, and accents of neon blue with his layers of jewellery.

Oh, and the book was on bondage.

"You know why I'm here," I said, crossing one ankle over the other in an attempt to look more casual. It was better to match Soren's vibes when possible.

"And you didn't bring gifts. I expected to be showered in gifts to make up for your cruel words on the phone."

Internally, I cursed. Externally, I kept my demure smile on my face.

I should have thought things through this morning. The way to butter Soren up was to bring gifts and wear bright colours. My pantsuit today was black, which was the most boring shade. He despised it.

"I apologize. With the task that you laid out, I haven't had time to find the perfect gift. I do need some information to help in my completion of the task, if at all possible."

"Always so formal," he said with a snort.

His fingers waggled to gesture me closer, and I sat down on a chair near him. This close, I came to the chilling realization that his latex pants were actually latex chaps, with a very tight pair of briefs underneath. If he got up and turned around, I was going to have to bleach my eyes.

"You are a client," I said. "Formality is expected from me."

"I suppose so. What do you need today?"

There was a gleam in his eyes—they were golden, the orbs truly shining. Soren was a male gold pack omega. They were considered the highest threat of all, because they could go around impregnating women and creating rogue alphas like crazy.

Which was exactly what he did. On purpose and illegally.

His money sheltered him from being exposed, especially because no one knew he was gold pack. Any time he left his house, he wore illegal coloured contacts. He didn't bother putting them on with me, because I knew one of his sons who was in my brother's pack.

"Are you aware of how my mother knows Noah Connolly?"

Soren laughed. "Ah yes, poor Edith. She's really gotten wrapped up in them, hasn't she?"

"I wouldn't know. All I know is she sent me to his house for a job, and he gave me the task of finding Kiara Connolly." I raised an eyebrow at him. "Which I can't do because that would be going against your instructions. What am I supposed to do in this situation?"

He snorted. "Well, Leigh-Leigh, who do you fear more?"

My blood ran cold. I didn't have an answer for that, because both of them were blackmailing me over the same damn thing—but my mother had an additional threat hanging over my head. What was I supposed to say?

"Let me flip that. Who do I care about more?" I asked, doing my best to hide my panic. "And the answer is Kiara. I had to dark bond her, so I'm going to do whatever is best for her in the long run."

"So, you're going to follow my instructions," Soren said.

"No. Not unless you tell me what you need her for."

He snapped his book closed and grinned, standing up from the circle chair. I averted my eyes, but he didn't turn. He strolled closer to me, fanning himself with the thin paperback.

"You're demanding today, and I'm not particularly a fan," he said. "But I'll give you a pass this one time because you're protecting your new omega. I will not, however, be telling you my motivations. You know I like to keep an air of mystery about me."

I grit my teeth, holding back more demands.

"I'll give you one hint though: what is it that I like to do most? That's my entire motivation behind sending Kiara your way. Plus, I thought you would be more fun if you bonded an omega. Not the case. A shame, really."

His grin revealed shiny white teeth, bleached to an almost unnatural perfection. What he liked to do the most was stir the pot, disturb shit, and, oddly enough, protect omegas.

Did he think I was capable of protecting her without his help? I was well-equipped and organized, but not enough to take down a beta crime family. I wasn't a goddamn criminal like him.

Or was this simply his way to stir the pot and entertain himself?

"It's hard to have fun when I'm under so much stress," I muttered.

Standing, I smoothed down my pants and peered around the library. It had high ceilings and plenty of cozy chairs, but I imagined there would be a layer of dust on the books if Soren didn't employ a large cleaning staff. The man didn't actually read tomes like Pride and Prejudice, even though I spotted four different editions of the book on a nearby shelf.

"Stress is of your own making, my dear," Soren said, clapping a hand on my shoulder. "Stop creating it, and you'll be so much better off."

Yeah. Says the billionaire who can afford to throw money at all his stressors.

"What sage advice," I said, trying not to sound sarcastic. "I'll be sure to take that under advisement."

He beamed. "Perfect. I'm glad I could help. Lyra will of course show you out, and I believe she has some paperwork with a couple of tasks I'd like you to complete in the next couple of weeks. This was a wonderful visit. We should do this again—except next time, don't wear those ugly clothes into my house."

I really should have pulled out the bright red suit I had in the back of my closet for Soren visits. Dash would have gotten a laugh seeing me in it, but maybe Soren would have given me more information if I'd catered to him a little better.

All I got out of this was a headache and more work put onto my docket.

Perfect.

I had to at least make an effort to 'find' Kiara until I got myself out of this mess. I spent the afternoon making calls, trying to find out if anyone had a clue where she was. No one did, and I got a sense of satisfaction from sending that text update to her father.

By the time I got back to my condo, I was more than ready to bathe off the day and spend an evening curled on the couch with my omega.

It was so damn domestic.

The second I walked in the door, I discovered the evening was not going to be anything like that.

Kiara was twirling around the room in a t-shirt dress, a bottle of alcohol in her hand. "Leighton!" she squealed when I approached.

She flung herself into my arms so aggressively the half-empty bottle spilled over the edge, splashing onto the floor. I caught her with a small sound of surprise, glaring over her shoulder at the men in my living room.

Their entire pack was here, and they'd let her get wasted. This was not a sober woman. She was rubbing herself on me like a cat in heat—or an omega in heat. Coconut and chocolate hung heavy in the air, overpowering all their scents.

"How much of this have you had to drink?" I asked, taking the bottle from her.

It was whiskey. Half empty, but it had been full in my liquor cupboard. She better not have drank it all herself.

"Just a couple sips," she said, beaming.

"It was more than a couple sips," Dash said.

He was tipsy too, a glass in his hand as he swirled the amber liquid.

I glared at Mercury and Ambrose, noting they both had glasses too. They weren't sloppy like Dash and Kiara, though. They better not be. My omega was in danger, so leaving her without mentally sound protection would get their heads kicked in.

"Why is she drunk?" I demanded.

"Can we tell the fun police to leave?" Dash sauntered over to Ambrose, leaning over the back of the couch to put his chin on his head. "The sirens are giving me a headache."

Kiara was still clinging to me, so I ignored the alpha and manhandled her onto the couch. She bounced right back up, and her tits bounced with her. They were almost spilling out of the top, which definitely wasn't secure enough to handle her drunk. She was wearing a low-cut t-shirt dress that wasn't among the clothes I'd bought for her.

"I want to stand," she proclaimed.

She swayed but was mostly stable on her feet. I moved around her and collapsed onto the couch instead. Ambrose held his cup out in front of me and I took a sip, savouring the burn as the alcohol went down. Then I handed it back.

Loss of control wasn't my favourite.

"Someone explain to me what's happening here."

"She'd never had alcohol before," Mercury explained. "Of course, Dash took that and ran with it. Usually I'd put a stop to it, but I'm curious if being drunk is going to bring out her stabby side. It would be nice to prove that she's dangerous."

Kiara pouted, placing her hands on her hips and glaring down at Mercury. She didn't look dangerous. She looked adorable, and Mercury looked away with a grumble.

"Mercy has been mean to me all day," she said. "Nyla only stabbed one person. I thought it would work! We're not going to hurt anyone else unless they deserve it."

She patted Nyla, holstered at her hips beneath the dress, and frowned.

"Nyla says that Mercy might deserve it."

I snorted, taking in Mercury's horrified look.

"He might," I agreed, "but let's make that decision sober, OK?"

She shrugged, going over to the TV and bending over in front of it. All of us alphas released a collective groan—in Mercury's case, it was stifled like he could really pretend he wasn't attracted to her. Kiara bounced back up with a game controller in hand.

"Dash showed me video games, too! And he bought me more new clothes—not that the new clothes you got weren't wonderful, but Dash got even more. Plus he gave me one of Ambrose's shirts. Oh, and he got me this."

Her free hand grabbed the hem of the t-shirt dress and lifted it as the rest of us watched with wide eyes.

Should I have stopped her?

Yes.

It would have been as simple as a command, and she would have been forced to stop. My brain didn't work fast enough, and when I saw the lace barely covering her pussy I lost all ability to speak.

The expensive lace bodysuit cut high on her hips, hugging her soft curves. Its built-in bra was see-through, putting her nipples on display along with the rest of her body. My mouth fucking watered. The guys' auras were flaring, scents getting stronger.

Kiara moaned, her eyelids fluttering shut.

Nope. Time to put a stop to whatever was happening here.

"Pull your dress back down, Kiara," I said.

Her lips pursed. "No."

"Pull your dress back down. Now."

The command forced her hand despite her whine. She was going to thank me for that one when she was sober. Her dress fell back down to where it rested at mid thigh, and we were all able to breathe easier again.

Dash had started toward her to do God knew what, when a knock on the condo door interrupted us.

My nose crinkled, and Ambrose stood first. "I'll get it."

I had no idea who it could be. Liberty, maybe? She usually called first, and we'd chatted during the day. Not many people knew where I lived other than her. Even my brother knew not to come to my house.

The front door creaked as it swung open, followed by Ambrose's shout and the thundering of boots across the hardwood. I jumped to my feet, backing toward Kiara until the badges on the black tactical units registered.

It was the fucking police.

TWENTY-ONE

KIARA

The gentle buzz of alcohol through me came to an abrupt end.

Adrenaline took its place as a dozen men stormed into the apartment, wearing all black with guns up and pointed around. Their attention focused on me, pushing past Leighton so they could grab my arm.

I shrieked, fumbling for Nyla at my hip until Dash's hand on my wrist stopped me. He'd been the closest, and now... he was the only one they weren't yet putting in handcuffs. My throat dried as I saw Leighton on her knees, hands in metal cuffs behind her back.

"They're not going to hurt you," Dash said urgently. "Don't, Kiara."

My hand dropped from where my blade was hidden. He was right. The grip on my arm was gentle, the eyes full of concern. This man was a beta. What were they even doing here, though?

If I was taken into custody, my father would find me.

Tobias would find me.

I'd have to go back, and Leighton wouldn't be able to save me if she were under arrest.

I still shied away from the beta man but let him lead me toward the condo exit. Dash's harsh laugh drew my attention back, my footsteps stalling.

"I fucking dare you," he said, holding out his arms for the cuffs. "Do it. See what happens. You know who I am."

The man trying to cuff him hesitated, looking over to someone else.

I didn't go with the beta man, watching the exchange nervously. If Dash wasn't arrested, he would save me. Right? He'd claimed he wanted us to join his pack, but would that not matter now that this was happening?

The supposed person in charge sighed. "For fuck's sake. Don't cuff him, and let his packmates free too. We only need Leighton Winston. She's the one alleged to have dark bonded that omega. If we find out it was you that made that bond, we'll be coming for you, Dash."

Dash laughed. "I didn't make the bond, and Leighton's bond isn't illegally created either."

"It's not registered, and the omega has injuries all over her. We're taking her in for an assessment by the seers, and Ms. Winston is in custody until further notice."

"I asked for the bond," I said, ripping free of the beta's grip. "Why are you arresting her? I asked for it."

The man looked at me. That one was an alpha, his eyes holding something that bordered on warmth, but was still oddly cold. "The seers will be the ones to prove that, Miss."

My arm was grabbed again. This time the beta hustled me out without pause, barely giving me time for my head to stop spinning. I couldn't tell if that was the alcohol or the situation. I did know that Leighton was doing her very best to send me soothing emotions through the bond, trying to tell me everything was going to be OK.

It didn't feel like it was going to be, and with every step away from her I grew twitchier with the desire to stab someone.

My alpha needed to be with me. I didn't like it when she wasn't.

"Where are you taking Leighton?" I asked the beta man.

He looked over his shoulder at me. We were wandering down the hallway away from the chaos, headed for the elevator. "She's going to be questioned. Did she coerce you into the bond?"

I shook my head vigorously. The slight sloshing of my brain was absolutely a result of the alcohol. Considering my first time getting drunk was ending like this, I wasn't keen on repeating the experience anytime soon.

"She didn't. At all. I gave her permission—she didn't even want to bond me at first, but I asked for it."

"They're going to ask you that question again and plenty more at the Institute. This is for your safety. It's taken very seriously if a normal omega is coerced into a dark bond."

"There was no coercion."

"If that's the case, I'm sure the Institute will determine it."

He didn't say anything else. I didn't trust the Institute. Not with who my father was. His ties to alphas and omegas weren't that strong, but he did have some. Was it enough to steal me out from under the Institute's thumb?

Why was I alone with this guy, anyway? Shouldn't I have an entourage of more than one person?

Heart pounding, I stopped abruptly. The beta man almost pulled me over when he kept going for a couple extra seconds. "Is something wrong?" he asked, his eyebrows drawing together.

I couldn't trust him. I couldn't trust anyone.

"Let me go."

He did, which was points in his favour. I backed up. "Can I go to the Institute myself?"

"I need to escort you…"

"An escort isn't necessary," I said.

"Miss, it's my job."

I bit my lip, glancing back over my shoulder. They hadn't taken anyone else out of the unit yet. Were they waiting for me to get downstairs? Did they expect Leighton to influence my answers to questions? It was a good protocol to have in most situations, but it was causing panic to creep up my spine.

My hand was resting on Nyla again. They hadn't checked me for weapons. I guessed it was because I wasn't considered a threat… but I was.

I'd stabbed Ambrose.

Killed Jonathan.

"I want Dash to come with me." I wasn't sure who I was going to ask for until the words came out.

The beta man lifted an eyebrow. "That's against the rules."

"I don't care. I'm not going unless I have him."

He pressed a button on the radio clipped to his vest. "She wants Dash Loranger. Won't leave without him. Please advise."

Dash strolled out of the condo a minute later, a grin on his face. He was still acting that goofy amount of tipsy, but I was sure he'd sobered up from the panic the same way I had.

Or maybe not. He didn't seem to feel things like panic.

He made to put his arm around me, but the beta man stood between the two of us with a shake of his head. "No touching. You shouldn't even be allowed to come."

"Kinky," Dash muttered under his breath.

I snorted. The beta man didn't find it as funny as we did, herding me in front of him and into the elevator.

We were silent as we rode down to the parking garage. A black sedan waited. The beta man slid into the middle seat in the back, continuing to prevent Dash and I from touching each other. A man in a suit drove the car, while an omega woman with a wide smile turned to face the backseat.

Her smile faltered when she saw Dash, but she focused on me. "Hi, honey. I'm Selena, your Institute contact. We're going to make sure you get taken care of while we work everything out. No matter what you say to me, you're not going to get into trouble. If your alpha told you that you would, that's a lie."

I glanced over at Dash. He was amused by her, but unconcerned.

Selena's words weren't exactly true. I was pretty sure I would get in trouble if I admitted to stabbing multiple people. She was trying her best, though.

"How long will it be until I get to go back to Leighton?" I asked.

Her gaze flicked down to my throat. "You seem eager to go back."

"She's my alpha, and I asked her to bond me. She's also not the one who gave me the bruises."

"OK, honey. If you say so. We'll get into some more questions once we get to the Institute building, after the seers have taken a look at you."

Her tone had a hint of condescension. She didn't believe me. The bruises were going to be hard to explain, but I think what was harder for her to grasp was why any omega would ask for a dark bond.

My gaze strayed to Dash again, but this time he had a sour expression on his face as he looked at Selena. She'd turned to face the front, and we spent the rest of the drive in tense silence.

The seers were nice.

The rest of the staff weren't.

"Check again," Selena instructed.

My aura was being probed by the Institute's seers, trying to prove that Leighton had dark bonded me without permission. That wasn't what they were going to find. I'd given permission enthusiastically. The ones who could see my aura would know that.

This was the second seer who'd checked me over because Selena was confident they were all wrong. I had no idea why she was so set on being right. Shouldn't she want me to be happy with my bonded mate?

"There is no evidence that the dark bond was forced," the seer said again.

The seers were dealing with her far better than I would have. I wondered if they often had to deal with people who didn't believe their findings. It wasn't as if Selena could double check their work.

Selena looked me up and down, loosing a sigh and then offering me a smile. It was the same one she'd first offered me in the sedan, and I'd since learned it was fake.

Big and fake.

"Well, then, let's move on to the interview. Grab me a coffee." She directed the request to the seer, and I gave the woman a sympathetic smile.

I was pretty sure she wasn't supposed to be a coffee-toting secretary, but Selena liked to make demands.

She led me down a hallway in the vast building we were in. Dash had been forced to wait in an office, but I caught his scent from here. It was comforting. That meant he could smell me too, and my family wasn't going to be able to whisk me away completely unnoticed.

The room we entered was small but cozy, with a couch across from an armchair and a small desk in the corner. It was what the therapist's offices looked like in the TV shows my mother watched.

I took a seat on the couch, leaning back into the sanitized leather, devoid of all scent except the lingering note of lemon cleaner. Selena perched on the arm of the chair, not at all relaxed.

"If you could give me a rundown of when Leighton claimed you, that would be wonderful, honey."

I didn't like her calling me honey anymore, not when it was so obviously patronizing. "We were at a park. I asked her to, and she bonded me like I wanted," I said simply.

The more details I gave, the more likely it was for me to reveal an inconsistency in Leighton's and my stories. Was I expected to tell Selena about my brother?

My family that I'd run away from?

Did they know who I was, and know my last name?

And then there was the matter of the bruises. I already knew Selena would require a response, and I'd have to lie. It wasn't Ambrose's fault he'd done it, and if I told anyone I'd stabbed him unprovoked…

"Was this before or after you received the bruises on your neck?" she asked.

I chewed my lip. "After."

"How did the bruising happen, Kiara?"

Lie, my inner voice urged. It didn't give me an answer on how I was supposed to make sure my lie was the same as Leighton's. We were bonded, not telepathic.

"My brother." The answer came to me suddenly. Selena did seem to want to protect me despite her abrasive way of doing it. If I created a story that was close to the truth, but not quite right, I might be able to work this in my favour.

Her eyebrow lifted. "Your brother?"

"My older brother, Toby."

I almost smirked at the shortened form of his name. Hearing

Leighton use it had been exciting, especially when I saw the tic in his jaw.

"Why did he try to strangle you, honey?"

"He's never really... liked me," I said. I pitched my voice lower, a little sad, and tried to appear dejected. It wasn't too difficult because there was a part of me that wished he'd been on my side. My childhood would have been easier if he'd been looking out for me. "When I said I wanted to leave to be with Leighton, he was angry."

Selena adjusted her perch on the chair and got out a notepad. "How did you get free?"

"There was a knife on the fireplace mantle. I sliced his arm with it and he let me go, and I ran back to her. We met at the park because it was close to my house."

I was weaving this story like an expert novelist, and it was believable. Probably. Hopefully if I had any tells, like the way Leighton tapped her nails, Selena wouldn't be able to peg them.

"Is there a reason you didn't try to register as silver status? She could have given you a normal bond if you'd gone through the process."

"I'm scared of him," I whispered. "And I trust Leighton with my life. She would never use the dark bond against me, so it made sense for us to do it."

"You're aware that this bond should have been registered right away, correct?"

"Yes, and I apologize. Sincerely. We just wanted to wait until the bruises went away. We knew you would think the worst of her, and I..."

Tears welled up in my eyes. They were easier to conjure than I expected.

"I didn't want her reputation to be ruined by me."

Selena's gaze flashed with regret, and she finally shifted to sit on the chair instead of the arm. As she continued to volley questions my way and I continued to maintain my perfect half-truth story, I wondered what she'd already done to ruin Leighton's reputation.

She had to have done something, otherwise she wouldn't look guilty.

And I kind of wanted to stab her for it…

But I wasn't going to.

Geez.

I had *some* self-control.

TWENTY-TWO

LEIGHTON

The police car sat parked on the street outside my apartment building.

To get there, we would have to pass through a crowd of reporters. They had cameras and microphones trained on the building, trying to get a good shot of me beyond the glass. I had handcuffs snapped around my wrists, and I wasn't afforded the courtesy of hiding that from the world.

This was a new low for me.

My reputation was trashed. Shot to complete hell. No one would hire a fixer who couldn't even fix her own life. That wasn't the worst of it, though.

Mother was going to hear about this.

It didn't look like Kiara had been dragged out the front of the building like I was—there was no buzz from the reporters, they were all half-asleep waiting for the story to show up until they'd spotted me. Hopefully that meant Mother wouldn't know *who* I'd dark bonded, but Tobias was bound to figure it out. The pieces were all out in the open now.

"Are the metal bracelets really necessary?" Ambrose growled as he followed behind me and the few cops who shoved me forward. We hadn't yet breached the front doors, and thankfully the reporters hadn't gotten inside.

Dash had gone with Kiara. Thank fuck they'd let him when she'd asked, because I'd been half convinced this was a ploy to get her back into her brother's grasp. Mercury and Ambrose had stayed with me, even to do this horrible walk of shame.

The reporters were eating it up. I heard some shouts that told me they were already running with the story of an illicit affair between Leighton Winston and her brother's rejected scent match pack.

They weren't wrong, but I wasn't looking forward to the fallout of that being added to the whole chaotic situation.

"She's in custody for the time being," the man in charge barked. "This is a serious offense."

"That she hasn't committed," Mercury said. "You're actively destroying her life."

I was surprised he was willing to defend me. So far, Mercury had only been along for the ride. He was trying to keep his pack together more than anything else, and he didn't need me for that.

"We'll see what the Institute determines," he countered.

"And then you'll see what our lawyers can do to you. The damages your organization will have to pay are astronomical. I'm sure you'll be fired. Remember what happened to the man who led that little raid on Dash's studio?"

Mercury wasn't even being discreet about his threats.

The GPRE had raided the Dirt with Dash studio during a rather... controversial broadcast a couple of months ago. That case was still in the courts, but the Loranger pack's lawyers were suing for destruction of property, arrest without cause, and impeding free speech. Oh, and emotional distress.

I'd seen them at the GPRE headquarters and Dash had almost been pleased to be arrested. No distress present.

Needless to say, the person who'd ordered that action was now on unpaid leave.

"Your threats aren't going to stop me from doing my job."

"Enjoy your unpaid leave."

We exited the building then. Muffled shouts grew clamorous, and it was hard to keep my head high when I was the centre of attention. I was no stranger to it, but it usually wasn't this loud. Microphones were shoved in my face, requesting my comments. I turned away from them all.

That was the advice I gave my clients. Don't let them force you into speaking in a stressful situation. It's better to look like you're snubbing reporters than to say something you haven't thought through.

No one ever listened to that one, but I at least was going to follow my own advice.

When I was helped into the back of the cop car, Ambrose was stopped from following me and Mercury never tried. He faced the crowd of vultures instead, acting as my own PR manager.

He better not say anything that would bite me in the ass.

I didn't get a chance to hear his speech because the car pulled away from the curb. Ambrose was jogging down the street to catch a cab, and we left all that behind.

"Kiara didn't tell me how she received the bruises on her neck," I said for the fifteenth time.

Just my luck, the woman interrogating me was an old friend.

OK, friend is a gross overstatement. I got her demoted from the GPRE—which was the only reason she was working here— and she was trying to twist my words to fit her agenda.

"Are you sure about that?" Jennika asked, leaning across the metal table like she was ready for me to tell her a secret.

I raised an eyebrow. "Does anyone know about the conflict of interest here? If you wanted to get demoted again, we could arrange it."

She scowled and sat back. Her back was always ramrod straight, the poster child for good posture. There were a few more wisps fraying from her slicked back ponytail than there had been the last time I'd seen her, but I guess stress came with the demotion.

And the pay dip.

Poor her.

"Please answer the question, Ms. Winston."

"Yes, I am absolutely certain my omega didn't tell me how the bruises on her neck appeared. All I know is she came to me with them and asked for the bond. I gave it to her."

My fingernails clacked against the metal table, my wrist movement impeded by the handcuffs. They were going to take them off in this interrogation room, but Jennika had recommended I be shackled to the middle of the table instead.

"Will Kiara have the same story to tell?"

"It's not a story, because it's the truth. We've been around the block five times by now, Jennika. Your seers have finished looking at her, and they'll reveal the truth that none of us can see. The dark bond was created with permission. End of story."

"Seers can't tell if it was a coerced bond."

I sighed heavily. "No, but my omega would tell you if it was a coerced bond. That's why we're separated, right? So she can feel safe from me?"

"Your story doesn't line up." She leaned across the table, placing her hand on top of mine and making me snarl. "A bitch like you couldn't love an omega enough to bond them and torpedo your own reputation."

She whispered the words so quietly none of the recording equipment in here would pick it up.

I ignored her.

Of course I was known to be a frigid bitch, but Jennika didn't know me any deeper than that. I was furious about my business being ruined, but would never blame Kiara for ruining that. I would do this all over again, the exact same way.

But did Kiara feel the same way? She'd had limited choices in alphas and not much time available.

Gritting my teeth and showing a hint of my weakness to my interrogator, I shoved the thoughts away. If Kiara didn't want me, she never would have sung beneath my tongue or thrown herself at me when drunk. These doubts were the result of being able to feel her mild anxiety but being too far away to comfort her.

Jennika smirked. "So what do you get out of bonding the omega?"

"Love and affection," I answered.

"You could have had that with a normal bond if you'd registered as silver status."

"We all know how long the process is to register as silver status."

There were hoops to jump through. More for omegas than for alphas. Once you were registered officially, your biology shifted to allow you to find a scent match among other silver status singles. You could also bond a single omega in a normal bond. That wasn't something I could do as a packless, but not silver status, alpha.

The biology and 'magic' governing bonding mechanisms was hard to understand unless you were a researcher. Most of the population didn't get into the nitty gritty.

"Wouldn't you have waited if you really loved each other?"

It was pointless entertaining Jennika, but I didn't have my normal level of cool. Having her poking at the legitimacy of my bond with Kiara irritated me to no end.

Ironic, because it wasn't the most legitimate of bonds when it came down to it.

"She trusts me," I said coldly. "Which is why she was comfortable with a dark bond."

"The level of trust it takes to ask for a dark bond... How long have you two known each other?"

I glared at her. There was no way I could answer that question. The truth would be absurd, raising red flags. A lie would open us up to story inconsistencies.

A single knock rapped on the door. It opened without waiting for a response, saving my ass and revealing... a lawyer. Not my lawyer—Jasper was a multi-talented guy and had gone to law school after deciding being a doctor wasn't his calling. This lawyer was much higher-powered, wearing a three-piece suit that cost upwards of five grand.

"I'm Ms. Winston's legal representation."

I had to hope I wasn't paying him. I was on the high side of well-off, but my mother was the rich one.

Jennika stiffened, her face a mask of false niceness. "Ms. Winston didn't make me aware she was waiting for her lawyer."

"Now that I'm here, you're going to need to leave and give me a moment with my client."

She knew the law but took her sweet time getting up and gathering her paperwork together. Offering me a smile, she patted my cuffed hands again. "We'll get back to the questions in a couple of minutes then."

It was all I could do to resist another growl. The more erratic I seemed, the more likely I was to be condemned.

The door slammed behind her, leaving me alone with my new lawyer.

"Mercury send you?" I asked, leaning back in the chair. My cuffs jangled against the metal table.

"He informed me that getting you and your omega out of

custody is my top priority, so I hope you haven't made it harder for me to work. What did you tell her?"

He didn't bother with introductions, and I didn't care. The man was a lawyer way above my pay grade, and he'd get me back to Kiara. That was all that mattered.

I gave him a rundown of the last couple hours spent in this interrogation room with Jennika. Then he knocked on the door to indicate we were done, and sat down in the uncomfortable metal chair beside mine. "We'll get you out of here within five hours. Probably two. Based on what they found down in the Omega Safety Division, they have no reason to hold you. If you want to sue, we can make it happen."

Jennika opened the door before I could respond.

My grin wiped the smirk right off her face.

Bitch already knew she'd lost—and maybe gotten another demotion out of it too.

TWENTY-THREE

DASH

The Omega Safety Division was committed to—you guessed it!—omega safety. It would have been hypocritical as fuck if they'd kept Kiara against her will after they were finished with their questions. Selena, the big bitch in charge, seemed tempted to do it anyway.

When Kiara demanded to leave, though, she couldn't say no.

I wouldn't have been able to say no either.

My little omega was quite the actress. I'd heard the heaving sobs and begging from the office they'd stuck me in to wait. *"Please, Selena, don't make me stay here. I miss Leighton. What if my brother finds me here?"*

I wasn't sure what she'd said about her brother, but Kiara was smart enough to avoid mentioning her part in one of the bigger beta crime families in New Oxford.

A second later Kiara appeared from the room where she'd been getting her interview and rushed to me. She followed my scent so easily, it must have called to her like a beacon. We were meant for each other, definitely.

"Where's Leighton?" she asked breathlessly when she entered the office.

Was I a little jealous she didn't spend a moment simply being excited to see me? Yes, absolutely.

"On a different floor. Would you like me to take you there?"

"Please."

"So polite," I purred, standing and stretching.

Her gaze travelled down my body and back up again. That made me feel a little better.

"I figured polite was the way to go with you," she said. "Would you have taken me if I was demanding?"

She crossed her arms over her chest, drawing my attention to her cleavage. I didn't hide how I stared at it. There were so many things I could do with tits like that. I was most excited to try teasing her nipples until she begged for more. Oh, and having her wrap the soft flesh around my cock until I spurted all over her pretty face.

My cock plumped up and I blatantly readjusted it.

"Maybe," I said. "I like you both ways. Hearing you say please makes me desperate to have you begging for more, though."

"Now isn't the time. Leighton is still arrested."

"My family's lawyer is well on his way to freeing her from that predicament. There's nothing we can do to rush the process, so there's no need to cut off my fun."

I smirked, leaving the safety of the office and heading through the hallways to the elevator. I gave a wave to Selena, hoping we wouldn't be seeing her again. Kiara seemed to share my testament, avoiding giving any sort of final farewell.

We weren't the only ones in the elevator, the steel box holding a couple of Institute employees, so I tugged her to the back and stood against the wall. "P2 for us," I said to the person closest to the buttons, nodding when he thumbed it.

"Isn't that parking?" Kiara asked, confused.

"It is, sweet omega."

I pulled her backside to my front. My erection pressed against the small of her back. I was so much taller than her. My chin could rest on her head.

She let out a soft hiss as I discreetly palmed her breast, removing my hand as quickly as it arrived. "What are you doing?" she whispered.

We were in close quarters with these people, but there were a couple of gossips at the front of the elevator. Their chatter would make hearing our conversation difficult.

"Am I doing something?" I asked innocently.

I slid my fingers down her arm to grab her hand, placing it on the holster where her knife sat beneath her dress. They hadn't taken it from her. If they had, she would be an anxious mess right now.

"If you think I'm doing something uncouth, feel free to let me know. Violently."

Her breath hitched. My fingers trailed back to the curve of her ass, then teased the hem of the t-shirt dress. I was playing a dangerous game. Her perfume would give us away the second it heightened, but she was fighting her arousal. I loved a little risk, whether it was the risk of being caught... or of being stabbed.

Is she going to do it?

I wanted to feel the bite of that steel in my flesh again, same as how I'd taunted her into it the last time. It helped me feel alive after so many years of being dead inside, hiding behind alcohol and sex.

My fingers slipped beneath the dress to caress the bare skin of her ass, but I didn't go further. That would be beyond the limits of an omega's control. Even with this she was stifling a whine, the sound coming out strangled from deep in her chest.

The chatty employees got off, leaving us with only quiet people, waiting impatiently for their next destination.

It increased the risk.

Upped the ante.

We descended with my hand squeezing and stroking her ass, stopping every couple of floors to let people on and off. By the time we reached the lobby we were alone, heading down to the parking level.

I plunged my fingers down to gather her arousal, groaning at how wet I found her. "You're soaked, little omega. I'm surprised your scent didn't spike. Let me smell your arousal now."

Coconut and chocolate bloomed in the tiny, confined box and she groaned.

Then, the tip of her knife nicked my skin.

She'd grabbed it from under her dress and was holding it openly, the blade in danger of plunging into my stomach.

I hissed, bucking against her to gain some friction on my cock.

"We shouldn't be doing this," she murmured. "Leighton was furious when you slept in the sheets I'd come on. How would she feel about this?"

I grinned, circling her clit with my thumb. "I don't really give a fuck. She can punish me for it later. She knows what I want, and she's well aware I'll play dirty to get it."

The knife didn't dig any deeper. Not even when I teased her entrance with my finger, threatening to slide the digit inside her.

The elevator dinged open on P2, and I pulled back from her all at once. My hand caught hers—the one that wasn't holding her knife—and I led her out and around a corner. In the long hallway that led to mechanical rooms and possibly an emergency exit, a light was burnt out. It left us shrouded in darkness.

I pushed her back against the cold cement wall and leaned in close enough our lips brushed together. The knife was at my throat in a second.

This time, my breath hitched.

Her eyes were so big and blue and dangerous, in more ways than one. Her hand trembled on the knife, but she kept it pressed close to me like she kind of wanted to but wasn't willing to commit.

"If I die like this, it'll be a good way to go," I whispered.

I leaned forward to slam our lips together. The blade sliced me, but not deep enough to kill. Only enough to hurt in a way that lit my blood on fucking fire. She gasped into my mouth, giving me full access to plunge my tongue inside and explore.

Kiara tasted like coconut. It wasn't fair for an omega to taste so good, and if I hadn't been obsessed with her before, I sure as fuck was now.

When I pulled back, a tiny trail of my blood slid down my collarbone from the wound she left behind. It was superficial and would heal with a simple flare of my aura. I didn't do it, because I didn't want to scare her.

Her eyes were wild, staring between the knife and my neck. "What are you even doing?" she asked. "I could have... I could have killed you."

"Then I would have died."

"I'm not... You... It's wrong for me to enjoy holding your life in my hands. The thrill I got..."

She flung the knife to the ground. I didn't wait for her panicked whine, diving down to pick it up and press it back into her palm.

"I'll tell you a secret, little omega," I purred, leaning in and licking along her jawline. "I don't think it's wrong at all. I think it's sexy."

Kiara glared at me, but it was half-hearted. "You're trying to turn me on by calling me sexy and not unhinged."

"I was turning you on regardless."

I yanked her dress up high enough that it revealed her lingerie underneath. She might never have put it on if she hadn't been drunk, but she wasn't drunk anymore. And she was the one with the knife.

The tiny scrap of fabric covering her pussy had already been displaced by my teasing in the elevator, and her thighs were soaked. I forced her legs apart by shoving my thigh between them. She drenched my leg almost immediately. I was going to be covered in my omega's scent when we picked Leighton up.

Wouldn't she just love that?

"You're going to come for me, or you're going to stab me until I stop touching you," I murmured. "Take your pick."

I sunk a finger into her pussy, her channel clenching tight around me as she gasped. Her slick made an obscene squelching noise every time I thrust my finger. I used my other hand to stroke her clit. Her moans echoed in the hall, announcing to everyone who walked by that there was an omega being pleasured down here.

When she brought her free hand up to smother her cries, I smirked.

"You could have just asked me to kiss you, little omega."

"I don't want a kiss," she gasped.

I leaned in, only to be stopped by the blade.

She knew how to use it. This time it was pressed against my clothed cock, which pulsed at the threat.

"You're serious about no kissing," I murmured. "Got it."

"Leighton hasn't yet," she said.

"She hasn't... kissed you? I do recall her kissing your pussy until you screamed her name. There was no mouth kissing involved in that?"

Kiara shook her head. "You stole one kiss, but I'm not giving you another."

I wanted to be there the first time Leighton claimed her mouth, but I doubted the other alpha would let me. A damn shame. I would be happy if I got a seat in the other room though, like I had the first time Leighton had touched Kiara.

Letting her focus on keeping herself quiet, I put all my effort into making her scream. I worked in a second finger, curling them to hit the spot that had her arching off the wall. Her clit was being downright abused, though I took a second to shove her dress up even farther, baring her tits.

Only that thin, translucent lace kept her from being naked in front of me. I sucked on her nipple through the fabric, her grip on her knife going limp as her pleasure built.

All the better. I didn't need her spasming when she came if she was in the perfect position to cut off that delicate part of me.

"Are you going to come for me, little omega?" I asked, my lips barely detaching enough to mumble it against her breast.

"No," she said.

Her body was tensing though, telling me how close she was to release. There was no way I wouldn't push her over the edge. Unless she did use her knife on me, after all.

"You are."

I kept working her just right until she screamed against her fist. If anyone else was on P2, they would have heard her. If they didn't smell her first. God, an aroused omega was a scent like no other. Especially her. When her body stopped convulsing and she slumped against the wall, I worked her t-shirt dress down to cover her again.

Then I licked my fingers clean, because how could I let all that slick go to waste?

She had a pout on her lips as she watched me.

"If Leighton asks, I came for her. Because I was thinking about her, not you."

I grinned. Considering my history of being rejected, maybe that should hurt. It didn't, because if she had to say 'if Leighton asks,' that meant it was a bluff.

Kiara was thinking of me the whole time. I was in.

And in for a spanking from Leighton. Maybe ball busting? I didn't know what she was into, but I was flexible. The punishment for touching her omega was going to be just as sweet as the orgasm I just stole.

TWENTY-FOUR

LEIGHTON

There was one thing about my life that was inevitable.

Mother would always meddle. Sometimes she meddled for seemingly no reason—though there was always some ulterior motive going through her head. But sometimes, I could see her interference coming from a mile off.

Like tonight, when I'd been publicly arrested for dark bonding a normal omega and my brother's rejected scent matched pack had been found at my condo.

It was a minor miracle it took her hours to arrive instead of minutes. Mercury's lawyer was close to getting me released from custody when the interrogation room door burst open and Edith Winston stood there in all her glory.

I tried to keep my expression impassive, even as my stomach turned with the desperate need to see Kiara and make sure she was alright. Mother's arrival was only keeping me away from her for longer.

"I need to speak with my daughter," she said, not a smile in sight.

Jennika had the good sense not to hesitate before getting up out of her chair and leaving. The lawyer paused until I gave him a nod, and then we were alone.

At least I was no longer handcuffed to the table. My representation had insisted on having them removed, considering I'd never exhibited dangerous behaviour.

"What do you have to say for yourself?" she asked after a long pause.

Despite it being the middle of the night, her attire was immaculate. Her makeup, perfect. She'd never leave the house unless it was, not even for this kind of PR emergency. We had the same colour hair, but hers was kept in a straight, precise bob. Maybe our features had once been similar, but she'd had enough plastic surgery that it wasn't the case anymore. Anything to keep herself from aging.

Had she spent time figuring out who my omega was, before she'd come to visit? Kiara hadn't been on TV, so her and Noah Connolly might not have put the pieces together yet.

Then again, Tobias had probably run right to his father and informed the man that I was the one who darked bonded Kiara right in front of him. That's if he hadn't found my identity before I'd been splashed on the evening news. Maybe he was the one to tip off the authorities and the press.

"The situation got out of hand," I said.

I wouldn't apologize. Not for saving Kiara's life. An apology automatically gave Mother the upper hand, and I couldn't give her any more leverage.

"You lied to me, Leighton. I'd say you let the situation get out of hand."

"There were no lies."

"You dark bonded the Connolly daughter."

Her carefully constructed facade cracked, her jaw clenching. Manicured fingertips tapped against her leg. The woman was never twitchy, so I could only surmise this situation could—or already had—fuck her over in a big way. She was almost anxious on top of being angry.

"I didn't lie about it. No one ever asked," I said.

I was pushing my luck, but I was both curious and fed up. Curious because I'd never seen her so close to a breaking point before. Fed up because I'd done everything she asked since I was old enough to understand words—yet it was never enough. And just when I'd established myself as an independent contractor who didn't need her support anymore, she'd found the perfect blackmail to keep me under her thumb.

"So you think it was appropriate to withhold that information after you took on the job of finding her? You've made me look incompetent in front of the Connollys. On top of that, you're all over the news. You and the Loranger pack. You dark bonding an omega. Do you have any idea how that makes us look?"

Her voice rose at the end, nearing hysteria.

I'd finally discovered something she feared. This situation terrified her more than anything else in the world, or she wouldn't be reacting at all. She'd been emotionless through every prior family drama, whether it was something that hit the news or not.

"The story will blow over. I dark bonded with permission. My lawyer was minutes away from getting me out of custody because they have no proof to hold me on," I said.

Mother's lips curled up into a snarl. "That's the Loranger pack's lawyer, not yours, which is only going to fan the flames of these nasty rumours. And the dark bond will not '*blow over.*' Not with the media and certainly not with Noah Connolly."

"It isn't as if it can be undone."

"No, but you're going to fix it, or you're going to die."

If I hadn't been sitting, I might have swayed from the shock.

My eyes widened as I watched Mother's face. Her eyes were as flinty as always. She was dead serious.

"Do you plan on killing me?" I asked.

"You're a foolish fucking child. He will. Not me, but him. If you die, the bond is no longer an issue. You'll do as I say to save your own life."

She crossed her arms over her chest, lips pursed. She was collecting herself as I watched, once again hiding away the reactions that made her vulnerable.

"I can keep myself safe from the Connollys," I said.

"You'll do as I say, Leighton, or your brother's secret airs on national news. If you don't listen to me, his life is going to be turned upside down and you'll be too dead to help him."

It was as serious as I'd ever seen her. Glaring across the tiny interrogation room, I gave in to her demands. For now. She wouldn't leave until I'd agreed to her plan, and I needed to see Kiara.

"How do you intend for me to fix this?"

"You and Kiara are going to join the pack of Kiara's father's choosing," she said.

I almost barked a refusal at her. That wouldn't have gotten me anywhere. She would only dig in her heels, threatening the people I cared about more vehemently. She must have seen the visceral denial in my gaze, because she narrowed her eyes.

"You'll meet with them in two days. A public date. This will help with our family's reputation, while also appeasing the Connollys. I can't have a female alpha daughter with a dark bonded omega. It's frowned upon highly enough when a male alpha does it. Females are held to a higher standard, Leighton. You'll answer the phone when I call and go to the location I give you at the time I say."

She didn't ask if I understood or agreed.

It was implied that I had to.

"I also expect you to stop associating with the Loranger pack. Their lawyer will get you out of this place, but that's as far as your association goes."

That wasn't going to happen. Neither was Kiara and I joining some random pack of alphas who were likely criminals. Right now I was helpless to speak, rage simmering beneath the surface. I was holding myself together outwardly. She'd taught me that.

"Then I suppose I'll speak with you soon," I said plainly.

Mother scoffed and turned on her heel. Her composure had been carefully gathered again. She pulled open the door and strode out without another word to me.

I wanted to break down, to scream into the void and throw a chair against the wall. Instead, a smug-looking Jennika reentered the room, followed by Mercury's lawyer. I kept my mouth shut and let the lawyer and Jennika settle back into the irritating back and forth they'd been doing before. I thought only of Kiara.

There was nothing in this world that she was more scared of than going back to her family.

I'd felt it when they'd taken her away from me—she'd been scared to go alone. If I hadn't been indisposed, she would have asked for me, but it was good to know her second choice was Dash. I bet he'd gotten an ego boost from that.

She was less scared now. *I hope they took her home to get some sleep.* My body was weighed down with tiredness, and I hadn't been the one drinking before all this happened.

Plus, she would be safer at home than she was here, and all I wanted was for her to be safe.

If I had to dig into the dredges of my mother's life and tear it to shreds to meet that goal, so be it.

Bitch had it coming, anyway.

TWENTY-FIVE

MERCURY

"Took you long enough," I snapped as our lawyer let Leighton out of the interrogation room. It had taken hours after he'd arrived—and the intermission while Edith Winston said her piece to her daughter hadn't helped.

The wait was long enough we'd sent a dishevelled Kiara home to sleep because her yawns had become contagious. Luckily, that was before the arrival and subsequent quick departure of the manicured bitch from Hell. She'd shot me a disdainful look when she'd passed me in the lobby.

Both Ambrose and Dash were home with Kiara because Dash had proven he couldn't be trusted alone with her. I didn't think either could be trusted at the end of the day, but she wasn't comfortable with me. Besides, I was the bullheaded one who wouldn't let these assholes get away with locking Leighton up for no reason.

Ambrose's dominant streak began and ended in the bedroom—he wasn't a fan of conflict in real life. Dash was more likely to get himself locked up than get Leighton out.

"There are some hoops we had to jump through," he said. "They wanted to do more interrogations, but they had no grounds to hold her. These Institute people aren't as familiar with the nuances of the law as they should be, so I had to do a few lessons."

I couldn't fault him for that, but I kind of did.

"I'm out now, and that's more than my lawyer probably could have done for me this fast," Leighton said with a shrug. "On that note, you better be paying him because I can't afford him."

I scowled. "He's on retainer for all of the Loranger pack's legal needs."

"Are you counting this as one of the Loranger pack's legal needs?" she asked.

Her eyebrow lifted. It highlighted the dark bags under her eyes. It was late in the evening and the last few days had held more than a small amount of stress. She needed sleep.

And I should not be worrying about what she needed.

Leighton was only my problem because Ambrose and his goddamn sex drive had made her my problem.

"It became one of our needs the second you were arrested while we were all present at your condo," I said.

I bet Ambrose would have called our lawyer regardless. So would Dash. The only one with any reasonable thought in their brain was me.

"Point taken," she said.

My lawyer bid us goodnight, promising the paperwork for the civil suit we were about to file would be complete within a few days. It left us standing in the middle of a nearly abandoned office. Only a couple of people were still on duty, and they were more interested in their paperwork than us.

The law never slept.

Pulling out my phone I sent a text to the private car company I used on occasion. I'd cabbed over, but there was no way I was getting in a cab at this hour. Not with Leighton.

Again, stop fucking worrying. She's not pack. You can't let her into your little swirl of overprotective thoughts.

"Car will be outside in fifteen," I said.

"I'm definitely not waiting up here."

She strode to the elevator without waiting for me, her heels clicking on the tile. They'd let her put on shoes before she was taken out of the condo, and she'd chosen heels. To get arrested in. This woman was something else.

It bothered me immensely that I hadn't known she was the one Ambrose had been with all along. They only saw each other once a week or less, but he always came home with a quirk to his lips, his body relaxed. Before we'd put a halt to our relationship, I'd always done my best to please him better than she could the next night—jealousy razed through me at the thought of her being *better.*

Once we'd stopped sleeping together, the jealousy had been worse. There were no opportunities to prove myself.

But I wasn't jealous enough to try to ban him from relationships outside the pack. It wouldn't be fair.

"Are you coming?" Leighton asked, her foot blocking the elevator door from closing.

I hadn't realized it had arrived.

I joined her in the elevator and crossed my arms over my chest. Being in close quarters with her had me sucking in breaths of her scent, vanilla cream lingering in my nose. It bothered me how she had traces of scent from the men who had arrested her.

They shouldn't have touched her.

I shouldn't have let them.

And those thoughts were preposterous. Leighton was a grown woman—an alpha, who could take care of herself.

Ambrose's words echoed in my head. *"He's an adult. He can handle himself, baby."*

He'd been talking about Dash, but it was dawning on me that I went overboard on protecting more than just the one packmate. My desire to protect also extended to Leighton and the omega.

Not allowed.

We stood in tense silence all the way down to the lobby. The security guard had to let us out at this hour, the front doors locked. We waited on the street. At this time of year, even the middle of the night was warm enough to be comfortable.

Leighton kept reaching into her pocket for her phone, but she didn't have it. The device had been left behind at the apartment.

"Get some sleep before looking at your phone when we get back," I said.

She palmed her pocket and glanced at me. Her expression was pinched with stress. "I'll have a lot of messages."

"Yes, and they can all wait. As far as they all know, you're still in police custody without access to a phone."

"There are circumstances—"

"I will personally stop any circumstances from entering your space until you've slept."

The hired car pulled to a stop at the curb, a familiar driver waiting behind the wheel. I opened the back door for her and she slid across the plush leather. I gave her address to the driver and raised the clear partition, giving us some privacy to speak freely.

"This situation is more complicated than I want it to be," Leighton admitted. "My mother isn't the only influence I have to deal with."

Kiara's family was another, but there might be even more. I wouldn't know because I hadn't given her the opportunity to let me in.

"So, let me help you."

Offering help was the wrong move. The right move was to cut

ties and get my pack out of this fucking mess. They'd get over the heartbreak.

Or maybe not.

Dash had never gotten over Leighton's brother, not until meeting Kiara and seeing Leighton in a different light. Who could say that his wallowing wouldn't happen again? Seeing him alive—and not a husk of a man living on alcohol, sex, and a hyperfixation on various hobbies—was enough to warm me to this dark bonded pair.

And it wasn't only that, but I was going to continue to pretend that was all.

"I don't need any help," Leighton said.

"The tension in your shoulders says you do."

She glared at me but worried her bottom lip between her teeth. I found myself hoping she accepted the offer. We could make everything better. There were very few things Dash's family money couldn't fix. I also came from a prestigious family name, but with four siblings my trust fund was a little sparser. Dash was the sole heir.

"My mother is blackmailing me," she said quietly. "I've come to accept it, but this situation with Kiara has messed everything up. What my mother wants is conflicting with what she needs, and that's before mentioning that there's someone else also blackmailing me."

I tried not to let my aura flare, but it did. The intensity shattered the serene quiet of the car and the deserted streets. Our driver glanced back in alarm, and I offered him a tight smile and a nod.

It didn't take long to get my anger back under control, and he stopped paying attention to us back here again.

"What are they blackmailing you with?" I asked.

She shook her head. "Not my secret to tell. But they both know the same thing, and it can't become public knowledge."

There was only one person in the world that Leighton would allow herself to be blackmailed over.

Her brother.

Maybe two people, now that she had a bonded omega.

"Can we eliminate the evidence?"

Cringing, Leighton shook her head again. "No. The evidence is all over the place, kind of. Mother figured out how to connect the dots."

I was running through possibilities of what this secret could be.

We pulled up out front of her apartment building and I tipped the driver. Leighton was already unlocking the building's front door when I caught up to her. No reporters had been ambitious enough to camp out here overnight, especially since the story had already broken, so we didn't get hassled.

"We're going to figure out how to fix this," I said.

She waved me off, holding the door open to let me in after her. The 'up' button lit up red when she punched it to call the elevator. "I shouldn't have told you about that," she said. "You could be the ones to blackmail me next if you find out, and then I'd have even more problems."

"I'm not the blackmailing type."

Her heels clicked as she stepped into the elevator and turned to face me. "Dash is."

"He's not the one who knows about this."

Both eyebrows lifted in surprised, her lips parting. "I assumed you planned to tell him. Don't packs tell each other everything? I'm surprised you didn't already know about the blackmail, considering I gave Ambrose some details."

With my panic and subsequent anger over him being stabbed, he hadn't had a chance to get into it. And he wouldn't have. Ambrose respected her privacy too much.

"Not my secret to tell," I repeated what she'd said before.

Her arms crossed over her chest. "I don't believe you."

"Do or don't. You already told me and you can't take that back, so let me help you."

This was pathetic. I was practically begging her to let me help, and I couldn't put my finger on why. Leighton was going to ruin our pack the same way her brother had years ago. However, it was the kind of destruction I couldn't look away from.

"I doubt you can, but if you're going to insist on trying, I guess I can't stop you," she muttered.

The elevator dinged and we got out. Her front door had a boot print on it where the police officer had kicked it in and shoved past Ambrose. All her neighbours would be able to see what happened—as if they hadn't already witnessed the whole thing on the news. My statement outside the building had only been able to do so much.

My speaking on her behalf had fanned the flames of certain theories that had lain dormant for years.

One popular gossip blog was insistent that Leighton's brother had rejected us because we'd been caught cheating on him with her. Apparently he'd been 'devastated' and 'retreated to the suburbs to avoid reminders.'

That gossip blog was the same one that was confident Prey Nightingale and the Crimson Fury pack were carrying on a sordid affair under the guise of their public dispute.

If you'd ever met any of those actors, you'd know that was a crazy idea. They had the sexual chemistry of a bag of grapes.

I followed Leighton into the apartment without being invited. My pack was here and I doubted they were leaving until the situation was resolved. We kept our footsteps light as we wandered into the apartment, not wanting to wake anyone up.

Kiara was in the master suite, with Ambrose snoring on an armchair like a stationed bodyguard. My heart clenched.

How did he trust her to sleep in the same room as him?

Her knife glinted on the bedside table, inches from her outstretched hand.

I turned away, expecting Leighton to wander into the suite and shut the door behind her. She didn't, instead following me out into the living room. Dash wasn't here, but a light shone under the door to Leighton's office, the gentle clacking of keystrokes easy to hear.

"I'm going to make some tea," I said. "Assuming you're not a heathen, and you keep tea bags handy."

She rolled her eyes, nostrils flaring as she peered at the closed door. When she found out what Dash did with Kiara... I wanted to witness what she did to him, because it was probably going to be hot.

Fucking hell. Thoughts like that have no place in my head.

"Of course I do. Cupboard above the kettle. Make me a mug too, chamomile with a touch of honey."

It was an order.

Why did an order to make her tea have my cock chubbing up in my pants?

I only subbed for Ambrose.

"Got it," I said, clearing my throat and turning to the kitchen.

She strode across the living room to the office and I put on the kettle, ignoring my mild arousal in hopes that I could pretend it never existed.

Leighton was going to destroy us.

The best thing I could do for the pack was help her so we could all be off on our separate ways.

TWENTY-SIX

LEIGHTON

Dash had too much of Kiara's scent on him. I'd caught it the second I opened up my senses, and I had a feeling he'd taken advantage of my temporary incarceration.

He better not have taken advantage of Kiara. I'd always considered myself a peaceful mediator, but I wasn't above murder, after all.

I wanted to slam the door to my office open, but instead gently turned the knob and slipped inside. It was far past the middle of the night. I wouldn't risk waking Kiara or angering my neighbours, who I imagined were less than pleased to be living next to someone who graced the New Oxford evening news with her arrest footage.

He was too focused on the computer screen to notice me. The website he was on looked like a database, and it looked official. His fingers tapped away at the keys, multiple windows popping up and vanishing again, some full of lines of code.

"What are you doing?" I asked.

Dash didn't answer.

I moved closer, assaulted by coconut and chocolate mixed with the chaos of his peachy spring rain scent. They'd been up close and personal. If he hadn't wanted me to immediately find out, he should have at least showered.

"Dash," I said, placing my hand on his shoulder.

He jolted, swinging his head to look at me with wide eyes. "Fuck. Give a guy some warning."

"I spoke when I entered the room."

His nose crinkled. "Didn't hear that. I have to finish this."

He tried to turn back to the computer, once again cycling through windows at a ridiculous pace. My fingers dug into his shoulder. "I want you to explain why you smell like my omega."

"I'm in the middle of something."

His voice went higher, spiking with irritation. I growled low in my throat. "It's not important. Do you realize it's like three a.m.? Whatever it is can wait until morning."

"No. It has to be done now."

Paying more attention, I noticed his leg was bouncing and his hands had a hint of a shake in them. His shoulder was rolling sporadically where I held it, trying to shake off my touch. With the day weighing me down, I wasn't sure what to make of him. He was known to have mood swings. I got the feeling if I interrupted him again, he would snap.

That kind of spat wasn't something I could afford at the moment, no matter how annoyed I was at his close contact with what belonged to me.

The soft creak of the door opening again had me stepping back. Mercury took one look at Dash and sighed, placing a plate of cut fruit and a bottle of water on the desk beside him. His packmate glanced over at the sustenance, grunted a 'thanks,' and ignored the food.

When Mercury left I followed him out and back into the

kitchen, grateful to see my tea already brewing on the counter. "Do you know what he's working on?" I asked.

Mercury shrugged. "Not a clue. He gets like that, though. If you interrupt him, it's not a good time for anyone involved and he tends to forget to eat, drink, and sleep."

"How long does it go on for?"

"However long he needs to finish what he's doing, or until the hyperfixation runs out. It kind of depends. There have been a couple times where he hasn't surfaced for a month."

My lips parted. "A *month*?"

"His body forces him to sleep after a couple of days, and we keep him fed with foods he can pick at sporadically when he remembers."

"What was he doing for the month?"

"During one of the month-long stints, he paid a hacker to teach him everything he knows and grade assignments like it was a university course."

Hacking made a lot of sense considering what I just saw him doing on that computer. It couldn't be legal.

"Should I be worried that he's currently on a computer in my house? Am I going to have the cops busting down my door again?"

Snorting, Mercury pulled the tea bags from both of our cups and gave them a stir. "Doubt it. I don't know much about code and the dark web, but he seriously learned from the best. He's not going to get caught."

"Better not," I muttered, looking over my shoulder at the closed door.

Mercury pressed the warm mug of chamomile into my hands, and I sucked in a deep breath of the calming fragrance. I got hit with his scent too. It bothered me how his cinnamon was almost more calming than the chamomile. He smelled like an old library with cinnamon buns baking amidst it all.

I took a tiny sip, the hot liquid burning my tongue.

"I'm going to sleep on the couch, if you don't mind," he said, tilting his head toward the living room.

Oddly, I didn't. These men had invaded my space—so had Kiara, for that matter. Having them here didn't feel cramped or overwhelming, though. It made the well-equipped apartment I'd lived in for so long actually feel like a home.

"Go ahead. Doubt I could get rid of you," I said.

The mug warmed my hands as we leaned against opposite counters in companionable silence. When we'd each sipped our way through half the mug, I pushed off and headed into the master suite without another word.

I woke up covered in omega.

Kiara's leg was thrown over mine, one arm draped over my chest as her nose pressed to my neck. I couldn't tell if she was a hundred percent awake, but she was grinding her clit down on my hip, slick drenching me. Little moans broke the mid-morning silence.

My hands went down to her hips, finding her naked except for the shirt she was wearing.

The shirt smelled of Ambrose.

Why was she wearing his clothes? I was caught between irritation and arousal at the thought of him claiming my omega by giving her an oversized t-shirt to sleep in.

"Kiara," I murmured.

My fingers dug into her delicate skin to stop her grinding. Her whine was louder than her moans had been.

"Alpha, make me come," she said against my neck.

Her little tongue darted out to lick my skin and I groaned. My gaze slid over to the armchair where Ambrose had been when I'd come to bed.

Our gazes locked, his eyes dark with hunger. He couldn't see much beneath the sheets, but he could hear her and fuck, could he ever smell her. And me. I bet my scent was rising with every second.

"We're not alone, dove," I said.

Her hips pushed against my hold and I let go. She ground against me again, her movements erratic. Teeth scraped at my neck and I hissed, eager to feel the bite but conflicted about whether I wanted it with the audience. Even Ambrose, who'd seen me at my most vulnerable. Kiara still didn't belong to him.

"Look at me," I commanded.

She pulled back instantly, a pout on her face at having to listen to my order. "What?" she asked.

One of my hands grabbed her chin, carefully turning it so she faced Ambrose. "Are you doing this because you want him to see the show, or because he's inconveniently present and you didn't want to wait for him to leave?"

Her sapphire eyes were darker with lust as she stared at him. I felt her run her fingers up the side of my body until she could cup one breast, the touch gentle and unsure.

"Answer me, or you're not coming," I said.

"Both," she said.

I barely held back a curse.

Danger alarms were going off in my head. My omega couldn't get attached to another alpha, because then our only option would be to join their pack. If I joined Ambrose's pack, it could spell disaster for so many reasons. More than I could even count.

But maybe...

Slipping out of my mother's control was the only way to get out of this situation. Without her threats hanging over my head, I doubted Soren would care who I bonded myself to.

If we got out of this, I might be able to have it all. My brother's secret, safe. Kiara. Ambrose. The rest of the Loranger pack. It was better if I didn't get my hopes up, though.

"If you want to give him a show, then give him a show. Take off the shirt," I said.

My mouth was clearly not cooperating with my mental alarms or my demand to keep low hopes.

"I'd rather it stayed on, actually," Ambrose said, voice gravelly as he shook off the last dredges of sleep. "You know I love the tease, doll."

All my muscles went tight. I didn't know how to respond to that. I couldn't be Ambrose's doll and Kiara's alpha in the same moment. The two sides of me were so discordant there were no similarities at all.

Right?

Kiara sat up, her knee sliding between my thighs as she kneeled over me. Her bare pussy slicked up my leg and there was pressure on the apex of my thighs, clothed only in thin satin sleep shorts. She tentatively rubbed herself against me with a swing of her hips back and then forward.

I groaned when her leg brushed my clit, sending tingles of arousal ricocheting through my body. I grabbed her hip with one hand while the other pushed under her shirt. It rode up enough to give Ambrose a hint of a view.

"Fuck, Kiara," I said. "Do you even need your alpha to make you come? You're doing a pretty good job all on your own."

She whined, bracing her hands on her thighs and grinding again. "Are you not going to touch me?"

I didn't answer, cupping one of her breasts and tweaking the nipple. Kiara's scent spiked and her hips moved, faster this time, and not pausing. With every swing of her hips, her tits bounced and I played with them.

"Alpha," she whimpered.

Her head was thrown back, exposing the pale column of her throat. My mark was on display, facing Ambrose and giving him a clear view of how she was mine. I growled, getting rougher with her as I forced her to continue moving against me. The teasing rubs of her thigh against my clit were a bonus, but the real fun was in watching her get wound up.

"Please," she begged, her hand sliding down to touch herself.

I caught her wrist. "You can make yourself come doing this, dove. Be patient."

"I don't thi—"

"You'll come."

My words were a bark, but not a command that forced her to obey. Could I force an orgasm with the dark bond? Possibly. I wasn't sure it would be pleasant for her, though, and that was the whole point.

She moaned, moving faster on me and keeping her hands on her thighs. Her nails dug into her skin, but the tiny sparks of pain only seemed to spur her on more.

Sweat was beading on her forehead, and I was moving under her to meet her thrusts by the time she paused. Her head tilted back, and watching her lips part on a cry was the sexiest thing I'd seen in my life. I felt her body spasming above me as she came, and I rubbed her clit to draw out the orgasm until she was oversensitive and pulling away.

I was expecting her to be tired after I'd forced her to make herself come with little to no help from me, but she was anything but.

She was ravenous, a smirk curling her lips as she crawled off me, leaving my thigh a slick mess. When I made to move, she put her hand on my shoulder and held me down. I growled. "What do you think you're doing?"

"I did as I was told. Don't I get a reward?"

"When did I ever say anything about rewards?" I asked.

She dropped to her hands and knees and crawled down the bed, pushing the remaining blanket off my legs as she went. Her body ended up between my legs. Her ass was in the air, bare and on display for Ambrose.

He was sitting perfectly still on the armchair, not even adjusting the bulge in his pants or freeing his cock to let it breathe. He was always a patient bastard.

Kiara touched her fingers gently to my thighs, hesitance suddenly slicing through the bond with a fiery intensity. I closed my eyes and breathed in.

Dangerous little omega. That's what she was.

She'd be able to manipulate me until the end of time because I couldn't say no to her when she was nervous.

"Fine. Reward it is. What do you want for your reward, dove?" I asked, already knowing the answer.

She grinned. "I want to taste you."

"Is that all?"

"I want you to come all over my face." She paused, more of her nerves invading her happiness. "If I can make you."

Ambrose chuckled, and she looked over at him. "Anything you do will be enough to make my doll come, princess. I can give you instructions, if you'd like. I know exactly how she loves to be tasted."

Kiara's growl didn't surprise him, nor did it surprise me. She liked Ambrose being here... but she didn't like that he'd fucked me. Or maybe she just didn't like how he'd fucked me before she had and was rubbing it in her face.

He'd conned her into losing all her nervousness, competitive drive taking over her movements. "I don't need *your* help," she hissed.

She caught my sleep shorts a second later, pulling them down my legs and burying her face between my thighs.

"Fuck," I cursed, reaching down to grab a fistful of her hair.

Kiara didn't have a clue what she was doing, considering how inexperienced she was even with her own pleasure. It didn't matter. Call it omega instinct driving her, or competitive spirit, or because we were fucking perfect for each other—from that first stroke of her tongue I was rocketing toward an orgasm.

I ground myself against her tongue, taking some of the work off her plate. My grip kept her in place as she moaned and squirmed, giving me a perfect view of the curve of her ass. The only thing that would be better is if it was hovering over my face, dripping slick into my mouth as she made me come.

"So good, Kiara," I groaned, crying out when she sucked my clit into her mouth.

She moaned against me, the vibrations making my back arch. I saw her hand sneak between her legs. One orgasm wasn't enough for her, and I was eager to see how quickly she got herself off while she was making me come too.

A glance at Ambrose confirmed he was still watching, but not doing anything about his own arousal. He had a little self-satisfied smirk on his face, though. I bet he thought he was the behind-the-scenes puppet master of it all. In a way, he had helped orchestrate this part by eliminating all of Kiara's shyness in a way I never could.

But I was Kiara's alpha, not him.

This possessive streak was... unexpected.

"Are you going to come for me again, dove?" I asked, tightening my grip in her hair.

She moaned. "Yes, Alpha."

"Just for me?"

"*Yes.*"

"Guess we don't need Ambrose here anymore then, do we?"

Her whine came from deep in her chest, combining with Ambrose's flaring aura and answering growl.

"Get out," I demanded, settling my gaze on him as I shoved Kiara's mouth back against my pussy.

"Really?" he asked, his jaw ticking.

"Out."

He rose from the armchair and I couldn't help looking at the bulge in his pants. If this had been any normal time with Ambrose, I would have been taking care of that for him. His aura pulsed with arousal and annoyance as he stalked toward the door. The heavy smokiness of his scent draped across me, and part of me hated how I was conditioned by it. Ambrose's scent could only turn me on.

"You're going to pay for this later, doll," he promised.

His dark gaze landed on her exposed ass as he opened and closed the door, leaving us alone.

Kiara hadn't stopped sucking my clit, and something about turning the tables on Ambrose to claim her was sexy.

Fingers tugging her hair, I continued to grind on her face until I came with a choked moan. Seconds later she came too, her body shuddering and the air filling with her sweet scent. I slumped back onto the bed, letting her crawl up to lay beside me, her body wrapped around mine.

Her breathing was heavy for a while until it settled down to an even pace. Her soft cheek rubbed against my shoulder, fingers stroking my stomach. Even at rest, she had to be moving.

"Why did you kick him out?" she asked.

I tilted my head, smiling.

"Because you're mine. I wanted to experience your first time making someone else come, and I didn't want him here for it."

She blushed. Her head lifted from my shoulder and she looked sheepish. "So, you want all my firsts?"

"All the firsts I can take. I won't expect to be the one to knot you for the first time—toys are less comfortable than the real thing, from what I've heard."

If she hadn't had the option of a real cock, then it would have been a knot toy for her first time. Which I guessed meant I had come to terms with her first cock being... one of theirs.

Kiara ignored the connotations of my statement, and so did I. Though, I did curse myself internally.

"Dash stole a first from you," she admitted.

My chest rumbled with a low growl. "What first?"

"Kiss. He caught me off guard when he..." Her cheeks flared vibrant red, her thighs sliding together. "When he was fingering me in the parking garage. I didn't let him do it again, because I wanted to kiss you first."

Fingering in the parking garage. That explained why he was covered in my omega's scent. I wasn't sure if I should be angry at him for having her in public like that, or horny because of how hot thinking of the scene got me.

"I'll punish him for that," I murmured. "Especially if you didn't like it."

She whimpered. "I did like it."

He was still getting punished. I had some ideas in mind, and I shouldn't be so enraptured by them.

"Well, since you enjoyed his kiss, that just means you'll love mine that much more."

A purr rumbled through me and I grabbed her hips, forcing her over to straddle me. Her thighs were around my hips, her slick making a mess. I wrapped my arms around her and pulled her down so we were chest to chest, her forearms braced on either side of my head.

Her pupils were heavily dilated.

This kiss was going to be enough to necessitate another orgasm for my little omega.

I didn't know how to make this a perfect first kiss between us. Going slow might have been a good start, but I couldn't. Not when she was right there, reacting to my purr and my presence.

Our lips crashed together in a kiss I'd been desperately waiting for. She mewled against my lips, letting my tongue stroke hers. I tasted and teased and made it the best kiss of my life—and hopefully the best of hers. I didn't let up on my focus until she was whimpering, need spiking in the bond.

Then I made her come again and let her slump beside me, our lips finally breaking apart. I could stay like this with her forever, bodies sharing heat under the cool air of the AC.

Her stomach grumbled as she pressed against me and I sighed. Cuddling would have to wait. I couldn't leave her hungry, nor could I avoid my responsibilities any longer.

We wouldn't end up with the pack her father wanted her mated to, but I'd need to start digging now if we had any hope of unravelling this chaos before all hell broke loose.

"I'll get you some food," I said, pressing a kiss to her temple and hauling myself out of bed.

She mumbled something about getting up, but followed it with a yawn.

"Sleep some more. You need it after yesterday."

"So do you," she protested.

Her head was already resting on the pillow, cradling it under her arm as her eyelids fluttered shut.

TWENTY-SEVEN

KIARA

I hid in the master suite for as long as possible, even after I'd woken up from another short nap.

How was I supposed to face Ambrose after that?

I'd stabbed him, and now it was obvious I was aroused by him, which was absurd. My whines had been clear desperation for him, and I hadn't been shy with showing off my assets.

My bondmate didn't bring me the food she'd promised to get—I assumed it was to draw me out to the living space. There were things to talk about. She'd gotten arrested because of me, and I had no clue what we were going to do about my father.

I'd thought ahead to getting a dark bond from someone relatively powerful.

Beyond that?

I guess I'd just assumed my mate would deal with it, and I hadn't thought I'd be worried about my mate's safety in the situation. Originally, I wasn't anticipating *liking* the person who bonded me.

Peeking my head around the corner and into the kitchen revealed that only one person was present in the room. He was the one I wasn't sure how to act around, because he didn't like me much: Mercury.

His lean body relaxed against the counter, a mug cupped in both hands as he stared off into space. He didn't notice me, giving me plenty of time to observe.

The man had long auburn hair that hit the middle of his back, but it was secured in two French braids. They were smoothed with some kind of gel, ensuring that he didn't have flyaways or frizz and could look extremely put together.

He'd changed into something different than yesterday, but it was still made of expensive fabric. There were ironed dark slacks and a button up short sleeve. The buttons weren't done up to the top, giving it a more casual look.

I caught a whiff of his scent without even trying. It reminded me of the unused books my father kept in his study—scholarly and comforting. The cinnamon hints took it far away from being an exact replica of that place. Maybe he smelled more like a used bookstore with a cafe attached.

Clearing my throat, I tried to temper my arousal as I stepped into the kitchen. His gaze snapped to me, all the calm fleeing from his posture and expression.

"I think Leighton made me some food," I said.

One hand on Nyla, I stepped over to the fridge and opened it. There was a plate of fruit and vegetables waiting for me, alongside some yogurt and orange juice.

Mercury didn't say a thing.

I grabbed the plate and hesitantly released my knife to load up the yogurt cup and grab the juice. My grip was shaky and I didn't take it into the breakfast nook or the living room. I sat at the kitchen island on a bar stool, facing Mercury.

He pushed off the counter to leave, but I caught the fabric of his shirt and pulled him to a stop. "Did you need something?" he asked.

His tone was almost chilly enough that I shivered.

"You don't have to leave just because I arrived."

"No, but I would like to, if you'd do me the honour of letting me go."

"Why don't you like me?"

He scoffed, yanking himself from my grip. I expected him to retreat, but he didn't. He came closer, leaning over me. I didn't shy away, and our lips ended up mere inches apart.

"It's kind of obvious, isn't it? You stabbed Ambrose. There's no reason for me to like you," he hissed.

"Ambrose forgave me," I whispered.

"I'm not Ambrose. I apparently have far more concern for his well-being than he does. With that knife you carry around, you could stab him again at any moment. Or me." His gaze darted down. "Do you plan on it, little omega?"

My hand had landed on Nyla subconsciously, without thought. I peeled my fingers off her hilt, giving a tiny shake of my head. "No."

"You could have fooled me."

"I'm not going to stab you."

"I don't trust you," he said.

I avoided eye contact, bouncing my leg nervously. With him so close, there were only so many places I could look. His lips, thin and curled into a frown. His collarbone, exposed by the way his shirt hung open. Mercury was invading my space and my senses, and I didn't like the way I was reacting.

Because I wasn't annoyed or angry.

I was aroused.

My heightened scent would hit him any second...

And I saw the moment it did, his nostrils flaring as he growled. I clenched my thighs together, resting my hands on them to avoid the urge to touch him. My reactions to alphas had been intense recently, and I couldn't figure out why.

Was I close to a heat? Was it this pack in particular that made me wild with their scents? Would I react this way to all alphas? I'd never had much exposure to alphas, so I couldn't know for certain.

"Fuck, I hate the way you smell," he muttered.

Old insecurities rose up, forcing me to lean away from him. He didn't let me retreat. His eyes slipped closed and he followed, inhaling deeply. I kept going, back and back until I unbalanced myself, letting out a yelp as my body tipped off the bar stool.

His arm banded around my waist and caught me, pulling me upright before I could fall. It brought me against his chest, his old books and cinnamon scent rubbing all over me. Mercury inhaled again, then let out a stuttering breath and stepped back.

"Be more careful," he said, as if it were my fault I'd almost fallen.

It irritated me, driving me to call him out.

"You're a liar," I said. "You don't hate the way I smell."

He gave me a wry smile. "Oh, I do. Just not for the reasons you'd think."

He left before I could demand an explanation. I squeezed my thighs together, ignored the slight ache in my stomach, and popped pieces of cut fruit into my mouth to fuel myself for whatever the day was going to bring.

"He's just... engrossed in it? And you don't even know what he's doing?" I asked.

I was peering into Leighton's office, which had been thoroughly taken over by Dash. We hadn't delved into the difficult conversations yet. My bondmate was deep in conversation with

Liberty and had taken the call into her bedroom to gain some privacy.

"That's about right," Ambrose said. "He gets like this."

Dash's fingers moved like lightning on that keyboard, typing away. He hadn't acknowledged us even though we were talking about him.

I moved out of the doorway, wandering over to the couch and sitting on the side opposite Ambrose. Mercury was sitting on the armchair with a scowl. Its intensity made my skin grow hot, because I wasn't sure what I was supposed to do.

He didn't like me.

It didn't matter, did it?

Leighton was my alpha, and she wasn't in his pack no matter how wound up we were getting with all of them.

"What do you think he's doing?" I asked, referring to Dash again.

"If I know anything about Dash, he's making sure Leighton never gets arrested again. Using whatever means necessary," Mercury said.

Leighton, finished with her phone call, came to sit beside me and passed me a bottle of water. Her body was angled to keep me mostly out of sight of the other alphas.

This was why Mercury disliking me didn't matter. We were both too possessive, our instincts screaming at us. Trying to include a pack in this bond would only end in flames.

It was irrelevant how I kept thinking about the sounds Ambrose had forced out of Leighton. The begging. The moans. I wanted to know what she'd looked like in those moments, and a part of me wanted to see if he could make me cry out with the same intensity.

"Do you mean, like, illegal means?" I asked.

"Hacking isn't legal," Ambrose confirmed.

I nibbled on my bottom lip.

My family did illegal things all the time. I hadn't been exposed to much of it. I wasn't allowed to leave the confines of the house, except on rare and wonderful occasions.

One time, I'd been to the beach. Another, Mother and I had gone on a short walk through a park. Both times had been after I'd shown success in one of my tasks. I'd played piano flawlessly in front of Father's business associates. I'd aced an etiquette test my tutor had given me.

Even then, I'd known I was being rewarded with scraps.

But it was all I had.

Considering the dark bond situation, I was aware not all of my world views were accurate. My father had wanted me to believe what he believed, and there were some things I'd thought couldn't possibly be false. Like dangerous omegas getting dark bonded.

I wasn't sure how to feel about Dash doing something illegal.

Then again, stabbing was illegal and I'd done that.

A sharp laugh came from Leighton's office, followed by the chair rolling across the floor and footsteps. Dash appeared in the doorway, a tooth-baring grin on his face. "I fucking found it," he said.

Everyone stared at him.

His grin lessened and he crossed his arms over his chest. "Are you not excited?" he asked.

"We don't know what you found," Leighton said dryly. "You're going to have to enlighten us before we can get excited."

"The person who told the police that you'd dark bonded an omega. I found some other shit too, but it's irrelevant."

"Wouldn't it have been my brother who told?" I asked. "He's the only one who knew."

He hadn't known who Leighton was, but he had venues to get information like that. Tobias was resourceful. I didn't know how much was truth and how much was taunts, but he said he was the one who'd set up my arranged mating.

"He wasn't about to go to the police himself. They don't want anyone to know who you are, because as soon as others know Kiara Connolly exists, they're far less likely to be the ones to get to you first."

My nose crinkled. "Should I have told the Omega Safety Division who I am?"

"Of course not," Dash said.

"I'm confused."

"Get to the point, Dash," Leighton said. "Why is this guy important?"

He blinked. "He's not. Who's coming with me to beat the shit out of him?"

Mercury groaned, standing up and walking over to Dash. He grabbed his arm, manhandling him until he was down on the couch beside Leighton. "Sit the fuck down. You need to eat something substantial, and we're not beating anyone up."

Dash growled but stayed put. "Of course we are! He torpedoed Leighton's professional reputation and put Kiara through a traumatic experience. He deserves it."

"Do not move from this spot," Mercury commanded.

Despite Dash being the pack lead, he huffed and listened to the command like a scolded child. Mercury vanished through the French doors into the kitchen.

"Thank you for the thought," I said hesitantly, reaching around Leighton and putting my palm on Dash's knee. "Beating him up isn't necessary."

His grumbles immediately turned to something akin to purrs. Leaning forward, his hand came down over mine and he peered around Leighton with a grin. "Are you sure? You're a violent little thing. I thought you'd want to help."

Ambrose and Leighton let out twin growls.

"I..." Trailing off, I shrugged. "Maybe, but it's probably better if we don't let me near people with a knife."

"Definitely better," Mercury muttered, appearing with a plate of food. He shoved it at Dash. "Eat. If you pass out from lack of sustenance, I have to deal with that and it's not my idea of a good time."

Keeping one hand on mine, he used his other to shovel food into his mouth. I should have pulled my palm from his skin, because I was no longer thanking or comforting him. I let it stay, relishing the warmth that spread through me at the touch.

Leighton didn't seem to mind me touching the other alpha either, so I pushed out all my worries and just… enjoyed.

TWENTY-EIGHT

LEIGHTON

There were two things that I desperately needed to do before the sun set in the sky tonight.

One, I had to tell Kiara about my mother's blackmail and her threat. I'd have to admit that I wasn't quite sure how to fix it. Then, without telling her how, I had to reassure her that she would never be going back to her family.

Two, I had to return the ten missed calls from my concerned younger brother and his pack, who had seen me get arrested on the news last night.

Like the coward I was, I opted into the easier task first.

My brother's phone rang only once before he answered. "Leighton? Why the heck didn't you call me?" He was breathless.

"I'm calling you now," I said dryly. "I was a little busy last night."

"I have it on good authority that you've been out of custody for at least eight hours. You couldn't even send me a text?" I could almost see the dissatisfied pout on his lips.

My brother Marlowe was three years younger than me, and far more fragile. Even if he hadn't revealed as an omega, he would have been fragile. A ball of anxiety with a history of depression, his childhood had been rough. Rougher than mine, because I had a more abrasive personality while he wanted to believe the best of everyone.

"Sorry," I said. "There's a lot going on."

"I guess between having an omega and having the Loranger pack, there would be."

He didn't sound bitter—I hadn't expected him to. Lowe had a pack who loved him dearly despite him not being their scent match. His choice to reject the Loranger pack was the only reason he hadn't been smothered under the weight of Mother's expectations.

Marlowe did sound exceptionally curious, though.

"Ambrose and I have been sleeping together for years." I addressed the elephant in the room first.

Only the soft sound of fabric moving came from down the line. None of his pack were present wherever he was—I doubted they could stay that quiet. Most of those assholes would probably tease me for my secret affair.

"Why didn't you tell me?" he asked quietly.

"Well, it's a little awkward."

"But we're family. It's not like I was actively pursuing them. I already had my pack. Unless..."

He trailed off and I cursed.

"God, no. We met unintentionally a year after you'd packed up with your guys. That's when it started."

Marlowe laughed. "OK, good. I don't think I could be mad if you'd been together earlier than that on a logical level, but I might have been mad anyway."

That was fair. Before he'd formed his current pack, his instincts would have been telling him that Ambrose and the rest of his pack were his. The scent match was a bit of a biological imperative.

"I never saw any of the other members of the pack in any non-official capacity until recently," I said, explaining further.

"Until the omega, right? They didn't say anything about the omega on TV. Only that they were investigating whether the dark bond was taken without her consent."

I hadn't watched the footage yet, but I'd assumed that was the case. If they'd gotten into details about Kiara, I was sure one of the guys would have told me by now. While I didn't have time to watch the news relating to my arrest, they'd had nothing but time.

"Oh, and Mercury spoke up for you outside your condo building. That was unexpected."

Shrugging, I fumbled for an answer when I realized he couldn't see me. "It was."

It should probably be a top priority to find out what Mercury had said, but I couldn't bring myself to. We were in a good place. He'd offered his help. I'd grudgingly accepted. If he'd said anything rude to the reporters last night, I didn't want to know right now.

Even speaking up for me, I didn't doubt that Mercury could find a way to be low key rude.

"So are you going to tell me why you dark bonded an omega? I know you would only do it with permission."

"I did have permission," I confirmed. "That's why I'm not in custody anymore. I can't tell you why I bonded her. It's too complicated and I don't want you involved."

"You sure?" he asked. "You helped me out a few months ago. Mercury and Dash did too. If you guys are in some trouble together..."

If we were face to face right now, he would have been putting on his best pleading pout. He liked to help.

Unfortunately, Lowe was better at helping with baking

cupcakes and hosting a yoga retreat. Dealing with a high-powered crime family was beyond the capacity of him and his pack. Well, maybe not his pack. They'd done some contract security work and some less above-board jobs.

I wasn't going to put them in danger, though. There was no way I was risking it when this whole situation had come about because I wanted to keep them all safe.

"If there's anything you can help with, I'll call you," I lied.

He sighed. Marlowe knew me too well to trust that statement. "Okie dokie. Do you love her, then? Or them?"

My lips parted.

Fuck. Love?

I didn't know if I was aware of what it felt like to love someone who wasn't family. Lowe was the only person on the planet I'd openly claimed I loved. Not even my mother made the cut—why would I love a manipulative bitch?

In the rapid chaos of the days since I'd met Kiara, I'd barely had a chance to settle into my bond with her. Let alone consider what else it could mean to have this warm sensation in my chest.

"I bonded her, didn't I?" It was a non-answer. Marlowe knew that. He would also let me off with it, because it wasn't in his nature to push.

"You did," he confirmed with a laugh. "Is a bond with the Loranger pack next?"

Why did I like my little brother, again?

"I called to tell you that I'm safe, not arrested, and don't need you to call in reinforcements from any of your old high society friends. I've really got to go now, though."

He let out a small giggle this time. After this many years, he was used to my avoidance tactics, and this was one of them. "Well, thanks for checking in. Keep me updated on whether you can make our coffee date this month."

Our monthly cafe meetup was the highlight of my month, but

I might have to skip it for the sake of keeping Kiara safe, this time around. I had a couple weeks before we were set to have it, though. Everything may have blown up by then.

"Will do. Love you, Lowe."

"Love you. Stay safe, OK?"

Throat tight, I choked out a quick affirmation before hanging up. "Of course."

Of course I would try. That didn't mean it would work out in my favour.

For the next task, I sat my omega down with a plate of food at the kitchen island. I had a breakfast nook and dining table, but something about piling us all into the kitchen felt more... homey.

And less formal, which was better for a potentially tense conversation like this.

Kiara watched me as she pushed bites of mashed potatoes past her lips, sipping her smoothie. Ambrose was holding an ice pack against her neck, the bruises hurting her less than they had the previous day. He was caring for her almost more than I was—I saw his guilt every time he focused on her neck.

"My mother is blackmailing me," I said, leaning against the counter and starting with the most imperative facts first.

Mercury was unsurprised after our conversation last night.

Ambrose frowned. "That's not who you told me was blackmailing you."

I shrugged helplessly. "I'm also being blackmailed by Soren Rosania."

This time Mercury's eyes widened, and he whipped out his phone. Dash was here too, but he didn't care about the discussion from what I could see. His fingers were tapping the keys of his laptop. I hoped he hadn't gone down another rabbit hole. I *really* hoped he hadn't hired someone to beat up the guy who turned me in to the cops.

"Soren's blackmailing you?" Kiara asked, fork frozen halfway to her mouth. "But... he helped me. He sent me to you."

"He did that because I have no choice but to do what he says. He knew who you were the whole time, and when I tried to get rid of you he said that I couldn't."

"What does he have on you?" Kiara demanded.

Her body was trembling. Fierce protectiveness and anger projected through the bond. I locked eyes with Ambrose over her shoulder, and he stepped forward and started up a purr for her.

It calmed her fury just enough that we could have a reasonable conversation.

"It's not my secret to tell, but it would ruin multiple lives if it got out. My mother and Soren have the same piece of information—but my mother has a tiny bit more that would make the consequences infinitely more horrible."

"If Soren wanted you to keep me here, what does your mother want?" Kiara asked.

I inhaled deeply, trying to count through a full breath. This was the part that I had to say delicately. It would scare her, but I could calm her. We were mates. That was my job.

"My mother sent me to do a job for your father. He wanted me to find you. Obviously, he knows now that I've had you all along even though I lied to keep that hidden the first time. Considering the dark bond, they want something else."

"What?" Kiara breathed, not letting me take a break in her desperation to know.

"Mother has informed me that we are to go on a date with the pack of your father's choosing. After an acceptable amount of time and public dates, we're both going to join that pack."

"That's not fucking happening," Ambrose growled.

I glared at him. His purr had stuttered and wasn't properly

soothing my omega anymore. "Obviously. My mother nearly fell apart when she visited me when I was arrested. There's something there for me to exploit. I just need to figure out what."

Dash looked up from his laptop, lifting an eyebrow. "Doubt you have time for that."

Kiara shook. This time it wasn't anger but fear, her coconut chocolate scent going sour with it. I stalked around the island to press myself against her side, purring.

"I'm not going to let you go back there, dove. Neither of us is bonding that pack."

She clutched me with one hand. Ambrose let the ice pack slip down from her neck, putting it on the counter. We were both crowded close to her, and while the big alpha's presence hadn't been enough to soothe my omega, it was helping me.

"I just didn't realize... how much control they had," she mumbled. "This felt like a different part of the world. Us, together. I guess the arrest should have been a wakeup call, huh?"

My lips pressed to her hair. It flowed down over her shoulders today, matching the gentle flow of the dress she wore.

"I'm sorry, dove. I had to tell you, because we might have to go on the first date."

It was the final bit that I knew could make her shatter, but she didn't. She took a deep breath, sitting up straighter in the chair and grabbing my hand.

"A public date?" she asked.

"That's what my mother said. Private dates don't do anything for her image, so she'll want everything public."

"We can do it, then. But I'm bringing Nyla."

I ran my fingers against the knife, hidden in its holster around her hips today. She could barely take four steps away from it without getting nervous.

"You can bring Nyla wherever you want."

She smiled at me. "Thank you. What's the plan to get out of bonding the pack, then?"

Shaking my head, I pulled out her stool and gestured for her to get off. "Not your problem. I'll handle it. Ambrose and I are going to brainstorm, and the rest of you can go relax and behave. Dash might be best off if he got some damn sleep."

Dash rolled his eyes, grabbing his laptop but not looking at all like he was about to take a nap.

Kiara turned to me with pursed lips, and I gave her a chaste kiss. I tried to ignore how it reminded me of what my brother had said.

Love.

Then she was gone and I was able to pretend, once again, that there weren't any of those feelings swirling around.

TWENTY-NINE

KIARA

I trusted Leighton.

Maybe I shouldn't—the people who wanted me to mate this pack had information on someone close to her. I assumed her brother, because she didn't seem to care for anyone else. Why would she risk his secrets getting out? I was a mate she hadn't wanted. I was inherently less important to her than her family was.

Yet, I trusted her with my life. She held it in the palm of her hand and had since before the dark bond had marked my neck.

Nibbling on my bottom lip, I wandered out of the kitchen and into the living room. My ass had almost hit the couch cushions when there was a sudden whoosh of air and I landed on a pair of thighs instead. Hands gripped my hips and I looked over my shoulder at Dash.

"What are you doing?" I demanded.

"You're the one who decided to sit on my lap," he said with a smirk.

Mercury rolled his eyes from the armchair across the room. Ambrose was in the kitchen with Leighton.

"You weren't sitting here when I decided to take this seat."

"Wasn't I?"

He didn't let me rise, forcing me to remain perched awkwardly on his knees. When I tried, he held me down by the hips despite my little growl of irritation.

"Dash, let her up," Mercury demanded.

One of Dash's hands slid up from my hip. He rubbed across my stomach and then cupped my tit in his palm. I couldn't help but gasp, and Mercury hissed.

I tried again to remove myself from the seat I hadn't wanted, but Dash pulled me back further. My back landed on his chest, my thighs splaying wide on either side of his as my ass slid back. There was a bulge in his jeans, and I was now rubbing against it through no fault of my own.

"For fuck's sake, Dash." Mercury stood and stalked over to us.

He grabbed one of my hands, trying to extract me from Dash's hold. The pack lead wasn't letting me go easily, though. I ended up suspended between the two alphas, Mercury leaning closer so he could reach my shoulder instead.

Closing my eyes, I fought down the rush of arousal. They would smell it, damn it. They would know that it turned me on to be trapped between them. It shouldn't. This was wrong when Leighton was my bonded alpha and I'd stabbed their pack mate.

Tell that to my pussy.

A guttural whimper ripped from my throat as slick pooled between my legs. An ache built in my core, cramps making me desperate to be filled.

When I opened my eyes, Mercury had a hand over his nose and mouth like my scent was offending him, but he was still there. So close. His cinnamon and old book scent was invading my space and spiking with arousal just like mine was.

Dash's cock was rubbing against the curve of my ass, and he was far bolder than Mercury. He had his nose buried in my neck, huffing deep breaths. His hands were exploring places they shouldn't, but I didn't want to stop him. Couldn't have stopped him if I'd tried, not with the wash of pheromones.

"Dash," Leighton's voice rang out, cutting through the haze of lust.

I snapped my head around to look at her, letting out a little whimper when I caught sight of the way her pupils dilated. Her green irises were almost engulfed by the black. My alpha's scent was spiking too, vanilla and cream making me squirm in Dash's lap.

That didn't help the predicament we were in. Dash only held me tighter to him, rutting up against my ass, and Mercury's aura split the air, bringing a rush of his scent with it. I wanted to clench my thighs together to stop the gush of slick and relieve some of the pressure, but there was no way for me to move my legs like that. Not while I was trapped against Dash's chest.

Leighton stormed over to us, shoving Mercury out of the way. He almost seemed relieved to be removed, his long legs taking him to stand on the opposite side of the room.

Then Leighton leaned over us, one hand on the back of the couch and one fisting Dash's hair.

I swallowed all the sounds I wanted to make. It took so much concentration, I almost didn't notice how Leighton looked at Dash.

She looked like she wanted to spank him. Like she would have fun doing it.

"You're not supposed to touch my omega," she growled.

I brought a hand down between my legs. The ache was too much. The scents were overwhelming, and I liked being fought over. It brought out something... primal. If my alpha would fight over me, that meant I would be protected. With all these alphas fighting over me...

My fingers pressed to my clit through a single layer of fabric. The soft cotton of my panties was soaked, and my skirt was easy to push aside.

Leighton glanced down but didn't stop me. She pushed Dash's head back, exposing his neck. I leaned to the side, giving her more room to berate him, or whatever she was planning on doing.

"She came all over my fingers in the parking garage, though," Dash purred. He was unconcerned with being put in a delicate position. Was it because he trusted Leighton, or was he simply insane?

My alpha glanced to me and I sank my teeth into my bottom lip, rubbing myself faster.

"You're both brats," Leighton muttered. "I can't fucking believe you, Dash. You took advantage of me being arrested to steal my omega's first kiss."

Guilt washed over me, and I paused in pleasuring myself to probe my bond with Leighton. She was annoyed, but she didn't feel truly upset. There was no betrayal I could grasp in her emotions. Maybe it was buried too deep, and I was too unused to the bond.

But I did get arousal from both her scent and our bond.

It felt like she was turned on by Dash going behind her back and touching me.

"When else was I going to be able to touch her?" he asked with a shrug. "You're too possessive. I had to take what I wanted when I had the opportunity."

Leighton moved and Dash's breath hitched behind me. I shifted for a better view. There was one hand in his hair and another wrapped around his throat. The nails that Leighton had been tapping everywhere were now digging into his skin as she squeezed.

His eyes rolled back in his head. I would have been worried about her hurting him if I hadn't felt the jump of his cock against me.

Tentatively, I squirmed and rubbed against it. I slid my hand into my underwear, pressing a finger directly to my clit this time. No more barriers as I stroked myself.

A strangled moan left Dash, and Leighton looked down at me. She smirked. All her annoyance was focused on Dash, even though I'd played a part in the parking garage incident too. It didn't feel fair, but I didn't care.

"If I thought Dash had any sense of shame whatsoever, punishing him would be so much easier," she said. "It's harder to deal with him, because he's done plenty of embarrassing shit in front of the media and has never given a fuck about it."

"Like what?" I asked.

We were both ignoring how I was getting off on this.

On their mixed scents.

On the possessiveness.

I shouldn't have wanted to bury my face in Dash's neck and inhale his spring rain and peach scent, but I did. Almost as much as I wanted to bury my face between Leighton's legs and lap her up. I'd done it one time, and I was already addicted.

"He was caught with his pants down, once. In the hotel room of three beta women who were visiting New Oxford. I bet you can guess what they were about to do."

My teeth clenched but the barrier couldn't hold back my growl.

Three?

But he was *mine*.

And I was in fucking trouble with those thoughts, but Leighton had to have done it on purpose. She was fishing for my reaction, and I'd given her exactly the one she expected.

"There are a lot of incidents like that with Dash. He's a bit of a man whore."

My free hand reached down to grab his thigh, digging my nails in like I could claim him with a tight enough grip.

"In fact, he spends most of his time at an expensive club downtown, where he flirts and dances and finds people to hook up with in dark corners. I helped him keep a paparazzi picture out of the press, once."

That was too much.

The way I surged forward forced Leighton to let go of Dash. He groaned from the sudden lack of pressure on his cock, but I only got up for a second. Long enough to spin around to face him and settle my ass on his thighs. His arms came around me and he stared hungrily down the top of my dress as I leaned in.

All my attention was focused in one place.

My lips came down on his neck first, sucking at the tan skin as his head tipped to the side. Shortly after my lips, my teeth pierced his skin and he cursed. Leighton cursed too, her hand coming down on my shoulder as my haze cleared and the ache in the pit of my stomach intensified to an almost unbearable level.

Dash's pleasure washed through our fresh bond, melding with my pain and amplifying it. Everything was turned up by a thousand, and I needed more than his body against mine.

Teeth marks marred Dash's neck when I pulled away, and his pants were damp from his sudden orgasm. He stared at me with his eyes wide in wonder, his jaw slack.

"Alpha, I need to come," I murmured.

I almost curled over from the pain as I glanced between Dash and Leighton. Both of them were frozen. I didn't know which one I was talking to. They didn't either.

It was a different alpha who grabbed me from Dash's lap, letting me curl around him. Ambrose carried me with ease, his clothed cock pushing against my sopping wet core. He'd been in the room the whole time—Mercury had too. Mercury was glaring at me like I'd committed a sin, and maybe I had.

In the back of my mind, I knew what I'd done.

I'd claimed Dash.

Jealousy had overwhelmed me and I hadn't had any other option in my hind brain. My bite had created a temporary bond between us, faint beside the potent bond I had with Leighton, but present nonetheless.

"Ambrose," I said when he put me down on one of the armchairs. "Please."

A purr rumbled his chest. "I knew you wanted me, little omega. Spread your legs."

They splayed apart without thought. My dress rode up to expose my thick thighs, then further to show off the light lavender lace of my panties. His hands slid up my legs and grabbed the fabric, pulling it down my body to expose me.

There was a collective inhale from all the alphas in the room.

"Ambrose..." Leighton said, a slight warning growl in her tone.

He chuckled. "Doll, you kicked me out of your bedroom this morning. Now I want a taste."

"She's mine."

"And Dash is hers. Which makes her a little bit mine, doesn't it?" He peered over his shoulder.

My bondmate hadn't moved, her attention focused on us. Having Ambrose touch me didn't feel wrong—not right now. Not anymore. I needed someone to do it soon, because every breath I took was bringing me further into pain.

Coming was the only relief from this.

I knew it in every fiber of my being. An orgasm would bring me the sweet relief I needed.

"Touch me."

My plea reached all of them. It was for all of them—any of them.

"If you want to stop me, Leighton, then stop me," Ambrose said.

He knelt on the ground in front of me and leaned in, kissing each of my thighs. My legs wrapped around him and yanked him close. He growled but let me. Sensing my desperation, he didn't tease me or even wait for a response from Leighton.

His tongue drove into my pussy, and I threw my head back and screamed in sweet relief.

The rough, scarred skin of his hands held my hips, keeping me in place as I tried to grind down against his mouth. My vision went spotty as the ache finally subsided, relieved by the pleasure rushing through my veins.

I sobbed as he fucked me with his tongue, only able to focus on that until Leighton's hands came down on my shoulders.

She stood behind the armchair, glaring down at Ambrose. He only smirked, not pausing in his efforts to make me come. Efforts that were working—I was teetering precariously on the knife's edge.

"You're being bad, dove," she murmured. "Claiming another alpha? Letting one make you come? You came here wanting my dark bond, but apparently anyone would have been fine."

I whined, her words yanking my orgasm back from me. Panic flushed my cheeks. "No. No, I wanted the bond from you. You're everything I want. I love you."

Leighton froze.

I went bright pink.

That was a confession that had come far too soon. We'd known each other for days—not weeks, but days. She should have known better than to ask an omega something like that, in a moment like this. With Ambrose between my legs, I didn't have a filter between my brain and my mouth.

He didn't look surprised, sucking on my clit so intensely I sobbed.

"I don't think you know what you're saying," Leighton murmured.

"I mean—I..."

The orgasm hit me at that moment, cutting off rational thought. Slick squirted over Ambrose's stubbled cheeks and he drank it up. All the pain finally receded, leaving me panting through the aftershocks with an alpha between my legs and another behind me.

Dash was still so stunned he hadn't moved from the couch across the room. Mercury was gone, but I didn't think he'd been gone long. He'd watched the show. Cinnamon and old books was too potent for him to have vanished right when all this started.

Leighton tried to move away from me, but I caught her hand. Turning in the armchair, I peered up at her.

"I knew what I was saying, and I meant it."

Her expression morphed to match Dash's, stunned and unsure. It was impossible to tell what was going through her head, not even through the bond. She'd closed it off, for once. She was a quicker study than I was. I couldn't keep my feelings to myself if I wanted to—and right now, I didn't. I wanted her to feel just how truthful I was being.

"Let's not force her to respond, princess," Ambrose said softly.

He reached up and pulled my dress down to cover my bare pussy.

Leighton's lack of response made me nervous, even though I knew I was the crazy one. I was obsessive, possessive, and had basically forced myself on her at the end of the day. No one with a heart like Leighton's would have been able to say no to an omega in distress.

I wanted her to love me back, though, despite all that.

Ambrose helped me stand and I let him. My dress fell back

down to cover everything, hiding the evidence of what had just happened. All that remained was the slight sheen to my thighs and my discarded panties.

"How about we go for a walk?" he asked. "Upstairs. There's a rooftop pool."

I didn't want to, but being stuck in this apartment together wasn't going to do anything good for any of us. Space. They needed space. I didn't, but I was the omega. The anomaly. All I wanted was a chest to curl up on—Dash's or Leighton's, ideally, seeing as I was currently bonded to both of them.

Ambrose taking me upstairs would suffice. He'd forgiven me for stabbing him, and I felt nothing but safe and secure in his large presence.

"She claimed me," Dash said numbly.

It was the first time he'd spoken. Our bond flared to life, my aura working to calm him now that my own pain was soothed. He was panicked, but it didn't last long with my presence in and around him.

"She did," Ambrose agreed. "We'll be back in an hour. Then, you have to talk. Actually talk, with everyone sitting in different chairs and with no touching involved."

"Be careful," Leighton said, clearing her throat. "You shouldn't be seen with her. Don't leave the building."

Ambrose nodded.

He gently led me from the living room, letting me stop in the bedroom only long enough to grab a pair of panties. Then we left the condo, my stomach roiling—this time, not with discomfort but with nervousness.

THIRTY

DASH

I'd never... *felt* anyone like this before.

Sure, there was the pack. We had a bond. It was different, though. Kiara's presence in my head—in my body—was weak, but potent. She calmed me. Soothed parts of my psyche I hadn't realized had need of soothing.

I tried to bask in the comfort of it, but couldn't.

Now that I'd had this, I wasn't going to be able to let it go. If I had to, if I was forced to let this bond fade and never get another one, I would go insane.

Being rejected by my scent match had almost done me in. I'd never thought I would be claimed by another omega, but if I had a taste and then had it ripped away...

I brought my legs up to my chest and rocked, pushing down the uncomfortable feelings.

A joke. I needed a joke.

Or a focus.

Something that wasn't how Kiara had felt in my lap. How she felt in my mind. How she would feel being in my *life*.

Obsession was a dangerous game, I fucking knew it. I'd nearly fallen apart from obsession once. This time, it was Kiara's obsession and mine combined that was fucking combustible. We would explode from the pressure of rash decisions and need.

She'd gotten jealous and she'd bitten me.

I might have done the same damn thing, if she'd been mated to anyone other than Leighton. If she'd been fooling around with anyone other than my pack.

"I think she's going into heat soon," Leighton murmured.

Kiara got further away with every second, Ambrose and her vanishing to the rooftop pool. I wanted to run after her and have her purr for me. Fuck, I wanted Leighton to purr for me. There was no way she would. She was an alpha, and I was an alpha, and alphas didn't purr for each other.

"Why do you think that?" I asked, not looking up at her.

"She was in pain. That's why she was desperate to come. The heat hormones might have been why she was so jealous, too. I shouldn't have pushed her."

Leighton didn't sound regretful, though.

Was she eager to see me crash and burn? That's the path I was heading on, at this rate.

"I've never seen an omega close to heat before. Is there pain?" I asked.

She snorted. "You think I have experience? There's heat cramps, from what I've heard. I'm not sure if they're typically soothed by an orgasm, but that's not the kind of thing my brother would divulge to me."

I stiffened, gaze snapping to hers.

If I was going to be here, I had to acknowledge that Leighton may occasionally talk about... him. My scent match. The man who we should have been perfect for. The omega who decided we were anything but perfect.

I'd never been perfect to anyone in my life, but I should have been perfect to him.

Last time he'd been brought up, I'd been fine. That was before I was faced with the terrifying risk of being claimed... but then rejected.

"Fuck," I muttered.

I pushed up to my feet, intent on pacing. Leighton stood in front of me, stopping me. Concern swirled in the depths of her eyes. I'd avoided looking into her eyes for years, any time we saw each other. They were so much like his. Now I looked, though, and saw what I'd been missing.

They *were* different, after all.

Her eyes had flecks of gold, the green a hint more muted than his bright orbs.

"How do you feel about her claiming you, Dash?"

I scoffed. "How do you feel about her loving you, Leighton?"

I'd seen the look on her face. The shock and a hint of hesitance. I was fucking jealous and a bit angry, because it looked like she was tempted to deny she loved Kiara back. If that omega said that to me, I'd be tripping over myself to prove my affection in return.

Which meant I might love her.

Were love and obsession the same?

"You're deflecting," Leighton said, her voice a low growl.

"And you're not?"

"Fuck you."

"You don't want to, and I doubt she does either when the haze of this fucking upcoming heat blows over."

My mouth clamped shut. I wished I could take those words back, because they were a vulnerability I didn't need.

Leighton didn't give me a look of pity, though. The look she gave me was nothing like the ones Mercury and Ambrose had been giving me for years. She rolled her eyes and placed a hand on my chest, shoving me back down to the couch.

"If you think a bond mark can be brushed off so easily, I don't think I can help you," she said.

"It's going to fade," I rebutted.

I fought down the arousal I felt at having her hovering above me. At first glance, she was dainty. Her dominance was less 'in your face.' That made her all the more dangerous, and knowing she could ruin me turned me on. Her aura worked differently but would trump mine any day of the week.

"Sure," Leighton agreed. "But she gave it to you in the first place. Have you considered the meaning of that? Because I don't think it was inconsequential."

I'd never in my life been anything but inconsequential.

My parents had me purely so there would be a Loranger heir —not because they wanted a child. Dad and Pop's late wife hadn't been able to bear children, but when she'd died of cancer and their third pack member had passed away from grief right behind her, they'd shacked up with a twenty-year-old omega supermodel.

Mom.

She'd get anything she wanted, under one condition.

A child.

Just one, so the Loranger name wouldn't die when the remnants of the pack did.

So, I'd been born, the process as efficient and unemotional as creating a test tube baby. I was raised by nannies while Mom partied away her twenties and Dad and Pop worked themselves into early graves.

There was never a thought in any of their heads about me. I was their means to an end.

"Hormones are a powerful thing," I muttered.

I couldn't sit still, not with those thoughts swirling around in my head. My attempt to stand was blocked by Leighton. We ended up chest-to-chest, and my breath caught.

This whole situation was as dangerous as I'd thought. I'd pushed my way in, following my stupid whims and running toward the waving red flags, but they didn't want me. They couldn't.

What use was I?

All I did was push boundaries and fall apart at the tiniest hint of rejection.

Like right now.

Pushing past the female alpha, I headed for the kitchen. Mercury would be somewhere. He could be a barrier so I didn't have to have this conversation that Leighton was adamant about forcing on me.

Her hand caught my arm, and I ripped it out of her grasp with a hiss. Where she touched me heat seeped into my veins, vanilla cream lingering on my skin.

"You're not what I always thought you were," she said.

I forced myself to turn around, waiting to see the disappointment in her face.

Instead she wore a little smile, bordering on a smirk. She stared into my eyes, seeing everything I was good at hiding from the tabloids and the women I fucked.

"What am I, then?" I asked. Hearing the answer terrified me.

"I thought you were a whiny fuck boy who was angry my brother had the balls to turn you down."

My teeth sunk into my lip, holding back my wince.

"But you're broken."

"Wow, can't believe you figured that one out," I snapped sarcastically.

"You think you're unlovable and no one could ever want you."

She might as well have dug her nails into my heart, the muscle throbbing in my chest. Ambrose and Mercury knew what went on in my head. They'd known since the second we all decided to pack up, after Ambrose's parents had died in the fire and Mercury's family's pack had grown too dysfunctional for him to handle.

Neither of them ever pushed me like this or confronted me with the knowledge. I was pretty sure they worried that I would break apart and devolve even further. Not that it got much lower than fucking strangers in club bathrooms and drinking away my desperation for love.

"Fuck off, Leighton." My tone was sharp enough I was sure I'd made my point. She would turn and leave, and I'd be alone again. Loneliness of my own creation, this time.

She laughed.

A soft giggle turned into full-bellied laughter as I stared at her, stunned.

Tears streamed down her cheeks, and she pressed a hand to her stomach. I couldn't figure out why she was laughing.

What was funny?

I watched until the laughs subsided and she moved toward me. Every one of my backward steps were matched by her until I ran out of room to flee. My back hit a wall, a picture frame rattling from the force of my attempted escape.

Her front pressed to mine, from the thigh she shoved between my legs to the tips of her breasts rubbing against my chest. Our lips were inches apart, breath mixing. The height difference between us was so insignificant it was unnoticeable.

"Dash, get your head out of your ass."

They weren't the words I was expecting her to say this close up. My arousal leaked away, a slow removal of air from a balloon.

"What are you talking about? And what was so funny?"

"You're lonely because you think you're unlovable, and you think you're unlovable because you're lonely."

My brain pieced the puzzle together, trying to keep up with her.

"It's a self-fulfilling prophecy," she continued. "But that cycle is over. My omega claimed you, and you're not going to push her away like this. I won't allow it."

"What else am I supposed to do?" I blurted.

"Not sure how I'm supposed to know that," she said. "I can barely handle my own relationships. You've got to figure it out yourself."

I blinked a few times, each breath coming slower than the last. I'd been hyperventilating and hadn't realized. Her warmth and scent soothed me as I processed. Everything was overwhelming. Kiara being part of me. The dredged-up feelings of not being good enough. Leighton. Just Leighton, in general, was overwhelming considering my history with her brother.

She was patient.

She stayed against me, letting me figure myself out.

Mercury never let me figure myself out. I hadn't recognized how much it bothered me until right now. Being treated like this was a breath of fresh air. I appreciated everything my packmate had done for me. He was the entire reason I was still here instead of at the bottom of a pit of despair.

However, I needed this.

"I'm not used to working through my own problems," I admitted after a long pause.

She snorted. "Obviously."

"I'm also not used to having a woman between my legs in this manner. Usually I would be the one pressing them against a wall." I injected some humour.

Leighton responded by pressing her thigh up against me. My cock hardened and I choked back a groan. Oddly enough, this kind of input gave me more ability to focus in the background. My mind was whirring with possibility. How I could help get the dark bonded pair out of this predicament. How Kiara could be convinced to claim me again before this bond became a distant memory.

I had a few blissful seconds of brain work before Leighton's fingers dug into my cheeks, pulling me from it.

"You're never going to press me against a wall," Leighton promised. "And before you even get me in this position again, I owe you one hell of a punishment. You stole two firsts from me. Her first kiss, and her first bonding. Kiara has never bitten me."

My eyes widened, but she didn't sound angry about it. Her gaze focused on my fresh bite mark, staring in wistful arousal. I'd been antagonizing Leighton since the second I got here, and I bet that bite was going to be the thing that got me the worst punishment of all. Something I hadn't even been responsible for.

Something I would have begged for, if I thought I had even a tiny chance of getting it from Kiara.

Leighton pulled back, her fingers brushing against the mark from her omega.

"You look like you're less on the verge of a breakdown now, so I'm going to go do some more research on what the fuck my mother is hiding."

"And figure out how you feel about Kiara loving you?" I couldn't help the final tease.

She sighed. "I already know how I feel about that."

She left me in the kitchen to mull over my emotions, and I sank into my thoughts. It was refreshing to be given freedom to think for myself—even if I may not deserve it.

THIRTY-ONE

AMBROSE

It had just become impossible to detangle Leighton and Kiara's lives from our own.

Mercury would be freaking out, researching ways to make sure Dash didn't fall apart when the bond between him and Kiara faded.

It was no use. They were connected. *We* were connected.

And I was fucking ecstatic.

"How do you know there's a pool here?" Kiara asked when we got into the elevator.

She'd just bathed me in her slick, her scent all over me, and she was still mildly irritated that I knew more about her mate than she did. I hid my smile.

"I've seen the plans."

"So you've never... been there? With Leighton?"

I shook my head. "Before you, I'd never been invited to her condo before. I owe you a thank you, little omega. You gave me the in I'd been waiting for."

I ignored her little growl, stepping out of the elevator and swiping a keycard to let us onto the rooftop deck. At first we'd been sneaking past security to get in and out of the building, but before we'd left when Leighton got arrested, I'd found and snagged her spare set of keys. It was better to ask forgiveness than permission, and she had to have realized by now.

We weren't the only ones up here, with it being a sunny Saturday in August. Half the building was basking on the deck, but there were plenty of lounge chairs for everyone. With the fees Leighton paid to live here, I would hope it wouldn't be a problem.

I led Kiara over to a private corner, far from the pool and the couple of splashing kids playing in it. She settled on the lounge and I pulled over a simple chair, preferring to keep myself upright to watch the people around us.

Even this close to home, it was doubtful she was fully safe.

Having an omega in danger stoked the fire of my alpha nature like nothing ever had before. I would protect her. It was my duty.

"Why had you never been invited to her condo before? I thought she liked you."

I should have known she wouldn't let my comment go. I may still have the taste of her on my tongue, but that didn't mean she didn't view me as a romantic threat. Ravishing Leighton while she'd been alone in the living room may not have been the best plan—not that I would undo it. The female alpha had been mine first, and I wouldn't let an omega stampede over me in her efforts to make a claim.

"Leighton prefers to keep her distance from people."

She'd broken every rule she'd ever set with me when she bonded and fucked Kiara. To say I wasn't jealous would be a lie.

Kiara winced, pulling her knees up to her chest. I reached over and adjusted the drape of her skirt, not wanting the rest of the people up here to see anything beneath.

"She must hate me, then."

I barked a laugh. The sound was so sharp and sudden it drew

the attention of a few other pool goers. They were quick to look away when they caught sight of my scarred features, but the sting of rejection was so frequent I was numb to it.

"It's the opposite," I said.

"I told her I love her. Everyone heard it. That's not what she wants to hear... from the omega she was forced to dark bond."

Kiara's hesitance was endearing in a way that her sass wasn't. However, her nerves were misplaced.

"She was stunned, but not upset."

"And how do you know?"

I sighed. Peaceful enjoyment of anything was impossible with her constant fidgeting and talking, not that I should have expected to enjoy the blue sky and beating rays after what just occurred.

"I know that woman's reactions like I know the back of my own hand. You ask too many questions."

"I'm not used to them being answered."

Closing my eyes, I fought the urge to snarl.

She didn't talk much about how she'd grown up. Not to me. I didn't think she talked about it to anyone, really. Her childhood was like the night of the fire was for me—something she would rather forget.

I wanted her to be able to forget about it.

I wanted her so distanced from it, there wasn't a goddamn memory left. I would never get to that point with my memories, not when the evidence marked me for life. Not when I saw it in the mirror daily. But her? She might be able to replace bad memories with good, old with new.

"Your father didn't answer your questions?" I asked.

Maybe it wasn't the best idea to urge her on. If she broke down, my ability to comfort was... poor, to say the least.

She laughed bitterly. "He'd lock me in my room if I asked too many."

With her personality, I got the sense she'd been locked away often.

"Sometimes, being locked up was better."

This time I couldn't hold back the snarl. Her sapphire eyes widened, her cheeks flushed from the heat of the sun. I should have brought sunscreen. She was pale enough to burn in the hour we had to spend out here.

"Will you tell me why that was better?" I asked.

I wanted to turn my chair to face her head on, but I couldn't. Damn it, I was supposed to be protecting her, keeping an eye on everyone up here to make sure no one was snapping pictures or doing anything suspicious.

My focus kept wandering to her, the pain in her tone a beacon drawing me. We were cut from the same cloth. Trauma and pain. Not like the rest of my pack or Leighton.

I couldn't belittle what any of them had gone through, but it wasn't the same. There was something about being physically harmed by another person that did something to you. It twisted you up in a way nothing else could.

She hadn't admitted it yet, but the scar on her eyebrow had come from somewhere. Other small scars littered her flesh too. Nothing too noticeable if I hadn't been cataloging every inch of her when I'd seen her naked.

Whoever hurt her didn't want it obvious, and it wasn't.

I only knew because I recognized the pain in her expression.

"My brother," she whispered after a long pause. I strained to hear her voice over the screech of the children and the gentle hum of music from someone's speaker. "Tobias wasn't... nice to me."

"Did he hurt you, princess?"

I shouldn't have asked. It was prying, but she answered.

"Not often. Father wouldn't allow it because I was supposed to be perfect for whoever he gave me to." Her hand lifted, fingers brushing across her scar. "Sometimes, Tobias got carried away. It was usually only bruises. He told me not to tell Father, and I didn't. When I got this, it was the worst time."

I wanted to ask what he'd done but grit my teeth against the impulse.

This wasn't me. I wasn't the person to ask about trauma, not when I would never talk about my own. With Kiara I wanted to know every piece of her, good or bad, broken or healed. And I wanted to rain fire on the people who'd hurt her. I wanted it more than I wanted to kill the man who'd killed my parents and maimed me.

"It was actually an accident," she said. Those words were the quietest of all. "He shoved me and I fell against the corner of a table. I thought he would be worried when he saw all the blood, but..."

Her words stayed unsaid.

He wasn't.

The bastard could've taken out her eye or given her permanent brain damage, and he'd probably laughed. I clenched my jaw so tight my vision went spotty, turning my attention to the pool again. Coming out here may not have been the best idea, but I hadn't expected us to talk.

Her warm hand landing on my arm brought me out of the depths of my rage. "Ambrose, can you..." She trailed off.

I looked over my shoulder. She was glassy-eyed, her hair a mess in the breeze.

"Can I what, princess?"

"I fucked everything up, I think, but can we pretend I didn't? Can I curl up on your lap while we're up here?"

Pushing to my feet, I abandoned the flimsy plastic chair and picked her up from the lounge. She yelped, her scent spiking and drawing the attention of some people nearby. Once again, one look from me set their attentions elsewhere. I lowered us both down to the lounge, leaning back and letting her rest against my chest.

When her purr vibrated against me and her mussed hair tickled my nose, it was all I could do to shove down my arousal. I focused on anything and everything except her, except the invasive scent of chocolate and coconut. The needy, content sounds she made as she curled and half-dozed on me.

This was common behaviour for an omega with her alpha.

That's what I felt like.

Her alpha.

I didn't want this fantasy to end. Going back to the real world left a bitter taste in my mouth when everything was so perfect and domestic sitting beside this pool.

In the real world we had to keep her safe from people who didn't deserve her—Tobias, her father, Soren.

In the real world Dash might shatter into pieces and self-destruct, taking everyone in his vicinity with him. He'd done it before, when we'd been rejected by our scent match.

In the real world Leighton might never let this fly, no matter how much I loved her, no matter how much budding affection I felt for her omega.

In the real world, Mercury was an anxious, angry mess trying to keep all of us together in the way he thought was best. A way I disagreed with, despite how much I fucking loved him.

Kiara stayed on me until our skin was slick with sweat, the contact and the sun almost too much heat to handle. Our hour had been up for ages and I was sure one of the others would come looking for us soon when she finally sat up. "I have to use the bathroom."

"Let's go inside then, little omega."

I lifted her off me and placed her on her feet. When we walked across the pool deck to the glass entrance doors once again, I shielded her from view.

Those pink cheeks were mine to observe. Not anyone else's. Mine and my pack's.

And Leighton, but she was synonymous with 'pack' in my head now. She would never agree to join, but I could continue to hope, dream, and maybe even beg.

THIRTY-TWO

LEIGHTON

When my omega came back from upstairs, she was an absolute mess of anxiety. She'd been relatively calm through the bond for the past couple of hours. Now that she was no longer poolside and was facing what she'd done, she was flailing.

Kiara spent so long in the bathroom I wondered if she was ever going to come out.

She wouldn't look at me, staring at the floor as she wandered into the living room. I followed her, catching her before she could smash the buttons on the TV remote.

"Dove. We have to talk about it."

Her back went stiff and she glanced around the room. Dash wasn't in here, but he would be soon. After our chat, I bet he'd want to confirm how Kiara felt about things.

"I meant what I said," she murmured. "If you don't feel the same, I'd rather not know."

She'd already confirmed it before Ambrose had gently removed her from the apartment. To hear her say it again so confidently set my heart slamming against my chest.

Kiara was braver than I was. Maybe more foolish, as a result of her upbringing. It was irrational and unreasonable to fall in love with the alpha who dark bonded you to save your life. We knew so little about each other, it was laughable.

Yet, she was insistent.

With her proclamation, I couldn't live in denial anymore, but I also couldn't say the words. Not out loud.

"I don't *not* feel the same," I said quietly. I dropped onto the couch beside her, my hand resting on her shoulder. "And I believe you. That you meant it."

She looked at me with her scarred eyebrow raised. The remote was sitting on her lap and she was fiddling with the fabric of her clothing. "Saying that you don't not feel the same is incredibly confusing."

Letting out a short laugh, I shrugged. "Emotions aren't my strong suit, OK? I need more time to figure myself out, but I'm glad you told me. I was your only available option—I didn't want to pressure you into feeling more than you did just because we were bonded."

Kiara shook her head vigorously. "I would have picked you even if I had the choice of every alpha in the world."

Once again, her conviction floored me.

"Oh?" I asked.

Fishing. I was fishing for compliments and more, but I couldn't help it. Not many people wanted the driven lone female alpha. I was a last choice for most.

"I thought about it a lot while you were arrested. If I'd told them what really happened, it's possible they may have been able to help me and I wouldn't need you anymore," Kiara said. "Even if that hadn't been such a risk, I decided I wouldn't have wanted to try. I wanted to stay with you no matter what."

I'd considered the same. There had to be some people at the

Institute who would be able to help her. Was I willing to give her up, though?

Never.

"And where do I fit into that?"

Dash interrupted my moment of preening.

He leaned casually over the back of an armchair. I couldn't see his feet, but he was bouncing and there was a slight tapping sound. The man couldn't stop moving, except for—oddly enough—when I'd had him pressed between me and the wall. Once he'd stopped panicking, his body had been calm.

Despite his casual air, the question was anything but.

Kiara began to fidget—they were two sides of the same coin. Chaotic energy for both of them. However, where Dash was skilled at pushing people away, Kiara was eager to yank them closer.

"I claimed you," Kiara said softly.

Dash's hand went up to rub at his neck. His expression was unreadable, movie star handsome features blank. He hadn't bothered to put on the charismatic guise he wore in public, but he wasn't giving us his true feelings either.

I was just glad he'd thought through his true feelings. Based on what I knew about Mercury's micromanaging, he hadn't had a chance to do that in years.

"That doesn't mean much, in the grand scheme of things," he said.

Kiara stood abruptly from the couch, scowling. She managed to stomp surprisingly loud on the rug on her way across the living room. Crawling onto the armchair on her knees, she brought herself temptingly close to Dash.

Wide-eyed, he froze. My bondmate's hand slid across his shoulder blades and grabbed the back of his neck, hauling him close.

It was obvious what she was going to do before she did it. I could have stopped her with a simple command, but maybe Dash needed this.

Her teeth sank into the other side of his neck, a second claim.

Dash groaned loud enough it drew the attention of Mercury and Ambrose, both men poking their heads through the French doors from the kitchen.

Kiara whimpered too, the scent of her slick perfuming the air. She was creating a puddle on the armchair beneath her, but it wasn't my place to pleasure her at the moment.

"If it doesn't mean much, I'll keep biting you until it does," she said, her tone sharp with annoyance.

"Fucking hell," he muttered.

One hand went down to his crotch—I was assuming it was to readjust himself, though I couldn't see. He used his other to haul Kiara close. Their lips smashed together and he groaned into her mouth.

All our scents were spiking now, Ambrose and Mercury's included. I wanted to let this continue, see what would happen if Dash was allowed to do as he pleased.

Mercury had different plans. He grabbed Dash's shoulder. Kiara's irritation flared through the bond when her and Dash's kiss broke, and I assumed she hadn't hidden it from her expression. Mercury took a small step back before speaking.

"The omega is close to heat. Considering she has to go out on a public date in a few days, we shouldn't do anything else to push her closer to it."

He had a point. Sexual activity wasn't guaranteed to bring on a heat faster—so far, it seemed to be helping her with the heat cramps. However, Kiara hadn't spent much time around alphas in her life. Her body might react to having multiple alphas reaching peaks near her at the same time. It was impossible to know.

Dash hesitated, his gaze landing on Kiara's cleavage where her tits were pressed against the back of the armchair. Then he cleared his throat. "As usual, he's right."

Mercury paused with his mouth open. He closed it without saying anything, looking Dash up and down like he was foreign to him.

Tense silence hung in the air as Kiara's arousal dissipated slowly, along with the rest of ours. Mercury did end up being the one to break it, though not to say anything about the claim or the kiss.

"Dash needs to hack into some things for us. Edith is hiding something, and one of my contacts gave me an idea of what it is," he said.

"What's the idea?" I asked.

He shook his head. "It's unconfirmed. You can keep working whatever angle you're working, and I'll manage this."

My angle was going back through all the cases my mother had ever given me. She knew how opposed I was to working for violent criminals or corporate thieves, but I was discovering she hadn't respected that. Under the surface, plenty of the tasks she'd set me up with had been hiding crime.

I hadn't done my research.

Could I have turned them down, anyway?

Ethically, I should have, but I'd give up my ethics to keep my brother and his pack safe from their secrets. Maybe that was why I'd never dug too deep into it.

"I can start hacking right now," Dash said.

He took a step back from Kiara. My omega whined, a sound she tried so hard to stifle it came out like more of a breath. He tried to move back toward her, able to feel her upset almost as well as I was. Mercury blocked him, bringing them chest to chest.

"You need to eat first. And sleep. You stayed up all night figuring out who told the police about the dark bond, and you'll hyperfixate on this as soon as you start."

Dash fought with himself, glancing at Kiara and biting his lip. I realized in those few seconds that if I had to, I would demand he sleep and eat. I cared about his well-being, and it wasn't only because he was bonded to my omega.

It had a lot to do with my own affection for the damaged alpha.

"Fine," he muttered.

"If you promise not to jerk off onto my sheets, you can sleep in the bedroom," I said.

He managed half a grin. "No jerking off on the sheets. Got it."

His steps didn't have their usual bounce as he strode toward the hallway. However, he smirked at me before he vanished around the corner. "I'm just glad you didn't ban me from humping your pillow. That's how I prefer to get off, anyway."

Before my eyes had finished rolling, he was gone.

In the end, he'd shielded himself with humour, and I didn't know him well enough to be aware of whether that was a bad or good thing.

"Come on, dove," I said, making it a command for my needy omega. "We're going to lie on the pullout couch in my office. I've got some calls to make."

She followed me, leaving Ambrose and Mercury behind for the moment.

I brushed my fingers through Kiara's long hair, working out some of the less difficult knots. Others I left behind, realizing I needed to purchase her a brush of her own. What style was best for thick, gorgeous hair like hers?

My calls hadn't yielded results. Plenty of phone numbers for previous clients were now out of service, and those that still worked were answered by people who were utterly unwilling to chat. As expected. But the ones that were functional had been sent to Liberty, who wasn't as good a hacker as Dash but could still find some details that weren't public.

"What are you going to do if they try to kiss me?" Kiara murmured.

She drooped further against me, her back flush to my front. There had to be a heat coming, but I wasn't sure if she was aware. Omegas were clingy beings at all times, but it was something that got worse the closer they got to the sex-crazed days of heat.

"I won't let them," I said.

"But we're supposed to play the part. They'll want to touch. Anyone that my father wants an alliance with won't be…"

She trailed off.

They wouldn't be scrupulous, and we knew it.

"We'll be in public. That's what my Mother said. It's supposed to be public, to help my family's reputation. Apparently having a dark bonded normal omega is less scandalous if you're in a pack. In her head, at least."

"Kisses can easily be done in public."

"I promise they won't."

The thought of her being kissed by this pack of assholes made my entire body vibrate with rage. I'd had to acknowledge that my response was different with the Loranger pack. I'd been irritated at Dash touching her, sure. Same with when Ambrose had done it, but the anger wasn't all consuming. It was only a little hint of possessiveness, the need to remind them that she was mine first and theirs second.

"And what if they try to kiss you?"

I cringed. "I'll avoid it as best I can."

"If they touch you, I'll stab them."

My hand trailed down to find her knife at her hip, palming the sheath. "Maybe I shouldn't let you take your knife with you."

Her hand smacked mine away from the weapon, a low whine rumbling her chest. "Nyla has to come."

Despite how safe she felt around us—and I knew she did feel safe, because of the bond—she hadn't let it go for even a second. This piece of metal and wood may be the only friend she'd ever had.

"Behave yourself, then. I'm not above using my command on you, dove. I've done it before, to stop you from stabbing me and Ambrose—though I don't think that's necessary anymore. You gave me the ability to do it by letting me dark bond you, and if it's what I need to do to keep you safe, I'll take advantage."

The faint weight of the previous command dropped when I allowed it to. I had no reason to think she would stab either of us anymore. There was no need for distrust between us.

Kiara tilted her head to peer into my eyes, her tongue darting out to wet her lips. "Order me if you have to. If they kiss you, I'll stab them."

My fingers grabbed her chin, tilting it up until our lips were a hair's breadth apart. Her pupils dilated with lust, the sweet aroma of coconut and chocolate becoming the only thing I could taste or smell. I brushed my lips to hers for a second that left her panting, straining to follow me for more.

"If you stab someone, you'll be punished," I murmured. "I don't want to prevent you from defending yourself unless it becomes absolutely necessary, but we need to sell it, Kiara. Act like you don't hate the fucking thought of joining their pack."

"Punished how?"

"Ambrose's job is punishing people. He'll think of something."

Fuck.

He shouldn't be part of my punishment of my omega, but I couldn't help it. I couldn't get it out of my head, how he'd looked between her legs, his head clenched between her thighs. The two of us together would be able to dominate her so completely she'd forget her fucking name.

"His... job?" Kiara focused on that part instead, her nose crinkling.

"He works at a BDSM club called The Pointe Lounge. Do you know what that means, dove?"

She shook her head. Most times, she hid how sheltered she'd been. Occasionally it became extremely obvious.

"He's paid to tie people up and give them orgasms, among other things."

All the arousal in her expression fled, replaced by shock and fury. She squirmed on my lap, trying to crawl off the pullout couch—likely to go give Ambrose a claiming bite of his own. We didn't need more connections right now, not when the one she'd given Dash had caused a mental breakdown all on its own.

I held her tight, forcing her to look at me.

"Does that piss you off?"

Her growl was my answer. I'd always been a hint jealous of Ambrose's work too—but I was aware it was just work, and I didn't have the same possessive instincts Kiara did. I'd spent years pretending I didn't have feelings for Ambrose either. There was no room for jealousy when what we had was hidden beneath a facade of 'just sex.'

A facade that was showing larger cracks every day.

"Do you love him like you love me, then?" I asked.

The tension against my grip vanished and she blinked at me. Confusion swirled in her blue eyes, and she didn't answer rashly like I'd expected her to. The answer was thought out by the time she opened her mouth to give it.

"I could," she admitted. "With some more time. I regret stabbing him."

"Even though it did get you the dark bond in the end?"

She winced. "Yes."

"And what about the others?"

"Mercury isn't fond of me." It was a non-answer, a brush off. "But Dash... I claimed him, and I don't think it was all instinct."

Not for the first time, I considered what it would be like to entertain this idea. Sharing an omega with the Loranger pack. I would have to join them, and that was strangely appealing for someone who'd spent so many years alone by choice.

I didn't want to get my hopes up, though. If we couldn't get Kiara out from her family's grasp and me out from my mother's, there was no chance of a bond with them. Even if we did escape this situation, there was a ridiculous amount of baggage between us all, and I wasn't sure we could balance it.

"I'll be on my best behaviour," Kiara said, bringing the topic back around to the upcoming meeting with a pack. "You and Ambrose won't need to punish me. I know what's at stake. Nyla will stay in her sheath, but I can't guarantee I won't try to fight them bare handed if they touch you."

I chuckled, letting us both settle back and be comfortable once again. "Thank you, dove. With you, I would honestly expect nothing less."

THIRTY-THREE

LEIGHTON

My condo was cramped with bodies as the sun rose the next morning. Kiara and I shared my primary bedroom. Mercury took the couch, while Ambrose's bulk slept on the pullout couch in the office. Once Dash woke up from his six-hour nap in my bedroom —thankfully without coming all over my pillow—he'd settled in front of my work computer and started typing.

He hadn't stopped all night, it appeared.

An empty energy drink can was crumpled and tossed to the side, a box of crackers decimated with only crumbs left behind.

His fingers danced across the keys as he stared at the screen with a single-minded focus that I wasn't going to interrupt.

I wandered into the kitchen instead, watching my cell phone like it was an explosive device and waiting for the phone call that would set everything in motion.

"Did you sleep well?" Mercury asked.

He was the first to wake other than me, his voice heavy with sleep when he met me in front of the kettle. I reached for the pot of coffee but he shook his head, turning on the kettle and grabbing a mug and a tea bag from my cupboard.

"I've slept worse," I said.

Sleeping with another human being unnerved me. It was uncomfortable on a base level, and after helping Kiara fall asleep with my tongue on her clit, I'd struggled to fall asleep myself. The few hours I'd gotten had been fitful.

Mercury scoffed. "You've got a gorgeous omega in bed with you, and you're telling me that wasn't the best sleep of your life?"

I waited for him to backtrack on that statement, but he didn't. He grabbed sugar and honey from the counter and measured it out into his mug. The alpha was half asleep, for sure.

"Is that your way of saying you want to sleep with my gorgeous omega?" I asked.

The metal spoon clanged against the rim of the mug when he dropped it, cursing. He spun to glare at me, his half-lidded brown eyes confirming my suspicions. Not awake enough to be thinking.

"I do not want to sleep with that omega. She's objectively gorgeous, of course, but that isn't my opinion of her."

I shrugged, taking a slow sip of coffee. "Sure."

The rest of his pack was falling.

It was only a matter of time for him.

With a muttered curse, Mercury reached past me for the coffee pot. Our bodies brushed, my nose catching a breath of cinnamon and old books. Then he was gone again, his lean arm reaching up to grab another mug. He dumped a healthy serving of coffee into it, placed the pot unceremoniously onto the counter, and tipped the coffee into his mouth.

I watched his Adam's apple bob with every swallow, the muscles of his throat working hard to chug the delicious, tiredness-defying liquid. Before he was done I had to look away, trying to ignore the clench in my core.

Mercury was cold and abrasive at the best of times, but he was attractive. Especially when he let go of his leash for a second and allowed himself to do things that he usually wouldn't, like down an entire mug of coffee in a minute flat.

"Do you need some more?" I asked when he placed the mug back down. "I can make another pot."

His eyes narrowed and he shook his head.

I started another pot anyway, because if I had to deal with him along with everything else this morning, I might need a bit more caffeine myself.

Noon had come and gone by the time I heard from my mother. My phone lit up with her call and I didn't bother to make her wait for the third ring. I picked up on the first.

"Mother."

"Leighton. Your date is set. You'll be spending time with the Ashby pack tonight at an upscale club. They'll be expecting you at seven. Be there fifteen minutes early, and ensure your omega is dressed appropriately."

I bit my tongue against the anger that threatened to bubble up. She wasn't worth it, not when Dash hadn't found anything conclusive yet. At least, not anything conclusive enough for him to give us a straight answer. Neither had Liberty. We were at dead ends all around.

Mother didn't wait for my response. She hung up.

My phone immediately chimed with an address and reminder of the time. Ambrose peered over my shoulder at it. The club was popular, the same one Dash frequented to find beta hookups. That was a fact I wouldn't be telling Kiara.

"Who is your date with?" Mercury was the one to break the tense silence.

"Ashby pack."

His eyebrow lifted. Ambrose's surprise was similar. Kiara didn't have a clue who we were talking about.

The Ashby pack were wealthy businessmen. I'd thought they were completely above board—never had heard any evidence to the contrary, not even with my contacts. If they were agreeing to an arranged mating with a dark bonded crime family daughter, they had to have something going on under the table.

I just didn't know what.

That irritated me, because I'd been hoping something would slot together in my brain when I figured out who Kiara and I were supposed to mate. I had to have some hidden knowledge somewhere about my mother's criminal ties, I just couldn't figure out what it was, or where my brain was keeping it.

"Didn't know they were criminals," Ambrose rumbled.

Mercury muttered his agreement, his thumbs flying across his phone screen.

"If they're not criminals, who are they?" Kiara asked.

I jumped in to explain. "They run A/B/O Connections, which creates apps and runs events to connect alphas and omegas with betas so everyone can understand each other a little better. They're not an old money family. Their pack lead was born to a millionaire pack, but the other two were middle class or lower. The business was built from the ground up. With a bit more of an advantage than most people got, sure, but what they've done is impressive."

"It's nothing special."

Mercury's cold rebuttal had me blinking. He was staring at his phone, almost pretending he'd never spoken.

"Nothing special?" I asked, lifting a brow.

"Anyone with their resources could have done it."

That wasn't what the business magazines said. They touted Cordian Ashby as a man beyond his time, using growth strategies that led the industry. I'd never met him because his pack never had need of a corporate fixer. There was no minor white-collar crime to cover up, no playboy CEO image to tidy.

According to everyone except Mercury, they were perfect and groundbreaking.

I had a feeling I knew why Mercury didn't think the same.

"Would you like us to talk you up?" I asked, standing up from the couch.

His eyes narrowed, attention drawn from his phone. "What are you talking about?"

"Well, you're jealous that we're speaking highly of the Ashby pack."

"I absolutely am not."

Shooting a glance over my shoulder at Ambrose, he smirked. He knew Mercury better than anyone else on this planet, and he agreed with me. That meant I was right.

I walked until I ended up between Mercury's legs, my thighs forcing his knees apart. He looked up at me from his seat on the armchair, his phone laying on his lap as the screen darkened, and then went black.

"Is this some kind of intimidation tactic?" he demanded.

My grin widened. "Am I intimidating you?"

His cheeks were steadily growing pinker. The colour was cute as it rose to his high cheekbones. He glanced over my shoulder at Ambrose, trying for backup, but scowled when he received no help.

"Are you going to answer me?" I murmured.

Leaning over, I grabbed his chin and brought him closer to me. His eyes went glassy, sharp cinnamon scent swirling around me. His trousers bulged at the crotch, his cock straining to get free of its confines. Based on what Ambrose liked, I knew Mercury had to be submissive to him.

I hadn't expected his submission to be so easy.

"You're not intimidating me," he said.

My fingers slid down his chin to grab his throat. The groan he let out was echoed by a whimper from Kiara. I imagined she was transfixed on this scene, especially with her inching closer to heat.

"Maybe I'm not," I mused. "Maybe I'm turning you on."

Pressing one leg forward, I spread his thighs until I could rub my knee against his clothed cock. A wet spot formed and Mercury stayed frozen. He tried to choke down his sounds, but it was no use. Nothing could stop the stream of moans, especially not when he started raising his hips to meet me. He ended up humping my leg and I let him, because it was better proof than anything else that Mercury wanted this.

He wanted me, and he wanted Kiara.

It complicated things further, but I couldn't bring myself to care.

I pressed my knee to him and he ground against it. His hands clutched the arms of the chair, using them as leverage to help him move. My hand stayed wrapped around his throat.

He didn't stop until his breath was stuttering on a gasp. Those cold eyes were expressive in this moment, broadcasting his bliss as it soaked his trousers.

All of us were silent for a long moment as his breathing evened out. There was evidence of how I turned him on, now. He would have to face it.

Except his expression closed off and he yanked back from my grip. I stepped back just in time to avoid getting head butted by him abruptly standing.

Without a word, he stormed from the room. There wasn't anywhere to go in this apartment, really, but a second later the bedroom door slammed.

I sighed.

Fuck.

Pushing too hard was a recipe for disaster, and I'd known it.

Yet, I'd done it anyway. There was something about this pack that eliminated my ability to form rational thoughts.

"I'm going to check on him," Ambrose said.

His hand stroked through Kiara's hair—he'd watched everything from behind the couch, where Kiara was still sitting in stunned silence.

"Tell him I apologize," I said.

Ambrose snorted. "No, you don't."

I glared at him.

"You would do it again in a heartbeat, and he would want you to," Ambrose said. "He's in his own head. I'll get him out of it."

Thinking of how Ambrose got me out of my head, I fought back a blush.

I might need to change the sheets on the bed when they were done.

Again.

At this rate, I'll need more sets.

THIRTY-FOUR

MERCURY

I clutched the hem of my button up shirt, crushing the fabric into my sweaty fists. A headache pounded at my temples, and it felt like the tightness of my French braids was making it worse. Pacing across the floor of Leighton's fucking bedroom, of all places, I yanked the ties out of my hair and undid the braids.

Even with my curly mass of burgundy hair freed, my headache didn't decrease. It got worse, throbbing and pulsing until a familiar set of strong arms wrapped around me from behind.

Ambrose's embrace forced me to stop pacing.

"Deep breaths," he said.

He inhaled, long and steady. I mirrored him. We'd done this a thousand times before, both during scenes and in normal life.

It had been so long since I'd had him this close. Since I'd had his help and his comfort and his presence as a lover and not simply a pack member.

"Another one."

His command relaxed me. My brain fell into subspace instantaneously, despite there being nothing sexual about breathing.

I floated through time and space, breathing when he told me to and ignoring everything else.

It couldn't last.

Eventually the vanilla cream and coconut chocolate punched through Ambrose's blanket of hot iron and smoke. My cock hardened in my wet, sullied pants. The feeling of Leighton's hand was a phantom grip around my neck.

I pulled away from Ambrose, whirling to face him.

"What are you doing?" I demanded. "I'm not sure why you thought me walking away meant it was a good idea to follow me."

Tiny needles pierced my heart as I pushed him away, but he didn't budge. His face didn't twitch with annoyance or sadness or any emotion at all. Ambrose crossed his arms over his chest and stared me down.

I tried to win that staring contest, but couldn't.

My gaze darted to the side and I started to pace again. Footsteps pounding on the carpet, I wondered how long it would be until Leighton interrupted us. I'd invaded her bedroom. It was the only place with any privacy in this apartment.

I needed privacy.

I needed one fucking moment where I wasn't thinking about her or Kiara.

"Get out." I waved at the door. "I need..."

Trailing off, I growled.

What did I fucking need? There was nothing I could do that would dispel this fist of affection around my heart. I was already a goner, and because I hadn't saved us, we were all going to fall.

"You need to relax, baby," Ambrose said.

His tone was soft. When he moved toward me, I let him. He pulled me against his chest and I buried my face there, breathing him in.

There were very few things in this world that relaxed me. He was one of them.

"I'm fine," I muttered.

I very much was not.

"You're self-sabotaging."

"We can't end up with them," I said. "It won't work. Our pack is fine as it is."

Ambrose stroked my back with one of his big hands. I snuck my hands up underneath the fabric of his shirt, running my palms up his scarred back. He never let anyone else touch him like this. Except Kiara and Leighton.

"Tell me why we can't, baby."

He shuffled us over to the bed and sat down. Everyone's scent was on it. Dash, from when he napped last night. Leighton and Kiara, heavy with arousal. Me and Ambrose, now that we were perched on the edge.

It felt like a nest. Something I'd always wanted. A nest with my pack. It was something I'd given up on when we'd been rejected by our scent match.

"You know why."

"Tell me."

I couldn't disobey when he made it a command.

"The omega is under a lot of pressure, Ambrose. She can't know what she wants after such a sheltered upbringing. When she realizes she chose rashly and doesn't want us after all, our pack will fall to pieces."

My family's pack had fallen to pieces. No rash decisions necessary. They'd just realized after four kids and years of being bonded that they actually kind of hated each other. My childhood had been full of screaming matches and thinly veiled hatred between my parents.

A forever bond needed to be thought out, especially when it wasn't to a scent match.

It couldn't be decided on a whim. You couldn't fall for someone when outside pressure was pushing you to lock yourself in for life. Dash would do it, but if Kiara and Leighton ever decided they didn't want him, he would break.

If I let myself fall for them, they could break me too.

Ambrose sighed, leaning down to nuzzle his nose against my neck. I held back my moan—barely. Between Ambrose's arousal constantly lingering in the air and the sizzling chemistry I was ignoring with Kiara and Leighton, I was pent up. The one orgasm had been a breakdown, only heightening my desire. Not a release.

"Your fear is holding us all back," he murmured. "Especially Dash."

I stiffened, trying to pull away. He didn't release me.

"It's been getting worse since you broke off our relationship a year ago, not better," Ambrose continued.

He was right. Without him around to soothe me, I was more irritable and controlling. I trailed Dash like I was a suburban mom on a mission to keep her kid out of trouble.

And now I was the one in trouble, all because I couldn't actually keep Dash safe from this.

He was even handling it himself, kind of. I'd thought he would have broken down at Kiara's claiming, but he was holding it together for the most part.

"What are you saying, then?" I asked, letting my body slump against his.

"Well, for one thing, I want you back. I only let you break it off with me because you were insistent." His tongue slid along my neck and I shivered, gritting my teeth against my groan. "And you should let me take you out of your head the way I used to. It might give you some clarity."

"Yes."

The word released in a rush. He purred against me, the same way he'd purred for the omega.

"Good boy. You have no fucking idea how much I've wanted you to be mine again."

I *did* have a clue, because ending our relationship was the hardest thing I'd ever done. I'd hidden from the pack bond for ages, not wanting either of them to know how much it tore me up.

Ambrose stood, stretching his arms over his head. I counted out every breath as he went to the walk-in closet, holding up a tie.

"Can I?" he asked.

I nodded and he placed himself right in front of me.

Fabric covered my eyes, removing the sense I relied on most. Sight. There was only darkness, and tension left my body.

Ambrose was right, and I hated it.

I needed to get out of my head and give myself a moment where I could rationally think about whether I wanted Leighton and Kiara. Without the dread hanging like a noose around my neck, I might have a different opinion.

He knew I would, and so did I. Once I was freed from the constraints of keeping everyone else safe, I could admit what I wanted.

An omega.

Specifically, the only omega who'd been on my radar since our fated mate rejected us.

"Good boy. Let yourself relax. I'm taking off all your clothes, baby."

I had a moment of panic about this being Leighton's bedroom and not a place where I should be getting naked. Ambrose's skin on mine soothed the worry. His scent was sharper and more potent than usual—partially from his growing arousal, but partially because of my lack of access to my eyesight.

Each piece of clothing was carefully removed from my body until only my bare skin remained. I shivered from the AC-induced chill, but my lover's hands were quick to warm me.

He touched every inch of me. Tweaking my nipples, skimming my abs, gripping my thighs. He touched everywhere except where I wanted him. My cock and my ass.

"I wish I had my tools with me," he said in a husky rasp. "You deserve one hell of a punishment, baby."

My skin pebbled with goosebumps and I shivered.

"Sorry, Sir," I whispered.

His lips came down on mine and I moaned, desperate for the kiss to deepen. It had been so long since we'd touched like this, so long since I'd had this freedom. Since I'd had him.

I loved him so fucking much. It was why I'd done everything I could to save our pack from the fate my family had suffered.

Stupid as that may have been.

Ambrose kept the kiss soft, moving back before I could plunge my tongue past his lips. "Fuck. I've missed you. I know you were trying to keep Dash safe, but I never want you to deny me again. OK?"

"Never," I said.

It was too soon to promise. If things with Kiara and Leighton fell apart—or worse, if Kiara ended up back with her father—Dash wouldn't make it. He wouldn't. I knew him. We'd be back in the same situation as we were before, but worse. Our relationship would hurt him, and yet…

This time, I didn't care.

I needed this. *Me*. What he needed? He could find it himself.

"Where do you want my cock?" Ambrose asked.

"Everywhere."

He chuckled and I heard him unzip his pants. The sound was grating, teasing me with what I couldn't see. My memories of his cock were crystal clear from all our years together, but it had been so long I wanted a refresher.

His body heat returned in front of me, close enough to warm me but not touch. He grabbed one of my hands and I gasped when a slick liquid coated two of my fingers. I wasn't sure if it was technically lube or not, but it would do for our purposes.

"If you want my cock everywhere, you're going to prep your ass while I fuck your mouth."

I whined, barely waiting for him to lead me to kneel on the floor. The carpet was abrasive beneath my knees, and I knew I would have rug burn by the time we were done. Propping myself up on one hand, I slid the lube-coated fingers back and plunged both into my ass. The stretch was uncomfortable after so long, but I didn't care. Need threatened to overwhelm me, and I didn't even have his cock in my mouth yet.

Ambrose was gentle as he maneuvered me into position. I didn't have to think about how to make the position work. He did all that. What I had to do was rock back onto my fingers as they stretched me, my lips parted, waiting for his cock to land on my tongue.

His rough, scarred hand cupped my cheek when he had us both in the right place. Salty smoke exploded on my tongue, his scent melding seamlessly with his taste. I moaned around his tip and he took it as the invitation it was.

My mouth was suddenly full, his flavour reaching the back of my throat. I swallowed eagerly, but he didn't test my deep throat skills yet. He fucked my mouth slowly, one hand on my cheek and one tangled in my messy hair.

"Take what I give you. Good boy."

I groaned, trying to take more but failing when his grip tightened.

"You're not in control of how much cock you get, baby. If you need more, put another finger in your tight hole."

Two fingers were still a close fit, and usually I would give myself more time to adjust before adding a third. Today, I was impatient and irrational, traits that weren't often associated with me.

My moan broke on a whimper when the third finger was borderline uncomfortable. The stretch was almost too much without working up to it, but it gave me a sliver of what I wanted.

"Don't hurt yourself," Ambrose cautioned. He shifted, his cock going deep and making my eyes roll back. Then I felt the crack of his hand across the globe of my ass. "I don't want you in pain unless I've intentionally caused it."

"More," I moaned, the plea muffled around his thick length.

He pushed in deep again, letting me swallow and gag on it this time.

Each thrust was faster and rougher than the last. Hitting deeper. Making me a fucking mess. I loved each one a tiny bit more, and my cock throbbed between my legs. The faint discomfort of my fingers had faded and now I was lost in pegging my prostate and chasing an orgasm I knew Ambrose wouldn't let me have.

Sure enough, my tip had smeared a trail of precum across my abs when he pulled back and removed my fingers from my ass.

I was still blindfolded as he picked me up and tossed me on the bed. I tried to flip over onto my hands and knees, but he held me down on my back. My legs were lifted and pushed, folding me near in half. His warm body came to rest over mine, his cock prodding my hole.

"Tell me what you want," he growled.

I sobbed, straining to get him inside. As my lips parted to beg, an unwelcome image flashed across my closed eyelids.

Leighton, in the same position I was in.

Did they fuck like this?

Ambrose demanded begging—I bet he demanded it from her too. Did she give it to him easily, or did she resist until he snapped?

Then Kiara was there in my mind, and my cock fucking pulsed. Her ample tits were out and waiting to be fucked the way

I'd wanted to when I first saw her. That stupid knife was strapped to her thigh, reminding me of how easy it would be for her to use it. Why did that turn me on?

Sensing my sudden closeness to the edge, Ambrose grabbed the base of my length and squeezed.

"Baby, speak. Now."

"Fuck me," I whimpered, trying to banish the women from my mind.

It was impossible with their scent all around us, making this reunion about more than Ambrose and I. This was about the potential for us as a pack, and how much I wanted to say '*fuck the barriers*' and claim Kiara and Leighton in one fell swoop.

"That's not how you ask."

His cock was teasing my entrance, slightly cool from the lube. I had no idea when he'd coated himself. Without my vision, everything was touch and sound and smell, and I hadn't felt him move.

"Please fuck me, Sir."

Ambrose's lips crashed to mine and his cock pressed inside. It was a tighter fit than my fingers and somehow so much more intense. He shifted slowly to take me an inch at a time, likely for a double purpose: he knew how long it had been since I'd done this, and he loved to tease the fuck out of me.

He murmured a few curses under his breath as he rocked, tasting himself on my tongue. "I love you," he groaned when his balls came to press against my skin.

A year of denying it hadn't done anything to lessen how I felt about him. I'd sacrificed this closeness, this attention, for the hope of one day finding someone who would bring us together in the way a fated mate should have.

"I love you too," I whispered against his lips.

Kiara had helped bring us back together.

I had to admit that, even though I knew she was still just as likely to tear us apart. The situation wasn't easy, and Dash wasn't any less prone to breakdowns, but I could finally fucking hope.

"Now take my cock like a good boy, baby."

"Yes, Sir."

Emotional intimacy fled with those words, and I sank into the space he forged for me. The space where time had no meaning and emotions could wash over me with no consequences. If I cried, I cried. If I laughed, I laughed. There were no barriers to how I was allowed to feel with him in this space, not like the real world where I kept my exterior appearance in a stranglehold.

By the time the orgasm exploded from the base of my spine, I was pretty sure I'd gone through every one of the human emotions.

I was certainly past caring about how I sounded to the women waiting out in the all-too-nearby living room.

I begged Ambrose to come in me after I'd made a sticky mess of my chest. He obliged, only pausing to yank my blindfold off.

His head relaxed back, exposing his scarred throat and the tight clench of his jaw. Then he pitched forward as his hips stuttered to a stop, his body curling over mine. Hot breath teased the hairs of my Adonis belt, threatening to make my cock thrum to life again. He stayed unmoving, clutching me, for so long the world was starting to rush in.

Then he lifted his head, a quirk to his lips.

"I missed you, baby."

If there hadn't been tears when he was fucking me, they were certainly falling now. To stop him from seeing, I pulled him close for a kiss, but we tasted the salt of them on our tongues.

If Ambrose dared ask, I'd blame it on sweat.

But he knew. He knew how much I missed him and how much I needed him. He'd been waiting for me to admit it since the day I told him we had to break it off.

When I felt capable of thinking in Leighton's presence again, I redressed and made a decision. Leighton and Kiara weren't going to some other pack. If they had to join any pack, it would be ours and ours alone.

THIRTY-FIVE

KIARA

Dash dressed me. He'd laced up the back of my dresses' corset top and fluffed the sleeves to look ethereal. The dress had been brought by his personal stylist, along with a makeup artist who'd spent a mere thirty minutes making me look like I'd come from another planet.

Leighton had informed me I was overdressed. Even Dash had admitted it, while still insisting he wanted to dress me in this.

I didn't care.

This was the kind of dress I'd always wanted to wear, but never been able to. Father had given me clothes that were feminine, yes, but modest.

This was not modest.

The bust was so low cut my tits were almost spilling out, the fluffy sleeves barely holding it all together. Beneath the laces of the corset back was nothing but skin. And the skirts were somehow translucent from mid thigh down, exposing the curves of my legs despite the many layers of cloth. My knife hid in the holster around my waist, invisible to prying eyes.

"I want to dive under your skirt," Dash said in wonder, stepping back to peer at his handiwork.

My hair was up in a simple updo that he'd done—claiming he'd once watched ten hours worth of wedding hair tutorials as a procrastination tactic.

"You're going to dive right back into researching my mother's shady business practices," Leighton said.

She rolled her eyes but had a new appreciation for the extravagant alpha. We almost hadn't been able to detach him from the computer in her office, but the words 'undressing' and 'Kiara' in the same sentence had done the trick.

"I've got to see you ladies out the door, first," he said. "It's the gentlemanly thing to do."

His grin didn't quite reach his eyes, and occasionally his hand would brush against where I'd marked him. I felt his anxiety through our newly formed and weak bond, but I didn't know how to help. I'd been the one to create the emotion by bonding him unexpectedly. I figured it was best to let him work through it without interference from me.

"You're going to see us out to our date with another pack?" I asked.

When I crossed my arms over my chest his gaze dropped to my cleavage with obvious appreciation.

"I have to make sure they're aware you'll never be theirs."

My heart fluttered in time with my pussy. The arousal swamping me was frequent and intense enough that I worried about an upcoming heat. The signs were compounding—even the alphas had noticed them—and I was about due, but this really wasn't the time. Not while I was at risk of ending up in the beds and lives of this Ashby pack that I'd never met.

Dash stepped over to me and held out an arm. I glanced over at Leighton, seeking permission before I linked mine with his.

She nodded, hunger in her expression as she focused on the

point of contact between Dash and I. Leighton was dressed down, more appropriate for the high-class club.

While my dress fell in layers of baby pink to cover the white sneakers on my feet, hers was skintight. The white fabric went up to her neck but was sleeveless. It was floor-length, but had a slit running high enough to expose most of her left thigh.

Her nipples would have been exposed if the dress had been even the tiniest bit thinner. Even now, if I stared intently enough, I thought I could see the dusky pink outlines.

And I *was* staring.

My gaze lifted to meet hers, a smirk waiting on her lips.

"Are you ready to go, dove?" she murmured. "Or did you need someone to go under that dress after all?"

I flushed with embarrassment, shaking my head and clutching Dash. "No. We'll be late."

That was the only reason I didn't beg someone to do it. I would prefer to have one alpha's tongue on my sex while another stopped me from falling over, but we didn't have time.

Dash's lips brushed against the dark bond Leighton had left on my neck. The motion made me gasp—it was brazen, to touch another alpha's bond, whether I'd claimed him or not. He smirked, his confidence flitting in and out of existence now that I'd made him vulnerable.

"Hurry back, little omega," he murmured. "I'd like you to suffocate me with this tulle when you get home."

Leighton cuffed him on the back of the head and pulled him away from her bond mark before I had a chance to process that. "You know better than to touch her there, Dash," Leighton said.

Her fingers trailed over one of my marks on Dash's neck and he stiffened and groaned. I didn't feel possessive over the claiming bond, oddly enough. I wanted Leighton to sink her teeth into him too, to make a matching set.

"Fucking hell," he muttered, flinching away from the touch. "You're going to kill me."

"Then walk us out. We really shouldn't be late."

Her casual air cracked for a second, and I saw her worry. If this didn't go well, it wouldn't be us that suffered. Not right away, anyway. It would be Leighton's brother. The scent match mate Dash never got to have. As much as a little animalistic part of me insisted he deserved what was coming, most of me was sympathetic.

My mates all cared about him.

Yes, that annoyed the fuck out of me.

I could get over it.

True to his word, Dash walked us to the front door, but no farther. He should be seen with us as little as possible. It would be a miracle if Leighton's mother didn't already know the Loranger pack were still around us, but we wanted to be discreet nonetheless.

Before either of us had crossed the threshold, he stopped. His chin brushed the top of my head—a scent mark. I would be drenched in spring rain and peaches while we met with the Ashby pack, making it very clear I had someone else I belonged to.

Or, more accurately, someone who belonged to me.

Popping up onto my toes, I pressed my lips to each of the marks I'd left.

His long, low moan had Ambrose poking his head out of the bedroom and rolling his eyes. He and Mercury had said their goodbyes to us already. Awkward goodbyes, because we'd all heard Mercury getting railed, but apparently we weren't talking about it.

"Make sure you don't bond with anyone else." Dash meant it to be teasing. Instead, it was desperate.

I grinned. "I might stab them, but there won't be any claiming."

Relief flitted through his green eyes, and then Leighton was there. I leaned back against her warmth and she held me. Her head tilted ever so slightly to the side, exposing the curve of her neck.

Dash watched her pulse, swallowing.

"Do it, if you'd like," she said.

He was on her in a second. Dash's hands were careful to stay on her waist, avoiding any area that could be considered sensitive. That fresh, fruity scent grew in intensity as he rubbed it against Leighton's neck too.

When he stepped back he was holding both hands in fists at his side. "Give them hell, ladies," he murmured.

"I don't think Kiara has any other setting," Leighton said.

Before I could make my indignation known, the condo door was shutting behind us and we were making our way to the elevator.

We were walking straight into danger, and the fear making my pulse pound was too intense to ignore.

The chauffeur left us at the entrance to the club, no doubt reporting back to Leighton's mother. We hadn't spoken to each other in the car. There was too much risk of our conversation being overheard, and any of our words could be twisted against us.

Even here, I was scared of prying eyes and whispers. My skin crawled as we walked up to the hostess stand. Leighton gave the Ashby name—their pack lead was called Cordian. There were two other members. A simple, small, three alpha pack.

When the hostess began to lead me inside, I froze before we could cross the threshold.

We were already later than Edith wanted. The hands on the Roman numeral clock above the entrance were showing ten to seven.

But I couldn't move.

"I've been here before." Leighton's commanding tone stopped the hostess in her tracks. "We'll find the table ourselves. Thank you."

The hostess looked about to complain, but something about my bonded mate stopped her. Leighton's aura hung in the air, denying all refusals of her will.

We went inside on our own and the hostess didn't comment.

I didn't register anything about the dimly lit lounge before I was pulled into a dark hallway right beside the entrance.

Vanilla cream filled my space and I sucked in a deep breath, realizing that my breathing had been shallow and quick. Her hands stroked my cheeks, forcing me to look up at her.

"You're scared," she said softly.

"No." The word wobbled, betraying how false it was.

"You're allowed to be scared, dove. I know your father didn't treat you well, and you don't want to go back. We're going to fix it, whether you trust me to or not."

I shook my head, grabbing her hips and pressing myself into her chest. Her arms came around me, one hand cupping the back of my neck.

"I trust you, but I'm still scared. Tobias... he told me he comes to places like this. What if he's here?"

A purr rumbled through her, soothing something in the deepest recesses of my mind. I relaxed, almost slumping against her.

"He won't be. They wouldn't dare risk someone realizing the two of you are related."

It was a good point. Tobias and I had the same eyes. Anyone who'd met our father would know his were the same shade as well. It was easy to see when we were side by side, but harder to pinpoint when we were apart.

"And if he was, dove, I wouldn't let him stay."

"But your mother wouldn't like that."

She chuckled darkly. "I'm discovering there are plenty of things I would do for you that my mother wouldn't like."

I wanted to ask about her brother—what happened if he was brought into it? If the blackmail was dangled over her head again. I kept my mouth shut, because I wasn't sure I was ready for the answer. She wouldn't choose me. We'd known each other a mere blink of time, and her brother was family.

I didn't mean anything in the face of that.

"Are you ready to go find them?" she asked.

Fear still swirled in my head, but my response was far less visceral. I could call this about as ready as I would ever be. My feet were willing to move—an overall improvement.

I nodded and she led the way through a maze of tables and dance floors. My attire drew attention. We'd expected it would. Wanted it to, even, because people would be more likely to snap a few pics and make this a page in the gossip column. At least, that's how Leighton had explained it to me.

I was sure I'd heard a few shutter clicks when we found a table of three men seated on the far end of the lounge.

They were objectively handsome. All wore suits in plain colours, looking about as generic as they could get. Only one stood up when we approached, clearly familiar with my bonded.

"Leighton Winston," he said, extending a hand out. "A pleasure. I've heard a lot about you."

His attention flicked to me, gaze catching on the dark bond on my neck. I wore it proudly, though many would try to hide it.

They were considered poisoned bonds, but not by me. Not when it was given by Leighton, at least.

"Same to you," Leighton said. There was an air of professionalism about her. Shoulders pulled back, expression flat with a pacifying smile. "This is my bonded mate, Kiara."

She didn't give my last name—all the better, I never wanted to hear it again.

I didn't extend a hand, only nodding. The Ashby pack member didn't seem keen to shake mine either. He gestured into the booth and I slid in first, followed by my mate. He sat on the other side, alongside his pack.

"My name is Cordian Ashby," he said. "Pack lead."

I could have guessed, considering he was doing the talking for his pack. His expression was as blank as Leighton's, but his packmates gave more away.

"These are my packmates Hideki Kimura and Noel Smith."

The one he pointed to as Noel was dainty in his beauty. He had a face like the men in the fashion magazines my mother kept around the house. His lips kept twitching, threatening to pull up into a sneer.

Hideki was bulkier, taking up the most room on their side of the bench. The plain suit was bulging at the arms, far too small for him. I had to wonder if it was what he usually wore or something pulled from the depths of his closet specifically for the occasion. He had one hand in a fist on the table, clenched so tightly his knuckles were white. His expressive brown eyes were focused in a glare.

There was hatred boiling in their depths. *At me?* It was me he was glaring at.

I pressed closer to Leighton, placing a hand on Nyla at my hip. I wanted to stab the dislike right off their faces, replacing it with fear. I had a feeling I would enjoy it again, unlike the sick feeling I'd gotten when I'd stabbed Ambrose.

But I wasn't allowed.

Best behaviour, or she was going to command me to behave anyway.

"It's a pleasure," I said quietly.

I used the passive tone of voice I knew to use with my father. If I spoke too loudly or with too much force, he would tell me off. *'Women are supposed to be quiet and listen,'* he said. But when I'd grown into my designation, he'd amended his statement to say that was what omegas were supposed to do.

I'd believed him, to an extent. His beliefs were extreme—it was impossible not to know, even considering my minimal exposure to the outside world. I'd assumed that they had a basis in reality.

From my time outside my family home, I'd now learned that was untrue.

Very few people thought like he did. At least, very few people I'd met. I might have been lucky in my real world experiences.

"A pleasure indeed," Cordian said when his pack didn't give an acknowledgment. He didn't sound as if he thought this was a pleasure.

We stared at each other without talking for far too long. The silence had me uncomfortable, fidgeting in my seat. I played with the frills and layers of my dress, turning my gaze out to the club. It had dance floors, but wasn't what I'd expected a club to be like.

Then again, it was high end. Expensive.

Exactly the kind of place Tobias would spend his time. I visibly shuddered, leaning into Leighton. It might be better if I didn't observe everyone coming and going through the club. I'd grow more and more paranoid about the next person being my brother, no matter how unlikely.

Leighton's hand came down to rest on my thigh, squeezing. "Why don't we chat business?" she suggested. "Something to break the ice."

Cordian gave a sharp nod. Neither party wanted to break the ice—and I had to wonder why. They were wanting to bond me as a mate. Did they simply not care about what we had to say, and were only doing the date for appearances? Or was there something deeper than I could see?

"You have a storied career," he started.

I tuned out the conversation, catching bits and pieces about things Leighton had done. She saved reputations, some that didn't necessarily deserve to be saved, and stopped corporate chaos before it hit the news. She worked behind the scenes, preventing the public from seeing the bad side of alphas and omegas with money.

Most people would have been jaded and cruel in her position, but she wasn't. I respected that a lot.

They luckily hadn't included me in the conversation, leaving me to listen and nod along. Although, inevitably, my attention wandered. As minutes ticked by, the club was filling up.

There were plenty of booths like the one we were in, plus small circles of couches. A dance floor and lit up bar was in the middle of this room—but there were multiple areas. Plus, hallways off the main area looked like they led to private rooms, with bouncers guarding the entrances.

I curled closer to Leighton's side, inhaling a deep breath of vanilla cream. Dash's scent was layered over it, and if he were here the Ashby pack would know exactly which pack we wanted to go home with.

A head of blonde hair, casually styled, appeared in my line of vision.

I blinked a few times, wondering if sucking in his scent had conjured him.

But, no.

Dash was striding across the dance floor with Mercury on his heels. Both were wearing scowls, though Dash's was out of character for him. He spotted us and a grin slipped onto his face, but Mercury stopped him from coming over and interrupting our date. They instead settled on a couch within sight of our booth.

Their presence was like a comforting blanket. Leighton shot Dash a glare, but I was glad he'd come. I could focus on him when I got distracted, and I didn't have to worry about looking around and seeing something that I really didn't want to see.

My brother couldn't touch me. Not even a little bit. Not when I had so many layers of protection.

THIRTY-SIX

DASH

My pack tried to stop me, but it wasn't going to happen.

Not after I felt her through our tenuous bond. Pure terror had filled it for a couple of tense minutes.

It was an alpha's job to comfort an omega through that, and I hadn't been there. Leighton had been, but was one enough when the terror was that acute? Kiara deserved a full pack of alphas doting over her and comforting her.

"Don't rub your neck," Mercury hissed at me.

I removed my hand, the tips of my fingers coming back covered in concealer.

They'd gotten me to cover up my marks before leaving the condo, but that was all I'd let them sway me on. This club was my domain. I had every right to be here. Maybe it was more suspicious when I wasn't. Every weekend for the past couple of years had been spent bathed in wine and rum and betas.

Tonight I'd pretend to drink wine and rum, but the thought of meaningless sex with betas made me sick.

I was here for Kiara and Leighton, and they were the only ones I would have sex with.

Though, I was pretty sure Leighton didn't have sex planned for my future—she intended to ream me out and punish me in every possible way. The glare she'd sent in my direction told me that.

Relief had lit in Kiara's expressive eyes, and that was worth any punishment. Her relief, and the knowledge that they were both safe and sound despite the annoying presence of the Ashby pack.

"You're really good at acting, Merc," I teased. "You look just as annoyed as you usually do when you follow me around."

"I am," he said.

His tone was a little more growly than usual.

Mercury had taken on the task of babysitter years ago. I'd always been adamant I didn't need one, but I probably had. With the amount of trouble I'd gotten into under his watchful eye, I was hesitant to think about how much shit I would have been in if he hadn't been around.

That was why it wasn't unusual for him to be here with me. He never drank, but he always hovered.

Ambrose, on the other hand, never left the confines of our apartment or The Pointe Lounge. He hadn't come because it would rouse suspicions. The gentle giant had wanted to. I saw it in his eyes.

"Nah, you're glad we came tonight," I said. "You prefer to have them in your sights."

"Being involved with them is a recipe for disaster. I would prefer if we distanced ourselves, but I'm the only one with any rational thought left."

"Your rational thoughts seem to make you hard a lot in their presence."

He growled and stood from the short couch we'd claimed. "I'm getting a drink."

I grinned. If I had Mercury turning to wine to get through the night, I was doing my job. We needed him one or two wine glasses worth of drunk, in my opinion. Otherwise, his silly rational brain would get in the way of what we were here to do.

Protect Leighton and Kiara.

If they needed it. I didn't doubt that Leighton was capable on her own, but she was going up against one hell of a situation tonight.

"Hey, Dash."

A woman slid down onto the couch in Mercury's vacated place. Her arm was around me before I could shove her off. The previously appealing scent of honeysuckle and apple now grated on my nerves.

"Olanda. I'm not available."

I barely looked at her, but caught her plump lips push into a pout. The beta woman and I had a history. A short one that she kept trying to repeat.

Sometimes, it did repeat. I got up in my head so much, wanting someone to *want* me, and she was always there. At the beginning of the night, I told her to let me be, but by the time I'd downed a few drinks, when she was still by my side...

I shuddered.

Olanda represented my weakness, and I couldn't ignore the fact that she never had more than one or two drinks. She stayed sober and knowingly disrespected what I'd said before the alcohol.

"Do you have someone else with you?" she asked.

I flicked my gaze toward Leighton and Kiara without meaning to. Her eyes followed and she laughed. "Come on, let me take your mind off her. I know she's your scent match's sister, but you can't stay this obsessed forever."

I shrugged my shoulders so aggressively it shook her off, barely holding down the rumble of my growl. Prior to the live feed of Leighton facing down a criminal, that's what she was to me: my scent match's sister. Now she was so much more than that.

Yet, I couldn't fucking tell anyone.

Maybe coming had been a bad idea, but I wouldn't take it back.

"I'm not obsessed, Olanda. What I am is not interested in you. You'd be better off finding someone else to hang off of tonight."

She stared at me in blatant shock. Her leg was pressed to mine and I shifted away from the touch, burying myself against the far arm of the couch as discreetly as possible.

I'd never felt so itchy and uncomfortable before in her presence, but my mind was whirling now. What if she'd done what she did to me, to someone else?

Like Kiara.

I would be furious, so why wasn't I furious for myself?

"Are you serious?" she asked.

"Dead serious," I muttered, clenching my teeth.

With a huff, she stood. Finally. Her scent was cloying—if she'd been an omega, I would have had to cover my nose by now. It was a close call as it was.

"What the hell has gotten into you, Dash? We used to have so much fun."

I did have fun. Too much, with people I never gave a fuck about because they never gave a fuck about me. I wore my charm as a shield. Usually, I never would have said something so mean to her, whether it was running through my head or not.

I didn't know if I should come up with a bullshit answer or call her out for her past actions. Before I could decide, I was overwhelmed by the comforting weight of a familiar aura.

"I believe he said he didn't want to have fun with you," Leighton said coolly. Her hand latched around Olanda's bicep and she placed herself between us. "So why are you still here?"

My former bedmate's eyes widened the tiniest bit in surprise. She pulled herself from Leighton's grip, stumbling back into Mercury. He had a glass of wine in his hand, which he tossed back in one gulp as he moved Olanda farther away from me.

"There's no need to be so rude about it," she said. "I was asking why."

"You're not entitled to that information," Leighton said.

"I think I deserve—"

"No, you don't. I'd prefer not to start a scene, but I will."

Leighton didn't look prepared to start a scene. She wore a pair of white high heels, with her weight casually to one side. Her arms were draped along her sides, a picture of casual elegance. Any 'scene' would mess up her perfectly straightened black hair, and that would be a shame because it looked stunning on her.

Her aura was the only sign that she would fight a bitch.

It trembled, a bit. Kind of like how my aura flared outward when I was furious and had less of a handle on control. It was a threat, and if Olanda didn't feel it there was nothing that could save her from whatever Leighton planned to do.

Olanda did feel it.

Or she simply decided I wasn't worth her time. With another huff and a glare at me, she wandered back out to the dance floor in search of some other poor sap.

I expected the tension to drop when she'd vanished from sight, but it didn't. Leighton's aura continued to shudder.

An icy blanket draped over me when I realized I was as much the target as Olanda was. My skin broke out in goosebumps, but my cock throbbed in anticipation.

Have I finally done something bad enough for her to react?

I'd been waiting. I'd done a lot of bad things, so it was only a matter of time.

"Dash, why are you here?" Leighton asked without turning to face me.

"I'm always here on Sundays."

My cocky response was not appreciated. She growled and I chanced a glance at Kiara.

The little omega was sitting in the booth with the Ashby pack, but everyone's attention was on this scene. Her cheeks were flushed and her hand was resting on her hip. On her knife, like she was seconds away from using it.

Fuck. That was why Leighton had intervened. Maybe it wasn't because she was possessive over me, but because Kiara was. I should have gotten rid of Olanda faster.

"You've put a lot on the line to keep to your routine."

She finally turned to me. I swallowed, my throat dry as I scrambled for the glass of water I had beside me. A few gulps later and she was right in front of me, glaring down.

"Wouldn't it be more suspicious if I hadn't come?" I asked.

"Maybe. But you knew you were going to get hit on here. You spend your time banging any beta who will spread her legs. Did you seriously think I was going to stand by and watch someone rub themselves all over you?"

"I was getting rid of her."

"Then why do you smell like honeysuckle and apples?"

I inhaled sharply. Olanda's scent was everywhere, but Leighton's was so much stronger. "It will fade."

"You shouldn't smell like it in the first fucking place. Stand up."

It felt like her words pulled me up by a string on the top of my head. We ended up chest to chest, mere inches separating us.

The bulge in my pants was so thick it brushed against her, just like her breasts brushed against my chest. Her hand came around the back of my neck and she pulled my head closer until her lips were even with my ear.

"For the record, I'm furious I have to do this."

Vanilla cream created a halo around my head the next second when she brushed her chin against my neck.

A scent mark.

She'd marked me like I'd marked her.

It was almost enough to have me coming in my pants—which was an absurd reaction. This shouldn't be this arousing, but with her...

I moaned. She moved back. "My mother is going to hear about this little stunt, so you'd better fucking find something to shut her down. Got it?"

I would do literally anything she asked in that moment. My head bobbed and she sighed. She was back in the booth beside Kiara before I could process what had happened.

Honeysuckle and apples were only a memory.

There was only Leighton and an oppressive need to go jerk off in the washroom.

Mercury shoved me back down onto the couch before I could make my move to leave, though. He placed his empty wine glass on the table beside us and sat down with one leg crossed casually over the other. "No way," he said. "You get to suffer."

"I didn't realize you were such a fucking sadist," I grumbled. "I thought you swung the other way."

He rolled his eyes, staring at the women on their date with the Ashby pack. "I don't take pleasure in it, but you deserve some pain in your life."

"Asshole," I grumbled under my breath.

Regardless, I didn't try to argue. I let my head spin and my senses absorb Leighton's claim, watching the two of them with a fixation usually reserved for short-lived hobbies.

There would be nothing short-lived about my obsession with them. It would never end.

I already knew that.

THIRTY-SEVEN

LEIGHTON

The Ashby pack didn't say a word about the incident with Dash. I couldn't tell if my aura scared them off, or if they really didn't give a fuck.

Could be either.

Cordian was a pro at obscuring how he truly felt. Hideki and Noel weren't as skilled—both were angry. I wasn't a fucking mind reader, unfortunately, so I couldn't tell why.

My arm wrapped around Kiara's shoulders when I slid back into the booth. I pinched her bicep discreetly and she released her death grip on the knife. Her shaky inhale proved I was right to intervene. It was either that, or Kiara stabbing that beta woman.

Possibly in the neck.

"Is there anything you'd like to talk about?" I said politely into the silence. "We're supposed to be getting to know each other."

I'd rather I'd never met them in the first place, but I had to be cordial. I *was* being cordial, damn it. This was the best I could do.

"What do you and Kiara enjoy doing with your spare time?" Cordian asked.

He was good at playing along at this farce of civility, I'd give him that. None of the pack were keen to get handsy. For the most part, they weren't even wanting to make conversation.

I was suspicious they were here for the same reason we were—blackmail.

There was no obvious reason to blackmail their pack to bond with Kiara and I. She was supposed to be sold, and that was the opposite.

Grabbing my phone, I sent a quick text to Ambrose informing him of my guess. He could get started on figuring out the background here. It was supposed to be Dash's job, but of course...

My eyes met his.

He hadn't stopped watching since I left him behind, drenched in my scent.

I realized belatedly that Kiara hadn't answered Cordian's question, leaving us in yet another silence. Looking at her, I tilted my head to the side. I was careful to ensure my questions were simply questions, and not commands. I was still getting used to the power I had over my bondmate, and how easy it was to use. "Dove? Do you have an answer?"

Her sapphire blue eyes widened. "Um..."

What had she done when she lived with her father? She had to have hobbies, especially if she was never allowed to leave the house she grew up in.

"I enjoyed sewing," she said.

Her answer was given to me and not the Ashby pack, and she spoke in the past tense.

"Would you like to sew again?" I asked.

She shrugged. Her fingers danced over the concealed weapon.

I couldn't say I was surprised her chosen hobby involved needles.

"I can get you a machine," I said.

It would be at the house by the morning. Dash would make sure of it. My wealth wouldn't be enough to have a sewing machine delivered in the middle of the night, but his sure as fuck was.

"I never had a machine. Father wouldn't—" She paused, gaze flicking across the table at the bored looking Ashby pack. "All of my sewing was done by hand."

"And would you like to sew again?" I pushed.

Her bottom lip pulled between her teeth, and she gave a quick nod.

I sent another text to Ambrose. She would be getting a machine, along with a hand sewing set and all the fabrics an omega could dream of.

"What do you do in your spare time?" Kiara asked.

It was directed at me. Not the Ashby pack.

I was as hesitant to answer as she had been, for different reasons.

"I don't have spare time," I admitted.

"But you've had nothing but spare time since we met," she said, her eyebrows drawing together.

"I haven't been working, dove."

Not on anything that wasn't required. Soren and my mother took precedence. I despised them both, but the tasks they gave me had to be completed. It was forced upon me.

Everyone else, though? I'd turned down jobs left and right, and Liberty was getting paid double time to deal with the ongoing stuff. She barely needed any guidance—and thank fuck, because I hadn't had time.

Then again, a lot of my contracts were cancelled the moment my arrest hit the news. I doubted she had much to do anymore.

She was doing me a favour by not forcing business updates on me.

"Oh," Kiara said softly. "I'm sorry."

"Spending time with you is my preference anyway."

Coconut and chocolate made me wet and desperate, but I didn't like how the Ashby pack was getting a hit of it. I caught them shifting in their seats, their expressions caught between disinterested and appreciative.

Kiara liked having me to herself, it appeared. This close to her heat, everything seemed to set her off.

How long did she have before she was a needy mess? Should we consider heat blockers? I should have thought about it sooner, but I wasn't used to dealing with omegas.

"Excuse us," I said.

I hauled Kiara from the bench seat and she squeaked. The Loranger pack had a private room here, exclusively for their use. I wasn't sure which one it was, but I believed they were labelled—besides, their scents were a siren's call to me. I'd find the right one.

We whisked by the bouncer without a question from him. He'd seen my display with Dash, and it wasn't his job to ask questions.

The hallway with the private rooms was long and straight, doors lining either side. No sounds came from inside the rooms. They were fully soundproof. The establishment didn't want you having sex in them—in theory, a VIP server could pop in at any time—but they didn't do much to stop it, either.

"Where are we going?" Kiara asked.

Her scent was spiking more with every second. How much slick was wetting her thighs right now?

Without answering, I trailed down the hall until I found the door with Dash's scent all over the knob. The Loranger pack name was visible on a small plaque, even with the low light. I wasn't sure if it would be unlocked, but it was.

I pushed her inside in front of me and pulled the door closed.

Sliding the deadbolt home wouldn't do much—all the servers had keys—but it would give us a few precious seconds before interruptions.

Then I took in the room. It smelled like Dash, sure. But it also had other scents on the fabric of these lounges. The private areas that were rentable were cleaned frequently with scent dampeners, but they didn't need to use those heavy-duty products here. Only Dash's pack used the space.

Kiara let out a low whine, her expression flashing with pure rage.

"Let's make it smell like you, dove. Only you."

"And you." She sat back on the couch, her pink dress contrasting the red velvet.

I knelt between her legs, watching her cheeks flush as she shook her head. "Don't you want me to make you come?" I asked.

"Can I do you first?"

I glanced to the door, knowing we might have a limited amount of time. The omega should go first. Then again, if I made her come and then she made me, I might have to give her a second orgasm. She loved giving pleasure almost as much as she loved receiving it.

Hitching my tight dress up to my hips and dropping my panties to the floor, I crawled onto her lap. The material of her dress was itchy against my thighs and where it brushed my sensitive lips. Kiara's hands landed on my ass.

"You're going to leave a wet spot on my dress."

"I don't get as slick as you. I'd rather your dress be a little damp than ruin your makeup."

"Aren't you going to ruin your makeup?"

I smirked. "I keep my wits about me a lot better than you, dove. I'll keep myself as neat as possible."

She flushed and squirmed, but brought one hand around to brush her fingers across my folds. The touch was featherlight and hesitant, but I groaned all the same. Her scent was almost enough to get me off all on its own. I never thought I would have such a strong reaction to an omega.

"I'm not sure if I know how," she admitted quietly. "Isn't it easier to make you come with my tongue?"

I cupped her cheek in my hand and brushed her with my scent. Both of us made little sounds of pleasure. We would eliminate every other scent in here by the time we were done.

"You've been a quick learner so far."

"I mean... I haven't done much. It's mainly been people doing things to me."

Shrugging, I brought my free hand down to guide hers. Together we put a firm pressure on my clit and I rolled my hips, grinding against our fingers.

She watched in barely constrained awe. "This feels like cheating. You're still doing all the work."

"There's no such thing as cheating at sex, dove. We'll both come at the end. How we get there isn't important."

Her lip pulled between her teeth. Almost all the gloss was gone by now, her nerves keeping her fidgety. She was about to comment about it again—I could tell. I didn't give her a chance. My lips pressed to hers, which parted immediately to give me entrance.

She tasted sweet, like coconut with a hint of alcoholic bite. The coconut martini I'd ordered her was a perfect compliment to her scent.

Kiara went limp with desire, moaning against me, but my hand on hers gave me a solid surface to ride. It wasn't going to take long for me to come like this. She had no need to be worried.

"I should—" she gasped against my lips, but I cut her off.

"Stop talking."

The forceful command hung in the air for a second before

dropping. Most omegas might have been angry at me using the dark bond to boss them around in the bedroom, but not her.

Her pupils were so blown out they almost engulfed the blue of her irises. A low keening sound came from deep in her chest and she tried to buck her hips, in desperate search of friction.

"You should do what I tell you," I murmured. "Keep your hand right here." I squeezed it for emphasis. "And let me come for you."

All complaints had left her—finally. She tilted her head back and parted her lips, waiting for me to kiss her. There were hints of my red lipstick on her, but they'd be easy to tidy up.

Connecting us again, I worked myself up until her fingers were sliding through my folds in the mess of my juices. There would be a wet spot on her skirt, for sure.

"Are you going to come?" Kiara asked desperately, barely breaking the kiss. "Am I doing it right?"

I groaned. "Fuck, dove, there's no way for you to do it wrong. Slide a finger inside me, all the way, and curl it towards you."

I released her hand, stroking my clit myself as she did as I'd asked. My eyes were crossing with the orgasm before she managed to find my g-spot, so when she curled her finger like I'd asked...

"Fuck, Kiara."

My hips didn't stop moving until the last dredges of the orgasm had washed over me, nearly taking me into fucking unconsciousness. Her scent did things to me that I never could have anticipated. It made every orgasm with her earth-shattering.

"Alpha." Kiara's whine was the only thing that pulled me out of the post orgasmic haze.

She still needed me. Desperately.

"I got you," I purred, sliding off her lap. "Come."

The chaise lounge beside the couch was large enough for me to lay down on, and there was still room for her to straddle my head. I moved and positioned her trembling body until she was exactly where I wanted her. Layers of tulle covered me, obscuring my view of everything, including the task at hand.

It didn't matter, because I already knew her pussy like the back of my hand.

I was obsessed with her, and it was too early to say it back, but I was probably in love with her too.

Kiara didn't hesitate to strip her panties and settle her pussy down over my face, drenching me with her slick. I was wrong—there was no way I was going to come out of this without looking like a fucking mess.

Since I was going to be messy regardless, I might as well make it worth my while.

For her first orgasm, I only used my tongue. She rode it to completion within a minute, crying out my name as she reached her peak.

The second, I plunged one finger into her tight hole, curling it like I'd instructed her to do to me. When she came that time, she tried to lift off me.

I grabbed her thighs and held her down, lapping at her oversensitive clit. "Leighton—"

Her complaint cut off with a moan, her pleasure flooding through our bond. It was so easy to make her come. I couldn't come three times in a row without a break, but she only took five minutes to scream her way to another orgasm.

We'd been in this room for far too long. Fifteen minutes? Twenty? But there were still hints of beta scents in here, hiding beneath the hazy layer of coconut chocolate.

Plus, I knew if I could feel her pleasure through the bond... so could Dash.

And wasn't that the perfect torture for him?

She squirmed above me, trying to shake off my grip. I kissed her inner thighs, one at a time. "Are you going to let me up?" she asked, her voice a mere wisp of sound.

"No. You're going to come again."

Her little gasp was adorable. "No way."

"Yes. You're an omega, and I think you're close to heat... Aren't you?"

She shifted, and I imagined she was wringing her hands together, her lip pulled between her teeth again. "Um, I think so."

There were implications to that being the case, but now wasn't the time to think about them. "One more orgasm will take the edge off, then."

It may actually make it worse and push her closer. It was probably safer to leave her be, but I couldn't.

Kiara's slick was like a drug, begging me to keep going, continuing to taste her. Her emotions were a drug too, the heavy pleasure with a single thread of nervousness through it all.

My tongue slid along her slit from her clit all the way back until it was rimming her ass. She yelped, panic flowing through the bond with enough potency that I pulled back.

"Do you not like it?" I asked, squeezing her thighs in what I hoped was a comforting manner.

"No—I mean, yes, but... What are you doing?"

I grinned, wishing I could see her face.

I hadn't thought about it, but it made sense if she hadn't known this was an option. Her childhood had been sheltered, and I was her first for everything, except the firsts Dash had stolen.

"If you like it, I'll show you what I'm doing."

"I—"

Her body jolted and she let out a short scream when the door flew open. I tensed beneath her, but it was short-lived, because a hint of spring rain and peaches filtered through the haze of her scent.

He really didn't know how to listen, did he? I'd been taunting him on purpose, but he should have known to have some restraint. People would talk now that he'd followed us down this hallway. People were already talking enough.

"Dash..." Kiara's whimper was almost quiet enough I didn't hear it beneath the layers of her dress. "You had other women in here."

Her accusation had me growling my shared annoyance, but then I turned my attention back to her. Now that he was here, he'd get more torture—he could barely see any of her with the dress in the way. He could taste her pleasure in the air, though.

My tongue circled her asshole, knowing I would feel it if she truly didn't enjoy it.

She loved it, letting out a moan as Dash's footsteps brought him closer.

"I didn't know you yet, little omega," Dash said placatingly. "I would never bring other women in here now."

"What about that bitch who was touching you?" Her scathing complaint was lost in a moan when I plunged two fingers inside her pussy.

Dash was close enough to touch her, but he didn't. He knew better. "I was getting rid of her. She wasn't going to end up in here, I promise."

"But she's been in here."

He hesitated but didn't lie. "Yes."

"And now you smell like her."

"I smell more like Leighton than anything else."

"And you're hiding my marks."

Kiara's irritation was rising with every statement she volleyed at him. So was her pleasure. Her hips ground on my face with new vigour that she'd been too shy to show before. I explored her ass with my tongue and enjoyed the show.

"It wouldn't have been safe for me to come in here with your marks on display," he pleaded. "We don't want your family to know that you've claimed me."

"Why does *that* matter?"

She knew exactly why, but was furious all the same. Her instincts were warring with common sense. Unsurprising, with her heat on the horizon.

I wasn't able to stop her when she surged forward and grabbed Dash. Her body came to settle right back over me and I groaned, squeezing her thigh in my hand. She was going to do something irrational, but the alpha side of me loved to experience it with her. Her peak was close, I could tell, so I focused on that while she manhandled the other alpha.

"Everyone needs to know that you're mine," Kiara muttered.

Her scent got more potent. She was scent marking him.

Dash groaned. "Fuck. I shouldn't have come in here."

"Did you not want me to mark you?" Her voice went high-pitched at the end—a bit of righteous omega fury.

"No!" Dash exclaimed. "Christ. You know there are circumstances—"

"Come here."

Dash's scent was all over me, almost as much as Kiara's was. It was difficult to focus on my task when my own pleasure was building in my core, but I'd started this game. I was going to finish it. Needed to finish it, because maybe once she came again Kiara would settle.

I couldn't see what they were doing, but Dash moaned huskily at the exact second Kiara's pussy throbbed with her release. She cried out and arched her back, grinding down against me as slick drenched my face and neck. I was a mess, but with her desperate need receding I had to admit it was worth it.

When I'd moved Kiara's limp form off me and extracted myself from under her skirts, I found Dash slumped at the end of the chaise lounge. His eyes were half-lidded, a wet spot on his pants from his cum. There was a bite mark on each of his forearms.

She was the most possessive omega I'd ever met—and that was saying something. I fucking loved it, and from the way Dash looked reverently at the claims, I guessed that he did too.

Licking my lips clean of her slick, I reached out and brushed a hand across Kiara's hair. It was only a little mussed, unlike mine. "How did you like having your ass eaten, dove?"

Dash stiffened, and so did his cock. His recent release didn't do anything to stop him from perking up.

Kiara flushed. "It was really good," she mumbled.

I looked at Dash—I was sitting between them, cramped onto this chaise lounge that wasn't meant for three people. "I had to try it before Dash stole another first from me. Come here."

He surged forward, freezing when he got within inches of me. His breaths were heavy, gaze darting down to my lips and back up. "What do you need me for?" he asked.

Grabbing his chin, I leaned forward until my lips were right against his. Mine were swollen and red from my time under Kiara's skirt, and his were pillow soft, ready to be kissed. I leaned forward and did it, letting him groan into my mouth and taste Kiara on my tongue.

He wanted to keep kissing forever, but I moved him back with a smirk. "I just needed to taunt you. I'm going to get cleaned up, and then Kiara and I are going to go back out and continue our date."

Dash's eyes were glazed and he kept licking his lips, even after I'd gotten up and wandered over to the small sink and vanity mirror in the corner to tidy up.

I did the best I could to clean myself and hide the evidence of her pleasure—though there was nothing that could hide her scent. Nor did I want to cover that up.

Dash had to help my omega up and she leaned on me when I

came to take over. I helped slide her panties back up her legs. Then we left Dash by himself in the room. He was staring at the puddle of slick she'd left behind on the lounge like he wanted to lick it up.

It was a more successful tease than I could have imagined.

THIRTY-EIGHT

KIARA

It was a miracle I could walk.

My legs were so shaky Dash had to hold me up as Leighton fixed her smeared lipstick and wiped away the evidence of my slick. When he'd let go, it had only been because my alpha came to take over the job. I leaned on her as we walked back out to the main lounge.

"I'm going to get you some water and a snack," Leighton said, depositing me on the bench seat we'd left behind.

I glanced at the Ashby pack, but she didn't. She placed a kiss on my mussed hair and left me to make small talk on my own.

Maybe I would get lucky and they wouldn't say a word.

Cordian cleared his throat. With our scents layered onto each other, the alpha would have to be stupid to not realize what we'd been doing. I'd gotten the impression he wasn't stupid.

"I'm curious," he said. "Why do you want to enter into this arrangement? No offense intended, but the two of you don't seem... keen on adding members to your pack."

His gaze flicked to Mercury. Dash had yet to emerge from the private room. With the state Leighton had left him in, I imagined I knew why he was taking his time coming out.

"I don't."

With my brain hazy with pre-heat hormones and the aftershocks of coming four times in twenty minutes, I didn't have the capacity to lie.

Cordian faced me head on again, his eyes widened for one infinitely short second. All his efforts to conceal his surprise were wasted. His packmates gave it all away. The irritation I'd been feeling from Hideki and Noel the whole night faded away into mild confusion.

"You don't?"

"This arrangement is the last thing I want to do," I said.

"And yet, circumstances necessitated it," Leighton said, appearing with water and a small plate of salad and chicken. I hadn't seen anyone else in the club with food, but she'd somehow managed to get some for me. "We have no plans to deny you," she continued.

I slid over to give her room on the bench seat, watching the Ashby pack's expressions fall.

They wanted this as little as we did.

How odd. What was the purpose of conning both of us into doing this? I'd assumed I would be given to a pack who wanted me. There was some kind of exchange going on beneath the surface, but I wasn't sure what it entailed.

"Of course. Our bonding is important," Cordian said smoothly.

Too smoothly.

He was too perfect—he had to be hiding something.

"And why do you want to enter into the arrangement?" I asked, throwing his own question back at him.

His teeth clenched for a single second. Then his shoulder shrugged, too small of a movement to be intentional. It might be his tell—like Leighton's tell was the way she clacked her nails when she lied. His tell was that twitch of his shoulder.

"We've always wanted an omega, but the scent matching services didn't find a match for us. Instead of waiting longer, we decided an arrangement was the best option."

Cordian twitched again at the second part. Maybe he wasn't lying about the matching services. I knew about those, vaguely. They gave you a bunch of scents to test out in an attempt to find a scent match. Only rich people could use them, both increasing the chance of finding a scent match and increasing the likelihood of that match being... desirable.

Of the same station and level of wealth.

"I didn't wait for a scent match either," I said.

He glanced between Leighton and I, but I couldn't figure out his opinion on our dark bond. Did he find it disgusting? Intriguing? There was nothing, not even a twitch of his shoulder. He had an impeccable handle on himself.

"You two seem like a perfect match regardless," he complimented, "so I doubt you're missing out."

"We're not missing out," Leighton said.

A brief stab of guilt ran through me, because I'd taken that from her. The ability to have a scent match. Had she even wanted one, though? She hadn't been in a pack, or registered as silver status, so she wasn't able to find one as it was.

"Kiara is a stunning bondmate. The best one I could have possibly asked for."

I flushed at the praise from Leighton, placing my hand on her thigh in hopes it would steady my pounding pulse.

She took over the conversation from there, leaving me able to stay blissfully silent. I watched our companions, noting everything I could about how they acted. Cordian spoke for them, Hideki was the most antagonistic—though not openly—and Noel was hard to pin. Something akin to guilt crossed his features every once in a while.

"Would you be upset if we ended the evening here, ladies?" Cordian said after a painful amount of small talk.

There were no clocks in the club, but I had to guess we'd been here for hours already. I tried not to show how excited I was to be leaving. Unfortunately, I wasn't Cordian or Leighton. There was no hiding my smile.

"Not at all," Leighton said, sweeping onto her feet.

She helped me out of the booth next. The Ashby pack were just as quick to vacate. None of them made an attempt at a hug or even a handshake. They were almost averse to touching me. I was grateful. My skin was covered in Leighton and Dash's scents. They would only mar that.

"I'll reach out to set up a second date," Cordian said. He offered a hand to Leighton. She grasped it for a mere second before releasing. "Have a wonderful night."

They left before we did.

Dash had made it back to the couch he'd been occupying. He tried to stand when we were left alone, but Mercury forced him back into place.

"Let's go," Leighton murmured. "They'll meet us at home. They've made it their home too, at this point."

Her words weren't really bitter—just enough that she could pretend she wasn't pleased to have them there. I didn't call her out on it, nodding and letting her lead me through the busy lounge and back out into the night.

"Mercury is usually better at keeping a handle on Dash," Ambrose grumbled.

He'd greeted us with a snack when we walked in. Something

more substantial than the chicken and salad Leighton had gotten to refuel me at the club: ice cream. The snack of dreams, one I hadn't been allowed much of when I lived with my father.

"I do think he was trying to get rid of the beta woman," Leighton said.

She didn't sound a hundred percent convinced.

I was confident he was trying to remove her, but that wasn't enough. He was mine, and someone else had touched him. I wished my mark had been on display, because the bitch might have thought twice.

The rational part of my brain understood why he'd covered it, but the feral part that ran on instinct was furious he had. I'd bitten him *for a reason*. So no one else would dare to stake a claim. He'd disrespected the bonds by covering them up.

Which was why I'd been forced to give him two more.

"He shouldn't have gone at all, but none of us could have stopped that," Ambrose said with a sigh. "Hopefully, your mother isn't too furious."

"She will be." Leighton sighed, running her hands through her hair. "I'm tired, dove. Do you want to go to sleep?"

I shrugged, glancing back toward the door. Dash and Mercury had yet to arrive. I wouldn't be able to sleep until they did. They needed to be here, where there were no betas to try and claim them behind my back.

"I'd like to shower first," I said.

It was a good enough excuse. My skin was sticky with sweat and slick, and I'd rather wake up clean in the morning. Leighton flicked her gaze to Ambrose. "Of course. Ambrose, help her?"

My cheeks flamed. "I don't need help," I squeaked.

"You can't get that dress off on your own." Leighton smirked. "I figured I would shower too, so we can both go to bed clean. You use the bathroom attached to the office."

The dresses lace-up back seemed to taunt me. I couldn't

detangle the threads on my own. Maybe it would be better to slice the ties right off, but the dress was too pretty. It would be a shame to ruin it.

It would also be a shame to fall over myself in Ambrose's presence, but I wasn't used to being naked around him. He'd had his head between my thighs, but I'd been another level of desperate. I'd laid on his chest beside the pool, but that touch wasn't sexual.

How could it be anything but sexual with him undressing me?

Avoiding eye contact with the big alpha, I stomped into the office and through to the bathroom. My made-up face stared back at me in the mirror. With the layers of foundation, you couldn't see my embarrassed flush that well.

I pressed the back of my hand to my cheek.

The flush was still hot, though.

Ambrose appeared in the doorway, leaning casually against it as he scanned me from head to toe. "I'm sure Leighton will help you, if you insist," he said.

Biting my bottom lip, I shook my head. "No, it's fine. You can."

He hesitated for another second. That dark gaze peered into the deepest recesses of my soul, picking apart my motivations piece by piece. Why didn't I want him undressing me? I didn't even know why it felt like such an embarrassing thing, but it did.

No one except Leighton had ever undressed me.

Ambrose decided he liked whatever he saw in my soul. His footsteps—surprisingly soft for such a large man—brought him into the small bathroom until he stood behind me.

My breath caught. I saw both of us in the mirror, and he dwarfed me. His head towered above mine, brown hair pushed back from his face. His shoulders were immensely wider than mine, and his arms and chest bulkier.

He gently brushed the hair away from my neck, exposing my bare back to him.

"Lean forward, princess. Just a little bit. There's not much room in here."

I should have thought about that. I should have waited in the office for him to do this part. The undoing of the corset laces didn't have to be done in the bathroom... but maybe it was worth it, to watch in the mirror. His expression was set in concentration when I leaned forward, giving him space to work.

I held my breath waiting for his warm, rough hands to touch my skin.

They didn't.

He grabbed only the fabric, never any bare part of me. I stopped breathing any time he got close. I would feel the warmth coming closer only to vanish, leaving me bereft of contact I was increasingly desperate for.

As the top of the dress loosened, bit by bit, I grew more desperate.

Just once.

He *needed* to touch me.

I'd opened myself up to it by allowing him this close. I'd been prepared despite my nerves, and now he wasn't doing it.

"I think that's done, little omega," he rumbled.

He began to move back.

I panicked. "I need more help."

Our gazes locked in the mirror. His lips were quirked—he knew exactly what he was doing to me. Was he going to make me ask? Fuck, he was, wasn't he? He made Leighton ask. I'd heard it. It was ingrained in my memory in vivid detail.

"Do you?"

"Please."

"Alright."

He grabbed the fabric at my hips, slowly but surely working it down. I shrugged the sleeves down my arms because he hadn't made a move to help with those. He would have to touch me for that, but he was adamant about not letting me have so much as a caress.

When my dress pooled on the tile floor, he tried again to move back.

I darted out my hand to grab his arm, trying in vain to pull him closer.

"I don't think you need help with anything else," he murmured.

A low keening sound came from deep in my chest. It was sheer desperation. I didn't even know why I wanted this so much. It wasn't necessarily that I wanted to come. Leighton had taken care of me so thoroughly in the private room that I didn't need to.

It was the touch I needed.

Touch from *my* alpha.

Fuck, they were all mine. Even Mercury, in all his grumpiness.

"Whining won't get you anywhere." He pulled his arm away from me.

All-encompassing panic washed over me again. "Please touch me."

His retreat stopped abruptly. The slight smirk morphed to a grin as he crowded me up against the sink. My bare torso hit the cool counter, and I sucked in a breath.

Ambrose made it so he was everywhere, all at once. His hands landed on my hips. His chest pressed against my back. He even leaned his head down to press his lips to my ear.

And I could watch it all through the mirror.

"Good, princess. I was waiting for that please."

He hadn't stopped looking at me in the mirror. Neither had I. I couldn't. If I looked away, I didn't know what would happen.

"Thank you," I whispered.

What the hell was I thanking him for?

His teases were infuriating, but I could understand why Leighton liked them so much.

"You're welcome, little omega." He nipped at my ear with his teeth and I groaned. "Let's get you in the shower."

I'd forgotten about the shower.

That was the whole point of this, and I'd forgotten. I was grateful for the makeup still covering most of my embarrassment.

"OK," I said, reaching back for the clasp of my bra.

Ambrose's hand caught my wrist, shoving it down. I gasped.

"You were begging for my help. You're not doing that by yourself."

His hands lifted from my hips, skating up my sides until he could cup and lift both of my tits in his palms. With his arms wrapped around me, he was forced closer. A bulge in his pants pressed against the small of my back.

Knot.

My body wanted it, but a shiver of fear washed over me. I'd never taken one before—never been penetrated by anything more than fingers. That would change, soon. It was natural for an omega to want a knot, and my heat was coming.

But Tobias' words floated around in my head, trying to tear my comfort to pieces.

"Alphas are feral beasts. If you think you're going to enjoy your heat, think again. They'll tear you to pieces, little sis, because omegas are only warm holes to them."

He was wrong. A fucking liar. I'd known it then, and I was doubly certain now that I'd met these alphas.

It didn't stop the doubts from swirling.

Ambrose squeezed my tits, drawing me from the panic. I shouldn't be panicking. A knot wasn't going to happen right now. He was putting me in the shower, for fuck's sake. That was all.

"Princess, don't get lost in your head while you're with me," he said quietly. "Focus on me, and tell me to stop if you're uncomfortable."

His grip loosened and I panicked again, shaking my head. "No. Keep going."

He plucked at my nipples through the thin fabric of my bra, brushing his lips across the top of my head. "Alright. Let's get you in the shower."

He made it sound like it was a simple task, but that wasn't how he treated it. He took his time with me, fondling and caressing and making slick pool between my legs. By the time my bra was on the counter, my breasts freed, I was aching for an orgasm.

One I wasn't going to get.

Though he hadn't said it aloud, I knew there were no plans for anything sexual. He was going to undress me as sensually as possible, put me in the shower, and then put me to bed. I might be able to beg Leighton to make me come, but something about that felt wrong.

I wanted to listen to him.

If he said no coming tonight, it didn't feel right to go behind his back.

My panties were removed with an equal amount of care. He stroked his fingers along my pussy, but didn't give me enough stimulation to really matter. When they hit the floor he was on his knees on the tile, inhaling deeply to get a hit of my scent.

"Can you shower by yourself?" he asked.

He was the one on his knees, and yet I was the one who trembled. I was the one who was controlled.

"Yes," I said.

Ambrose stood, his palms grazing my bare flesh one more time. He pressed a kiss to my cheek and smiled. More of a smirk, really, because he knew he was in control. He'd made me beg for his touch and hadn't given me anywhere near enough.

"I'll see you in the morning then, princess."

I was still catching my breath when he vanished from the bathroom, closing the door softly behind him.

I showered in a daze, washing off the day with scent free soap. He was in the kitchen with his pack when I left the office and scurried to the primary bedroom, wearing nothing but a towel. I didn't stop to check in, or say hello. It was comfort enough that they were all here, and now I would be able to sleep.

Without putting on a stitch of clothing, I crawled into bed beside Leighton. She hadn't bothered with clothes either and was already halfway asleep.

Ambrose had taken his time with me.

"Goodnight, dove," she murmured, curling around me the way we'd taken to doing.

"Goodnight," I whispered.

For a while, I stared at the far wall, calming my pounding heart. And then, I whispered into the dark silence. "I want them with me during my heat. Them and you."

I didn't think she was awake. I thought my admission would be lost to the god of sleep, and no one would ever know.

But her mouth brushed against my skin and she chuckled. "Don't worry. I know."

She pulled me closer and I let the warmth of her body lull me, finally, to sleep.

THIRTY-NINE

LEIGHTON

The violent vibrations of my cell phone on the nightstand were enough to jerk me into wakefulness, but luckily not enough to wake Kiara. With a quiet curse, I grabbed the phone and hustled out into the hallway.

I was still yanking on my robe when I answered the call.

"What did I say about the Loranger pack?"

My mother's voice was chillingly cold. Had I ever infuriated her enough to get this tone?

The last time I remembered it, she'd used it on my brother. It was when he'd met his current pack—when she'd been forced to confront the fact that he was rejecting the Loranger pack (and their accompanying wealth) for real. For good.

"I believe you said not to associate," I said.

My voice was still husky with sleep. I padded down the hall, veering into the kitchen and settling onto a bar stool. The French doors to the living room were closed, so this was the place where I was least likely to disrupt anyone else.

"If you were listening to me the first time, why the fuck did you scent mark him in the middle of the lounge? It's on the front page of the gossip columns."

There was no explanation she would accept. It was in my best interests to apologize and beg forgiveness.

Dash better have found some of her secrets by now.

"He showed up on his own, and I reacted strongly. I apologize. It was instinct."

Mother hadn't been ruled by instinct for a single second in her entire life. Sometimes I wondered if she even knew what instincts were. She didn't have any of the motherly kind, that was for damn certain. I doubted she had any omega instincts either.

My fathers simply existed. They didn't care for her, nor she for them.

"It was unacceptable. We were supposed to be fixing your image, Leighton. Not making it worse."

I didn't respond. As expected, she kept going.

Oddly, her cool tone shifted as she spoke, becoming more and more... I wanted to say desperate. It couldn't be. Desperation had to be a trick, something funky happening with the sound coming through the phone. Edith Winston was never desperate.

In the middle of her tirade, the French door swung open. It hit the counter so hard I was surprised it didn't shatter, revealing a grinning Dash.

He was halfway through a sentence before he saw the phone up against my ear. I made a sharp cutting motion with my hand, and he snapped his lips shut.

Finally, he listened.

Was that the first time ever? Probably.

"You're clearly not listening to me," Mother said.

"Of course I was. Understandably, you're furious and you have my apology. It won't happen again. Regardless of what happened, the Ashby pack informed me they would be reaching out to set up our next date."

"You are going to publicly state that you have no association with the Loranger pack."

I couldn't help it. I laughed. Muffling it with my hand didn't work, so she must have heard it through the line. "If you insist, I'll do it. However, that's only going to bring a spotlight to the gossip because it will be such an obvious lie, it's laughable. It's exactly what I tell people not to do in situations like this."

She was dead silent. Dash was snickering, bouncing on the balls of his feet with a laptop clutched in his hands. Underneath his eyes were dark smears of colour, but he was invigorated.

It had to mean he found something.

I wanted this bitch off the fucking phone.

The line clicked dead, giving me my wish.

Her hanging up without so much as a complaint was a danger in and of itself, but it didn't matter if we'd made a discovery. I double checked the call was off, then hopped off the bar stool. "Did you find something?" I asked.

"Yes, I—"

I held up a finger. "I'm going to put my phone in the box."

Dash laughed, balancing the laptop on one palm and snatching my phone with his other hand. "Don't worry, sweetheart. The only one bugging you is me. Everything in the house is clean."

I had no idea when he'd had time to check that. He'd probably been sneaking around in the middle of the goddamn night, looking through my shit. It didn't annoy me as much as it should—Dash didn't seem to sleep easily, even when he wasn't hyperfocused on something.

Plus, I trusted him.

Around my home and around my omega.

I sighed. "I don't appreciate you bugging me. What did you find?"

"Your mom is in mountains of debt. Like, Mount Everest levels of it."

He beamed like he was delivering news of a lottery win. I grabbed the laptop from him and placed it on the counter before it fell to its death. Nothing on the screen stood out to me. It was a bunch of numbers and acronyms. I knew the basics of the code bookies used, but this wasn't normal.

"I'm assuming illegal debt, considering this shit is in code?" I asked, trying to tease the information out of him.

The rest came out like a fountain.

"I hacked the Connolly's accountant," he said. "I mean, they have a couple for different parts of their illicit business, but I hacked them all. And this one... this one was a gold mine."

He brushed his finger across the trackpad, clicking on things that made no sense to me.

"Gambling debts. It got me thinking—what would your mother do anything to hide? She would do anything to hide being flat broke. So I discovered that she's flat fucking broke. See that line right there?"

He jabbed the screen hard enough it shimmered.

"That's Edith Winston's debt. All your family's millions? They're fucking gone."

Dash tried to continue, but I stopped him with a hand on his shoulder. "Wait. How are you reading this? I don't see my mother's name anywhere."

Blinking, he clicked to a different tab, where he'd written out line after line after line of words and letters, some of them making absolutely no sense.

"It's a cipher. I thought it was obvious."

"Not all of us spent two months learning ciphers and code breaking," Mercury said with a yawn, coming into the kitchen.

Ambrose was right behind him, equally tired looking. We were all a fucking mess. At least Kiara was getting some good sleep.

"It should be something everyone learns," Dash defended.

Going straight for the coffee pot, Ambrose ruffled Dash's blonde hair on the way past. "Why would we need to learn it when we have you?"

"Are you sure you solved it properly? You could have a bit of a confirmation bias," I said, veering the conversation back on track.

Dash pouted at me. "Well, if you look at this series of numbers, it matches up with this series of letters which coincides with—"

"Actually, forget I asked. I'll trust your expertise on this one." The speed he was flipping tabs with was too fast for me to catch up. If I'd truly doubted him, I could have looked at it myself. My knowledge of ciphers was more base level than his, but I'd spent some time learning them to protect sensitive areas of my business. He said he had it right, though, so I wouldn't check his work.

I had way too much trust in the obsessive playboy alpha.

"Finally. OK, so your mother has been gambling at the Connolly's underground clubs for years. Since your childhood or possibly before, but the digitized records don't go back that far."

I was surprised criminals had digital records at all. The amount of hacks I'd seen while doing my job meant I knew that was risky as fuck. They had to be confident in their cyber security —misplaced confidence, considering a billionaire had gotten into them with a four-week crash course in hacking and eight weeks for code breaking.

"She loses a lot. Every time she goes," Dash continued. "Occasionally she'll win back some money toward the debt. See that?"

He jabbed the screen again. I placed my hand over his and held it, because if this laptop broke, we would be wasting precious minutes to get a new one. He glanced down at our fingers, turning his hand over so they were clasped.

"When she wins, she goes more frequently," he explained. "Multiple days in a row sometimes. She never keeps winning though. This woman is terrible at poker and has horrible luck betting on fights."

"Fights?"

My voice went high pitched. I clutched Dash's hand in a vice grip. Ambrose came up behind me and rubbed my shoulders.

"Yeah, like underground human fights, not super fucked up shit like dog fights or anything," Dash said.

He tried to go deeper into my mother's illicit history, but I wasn't listening anymore. I was reeling.

This was what I should have figured out sooner.

The connection point that made everything make sense.

Edith Winston was a gambler, and she'd bet on the fight that she was holding as blackmail over me right now. She'd been there —I bet she'd figured out a way to take those damn pictures herself.

Pictures of one of my brother's alphas, far before they'd met.

He'd killed someone in that fight, through no fault of his own. The guy was already injured, beaten up from days of cage fights. One wrong hit to the head and he'd gone down, convulsing. Anyone could see it was an accident, even from the photos.

The Gold Pack and Rogue Enforcement Agency wouldn't see it that way, not when the violent alpha who'd killed a man was a rogue.

Dangers to society, rogues were alphas who could break the rules that bound normal alphas. They could go feral, too, their auras turning them into mindless killing machines if they lost control.

My brother's alpha wasn't like that, but he wouldn't be allowed to live his quiet domestic life if the pictures my mother had got out into the world. He'd be imprisoned for life or worse for crimes that a normal alpha would only get a few years in prison for.

Mercury slammed a mug of coffee down in front of me, jolting me from the daze. I wrapped my hand around the handle, realizing my arms were shaking when I tried to bring it to my mouth. All three of them were staring at me, oblivious to the swirling shame and panic that threatened to overcome me.

I'd never wanted a pack bond before.

In this moment, I wished it was that easy. I wished I could open up a bond and let my emotions flow through, letting them experience how I felt. It was impossible to put into words, but I wanted them to know.

I'd never wanted anyone to know my feelings before, either.

"My brother's alpha," I said quietly. "She knows something about him that the world…doesn't. Something they can't."

Dash went stiff, the hand still in mine clenching tightly. "He's a rogue, isn't he?"

My brother's pack had three alphas, but they knew which one. It was obvious when you were aware of the history—and Dash had been obsessive over my brother for the first few years after he was rejected.

A week ago, I would have hesitated. I would never have confirmed that secret to the Loranger pack. They had hated my brother's pack for claiming their scent matched mate when they couldn't.

Today I didn't hesitate.

"Yes."

"That isn't the end of the world. It's not like rogues are tossed in prisons for existing. It would suck, but—"

"And what do they do to rogues that kill people?"

My question hung in a sudden, deathly silence. I cleared my throat, shakily bringing the mug to my lips and taking a huge sip.

"My mother has pictures of him killing someone in an underground fight. I don't know the context. I haven't asked him about it, because my brother and his pack don't know that she has this. I'm trusting that it was an accident and he's worth protecting, but the GPRE don't believe in accidents involving rogues."

"Why was he even in underground fights? I didn't think his situation was that bad before he met your brother," Ambrose said.

I laughed. It started as one short sound but devolved into full on guffaws.

Because wasn't that the icing on the cake?

He was in underground fights because of the other secret—the one Soren was threatening me to keep. The reason I was under the thumb of that fucking billionaire sociopath.

"Soren is his father. Is that explanation enough for you?" I choked out the explanation between laughs.

They didn't laugh, greeting me with more tense silence. As I expected. My breakdown calmed after another minute, and I sucked in a deep, uninhibited breath.

"Soren Rosania is gold pack." I said, glancing at my phone and hoping Dash was right about it only being bugged by him. "And he's the biological father of my brother's alpha. I don't know the whole story, but I do know that Soren is the reason he was there. I'm sure Mother would have figured out something else to blackmail me with if she didn't have this, but as it is, Soren is the reason I've been in this mess for years."

Mercury was thumbing his phone, staring intently like he was on the hunt for something specific. Dash had his head cocked to the side—he and Soren were similar levels of wealthy. Soren had gained his, while Dash was born with it. Ambrose was behind me but hadn't stopped touching me.

"I should have figured this out sooner, honestly," I muttered. "He did the fights, I was aware of that. When I'd seen those fucking pictures, maybe I should have dug deeper into how she got them. I thought she'd found them on purpose to manipulate me. It never occurred to me that she would have lucked into her blackmail material... by chance."

"There's no way you could have figured that out," Ambrose said.

I glared at him over my shoulder. "The pieces were there. I only had to fit them together. Noah Connolly even said that my mother had spent time in his casinos."

"I don't think the pieces were there," Dash said. "I just gave you a piece. You didn't have that one. It's not like your mother looks like she has a gambling problem."

Biting my lip, I pulled back an argument.

This back and forth wasn't helping the current situation, or Kiara.

I just hated that I'd been holding onto the threads of control for the past two years, and in that time I had ninety percent of the information I needed to solve the problem.

"I'm not sure this necessarily helps us," Ambrose said softly.

His lips landed on my neck and I sighed, melting into the soothing touch.

"Why doesn't it help?" I asked.

"It would have gotten you out of helping your mother with things if you had counter-blackmail, but your mother isn't our biggest issue. The Connollys are. They're going to come for Kiara no matter what. He's trying to do it in a peaceful way, currently, but if your mother starts refusing to help them, they'll turn violent."

"He's right," Mercury agreed. "Before we tell anyone about this, we need to find out how to handle the bigger issue."

"My brother won't stop until I'm owned by someone or dead."

I spun to face Kiara. She stood in the entrance to the kitchen wearing a fluffy robe that was too warm for the current weather. Her knife was clutched in her hand, unsheathed. Every inch of her trembled.

Dash got to her before I could extract myself from Ambrose's embrace. He felt her fear like I did. She leaned into him and let him lead her to a bar stool, where she sat.

As tempting as it was to move over to her, I let Dash stroke his hands awkwardly down her arms and purr behind her.

"Why won't he stop, dove?" I asked. "We could find something that's worth more to him than you are."

I hated talking about my bonded omega as if she were an object. Her family considered her to be one, though, and unless we killed an entire crime family, we would have to speak their language to keep her safe.

She shook her head. "No. You can offer trades or blackmail or anything. My father might let me go if you gave him something good enough, but Tobias won't. He hates me. He doesn't want me to be happy, and I think he'll go down in flames to make sure I'm not."

"He sounds like a real piece of work," Mercury muttered.

I had to agree.

Kiara shrugged helplessly, leaning back against Dash.

I sighed, brushing a hand through my hair. "Well, we've got some information on my mother, at least. That's step one. We'll figure out the rest. There's five of us and we've got a billion dollars to work with, after all."

More resources than the Connollys had. Not more than Soren, but he was a non-issue. He hadn't contacted me about my arrest. I pictured him watching this show with a bowl of popcorn, ready to swoop in and demand whatever he wanted at the least opportune times.

Kiara's big yawn cut the tension in the room, her body slumping. I laughed softly. "You need some more rest, dove."

She shook her head. "No one else got as much sleep as I did."

"You're an omega close to her heat. Keep your body well-rested, and go have a nap."

Her lips turned out into a pout, but she slid from the bar stool. "I just woke up," she muttered under her breath.

I didn't comment as she wandered back into the bedroom, but when I turned to face the others they were all smiling. Little grins quirked their lips, even Mercury.

If this didn't all fall apart… we might have a really good thing going here.

FORTY

DASH

I crossed my arms over my chest, staring at the sewing supplies that sat on the unused dining room table.

This was what Kiara had done as a hobby, and I'd spared no expense. The sewing machine was the best on the market, every fabric was high quality, and she had every item she could need to pick up the hobby once again.

Maybe it was stupid, but I wanted to test everything out before we showed it to her. It had been sitting in plain boxes on the table when we'd had our kitchen conversation, but with the heavy subject matter, she hadn't noticed before she went back to sleep again.

Except, I didn't know a damn thing about sewing.

Yet.

"I would advise against it," Mercury said.

I swung my gaze to him. He was leaning against the door frame, avoiding eye contact with his hands shoved into his pockets.

"It's better if we make sure she really does have everything. Sewing articles can only tell you so much."

"You shouldn't jump down a sewing rabbit hole right now, though. There are going to be more things we need you to hack, eventually, and I don't want to have to pull you out of a new hyperfixation. It's not pleasant."

"I'll pull myself out," I said.

Mercury sighed, pushing off the frame and strolling over to the table. He pulled out a chair, picking up a large hand sewing kit. "I can check this, if you're so insistent."

I sucked my bottom lip between my teeth, trying to place the feeling bubbling up in my chest. It was a little bit of annoyance, mixed with a lot of regret. My packmate didn't trust me, and maybe he shouldn't. But I wanted him to. I could be responsible.

Pulling out a chair beside him, I started fiddling with the sewing machine. The intrigue of dials and needles and thread did threaten to drag me under and make me forget about the world.

Kiara's need for me would be enough to pull me back.

"Dash..."

"I've got it," I bit out. "You don't need to baby me, Merc. She's my omega. The way I take care of her has nothing to do with you."

He didn't say anything. We worked side by side in tense silence for a long while. Ambrose and Leighton's voices came faintly from the office—they were trying to work out a plan. I needed some time doing mindless activities in order to think.

Then I could try to plan again.

"Do you wish I'd let you crash and burn?" Mercury asked.

I pricked my finger with a needle at the sudden question, cursing.

I turned to him. He'd put down all the sewing supplies, watching me intently.

Did I?

It was a difficult question.

Sometimes I wondered if rock bottom would have forced me to rethink my actions. I'd never reached it because Mercury was always there, hovering and ready to pull me out of trouble.

But I also doubted if rock bottom would have done anything good for me. I probably would have wallowed there, feeling even more like shit about myself and my life. It might have felt fitting —if my scent match mate didn't want me, how could I live my best life? What was the point of pulling myself out?

Without lived experiences, it was impossible to know.

"No," I admitted. "You're like an overbearing parent, but I'm scared to know what would have happened to me without you."

His shoulders relaxed. He tugged at one of his braids, half turning back to the task at hand. I stopped him with a grip on his arm.

"I don't need you anymore, though."

Mercury's eyes narrowed, flicking between me and the direction of Kiara. We all had an acute knowledge of where she was, just in case she needed us. Our protective instincts were raging around the delicate, dangerous omega.

"She could—"

"No. If this breaks me, that's on me. Not her, or you."

I worried my bottom lip between my teeth some more. After so many years being babied, I wasn't as confident as I wanted to be about my ability to self-regulate. But it was time. Leighton was right—my negative feelings were a self-fulfilling prophecy, and my guilt over being a burden to my pack wasn't helping.

"You know, I don't even know what you enjoy doing," I said. "All you do is run after me. What do you like?"

He blinked at me blankly. Mercury didn't know. Through the pack bond, usually locked up tight, I felt his mild horror at the realization.

"Since I don't need a babysitter anymore, you should probably figure that out. Or you're going to be really fucking bored. Maybe you can take up sewing like our omega."

Shaking his head, he looked at the table, filled to the brim with supplies.

"I don't think sewing is for me. I used to play chess. And fence and ride horses."

Wow.

Fencing?

People still fenced? Wasn't that like a medieval pastime?

I tried unsuccessfully to keep the amused grin off my face. "Fencing, huh? Sounds thrilling."

Mercury scowled, but it wasn't filled with his usual genuine annoyance with me. "Fencing is a respectable hobby."

"Yeah, if you lived in 16th century England."

"Fuck off."

I cackled, grabbing a piece of pale pink fabric. I was pretty sure I'd set up the sewing machine, so it was time to test it. My plan was to make Kiara a skirt. Had to be simple enough, right?

"Seriously, though," I said, using my phone to pull up a pattern for a circle skirt. "Buy a horse farm or something. We've got the money, and I'm not going to run myself into the ground if you leave for the countryside every couple of weekends. Or, God forbid, if you get a job."

His gaze flicked to the bedroom where Kiara slept. He wanted her. It was so fucking obvious. He wanted Leighton, too. Just like I did. The two of us had never had a common goal before, but assuming Mercury was willing to admit his desires, we finally did.

It was exciting and had me feeling closer to my packmate than I ever had. All the years of him trailing me everywhere, and it had never felt like the pack I'd dreamed of. We'd never been friends the way I wanted to be.

"Kiara might like the horse farm idea," I said slyly. "Doubt she's ever met a horse before."

"I'll have to ask."

"You might have to explain to her what kind of horse riding you do. Might need a full presentation on it."

He turned to me with an eyebrow raised, the hand sewing kit abandoned on the table. "You're trying to get rid of me," he said.

"This was a great bonding experience," I said. "But now that we've done the whole 'existential chat' thing, I know you're only here because you don't trust me. I'm not going to fixate or get snappy when someone has to interrupt me."

Mercury's disbelief was clear. I sighed. He might be right. Kiara couldn't make my brain work differently, and I did tend toward intense focus.

But wanting to be a good alpha for her could definitely change how I handled myself.

"And if I do snap, I'll take responsibility for myself," I clarified. "And apologize, or whatever. If I need your help with the apologizing bit, I'll ask. Fuck knows you've crafted a hundred apologies on my behalf already."

He pushed back from the table. I could sense his hesitance. Mercury letting me do things by myself was like a dad letting their kid bike without training wheels for the first time—a lesson in trust and letting them fall if they need to.

"I'm not going to create a set of presentation slides to explain my horse riding skills to Kiara, but I suppose I'll find something else to do," he said.

"Well, damn. I was looking forward to the presentation, too," I said teasingly.

Mercury rolled his eyes, looking once more at the sewing supplies.

I was going to be fine here alone.

I may not be a fully-functioning adult—the amount of times a week I forgot a meal wasn't healthy—but I could handle sitting at a table by myself for a few hours. Mercury came to the same conclusion, loosening the leash he kept me on.

Just a bit.

With the amount of shit I'd put him through, I was going to count any progress I got.

Turning on his heel, he stalked into the living room, closing the French doors behind him.

I beamed, turning back to my phone and my pink fabric.

Even Mercury was silently admitting that I could do it. Caring for Kiara the way she deserved was within my grasp, and I wasn't going to fail. Not when I was so desperate to please her.

FORTY-ONE

AMBROSE

The little omega had been asleep for hours, after already having slept through the night. It seemed like her body was preparing her for the extra physical stress of being in heat—which meant she was close. Days away, most likely. A week, if we were lucky.

Kiara's honey brown hair was flaring out around her head, tousled from the way her limbs moved in obvious discomfort.

I reached out a hand to stroke a strand back from her face, but paused before I could make the move to wake her up.

I'd thought she was having a nightmare—with her history, it wouldn't be unheard of. The things Tobias had probably done to her… it was him I wish I'd strangled, not her.

This wasn't a nightmare, though.

Her pale skin was flushed, sweat beading on her forehead. She'd tossed the blankets off, her bare thighs clenched together. Those plush lips I'd almost kissed last night were parted on a sigh—except it wasn't a sigh.

It was a moan.

Upon closer inspection her thighs were wet with slick where

they clenched, and her scent was growing harder to resist by the second.

My cock throbbed, my knot begging to slide inside her and make itself at home.

That wasn't my right. We weren't her alphas, yet. We wouldn't be until this mess was fixed and both of them were safe from the consequences of us being together. Only Leighton could help her by giving her the pleasure she deserved.

I breathed through my mouth as I moved back, ready to steal Leighton away from the calls she was making.

After last night and how I'd teased her, I should have known Kiara wouldn't let me make it to the door.

"Ambrose?"

Her voice was delicate, soft with sleep. I turned to face her, barely holding back a groan when I saw her sitting up.

With her thighs parted.

Exposing that pretty pink pussy I wanted to sink into. I bet she would feel just as good clenching around my cock as her walls had felt fluttering around my tongue.

"Yes, princess?"

If I was lucky, she would tell me to get Leighton for her. They could soothe her pre-heat ache together.

If I was *really* lucky, she would call me back and I would soothe her.

As it turned out, I wasn't lucky at all.

"Have you been with an omega in heat before?"

I stiffened, not enjoying the way my stomach tightened. "I have." I couldn't lie to her, as much as I knew the truth might send her into a rage—especially when she was this close to her own heat.

Never had I thought being a heat helper would come back to bite me in the ass.

Her little growl made my eyes squeeze shut, bracing myself. This could go one of two ways.

She could kick me out, her perception of me changed because I hadn't waited to have my own omega before helping in a heat.

Or, she could have a feral need to claim me as her own. She already had claimed me, she just didn't know there was a mark in the shape of her lips right over my heart.

"Why?"

I snapped my eyes open again. She was unexpected. Why was I surprised? She always was. "I was a heat helper. Some of my clients at The Pointe Lounge were mateless omegas."

Her nose crinkled and she patted the bed beside her. Hesitantly, I sat down on the edge, trying to keep my gaze off her nudity. It was impossible. Her bare skin was tantalizing, and I wanted to do far more than look.

Now, touch, I could resist.

Probably.

"Why would they want an alpha that's not theirs to help them through their heat?" she asked.

"They either choose someone to help them, or end up drugged to sleep through it. Spending too many heats unconscious isn't necessarily healthy, so if they haven't found a pack within a couple of years of their first heat, heat helpers give assistance."

"And why did you choose to be a heat helper?"

"Because I didn't think I would ever find you."

"What about Leighton? You had her. Is she worth less because she's not an omega? And Mercury?" Kiara was indignant.

I snorted a laugh. "Princess, I haven't been a heat helper in years. It was when I was far younger, before I was with Leighton or Mercury."

She flushed from the tips of her ears down her chest. I liked this much better than last night—the makeup had hidden her blush from me. I wanted to see every nuance of how she reacted to my words.

"Would you be a heat helper again?"

"Of course not."

"No, would you be... Would you be *my* heat helper?"

Blood rushed to my face and my cock at the same time, making me lightheaded. "You don't need a male alpha, little omega. There are toys. Leighton will give you a knot, and she has enough stamina to keep you sufficiently pleasured."

"That's not why I want you," she murmured.

I'd been hoping it wasn't—but hadn't dared to think it aloud. If she only wanted me to have an additional hand to satisfy her, I would have suffered through the pangs of not being wanted for real.

But that wasn't what I wanted.

I wanted her viscerally, desperately, painfully.

I wanted her teeth sinking into my skin, and mine punching through hers to claim her for good.

I wanted forever with the woman who'd forced us to face ourselves and the half lives we were living. Who'd plucked at the strings of my alpha instincts with her innocence and simultaneous ability to protect herself.

"Why do you want me, princess?" I asked.

She had to say it out loud, so I knew for certain.

"I might be falling in love with you."

Quirking one eyebrow, the other side twitched amidst the tight scarring. "Might?"

Her hands fisted the sheets, every second bringing more of her coconut chocolate scent into the air. More slick pooling beneath her, too. I should still get Leighton to help her. It shouldn't be me, not before I'd talked to Leighton and made sure she was OK with this.

Then again, I trusted them to handle their relationship as much as I trusted myself to handle mine with Mercury.

If I gave Kiara the knot she was desperate for right now, Mercury wouldn't be upset—which was the only reason I was even considering it.

Kiara wasn't yet in heat, so for her to be asking me for anything at all... they'd already talked about it.

"Maybe, if you knot me, it'll change to a definitely," she said.

Her cheeks were flushed but she was smirking, and that sass was enough for me to dive in and press our lips together.

She didn't hesitate to kiss me back. I knew she was new to kissing and everything else I wanted to do to her, but she didn't seem like it. Leighton had taught her all the ways to make me lose my mind with a kiss, and her omega instincts were taking care of the rest.

Kiara squirmed and groaned beneath me. I crawled onto the bed to hover over her, not breaking the kiss.

Her legs wrapped around my waist, wet pussy pressing against the bulge in my jeans. The whine she released ignited a feral part of my brain that I couldn't control.

"Good girl," I growled. "Rub yourself all over me, princess."

She bit my lip hard enough to draw blood, wrapping her arms around me and raking her nails down my back.

Such an animalistic little omega.

If she weren't so close to heat, and if this weren't our first time, I would have disciplined her for that. As it was, I was too thrilled to be the object of her desire. She would learn the next time.

"Ambrose," she whimpered. One hand trailed down to tug at the waistband of my jeans. "Off."

"Is that how you ask?"

I skimmed my lips down her jaw to her neck, scraping my

teeth against the skin. She keened and jolted against me, a new rush of slick drenching my thighs.

"Please! Please take them off."

With another quick nip, I drew back. Kiara panted and strained to follow me, but I kept her away with a hand on her shoulder. My belt landed on the floor a second later, but I paused before undoing my jeans.

"Princess, you're going to take them off for me."

Her hazy eyes cleared, showcasing their dazzling blue and the nervousness within their depths. Trembles wracked her as she reached for me, and I caught her wrist before she could complete the task.

My lips pressed softly against her palm. "You're nervous."

"I've never done this before," she said. "I was going to do it."

"I know, but I don't want you quaking with fear while you're undressing me."

"It was *not* fear." Her lips turned down into an annoyed little frown, and she pulled her hand away.

It probably wasn't. Nerves weren't fear, but I'd figured that my words would be enough to get her out of her head. Now she'd be adamant to prove me wrong.

I loved that I knew her well enough to know that.

"Does this look like fear to you?"

Her challenge was accompanied by her hand darting out to grab my waistband. All her hesitance was gone. My cock throbbed as she fumbled the button and zipper, pushing down the rough jeans to my mid-thighs.

Then she was face to face with the unconstrained bulge in my boxer briefs, an obvious wet spot where my tip pressed against the fabric.

Her fingertips grazed it and I bucked my hips forward. The wave of arousal was unstoppable at this point. I wanted to pin her to the bed and fill her to the brim with my cock, then my knot. My balls ached to rut her until I'd filled her up with cum a million times. The age-old desperation to *breed her* was crashing into me.

It was more intense than I'd ever felt.

I'd never wanted to breed an omega before.

"I need a condom," I said between my clenched teeth.

If I let her take the boxer briefs off, I wouldn't get one. Then, I really would be breeding her. None of us were ready for that, least of all her. She was so young and had just been freed of the control her parents forced on her.

Her sharp nails dug into my hips and I cursed, but stopped moving away.

I thought my self control was ironclad, but by God if she asked me to fill her up right now, I would do it. The consequences would flee my brain in seconds.

"You don't need one," she said, trying to pull me back.

"Kiara, it's risk—"

She shook her head. "They gave me an implant. Just in case. I want to feel you, Ambrose, I don't want you to knot me with a condom on."

Should we be trusting anything her father had done to her? No, we fucking shouldn't, but it was all the convincing I needed to stop trying to leave her. The nails gripping me loosened, leaving crescent marks behind, and she slid her hands down.

They were just breaching the waistband of my boxer briefs when the door creaked open.

If it was Dash, I was going to punch him in the fucking face.

We were pack, but in this moment, Kiara didn't belong to him. She was mine to knot. Mine, and...

I inhaled vanilla cream with a husky groan.

"I don't remember giving you permission to touch my omega," Leighton said. The door shut behind her, her light footsteps padding toward us.

I didn't turn to her, instead watching Kiara's face as she

flushed a deep red. Leighton's aura weighed on us, convincing us to do exactly what she wanted. I'd always found it sexy, and always been able to resist. Right now, I wasn't sure.

Kiara was her omega first, so if Leighton didn't want me to be dominant here, I wouldn't be. It would go against every one of my screaming instincts, but I could handle it.

"Do I *need* your permission, doll?" I asked.

She appeared in my peripheral vision, her robe fluttering to the floor and leaving her completely naked.

Fuck. She's been naked all morning.

Leighton hummed, coming over to stand beside the bed. Her torso pressed against my arm and I tensed, watching Kiara's reaction. She'd been furious when Leighton and I had been intimate before—granted, the situation was wildly different now. If we needed to ease her into it to soothe her possessive instincts, we could.

Not that I would ever give the female alpha up.

Our omega's reaction wasn't jealousy or rage, though. She began to purr, her hand sliding deeper into my underwear until she could grasp my cock.

I groaned. Her alpha's arrival had made her bolder.

"You should have asked me this time, Sir," Leighton murmured.

Leighton grabbed the hem of my shirt and pulled it over my head, leaving my chest bare. There was a familiar moment of panic. The scarring was so widespread it put people off and caused flickers of disgust to cross their expressions, however quickly. Neither of these women ever reacted to me like that, and this was no exception.

I still had to push down the desire to hide and not let Leighton see my marred skin.

"But from now on, you don't. I don't need your permission to touch her, either," Leighton continued. "Do we have an understanding?"

I nodded, grabbing her chin and giving her a quick, chaste kiss. "I can give either of you orders, but can't expect you to listen if I order you to do things to each other. Is that right, doll?"

"Yes. She's mine. You don't get to tell me how to touch her."

Kiara's hand squeezed my length, the pressure on the edge of pleasure and discomfort. I couldn't stop the moan. Having both of them was unravelling me.

"I understand," I grunted in response to our quick negotiation. "I'm sure we'll discuss this more later, but for now that's all that I need to understand."

Leighton smirked, her gaze sliding toward Kiara. "Are you getting a little desperate?" She teased me.

My hand slid from her chin to her throat, squeezing the delicate skin. She whimpered, clenching her thighs together. "Don't tease me, doll. You know I'll punish you for it later."

"Is anyone planning on touching me?" Kiara's complaint made me laugh.

"Princess, you haven't gotten my cock out yet," I said, glancing down. Her small hand was wrapped around my length, but she hadn't gotten further. "You have to listen before you get rewarded."

My cock bobbed free a second later, my boxer briefs pushed down as far as my jeans. Kiara swallowed down a whine, not quite confident enough to grab me now that she could see the length. She was only staring.

I leaned away from Leighton, holding Kiara instead. My cock slid along her folds, teasing me with her heat. "Good job," I praised. "Now, is there anything you want me to do to you, Kiara?"

She shivered.

"Fuck me, Ambrose. Fuck me and knot me."

FORTY-TWO

KIARA

Ambrose's cock was gorgeous.

I didn't know if cocks were supposed to be—I didn't know anything at all about this. The pack had touched me, but I'd never touched them beyond rubbing myself on them through clothing.

But it made sense to me that his cock was stunning, because the rest of him was.

His dark hair hung into his eyes as he hovered over me, not doing anything to hide his smirk. The stubble on his cheek had rubbed against my skin when we kissed, giving me an extra layer of sensation. He was broad and strong, with dark hair leading down his stomach to the appendage I had no idea what to do with.

It was obvious he was insecure about the scars, but to me they showed strength. I only had a few, and I'd gone through hell to get them. I couldn't imagine how strong he was to have that many and still be here.

I focused on his cock, peering down at it. The head glistened, and soon the shaft shone too from my slick. It was warm against me. Soft, with no hard edges like the rest of him had.

I guess that makes sense. It's going to be going inside me.

Oh, fuck.

Inside me.

All the way to the knot, which was bulging at the base. Thicker than the rest of him, it was a hint darker than most of his skin. Maybe a bit redder, too.

It was way too much to fit, but I wanted it.

I was borderline desperate to try.

That familiar, uncomfortable twist began in my stomach but shot down to my core. I tossed my head back, needing it to go away. He could make it, by fucking me the way I'd asked him to.

"Alpha, make him do it," I begged.

My vision was blurry with need. Leighton rounded the bed and crawled onto it, settling down beside my head. Her scent became more potent, smoky vanilla cream when mixed with Ambrose's desire.

"I can't tell him what to do, dove," Leighton murmured.

Her fingers stroked through my hair. She was aroused too—so much I could almost taste her core on my tongue—but she wasn't paying any attention to herself. Only to me.

I tried to turn and bury my face against her chest, but Ambrose's hand latched around my throat.

Adrenaline stampeded through my system. The bruising wasn't fresh, but was still healing. He was careful, but the light grip was a reminder of when it had been more—when I'd fucked up, and he'd almost had to live with the guilt of killing me for it.

Except this time, his eyes weren't dark and unseeing. They were dark with lust, his cock throbbing between my spread thighs.

And my reaction wasn't fear, aside from the millisecond of instinctual response.

It was arousal.

My head pushed up, bumping my throat against his hand in a bid for more pressure. He refused to give it, but I assumed it was only because of my injury. When he'd grabbed Leighton's throat, it had been roughly.

"Careful, princess," he said. "You're still hurt, but you need to understand something. Right now? You pay attention to me. I'm the one who's fucking you. My doll is going to tease you and comfort you, yes. But during your first time with me, I'm going to be your focus."

I nodded, the movement halted by his loose grip.

"You're *not* fucking me, though," I said, glancing down. "That's the problem."

His length hadn't been swallowed down by my pussy, so he and Leighton were both 'fucking me' about equal at the moment.

My snark wasn't appreciated. I hadn't expected it to be.

Ambrose growled, his fingers flexing with the desire to choke me. "You're a brat," he muttered. "If it's your first time, it may be uncomfortable, even for an omega. Would you prefer I didn't ease you into it?"

I shook my head. In my experience, easing in only meant the discomfort lasted longer. I wasn't sure if the principle applied to sex, but I was going to assume.

"Leighton, I need you to stop me if you don't think she can take it." Ambrose's voice was as husky as I'd ever heard it. His eyebrows were drawn together, a hint of concern in his expression. Every inch of him was tense and straining, ready to take me the way I'd been fantasizing about since these pre-heat cramps had begun.

Maybe before that.

I might have fantasized from the moment I saw him, or at least the moment I heard him fucking Leighton that first night.

"She can take it. She's an omega," Leighton said.

"That's why I'm fucking worried. I'm not fully... in control."

My heart skipped in anticipation. Using my legs wrapped around his torso, I slid myself up and down his length. The sensation was foreign to me—fingers were rougher, and tongues were softer. A cock sliding against my clit was a wholly unique sensation.

"I don't think she wants control, Ambrose. My omega wants a feral alpha and a knot. Give her both."

I did. She knew exactly what I wanted. I hadn't known how to articulate it. I wasn't sure if I could articulate anything, anymore. The pressure was building, the cramping uncomfortable and annoying when I knew it would be so easy to fix.

Ambrose's growl rumbled all the way down to his cock, vibrating against my clit. I cried out, digging my heels into his back and trying to position myself—I had to get him to my entrance, and the world would make sense again.

"Fuck," he cursed, removing his hand from my throat when his fingers tightened slightly. "At least make sure I'm careful with her. She's injured."

"You're the one that's going to be injured if you don't fuck her soon," Leighton said.

Her hand slid down to squeeze my breast, kneading the heavy flesh. It was a welcome distraction when she pinched my nipple, giving me another thing to focus on besides the unmet need in my core.

But then, Ambrose moved away, and I keened in protest until I felt it.

The head of his cock pushed through the resistance, sliding into me. There was a smidgen of discomfort from the unfamiliar stretch, but it had nothing on the cramping.

My cramps were soothed by his cock, so this was a win to me.

Plus, the *pleasure*.

My body slumped back onto the pillows, all attempts to hold

myself up failing. Leighton's hands smoothed over my upper body, her lips following in their path. Ambrose was growling between my legs. Sweat dripped from his forehead like he was already exerting himself, even though he'd barely given me half his cock.

Was it that difficult to stop fucking me?

If so, why was he *doing it*?

"Ambrose, more, please," I begged.

He released the base of his cock with a soft grunt, giving me another tiny piece of him. It wasn't enough. It wasn't all of him. It wasn't his knot.

"More."

This time, my plea was more of a demand. My legs tried to pull him closer, but my weak body was no match for his solid stance. He didn't budge.

I tried a different tactic, shifting my torso closer to him so his cock was forced to slide deeper. He sucked in a sharp breath, his aura flaring out abruptly. I froze. Another shot of fear ran through me. Was he angry? My pussy clenched around him regardless, because with Ambrose, his oppressive aura and smoky hot iron scent were more sexy than terrifying.

Ambrose leaned back, bringing both hands down to grab my hips. His scarred fingers dug into my pale skin painfully. The way he touched me today was in stark contrast to how he'd touched me last night—or, how he'd not touched me at all.

"You want more?" he growled.

I got the sense this was it. The end of his rope. No more trying to keep me comfortable. He'd acknowledged that we both craved more than sweet, soft sex. My body was made for rough thrusts, and getting a knot would soothe my aches.

"More," I whispered.

He slammed the rest of the way into me, his knot rubbing against my entrance so abruptly it threatened to slip inside. I screamed, throwing my head back and arching into him. My hands scrabbled at the blankets—one grabbed a fistful of the sheets, while the other clutched Leighton's thigh in a death grip.

This deep, he rubbed a spot inside me that Leighton had explored with her fingers. But this was different. A different kind of intense, because there was more than one or two fingers inside me. All of Ambrose's cock was, thick and throbbing.

My begging had eliminated the calm and collected man I knew. He wasn't the same person who'd refused to react to my taunts or quietly forgiven me for stabbing him.

He was an uncontrollable alpha now, and I was going to get everything I needed.

I knew my hips were bruising beneath his grip with every thrust, but that was a mark I would cherish until it faded. His cock sent an echo of pleasure through my core, staving off the cramping I'd been managing all week. We were a symphony of grunts and moans and growls, the occasional scream slipping out of me when his knot hit my clit just right.

Pleasure built, but the way it rose was different than it had before.

It wasn't focused in my clit but deep inside me, and when it hit, it hit hard.

"Oh, fuck!" I buried my face against Leighton's stomach, crying out as I convulsed.

Ambrose's hand grabbed my chin, yanking me to face him. My eyes were glassy, vision blurry behind the sheen of pleasure tears. "Don't hide from me, little omega. I told you."

Shakily exhaling, I nodded. He had. I couldn't hide in Leighton right now, because I had to give everything I had to my other alpha. I wanted to.

"Knot me, please. I want to feel that again."

"Princess, when I knot you, it's going to be even better."

I blinked away the tears, looking into the depths of his dark eyes. He was hazy too, his need showing in the way he continued to fuck me, even as we spoke.

"Please," I whispered again.

He groaned, seating himself deep inside me and rubbing his knot against my entrance. Slick drenched the bed beneath us, making his thighs shiny. My core was ready for him. I'd been ready since I first saw his knot, swollen with his arousal for me.

"Tell Leighton if it hurts," he demanded.

"Not you?"

"I'm not stopping if you tell me it hurts. I won't be able to unless she forces me. That's how out of my head I am around you, Kiara. I've never been like this around an omega before, in heat or not."

An involuntary little growl rose at the thought of those other omegas. They'd touched what belonged to me, but it was a small comfort that they never would again.

"I'll tell her," I said, swallowing.

It wouldn't hurt. Even if it did, the pleasure would outweigh the pain and I wouldn't let Leighton force him to stop.

"Good girl."

My entrance stretched around the knot as he slowly worked himself inside. I moaned and grabbed his arms, hoisting myself up to press against him. He released my hips to hug me close, letting the movement force his knot the rest of the way inside.

I was caught between a whine and a purr, some odd combination of both sounds rumbling through my chest.

Leighton had pulled back for now, her gaze burning into my side while she remained a comforting presence.

Ambrose's knot swelled a hint more, locking us together and triggering a weak, shaky orgasm that wasn't anywhere near enough. His teeth were grazing my neck, each breath a heaving endeavour as he fought back...

What? An orgasm? Or was he fighting against the urge to ravage me?

"I want you to come in me," I blurted. "Come in me and rut me until you come again."

It wasn't the sexiest way to ask—but it was enough for his entire body to shudder, hot cum mixing with my slick to warm my core.

"Princess," he groaned. His teeth were threatening to sink in now, and I wanted him to do it. It would complicate things so much our lives would be at risk, but I wanted it anyway. Fuck the consequences.

I buried my face against his neck, marking him with my scent and making sure I was covered in a heavy layer of his.

He purred, his hips bucking hard against me. It was the tiniest amount of movement, but made me light up. "So good," I moaned. "More, Ambrose."

There was no way for him to give me more. I thought it was impossible when he was like this, but he proved me wrong. His arms tightened around me, my tits squished against his chest and the pleasant sting of beard burn starting to blossom on my neck. His cock rubbed all the perfect spots and I had to close my eyes, because my vision was going starry.

"You're going to come for me again, princess," he grunted. "I'll make your pussy milk my cock dry. You'll be good and bred for me."

He slid a hand between us, pressing the pad of his finger to my clit. With his words I was already teetering on the edge—I didn't want to be bred, not really.

But at the same time, I did. The thought of it made me purr with pleasure.

His cum would be locked inside me until we were able to release each other, satisfying my primal need to be the perfect omega.

I lost myself in that thought and the final peak of pleasure. My teeth sank into his neck and the gentle thrum of a bond settled over me—weak, like the one I had with Dash. Temporary. I didn't want it to be, but it would do for now.

My body pulsed with my release, clenching on his knotted length and doing exactly what he'd said it would. I forced another orgasm from him with how tight I got, leaving me impossibly full of him.

I panted and moaned and rocked against him until he stilled. His lips pressed to the crook of my shoulder, every breath shaky.

And I didn't just feel his physical presence. He was open with his emotions, letting me feel every piece of him through our tentative bond. Ambrose held nothing back. Not any of his affection or worry or arousal.

Licking at the marks I'd left on him, I purred contentedly. It was even better when Leighton came up behind me, letting me rest on her chest. She helped Ambrose hold himself up as we snuggled and waited for his knot to free us from each other.

I was in no rush, of course.

He sighed when his soft cock slid out, making more of a mess on the already soaked bed.

"I'm not sorry I bit you," I said.

I hadn't apologized to Dash, either. There was no point in lying.

He chuckled, smoothing his hands over the irritated parts of my skin. The beard burn. Hip bruises. My pussy, swollen from experiencing that for the first time. "I was hoping you would claim me," he said.

"I want to have a bond with everyone who helps me through my heat. It feels right that way."

More than a weak, temporary bond was what I wanted. It was unrealistic. I knew that. That Leighton didn't resent me for this dark bond was miracle enough. I shouldn't test my luck by jumping into having an entire pack.

The bonds I gave would have to do.

"And who is going to help you through your heat, princess?" Ambrose asked.

His eyebrow lifted and he rolled over onto his side, laying beside me and Leighton.

"You, Leighton, Dash, and..."

I trailed off, and I swore a flash of panic went across Ambrose's face.

Mercury was the one of them I barely knew. He didn't like me, from what I'd gathered. I didn't want to lie and say I didn't want him during my heat, but it wasn't fair to make him feel... obligated.

"Mercury," I said quietly. "But he doesn't have to."

Smiling, Ambrose pressed his lips to my arm—the nearest part of my body. "Should I tell him you want him, little omega, or are you planning on doing that?"

I huffed. "It isn't like he likes me. Maybe it's better if I don't tell him anything."

"He likes both of us more than he lets on," Leighton said with a confidence I didn't possess. "But you're right. His pack needs to convince him to make an effort first."

The comment was pointedly for Ambrose. It was a burden that shouldn't be put on him, though. They were lovers. We were lovers. We couldn't use him as a go-between.

I didn't want to think about terrifying, awkward conversations right now. I'd just woken up but my limbs were heavy and I was about ready for a nap. Curling up between Leighton's legs, with Ambrose to my side, I purred until sleep dragged me under.

Just a small nap.

I deserved it, with the chaos last night had brought.

FORTY-THREE

MERCURY

Leighton's phone lit up on the counter before she'd returned from the bedroom. I glared at it, annoyed at the reminder that I wasn't alone in this condo, no matter how I pretended to be.

I wasn't jealous.

Not at all.

There was no way I was jealous about how they'd fucked Kiara together. Or about how she'd claimed Ambrose, leaving me as the only one in the pack without a bond. I felt the echo of her through our pack bond, now that she'd sunk her teeth into two of us.

I certainly *was not* jealous that her heat was coming, and I wouldn't be invited because I'd spent so much time being a cunt to her.

The rest of my pack would get to spend it with her. I couldn't do anything to stop Dash from being where she wanted him, and I'd finally acknowledged he might be able to make his own decisions about what he could handle.

"This is another dead end," I muttered to myself, clicking away from the web page.

Knowing Edith was a gambler helped a lot, and knowing what leverage she had over Leighton was extremely valuable. But, it didn't help with the bigger issue, which was the Connollys.

Did they have the same blackmail?

If we counter-blackmailed Edith, that was all well and good. We'd be at a stalemate.

Except for the Connollys, because they wouldn't care about Edith's story getting out. They'd reveal Marlowe's pack's secret to the world if we didn't listen, and then probably use nefarious means to get Kiara back on top of it. Leighton's life would be in danger—more than it already was.

I checked the message on Leighton's phone.

Liberty: meet me at the coffee shop? Got info

Leighton had mentioned Liberty was her assistant. I doubted the information was going to be too helpful, considering the jack shit Dash had found so far, but we could hope.

Picking up the phone, I stood from the bar stool and walked toward the bedroom.

Their grunts and moans and screams had stopped a while ago. However, when I turned into the hallway I hit a wall of their scent. I brought my hand to my mouth with a strangled groan, ignoring the steady beat of my pulse in my cock.

This was too fucking much.

Kiara was close enough to heat I could taste it. Coconut chocolate overpowered the vanilla cream and hot iron that were also lingering.

Yet, she was in danger and at this rate wouldn't be able to have the proper routine of nesting and fucking an omega needed—and deserved—during heat.

We need to fix this.

Pushing through the haze of lust and my own arousal, I knocked loudly on the door. It opened a minute later, Leighton pinning me with a glare. "She's sleeping," she muttered quietly.

And Leighton was naked.

Fuck.

I didn't look down, staring intently into her eyes. She scanned me from head to toe, no doubt noting the stiff bulge in my trousers and my spiking scent. Even my aura, which I usually had under control, was flaring.

"You got a text. Liberty has information."

She grabbed her phone from my hand when I held it out, vanishing back into the room without another word. The door stayed cracked and I stared at the thin opening, wondering if I would see Kiara through it. I'd just have to angle myself correctly, and maybe the bed would be in view…

Shaking myself, I stepped back from the door and was back in the kitchen by the time Leighton caught up.

She was clothed again in her typical work attire. A pantsuit in steel grey, expensive fabric. She had a high-neck black tank top tucked into her trousers, and her blazer was draped over her arm.

"Ambrose and I are going to meet up with Liberty," she said. "What she found could be helpful, especially if she doesn't want to give details over the phone. Dash is going to the Dirt with Dash studio to grab some things and record an episode. That means you're with Kiara."

I glanced toward the primary bedroom as if I could see her through the walls. "It would be better if Ambrose stayed and I went with you."

That way, I wouldn't do anything else stupid. I wouldn't dig myself deeper into the hole when it came to our relationship.

Sometimes my mouth didn't cooperate with the orders I gave it, and deep down, I still worried.

Kiara was under duress.

Were we a choice she'd made only because we were the only options? Was this trauma bonding at its finest? A bond like that wouldn't last. We were in too deep to get out now, but there was a part of me that wanted her to admit she wasn't sure about us. That way, I wouldn't let myself fall for her too fast.

"You're staying here," Leighton said.

Her tone was final, the persuasive weight of her aura behind her words. I bit my tongue against another complaint. I could handle it. Being alone in the condo with Kiara wasn't the end of the world.

With how hard she just got fucked, she might be asleep the whole time anyway.

"Fine," I said. "I'll keep looking into your mother. I'm scouring high society gossip blogs to see if there are any photos of her that hint at anything. Maybe the place she goes to gamble, or how she's still getting the money to do it."

"I wouldn't be surprised if she's committing white collar crimes, but threatening to expose those won't be any more or less damaging to her reputation than simply telling the world she's broke. She cares more about her reputation than anything else—even the idea of criminal consequences."

"Knowledge is power." *And I have nothing else to do.*

"True. Hopefully Liberty knows something useful."

Dash wandered into the kitchen then, his cheeks flushed and hair still dripping. The casual button up he wore was hanging undone, his jeans riding low on his hips.

When Leighton had disappeared into the bedroom with Ambrose and Kiara, he'd vanished into the shower, abandoning the sewing machine. Dash had always been shameless, but his cock had to be raw after how long he'd been in there.

"You've got the filming of your little internet show," Leighton said. "Are you ready to go?"

He smirked. "Are you my babysitter today?"

She snorted. "No. You're going to have to function without a babysitter."

Dash's eyes widened slightly. He glanced at me, and I shrugged. "She doesn't seem to believe you can get in too much trouble at the studio. I'm staying with Kiara, and Ambrose is going with her."

"Daddy, it's only you who worries about me," Dash said with a shrug. He slung an arm around my shoulders.

I cringed, pushing him off. "Christ, don't fucking call me that."

"Why not?" He teased. "You treat me like I'm your son, always making sure I stay out of trouble."

Dash had brought this up before, but after our conversation the weight of it was different. His green eyes were dimmer than usual, not holding that typical Dash sparkle like when he was intentionally stirring shit.

I'd lost myself in my desire to keep the pack together, and I'd been chipping away pieces of him too.

"Because you get into a lot of trouble," I grumbled.

"Maybe I won't anymore."

I didn't need to muse over Dash's self-sufficiency today, not when I was barely able to process this blossoming relationship with Kiara. It was a long time coming, though.

"Go get into trouble then. Or don't. Either way, I won't stop you," I said. "Just don't call me Daddy again."

He planted a sloppy kiss on my cheek. "OK. I'll do whatever you tell me to, Daddy."

I groaned, wiping it away with the back of my hand. "Someone needs to fucking spank him or *something*."

Leighton chuckled, and Dash went a little pink as he danced backwards.

At least I wasn't the only one getting dommed by Leighton.

Not that I was, but...

I kept feeling the phantom of her hand around my throat, and I wanted more.

"I'll be in the living room. Kiara can come and find me when she wakes up," I mumbled, taking my laptop into the other room and leaving those two to do... whatever it was they were doing.

For a second, I'd felt like part of a family. A functional pack.

And that was too dangerous to think when it could all fall apart.

Kiara stayed in the bedroom for so long, I was beginning to believe I wouldn't see her until everyone returned home.

I was both disappointed and relieved.

Then, the soft padding of quick footsteps reached my ears, and a moment later she appeared.

She was wearing a plush robe, her honey brown hair pulled up into a messy bun on the top of her head. Fluffy slippers encased her feet, leaving only a few inches of ankle bare. She was bundled up all the way to her neck, otherwise.

It was the middle of summer, and Leighton's AC wasn't cold enough to warrant that many layers, which could only mean...

Nesting.

This was the first Kiara had shown nesting behaviour since I'd been here. It must mean she was incredibly close to heat, which meant I should stay far away from her.

I wasn't given that option.

She came to a stop in front of me, a nervous little frown on her face.

"Did you need something?" I asked after clearing my throat. "Everyone else is out."

Kiara inhaled deeply, letting out a whimper. I pressed back into the couch, but that was the most effort I could put into getting away from her. I didn't *want to*, damn it. The only reason I shifted at all was because I should—it was the right thing to do for all of us. I may have acknowledged that I wanted Leighton and Kiara to join our pack and not the Ashbys, but that didn't mean it was wise for me to start courting them, or anything equally ridiculous.

"I can call them," I offered.

Her scent was a cloud of need around me. My reaction was uncontrollable, each breath bringing me farther away from the self control I cherished.

"I need you," she declared.

I choked, doubling over my knees as I began to cough. I'd almost hacked up a lung when she placed her hand on my shaking upper back. Every inch of me tensed in anticipation.

Should I turn her down? Yes. But no, because wouldn't that damage our relationship more? If she wanted me, I needed to give myself to her... but that could damage me, and then what?

Fuck.

Fuck.

Her hand fisted in my shirt, trying to pull it over my head. It was almost aggressive enough to rip it by the seams. Sitting up, I removed it for her without consciously having decided my next move.

Instead of touching me like I thought she would, she grabbed the shirt. Held it to her nose. Inhaled with a moan that went straight to my fucking cock.

Right. *Nesting.* She was on a mission to gather every soft item in this condo, and my shirt had caught her eye. My panic receded and I almost smiled at the demanding little omega.

Before it could fully form, she looked down at my pants and made a grab for the waistband. "I need these too."

"Why?" I asked, looking down.

They weren't a comfortable material, not even for the person wearing them. She wouldn't be cuddling with my pants.

Her teeth sunk into her bottom lip. "Um..."

She trailed off, but her hand began to tremble. Tears beaded in the corners of her crystalline blue eyes, threatening to spill over.

I wasn't sure I'd ever undressed so fast in my life. My body had barely moved, but I was handing her my pants, left only in my boxer briefs. I'd lifted my hips to remove them, leaving me still sitting while she stood in front of me.

Kiara held the pants to her chest, then rubbed them against her bruised neck. She was coating herself in a layer of my scent. I'd rather she got it straight from the source—from my body bracketing hers, my cock sliding between her tits so my release would drench her face and breasts.

This was better.

I had to convince myself it was.

Her gaze flicked down to my bulge and she clutched my clothes tighter. Her nostrils flared, pupils dilating.

"Can I have those too? Please?"

I groaned. At this point, I couldn't help it. She'd stripped me of everything else—I wasn't even wearing socks. Now she wanted the underwear I was wearing? They had a wet spot from where my cock had leaked precum onto the cotton.

"You probably—"

She almost started to cry again. I saw those tears coming, and there was no way I was going to let it happen. Standing up, I crowded her back and took in a healthy breath of her scent as I did. She was so aroused I almost ignored my inhibitions and helped relieve her, but I didn't.

Her chest brushed mine as I stepped out of my boxer briefs and gave them to her. She whined, swaying where she stood.

I didn't know if I could watch her inhale my scent directly

from my fucking boxers, but she didn't. She held them with the rest of my things and squeaked out a quick, "Thanks!"

The little omega was gone a second later, hurrying off to add a piece of me to her nest. A place I didn't belong, but wanted to.

So badly.

Taking a few calming breaths, I grabbed the base of my cock and squeezed. I was not going to jerk off, especially not while the two of us were here alone. There was enough control left in the deepest recesses of my brain for me to manage that.

I was going to find some new clothes to put on that Kiara hadn't commandeered for her nest, and I was going to forget about being stripped bare in the living room by a needy omega.

Though, I'd been stripped bare in far more than just the physical sense, and that was the most dangerous thing of all.

With a curse, I stormed into the office and pulled on a set of Ambrose's clothing, the oversized loungewear hanging from me. I tried not to hope that she would come back and strip me all over again.

Because that was ridiculous to want, when there was no way she would be comfortable enough to fuck me during her heat.

FORTY-FOUR

LEIGHTON

Liberty saying 'meet me at the coffee shop' didn't mean to meet at a literal coffee shop. It was code for a warehouse I'd purchased dirt cheap under a fake name. Not exactly legal, but some of the things I did weren't exactly legal either. As much as I tried to keep it above board, I was a corporate fixer.

Some illegal activity couldn't be helped.

The area Ambrose and I drove into wasn't the friendliest. While I'd been here plenty of times before, I was glad for the company. Similarly, I was glad it wasn't Mercury. He might have judged me too harshly for conducting business in this area of the Gritch District.

That was half the reason I'd denied his request to come along.

The other half of the reason was because I knew he had to spend some time with Kiara. My omega wanted him, and he either needed to tell her straight up that he didn't want her—a lie—or come to his senses and accept one of her temporary bond marks.

I would have been jealous about my omega bonding all these

other alphas when she hadn't yet claimed me, but I knew our bond was the strongest. An omega claim was a mere shadow of an alpha's claim.

There was a little part of me that wondered why she wasn't sinking her teeth in me, though.

"Where do you think Mercury is at with Kiara?" I asked Ambrose, turning into a grungy, graffitied parking lot. "I know I shouldn't be asking you."

Ambrose sighed and shrugged. He was scanning out the windows, looking for danger that I bet lingered in every corner. It was doubtful we'd be jumped. Not in the car, at least.

"He doesn't want her to bond the Ashby pack."

"Because he wants her, or because he knows it would tear Dash apart?"

"He wants her. He's acknowledged that to himself, but I don't think he's going to make a move until everything is settled. Mercury is aware he treated her like shit."

I hit a button on my keyring and a garage door pulled up on a warehouse in front of us. It was at the very back of the parking lot, hidden behind a couple of other rundown buildings.

"You heard that she wants him for her heat," I said.

"I can't force them together any more than you can. Leaving them alone in the condo is about as good as it gets. She'll have to tell him, and he'll have to accept. That's the only way the whole pack is helping her through her heat."

I worried that he wouldn't accept. I'd be furious if he hurt her feelings by rudely turning her down—because Mercury didn't seem good at kind denials.

It would be a setback, but one we could overcome.

The setback that we were struggling to overcome was Kiara's family and their insistence on having her bond the Ashby pack. We hadn't figured out what Kiara's father gained from that alliance, considering the Ashby's lack of criminal ties, but maybe Liberty had something.

I drove into the open warehouse, waiting until the garage door was closed behind us before turning off the car and getting out.

"This is where the two of you get coffee?" Ambrose asked dryly. He slammed the passenger door shut, raising an eyebrow at me.

The warehouse was nothing like a coffee shop. It was a wide-open space with not much going on. A couple of cars sat unused and broken down in the main room. They'd come with the purchase.

My heels clicked against the concrete floor as I strode off to the side, toward an office door with a boarded-up window. Swinging it open, I gestured for him to go through first. He did, but froze in the doorway. I had to skirt around him to see what it was that had stunned him.

Liberty sat perched on the office desk, her signature red bag of cleaning supplies beside her. A man was strapped to a chair beside her, an IV stuck into his arm. Jasper pushed up his glasses and crossed his arms over his chest with a sigh.

"Hey, Leigh," Libby said, hopping to the ground. "Didn't realize you were bringing company. Hopefully you trust Ambrose, but if you don't, Jasper might be able to inject him with something to fuck up his memory."

Ambrose stiffened and I growled, placing myself between him and my errant employees. Liberty chuckled.

"Who the fuck is this?" I demanded, gesturing to the guy in the chair.

He was surprisingly calm for someone tied up. Maybe it had something to do with whatever was running through that IV line. His eyes weren't hazy when he looked at me, scanning me up and down. He almost looked... happy.

How could anyone be happy to be strapped to a chair? Unless

this was some kink thing, but I got the sense it was more like a kidnapping.

"Reynold Carter," Liberty said. She spoke matter-of-fact, like I should know who he was already.

"You're going to have to go into more detail than that."

"The man who told the police about your dark bond with Kiara."

I glanced back at Ambrose with wide eyes.

Goddamn Dash.

Unless Liberty had hacked her way into this information herself, it was obvious that the most disobedient and chaotic member of the Loranger pack had tipped her off.

"Why is he here?" I demanded.

"Look, Dash thought he would have some information we might be interested in, and I agreed. A friend and I picked up Reynold from his house yesterday morning."

"And you've been holding him hostage?"

Liberty wasn't always the most above board. That candy apple red bag of cleaning supplies had seen some shit. Kidnapping was far beyond anything I'd seen her do before, though.

The amount of trouble we could get into if this got out... She may have given Soren and my mother more ammo than they already had against me.

"Hostage is a strong word," she said.

She reached out a hand to ruffle Reynold's hair. The man didn't flinch. I was struggling to comprehend what was going on here.

"We're helping him with a detox," Liberty clarified. "That's why Jasper is here. Torture and murder aren't really my wheelhouse, but I figured if we could give the guy something he needed, he might give us what he knows. As it turns out, he needed a detox and a ticket out of New Oxford to escape his debts."

The IV setup made a hell of a lot more sense now.

"Let me guess. A debt to the Connollys?" I confirmed.

"The one and only," Libby said. "And he had some interesting information from when Tobias came to give him a task."

Reynold glanced between Liberty and I before speaking. He shifted in his chair as much as he could while being tied down. "Tobias is a piece of work. He told me if I went to the cops about you, he would shave off some of my debt, so I agreed. Before he left my place, he took a phone call."

People would do a lot to pay down debts—my mother included. I couldn't blame him.

"On the phone he said he needed his sister back because she was the ticket to their family improving their position with the alpha crime families in the city. He said he set up something with the Belisle pack and it involved his sister bonding the Ashby pack. Since it was his deal, he wasn't pleased about you bonding 'the bitch'—his words, not mine—but you were valuable, and his father insisted on keeping you. They said something about paying off high society debts, but a lot of that was on the other end of the line. I didn't hear it."

I stared at him, turning the words over.

We already knew a lot of that, but I'd assumed the deal had more to do with Noah Connolly than Tobias. That made this worse. Not only did Tobias hate Kiara, but her escape and our dark bond had fucked up plans he'd made to better his standing with their father.

"Is there anything else you can remember about the high society debts?" Ambrose asked.

His hand went to the small of my back. I let him touch me, indulging in it. Liberty raised an eyebrow skeptically when she saw the casual affection, but didn't comment.

She'd be ribbing me about it later, I was sure.

Reynold shrugged. "They were a woman's debts. If they were

partially paid off, Tobias said they could count on the woman accruing more. I'm not sure what the potential payment was, though."

Ambrose's aura flared, filling the small room with hot iron and smoke. Reynold's eyes widened and he shied back against the chair, but my employees were unphased. "That's fine. I think I know."

They had been talking about my mother. That much was clear. I didn't know what the payment was either. Based on the accounts Dash had hacked into, my mother owed the Connollys so much money she would have to clear out all her accounts, sell off the houses, and then some, to clear her debt.

When Ambrose tilted his head toward the door, I nodded and followed him. Liberty hopped off the desk and tailed behind, while Jasper stayed with his patient.

"Your mother is paying off her debts by giving them you."

He stated it like fact the moment the door closed behind Libby. I faltered, a denial on the tip of my tongue. I swallowed it down, a myriad of emotion swirling through me. Betrayal, disgust, pain.

"I wish I could say that doesn't sound like something she would do," I said quietly.

Ambrose tried to hug me, but Liberty pushed her way in between us. I considered her my best friend, but I'd always kept her at arm's length—just like everyone else. Maybe my mother had fucked me up more than I thought. She'd damaged me as much as she had my brother, I just hadn't realized it.

"She's a raging cunt," Liberty declared. "But if they're paying off some of her debt in exchange for you, that means you're valuable. They wouldn't have entertained her if you weren't. That's a leverage point. Especially if Noah Connolly is the one who believes you're important."

Her hands clutched my shoulders, her brown hair loose and

wild. She had a smile curling her lips, the look in her eyes almost feral. The amount of work she'd been doing behind the scenes was astronomical—especially because she was aware of how many of my contracts had dried up. I wouldn't be able to afford to keep paying her forever, but she hadn't jumped ship. She'd dug in her heels and supported me.

Maybe she considered me as much of a friend as I considered her, even if I hadn't been a very good one.

Acting on impulse, I wrapped my arms around her and tugged her against me in a hug.

It was a weird feeling. The only person who hugged me on a regular basis was my brother, and not because I initiated them. He was a touchy person by nature. Kiara and I hadn't even hugged much, despite the cuddling and sexual activities we'd participated in.

Liberty squeezed me before pulling back with a grin. "Maybe the strange omega was good for you after all."

Touching moment or not, I growled at that. She laughed.

Ambrose placed his hand on my shoulder possessively, tucking me against his side. Once again, I relaxed under his affection, as unfamiliar as it was.

My mother may have sold me to fix her mistakes, but she wasn't someone who mattered to me. The betrayal didn't cut deep. I'd known for a long time that blood relations meant nothing to her.

"What if we went above Tobias?" I asked, glancing between Libby and Ambrose.

"To his father?" Liberty confirmed.

"Yes. We could offer Noah Connolly something he can't refuse. I have some expertise he wants, clearly. With a bit more research into the Belisle pack and their connection to the Ashby pack, I'm sure I could give him something better than that alliance."

"Won't Tobias come after Kiara, still? She seems confident she'll never be safe from him," Ambrose said.

"It'll be part of the deal. He won't do anything that would sacrifice his position in his father's empire. Noah Connolly will have to agree to keep Tobias away from us if he wants what we have to offer."

Did we have anything to offer?

Not yet, but we would.

Dash would be able to find something now that he knew what to look for. I trusted that more than I'd ever trusted anything—maybe more than I should. But he was falling for my omega as fast as she was falling for him, and if this was what we needed to save us all, then he would make it happen.

"It's a better plan than anything else I've thought up," Liberty said, glancing back at the closed office door. "But if we have to torture someone for information, I'm out. There was a brief period where Reynold and I really weren't getting along, and the idea of having to torture him was altogether unpleasant."

I snorted. "There's not going to be any torture. I'm not a hundred percent above board, but I'm not a monster."

Liberty cringed, pulling a piece of folded paper from a pocket in her jean shorts. "Less above board than you thought, I'm afraid. I looked into the jobs you told me to, and your mother was absolutely making you do illegal shit without telling you."

I took the paper, but didn't unfold it. Part of me didn't want to know the details. Mercury could look at it when we got home to see if anything was relevant.

For me, it was enough to know my mother hadn't respected a single one of my wishes. Not even the desire to avoid working for harmful criminals.

I'd told her outright that was something I wouldn't do—not even to keep my brother's secret. Marlowe would be furious if he found out I was hurting people to keep him and his pack safe.

"Thanks for looking into it," I said quietly.

She nodded, and silence fell over us.

This warehouse was oppressively hot with the August midday heat. It hadn't come equipped with AC, and I wasn't rich enough to install it, leaving us with little temperature control. Each breath of warm air made me feel heavier, tiredness weighing me down.

I could only run on desperation for so long.

"If you've got everything handled, we're going to go home," Ambrose said.

It made more sense for us to stay. Ask Reynold more questions. Do more work and research. I doubted I could convince Ambrose that I didn't need a nap, though, because I did.

He was taking care of me like he always had in the bedroom, but this time I wasn't trying to stop it.

"Reynold is slowly detoxing, and we'll send him off on the run when he's done," Liberty said. "If he remembers anything else, I'll contact you again."

"Thanks," Ambrose grunted on behalf of both of us, leading me to the car.

He opened the door and pushed me gently down into the passenger seat. I didn't complain when he took the keys from me. We were out of the warehouse and back on the road quickly, but the path he took wouldn't bring us back to my condo.

"Where are we going?" I asked.

The decrepit buildings and dirty streets of the Gritch District dissolved into a bustling commercial area. Ambrose kept driving in a straight line.

"Nowhere. But you need some rest, and it's going to be harder for you to relax when we're home."

"No it isn't."

"Kiara is days away from heat, doll. She might be needy, and if she is, you'll cater to her. Right now, she has Mercury to cater to her, so we can spend an hour or two driving around."

I wasn't sure how Mercury was going to cater to my omega. He still seemed to be trying to insist he didn't want her—that wouldn't go over well with her near-heat mood swings. If things devolved into absolute chaos, I was sure Mercury would call, and that soothed my nerves just enough to let my tiredness creep in.

Yawning wide, I tried to fight it back for no more than a few seconds. Then, I sighed.

"Fine. I'm not used to sleeping with another person. It's made it a lot harder—combined with everything else."

"Here, it's only you in that seat. Take a nap, and I'll wake you up when we're home."

I didn't complain again, drifting slowly off to sleep as I realized that Ambrose hadn't referred to it as *my* home.

Just home.

We were getting in deeper with these men every day, but I had to hope we'd just discovered the light at the end of the tunnel.

FORTY-FIVE

KIARA

I didn't want to leave my nest.

In the pile of blankets and pillows and clothing I'd built myself, everything was bordering perfect. There was no Ashby pack, waiting to take us on another date. No Tobias pulling the strings behind the scenes. No rejection like the one I was expecting from Mercury.

I was safe from all things.

It couldn't last, but I desperately wanted it to.

My nest was mostly complete to my brain's irrational requirements. I had every pillow I could find on the edges of the bed, crafting a barricade from the rest of the world. Blankets were draped on top and in the middle, over my fluff-covered form. I'd stolen the soft robe from Leighton's closet.

I would give it back, but I'd *needed* it. It was impossible to resist the compulsion, and when I tried, I'd broken down into tears and shaky, shallow breaths.

A few items of everyone's clothing were in the centre of the nest with me. It was the next best thing to having them all here. I was curled up with the clothes, occasionally rolling around in the comforting scents.

There was something missing—other than my alphas—but I couldn't put my finger on what it was. I'd circled the condo multiple times in search of something that could complete my nest, but nothing stuck out.

If I thought a simple failed search would be the end of it, I thought wrong.

The incompleteness of the nest rubbed at me more and more with every minute I spent in it. While it was still the most soothing place in the house, it wasn't the way it was supposed to be. It wasn't the perfect nest I longed for—not yet. It needed to be different. I just had no idea how.

Leighton had yet to return, so I couldn't beg her to help me. There was only one option to fix it as soon as humanly possible.

I had to go talk to Mercury.

My nerves stopped me until it was literally too much to handle staying in the nest. I'd had him strip down to nothing, and when he tried to refuse I'd almost started sobbing in front of him. Even in the preheat haze of nesting and desire, I was aware it was out of line. If unavoidable.

He wasn't my alpha, and he didn't want to be.

"Mercury?" I faced him in the living room, keeping more of a distance this time.

The auburn-haired alpha was wearing Ambrose's clothing. The oversized fit made him look smaller and softer than he usually seemed, but his brown eyes still didn't have much warmth in them. I avoided eye contact.

"Yes?" he asked.

"I need something for the nest."

"What do you need?"

Shifting my weight from foot to foot, I patted where Nyla sat strapped to my thigh. She'd been with me in my nest, so it wasn't her that was missing.

"I don't know," I whispered.

He sighed heavily. "How am I supposed to help you if you don't know?"

Those unbidden tears rose again—stupid heat hormones. I couldn't stop them if I wanted to. I tried to hide them this time, not wanting him to feel it was necessary to help me again. I'd turned half around to go back to my nest when he touched me.

His hand caught my arm, and I gasped. There wasn't any skin-on-skin contact with my robe on, but it was electric nonetheless.

Mercury was touching me.

On purpose.

When he tried to release me I whined, curling myself closer to him. Old books and cinnamon soothed my aches and made it less uncomfortable that my nest wasn't perfect. It made my skin tingle, the sharp cinnamon tickling my nose.

"Kiara," he breathed my name.

I turned to him, watching hesitance flit across his face, his tongue darting out to lick his lips. His jaw set and he released me, but again my eyes threatened a waterfall.

He cursed and swept me close to him, leading me over to the couch where we could sit down. I was tucked to his side, my head on his shoulder. I curled my legs up under me and sniffled.

"The crying isn't on purpose," I said. "I'm just... emotional."

"You're about to go into heat. It's natural."

His arm tightened around me, and I could have sworn I felt his lips ghost across the top of my head. "My emotions are manipulating you. I wouldn't fault you if you just let me cry it out."

"Leighton would kick my ass if I let you go off and cry by yourself."

"She wouldn't know," I countered. "And if she found out, I wouldn't let her hurt you for it. I know you don't really like me."

"I like you."

My laugh was a little hollow. "You don't have to lie to me. I ruined my chances with you the second I stabbed Ambrose."

I let myself continue to cuddle up to him—I wouldn't have this for long, and I wanted to take advantage while I could. Mercury kept me close too, almost seeming opposed to letting me go. We were silent for a while, but breathing together was enough to calm my hormones.

When I felt confident I wouldn't immediately burst into tears, I tried to get up.

He held fast, not releasing me from under his arm. As much as I wanted to stay cuddled, he didn't *need* to anymore. It wasn't fair to expect him to comfort me forever.

"I'm fine now," I said, clearing my throat slightly. "I can go back to the nest."

A flare of his aura split the air, accompanied by a growl.

It should have been terrifying, considering how close he was to me and how unhinged it sounded. My whimper wasn't because of fear, though. No, it was because slick was flooding my core and that tight feeling of need was again clutching my ovaries.

"Or I can stay here," I whispered. "If you want me to."

"Stay," he muttered.

I swallowed down my arousal and nodded. It was surprisingly easy to relax back against him. His scent blanketed me, not helping my body calm down after his outburst. Mercury's fingers absently stroked my arm, and I wished the skin was bare so I could feel the slight scrape of his nails and the softness of his long fingers.

My ability to stay still didn't last long. I got bored, anxious, twitchy. Every time I shifted he held me closer, preventing me from leaving his side.

With my body unable to fidget, my mouth began to spew words instead.

"You said you like me. Why?"

He heaved a sigh. I'd been avoiding looking at his face—from my position at his side, it was easy to curl up and stare at his knees instead. Now, I strained my neck to peer up at him.

His jaw was twitching, turmoil roiling in the depths of his eyes. Stubble brushed across his cheeks, but it didn't look natural on him. I got the sense he was usually meticulously clean shaven. His hair was messy too, twined into a single French braid that had strands falling out in a chaotic manner.

"Let me ask you something, little omega," he said, ignoring my question. "Why did you mark Dash and Ambrose?"

I flushed.

Had it been rude to place a temporary claim on his packmates when I knew he didn't like me? Absolutely. Especially since I hadn't even asked the packmates in question before doing it.

I'd been running on a combination of instinct and desperation.

Asking Leighton for the bond had been desperation to escape Tobias, at first. Biting the Loranger pack had been desperation to take a piece of what they had, before anyone else could.

I wanted to be a part of the casual affection they had for each other, despite the problems they clearly also harboured. Being around them felt like having the kind of companionship I always wanted, but had been denied by my father. Whether we ended up sating my sexual desire for them or not, I needed to be near them.

And it wouldn't have happened with just anyone, either.

The way they'd treated me had made it real. I was a person, with flaws, just like them. The flaws weren't ridiculed or dismissed, but almost... cherished.

"I... need them," I eventually mumbled. "But they're your pack first, so I know I'm not allowed—"

"What do you mean by need them?" He cut me off.

"They make me feel..."

There wasn't a way to describe it. Mercury was staring at me waiting for an answer, and I didn't have the words. All my years of tutoring to make me seem high class, and I couldn't find the proper word for the emotions that crashed over me whenever I was in their presence.

Including Mercury's.

I couldn't tell him that.

Instead I blurted something stupid, but true.

"I think I'm falling in love with them."

It was as irrational as my love for Leighton was—maybe more.

Mercury was silent for a long time. I began to fidget again, and this time he didn't tighten his grip. When the silence was so oppressive I needed to escape, I tried to get up once again.

At first, it seemed like he let me.

Then, he grabbed me by the hips and dragged me back down. Except this time, I was on his lap facing him. The robe wasn't built to hide my body when my thighs were splayed open, and the fluffy fabric opened to expose skin. A lot of skin, because I wasn't wearing anything beneath it.

My thighs were exposed, and the crack in coverage continued up to my pussy too. A sliver of my stomach was showing before the robe was once again properly wrapped to cover my breasts. I tried futilely to pull it closed at the bottom, only to be stopped by Mercury's long inhale and husky groan.

"You're in love with them?" he asked.

I blinked. His hands were on my waist. This was far too close.

"Falling..." I clarified, trailing off.

"And what if you're only falling in love with them because you're scared of your father stealing you back?"

"I'm not!"

Protective instinct surged and I tried to shimmy myself off his lap. It was a rational question, exactly what I would have expected from Mercury. Yet I was offended on a base level that he'd even asked.

They were mine.

That had nothing to do with anything else.

"Are you sure, little omega?"

"Of course I am. If I was attaching because I was scared, I could have attached to anyone. I could have been aroused by the doctor that treated me or anyone I talked to in the Omega Safety Division. I wasn't. Only your pack. Only ever you three and Leighton."

I'd never been more sure of anything in my life.

Mercury held fast to me, and all my straining couldn't free me from his grip. His aura was out, making him stronger than I could ever dream of being. We were alone here together, so maybe I should be scared of him holding me on his lap.

I wasn't.

I flourished under the attention, wishing he was holding me here so I could take a seat on his cock.

My heat was so close I could taste it. This would be about the time I would usually get locked in my room with the first dose of sleep medication, ready for me to take when the need got to be too intense.

"You're confident," he murmured.

I squirmed some more, but all it did was rub my pussy across the prominent bulge in his pants.

"It's the truth. Why wouldn't I be confident in that?"

He hummed instead of responding, trailing one hand down from my hip to slide across the bare skin of my thigh. I gasped, arching into the touch. Mercury took it away just as quickly.

I let my eyes close, hoping he would do it again.

He didn't, and I waited a minute full of long, tense seconds before I resorted to begging. "Mercy, touch me. Please? Or did you not want to?"

"Mercy? I thought you only called me that because you were drunk."

The alpha touched me despite calling me out for the nickname. His fingers trailed down my torso, tickling the flesh of the exposed part of my stomach.

"If you don't like me calling you that, I don't have to," I said breathlessly.

He growled softly, shifting until he'd pulled me to his chest and his lips were against my neck. "No, I enjoy it."

There wasn't time to savour the spark of exhilaration that lit inside me at his acceptance of the nickname. The ache in my core was compounding too quickly. I whined against him, opening my eyes, and nuzzling my nose into the crook of his shoulder.

"I need to come," I murmured.

His teeth grazed my neck and I moaned.

"No, you don't."

The realization of what he'd said was like the scratch of nails across a chalkboard.

"What?"

"You're on the precipice of heat. Any sexual activity could push you over the edge. Do you want to go into heat right now?"

I nibbled on my bottom lip. Was I completely against the idea? Not at all. From a practical standpoint, I should hold off. There was no telling when our next date with the Ashby pack would be, and we needed to continue to play that game until Leighton had figured out what else to do.

"I'll answer for you," Mercury said. "You don't. Your alpha isn't home yet, and you want your nest to be finished before you go into heat."

The mention of the nest was enough to have me shifting in his lap for an entirely different reason. He was right. It wasn't *finished*. "I need to figure out what it's missing," I said.

"Alright, little omega. Let me help you."

He released me and I bounded to my feet, brushing down my robe to cover myself again. My moods were changing faster than the winds on a tumultuous day, but trying to control it was pointless. Maybe it was good he'd shaken off the arousal for the time being.

Mercury stood up after me with an impassive look on his face. I paced the living room until he grabbed my hand. "Show me the nest, and we'll find what it needs."

I flushed but nodded, tugging him back to my nest in Leighton's room in the hopes that I could find what was needed to complete the makeshift place of comfort.

FORTY-SIX

LEIGHTON

I had no idea how long I slept, but I woke up to the sound of my phone dinging with a fresh notification.

The Ashby pack was ready for their next date.

Tomorrow night.

Sooner than we'd hoped for, but it was only a date. We weren't expected to bond them yet, so if we could find something suitable to offer Noah Connolly, we could go to him the morning after the pack date and put a stop to future ones.

Ambrose hadn't been anywhere near my condo, so we'd driven back in comfortable silence, his hand on my thigh and his jaw clenched.

We came home to find Mercury and Kiara curled together in the nest, fast asleep. Dash hadn't made it back yet, but there was an update text flashing on the lock screen of Mercury's phone. It confirmed everything was going well and he hadn't blown anything up—the man clearly wasn't used to being left to his own devices.

Ambrose and I didn't wake either of them, dropping onto the leather living room couch instead.

I flicked on the TV, trying to process what we'd learned. The plans we hoped would work to get Kiara out from under her father for good. The way I'd been making the world a worse place for years because of my mother's sins.

A mindless cooking show came on and I left it playing, staring blankly with my hands limp on my thighs.

After a few minutes of that, Ambrose laid his arm across my shoulders and dragged me into his lap. I relaxed against him. "Is this alright?" he asked.

It never would have been, before all this. Before Kiara. I'd fled like a demon was on my tail after every encounter at The Pointe Lounge. I stayed exactly long enough for aftercare to bring me out of my typical slump, and then I was gone. There was no excessive cuddling or time spent on the couch watching pointless television.

I'd been bleeding him dry, never giving anything back.

Why does he even want me after all that?

His dedication to me was part of the reason I was so comfortable entrusting Kiara to him, even after the incident.

"It's fine," I whispered.

He released a heavy breath—relief, I imagined.

"I kind of treated you like shit." My admittance was sudden and Ambrose didn't respond right away.

The cooking show rated and scored the final dishes of phase one, and when they'd moved on to phase two he spoke. "I'm no saint, Leighton. I should have told my pack about you. My secret is probably the reason Mercury is so resentful now—he cut off our relationship for Dash's sake, but I wasn't willing to give up what he was. I wasn't willing to give up him or you."

"He's in my omega's nest with her, so he must be overcoming that bitterness."

Ambrose chuckled. "Maybe. Slowly. He was alone for a year,

letting himself go under to save a drowning man. If I hadn't been selfish and kept seeing you, I might have been disgruntled too."

"I can't see how you're not, after so long of seeing me. I didn't treat you like a human being. You were more like..." I trailed off, sighing and sliding down to lie on the couch, half my body in his lap. "A convenient cock and an escape from life."

Drama unfolded on the show—a squabble about stolen ingredients, or something. I wasn't paying much attention, but Ambrose waited until it was done before he spoke again.

"I was happy to be that for you, Leighton. Did I want more? Yes, I did. But I knew you weren't ready, and I didn't want to push."

"I doubt you felt good about it."

"No," he admitted. "Every brush off hurt, but I would do it all over again in a heartbeat."

My pulse pounded faster. I turned in his lap, staring up at his scarred jaw and stubbled cheeks. His body was taut. He was trying to resist the temptation to free the words clinging to the tip of his tongue.

If this had been a month ago, I would have let it rest. I wouldn't have wanted to know—there was no part of me that was ready for an admittance like the one he was currently holding back.

Now?

I craved it. I'd gotten a taste of having someone close besides myself. I'd gotten a taste of Kiara invading my head and space, and I liked it, damn it.

"Why would you do it all over again?" I whispered, giving him permission to say it—if he was as ready as I was.

"Fuck, Leighton. I love you. How could I not?"

His thick fingers stroked through my hair, his other arm resting over my relaxed body. I sat up, untangling myself from him, only to press closer once again.

Our lips brushed and he groaned, deepening what was meant to be a simple kiss. We devoured each other, ignoring the cooking show for real. When we broke apart we were panting, and his warm brown eyes exposed every soft piece of him I'd been ignoring for years.

"I..." I trailed off, the words lodging in my throat.

Shit. I thought I was ready to say it, but I couldn't. The circumstances were rushing in again. Kiara's safety. Mine. Theirs. It would be safer for all of them if I kicked them unceremoniously from this apartment—it would have been better if I'd done that from the beginning.

Maybe I'd still need to do it, and I wouldn't have the guts to even try if I cracked now and told Ambrose what I wanted to say.

Ambrose sighed, his lips landing on my nose and then each cheek. "I'm just grateful you didn't flee the scene after I said it, doll."

"You know how I feel," I murmured.

He nodded. "I do. When the dust settles, then we can work on your ability to say it out loud. I've made you say plenty of other things you never thought you would say."

My cheeks flushed. I settled back down on his lap, taking comfort in his warmth and closeness and reminding myself of the truth in my head.

I loved him.

And Kiara.

Dash and Mercury were next, if we continued on this trajectory.

Yet, I couldn't find a single internal problem with that.

Dash crashed into the condo with a grin on his face.

"I made it back alive!" he proclaimed, tossing his keys onto a console table in the living room. He was definitely going to forget where he'd left them the next time he needed to leave. The man was pure chaos.

Ambrose rolled his eyes, kissing my head and lifting me off his lap to stand. "Proud of you, bud."

"Bud?" Dash wrinkled his nose. "Now you sound like my dad. Do I have to call you Daddy too?"

"Please don't," Ambrose said.

Dash observed him, seeming to decide if he wanted to test him. "Anything you want, Daddy," he said eventually.

Ambrose, halfway to the kitchen, let out an irritated groan. "You're evil. I never should have let you have pack lead."

Snickering, Dash flopped down onto the couch next to me. His arm slung casually over my shoulders, like it belonged there. I let him bask in the touch until Mercury came out into the living room. He was tired, blinking the haze of sleep from his eyes, with a disgruntled expression on his face.

"Kiara heard Dash come home. Wants him," he muttered, narrowing his eyes at his packmate.

Dash tried to release me and leap to his feet, but I didn't let him. My hand came down on his upper thigh, right where his thigh met his hips, and I held him down on the couch. His lips dropped into a pout. "She wants me," he said.

"Yes, but cuddling her in her nest would be a reward. And you know what you don't deserve?"

I paused, waiting for him to tell me. He bounced on the cushions. If he'd tried he could have dislodged my grip on him and stood, but he didn't. Spring rain and peaches grew heavy in the air as a bulge grew in his pants. Mercury sighed and vanished into the kitchen.

"A... reward?" he said hesitantly.

"Exactly. Why would you get rewarded when you haven't been punished yet?"

A full-body shudder rolled through him. His green eyes locked with mine, his movie star handsome features softened with desire. He nibbled his bottom lip.

"Punish me, then," he whispered. "Because I want to be in the nest with both of you."

I could have teased him—I'd never said anything about cuddling in the nest along with my omega. He was being vulnerable, though, and I didn't want to risk embarrassing the normally shameless alpha.

"Don't you want to know what punishments I have in mind?" I asked.

He shook his head. "You could do literally anything to me."

It was my turn to shiver. Standing from the couch, I watched Dash tense. Instinct told him to get up, but he waited.

He was being surprisingly good, considering he was usually a huge brat.

Would it last?

I didn't want it to. I wanted Dash to rile me up like he always did.

"In that case, Kiara and I are going to do plenty of things to you before you get your release."

He popped up from the couch. That impulse was apparently too hard to ignore. He'd taken a few steps toward my bedroom when I grabbed him by the back of his shirt. He groaned.

"The more you rush, the longer you have to wait," I said.

Instead of letting me go first like I'd wanted, he glanced back over his shoulder with a smirk. My grip on his shirt released when he ran forward, sprinting down the hallway and into the bedroom. I heard Kiara's soft squeal as I followed much slower behind him.

When I got into the bedroom, Dash had his face buried between her legs. He was lapping up her slick, but spared me a glance and a grin as I closed the door.

"Get off the bed, Dash." I injected as much command as I could into my words, putting the weight of my aura behind it. Not a bark in the typical sense, but stronger than simple words.

He groaned, his hips bucking against Kiara's pillows, which were in a ring around the edge of the bed. My omega's eyes were rolled back, her hand gripping Dash's blonde hair. A little whimper left her as his tongue laved her clit.

I growled when he didn't immediately listen, and his attention finally snapped to me. His grin faltered, dropping into the nervous pout again. "Off the bed," I demanded again.

He had to extract himself from Kiara's grasp, but he did as he was told. Dash slid down off the bed, landing on his knees in front of me. I almost purred at that sight.

"Alpha, why did you make him leave?" Kiara whimpered.

Her fingers had already taken over for his mouth, swirling around her clit. Slick drenched her thighs. She was so close to heat—we shouldn't be doing this. This tension had built to a breaking point, though, and I wasn't about to let Dash fuck her through her heat without being punished first. He'd stolen her first kiss and been the first one she'd bonded.

Both honours that should have been mine.

"He's being punished, dove. Dash is just being a brat about it."

"But I want him to knot me," she said.

I strode over to my bedside table, opening the bottom drawer and pulling out a toy. It was a silicone cock in a vibrant shade of blue. Kind of matched her eyes, actually. At the base was a knot, same as the one a male alpha's cock had.

I threw it to Dash, and he fumbled but caught it.

"He'll use the toy on you."

Dash stared at the toy, a low growl rumbling his chest as he pouted.

I glared at him, stalking over to grab his chin. His growl died, pupils dilating. "Unless you'd rather leave," I said. "You're lucky

I'm letting you fuck her with anything, after the stunts you've pulled. What's it going to be?"

He leaned into the tight grip I had on his sharp jawline, licking his lips.

"I told you that you could do anything to me. You just have to make me."

His smirk was infuriating and sexy at the same time, and I grinned right back.

"I hope you know that making you is going to be fucking easy."

FORTY-SEVEN

DASH

I was already in enough trouble.

It was a mystery, what had possessed me to antagonize her more. I'd run ahead of her into this room, gotten a taste of Kiara that I'd been dying for, and growled at her.

Leighton was going to fucking ruin me.

And did I ever want her to.

"Should I, like, not fight back? I think that's the only way it can be as easy as you say," I taunted.

The aroused irritation in her gaze sent of a zing of desire through me. My blood boiled with the need to play with fire. I'd been burned before, but I loved being kept on my toes. It was the only way I didn't get bored.

"Fight back as hard as you can," Leighton said.

Her aura grew heavier, crushing me beneath the weight of it. My aura flared without conscious thought from me—my alpha side didn't enjoy being challenged. I was pack lead. The strongest in my pack, even though the position had originally been gifted without a fight.

I wasn't stronger than her.

There was something about her that brought me to my knees, even my alpha nature giving up the fight quickly.

She grabbed my shoulder and shoved me toward the foot of the bed. Kiara's pussy was in front of my face a second later. I leaned in, wanting another taste of her slick pink folds, but Leighton's hand wound through my hair. She yanked me away so hard, I whined.

"All you get to do is knot her with that toy," Leighton instructed.

The toy was still in my hand. It was thicker than me, but not longer. I would definitely be able to give her way more pleasure with my real cock than this fake one.

But part of my punishment was giving our omega what she needed without taking what I wanted. Leighton truly was a cruel Mistress, and I assumed this wouldn't be the end of my discipline.

Clamping my fist around the base of the toy, I rubbed the tip from Kiara's clit to her entrance and back again. My omega whined, one of her legs coming up to rest on my shoulder. Leighton purred, standing over us like a reigning queen.

I teased Kiara until she was squirming, her hips rising off the mattress in an attempt to get the dildo inside her. Then, I glanced at Leighton.

For permission.

She nodded, smirking.

Her enjoyment of my submission made me want to be good—for now. I doubted this desire to do as she said would last.

Using my free hand to readjust my cock in my pants, I held the knot of the fake cock in the other. The tip breached her entrance slowly, and she moaned. Her slick was so tempting I almost tried to lean forward and snag another taste.

"You like that, little omega?" I asked.

Kiara rose up onto her elbows, looking down at me with

adorable flushed cheeks. She was naked from head to toe, except for the knife holster strapped to her thigh. I couldn't decide if this was the sexiest she'd ever looked—she was too goddamn ethereal in everything for me to choose.

"More," she begged, her voice soft.

"Don't beg me, beg Leighton."

Her gaze swung, eyelids fluttering when I pushed another inch of fake blue dick into her pussy. She was clenching so hard on the length, maybe it was better it wasn't my actual cock. I might have embarrassed myself by coming in her pretty pussy right away.

"Alpha, please," she murmured. "Make him give me more."

Leighton grabbed Kiara's hand and brought it to her lips, leaving a soft kiss on the back of it. "This is a bit of punishment for both of you, dove. After all, you gave him a bondmark. You still haven't given me a bondmark."

Kiara's eyes widened and she sat up all the way abruptly. My grip on the dildo almost slipped and I cursed, pulling it out of her and grabbing her thigh with my free hand.

"Did you want one?" Kiara demanded. "We're already bonded, I didn't think my weak little bite would do anything to strengthen our bond..."

Having her sitting up had brought her soft skin too close for me to resist. I pressed kisses along her thighs, using my teeth to nip at her. It was a distraction from the temptation of her chocolate coconut slick, because I knew I wasn't permitted to taste her there.

I was already going to be disciplined enough.

But the longer she stayed like this, the more likely I was to say 'fuck it' and lap her up anyway.

"Do you want to give me one?" Leighton asked.

"Yes," Kiara answered instantly. "I just wasn't sure... I forced you to bond me, so I didn't know if you'd want more bonding.

And I thought it might complicate things. Like, with Ambrose, and how he insisted you were his too…"

My lips grew closer and closer to her core with every nip, every kiss. It was too fucking tempting. Leighton should know my self-control didn't extend this far. I inhaled deeply, groaning when I landed at the apex of Kiara's thighs.

"Dash." Leighton's tone was warning.

My tongue slipped out and tasted Kiara, the flavour of her exploding on my tongue. She moaned, thighs spreading.

Before I could taste her again, Leighton pulled me back by the hair. My cock throbbed at the rough treatment, and I stared up at her. "I thought you wouldn't notice," I said cheekily. "Seeing as you were ignoring me, and all."

Leighton growled. "You're a real slut for attention, aren't you?"

"You knew that about me already."

"Kiara, get on the bed. On your back," Leighton ordered.

Her omega scrambled to obey, crawling through the masses of pillows and blankets and clothing to lay up by the headboard. She kept her legs clenched together, depriving me of the best view in the goddamn universe.

"You're going to be on the bed too, Dash. But I want your ass up in the air."

I groaned. The dildo had somehow stayed in my hand through all that, Kiara's slick drying on the tip. Leighton released my hair so I could crawl up onto the bed, getting into a position that left me feeling exposed—despite the clothing still covering all of me.

"Lay down right between Kiara's legs," Leighton said. "Show him your pussy, dove."

Kiara's pink flush travelled down onto her chest at that, and she hesitantly spread her legs again. My mouth watered. Omega slick was addictive. I hadn't realized until I'd tasted her the first time, but I would never be able to get enough.

I leaned forward, knowing I was testing my luck once again.

Leighton's hand came down on my ass, hard. The impact was muffled by my pants, but it startled me enough I stopped.

"Ease the dildo into her, Dash, but don't touch."

The fake dick was the absolute last thing I wanted to ease into her. I would much rather have my fingers, tongue, or cock inside her, but I'd lost the privilege. Hopefully not for long.

I pushed the tip into her tight heat, eagerly watching as her pussy swallowed it.

Then hands reached around to undo my belt, and my cock jumped. Kiara whimpered, but I couldn't move while Leighton palmed my cock through layers of clothing. I could hardly breathe when she slid my pants and boxer briefs over my ass and down to mid-thigh, before leaving the fabric constraining me.

"Don't get distracted," Leighton murmured. "Our omega needs you to pay attention to her."

I sucked in a sharp breath.

Our omega.

Leighton had called Kiara that. It didn't feel real. Was she serious, or was that just something said to get me riled up in preparation for my punishment?

I decided I'd rather not know. Reality always had less of a shine than I wanted, and I wanted her and Kiara. More than anything I'd ever wanted before.

It was hard to believe, but I wanted them more than I'd ever desired my scent match. That wasn't supposed to be how it worked.

Sharp pain bloomed on my backside, the sound of the smack ringing through the air. I gasped, glancing back over my shoulder at a smirking Leighton. "Every time you get distracted, it's another spank. Do you want to know how many you're getting already?"

I shook my head, swallowing. The ass cheek she'd spanked

was smarting, but it was the kind of pleasure-pain I yearned for. Like when I'd antagonized Kiara into cutting me with her knife while I made her come. Pain made me feel alive.

The betas I'd fucked had never been able to give it to me. The few times I'd gotten up the nerve to ask, they'd laughed it off like it was a joke. Maybe I was a joke—an alpha that preferred a hefty dose of torment with his pleasure.

But Leighton didn't think I was, and neither did Kiara.

"If you don't want to know, tell me how much you think you can handle. We can split your punishment up if we need to," Leighton said.

"I told you," I said. "You can do anything to me. All I want is to end up in this nest after."

She lifted a perfectly shaped dark eyebrow. I caught the glint of satisfaction in her eyes. "You're more of a pain slut than I thought. Tell me if you need to tap out."

"I won't."

"You don't have to take everything today."

"I want to."

Maybe I was speaking too soon, considering she hadn't told me how much pain she planned on inflicting. I didn't really care. The risk of possibly having to tap out thrilled me. There was a reason I'd stacked taunt after taunt, antagonized her over and over again.

Kiara whined and Leighton's hand came down on my ass, hard.

"Make her come while taking your punishment."

I plunged another inch of the dildo into her, reaching my hand out to reverently stroke her clit.

Another smack.

This was going to be a challenge. Caught between the two of them, it was hard to focus. Vanilla cream swirled with coconut chocolate, hints of my packmate's scents lingering on the fabrics in this nest. I tried to hold my breath, not wanting to get lost in the sense of comfort and belonging.

Kiara's pussy took the fake cock, bit by bit, until the knot rubbed against her entrance. She mewled softly, trying to press down and take the knot too, but I didn't let her. Leighton hadn't told me to give her the knot she was desperate for, yet.

I was finally hesitant to earn more punishment.

Leighton's palm connected with my ass again and I jerked. Precum beaded at the tip of my cock, my knot aching with the need to please the omega in front of me.

Unfortunately, I was one hundred percent certain I wouldn't be rewarded with my cock in my omega today.

Today was about discipline.

"You're easily distracted," Leighton murmured. "Kiara, make sure he remembers to pleasure you, because this spanking is about to get a lot more distracting."

Kiara's hand came down to wrap through my hair, nails digging into my scalp. I groaned, choking when Leighton gave me the hardest spank yet.

The female alpha wasn't gentle with me. She wasn't soft, and didn't give me much of a chance to adjust. Her hands came down repeatedly on my ass, enough force behind each spank that I winced even while my cock pulsed. Faintly, I heard her counting.

I would have lost myself in only the feeling of the spanking if it hadn't been for Kiara's moans and whimpers urging me on. I was rough with her—if Leighton spanked me especially hard, the dildo plunged into Kiara with more force. My omega didn't complain, though. Her hands in my hair only pulled me closer.

By the time she arched her back and screamed with release, I was shrinking away from every smack. Leighton had to hold me in place. It hurt like a bitch. The only thing that was worse was the way my cock throbbed, eager for a touch and release.

"So, that was about half of the punishment I had planned for you," Leighton purred.

I groaned, my body slumping down to the bed. I glanced over my shoulder at my ass. It was bright red, some spots darker where bruises were forming.

"If you want to call it, you can still cuddle with Kiara in the nest tonight."

"I told you, I'm not calling it," I said, my face half-pressed against the blankets.

If that was *half* I wasn't sure how I was going to handle it, but I wasn't at my limit. To be honest, I had very little concept of where my limits existed, because I'd never had the chance to test them. Not like this.

"Can I have the knot?" Kiara asked, her voice wispy.

The dildo was knot-deep inside of her, slick drenching every inch of the toy. Her pussy stretched tight around the girth, and I would love to see how it looked swallowing down a knot—as much as I wished it was my knot sliding inside her.

Leighton hummed. Her hands rubbed circles on my raw ass, soothing the burn. "Fine. Since Dash isn't tapping out, he can have a little reward. Push that knot into her, and then you can taste her again."

Moaning, I dragged myself up from my slump. Having the best view was imperative.

"Fuck, little omega," I said, watching her pussy gush slick. "You're so fucking ready for this knot."

She nodded a few times, bright eyes locked on me.

"Please," she whispered. "Give it to me."

Her heat was coming, soon. There was a hint of desperation in her tone that would increase when the heat hormones washed over her. Since I'd paid my dues to her first alpha, I'd be able to see her through her heat with my real knot—not this fake silicone. If she would have me.

A flash of doubt made me hesitate.

Kiara flushed, her hand caressing my cheek. "I wish it was your knot."

Our bond flared to life, her emotions flooding in. The connection wasn't constantly open. I'd learned to shut it down, since it was weaker than a normal bond. But my doubt had seeped through, and she'd felt it.

"I wish it was too," I whispered.

Leighton's hand ventured between my legs, grabbing my balls in her hand. "Take your punishment, and next time it will be."

I stiffened, unsure what she planned to do with the crown jewels, but she just held them. Somewhat gently.

I pushed the fake dick forward, working it deeper into Kiara as she whined. Every bit stretched her further until I wasn't sure it was possible for her to take more, and then she'd taken the whole knot.

"Good girl," Leighton said. She tugged at my balls and I groaned, trying to shift away from her. She didn't let me. "She needs another orgasm, Dash."

"What are you planning on doing to me?" I asked, the question spilling out.

"Squeezing. Not too hard."

She gave a test squeeze. It was a different flavour of discomfort than the spanking, but I somehow translated it to pleasure just the same. That was unexpected.

When I didn't protest she kneaded me a little harder. I groaned, a full-body tremble wracking me, accentuating the foreign sensations. I didn't want her to stop, so I buried my face against Kiara's pussy, laving her clit with my tongue. The dildo could barely move with the knot embedded, but I pushed and released the base.

She seemed to like it, a high-pitched keening coming from her.

Her thighs came around my head, and I was pretty sure this was what it was like to be in heaven.

Between an omega's legs, her silky thighs tightening to pull me close.

Leighton behind me, testing out different levels of pressure on my balls, and occasionally giving me a smack on my abused ass cheeks.

I used my tongue expertly against Kiara's pussy, working her up until she screamed—and I grunted, because Leighton chose the moment of Kiara's peak to squeeze my balls extra hard.

But then her hand moved down to my cock, and I tried to pull away.

Not because I didn't want whatever she planned to give, but because I wouldn't last ten fucking seconds with her delicate palm jerking me.

"I'll come," I choked out. She'd ignored my movement away from her, wrapping her fingers around my length.

"You liked the pain that much?"

She couldn't see my flaming cheeks because I'd buried my face against Kiara's stomach. My omega was sated, gently purring in the aftermath of her orgasm.

Leighton didn't let me hide for long, grabbing my hair more gently than she'd touched me since we started. I was pliable beneath her, and she hauled me up until I was on my knees, my back to her chest. She laid her lips against my neck and my breath hitched.

Christ, she wasn't going to fucking bite me. *Alphas don't bite each other.* Just like they didn't purr.

Except her chest rumbled and I melted back against her. She held my weight with ease, one hand in my hair and the other holding my cock.

"I asked you a question. If you answer it, you can come."

I cursed under my breath. She could definitely see my blush

now, and so could Kiara. The omega's eyes were bright as she watched, the toy still knotting her.

"Yeah. I did," I admitted.

"No wonder you're such a brat, if you're this much of a pain slut too."

I didn't have any sort of rebuttal or comeback. All I had was a moan, because her hand slid down my length. She only stroked me three times from base to tip before I came.

My head swam, the orgasm wiping my brain but simultaneously not feeling like enough. I needed more after all the pain my body had endured—after how much I'd suffered to come, just once.

Leighton released me, though.

I wasn't getting another, and that was part of my punishment too.

"Lay down beside Kiara," she said in a soft tone.

I wouldn't have been able to stop myself if I tried. My body was jello, my limbs barely listening to my commands. All I could do was drop onto my hands and knees, crawling up to my omega and curling myself against her side.

My eyelids fell half closed as Leighton worked the knot toy out of Kiara. She moaned, but didn't beg for another orgasm. She turned to me instead, pushing her head against my chest. A blanket of tiredness draped over me, and I was half asleep by the time Leighton crawled off the bed.

"Where are you going?" I asked, a hint of panic sliding down my spine.

She couldn't just... leave me. Not after that.

She smiled, brushing a strand of black hair back from her face. I loved her smile—it wasn't something I'd seen before Kiara. I was used to her stern expression and frowns.

"We're not cuddling with a dirty dildo," she said dryly. "I'm going to clean it and grab a towel to tidy up some of the mess. I'll be right back."

"Oh," I mumbled.

Kiara hid her chuckle by pushing closer to me, our sweaty bodies curled against each other. Leighton spent a few minutes in the bathroom, coming out with a towel as promised.

I expected her to press against Kiara's other side when she joined us in the nest.

She didn't.

Instead, she laid beside me. Her side pressed to my back, and it wasn't exactly cuddling in the traditional sense, but this was closer than I'd dreamed of getting. The alpha didn't seem like much of a cuddler. It took far too long to calm down my racing heartbeat as she laid beside me, but eventually tiredness won out and I drifted off into a blissful nap.

FORTY-EIGHT

LEIGHTON

"There's no way she can leave this apartment," Ambrose said the next day, staring at Kiara.

She was curled up in her makeshift nest on a pile of blankets and clothes. My omega had barely spent any time awake since Ambrose and I returned home from the warehouse. There had only been the brief interlude of wakefulness with Dash. She'd stolen clothes from all of us, and insisted she always have someone in the nest with her.

Every time I touched her, her skin was flushed and hot. Her heat was no longer creeping in—it was sprinting.

"No," I agreed. "I'll go on the date by myself. They'll have to understand."

Kiara whined, one hand on her lower stomach and the other clutching the arm of a fluffy stuffed animal.

I hadn't had any in my house, but we'd received a large shipment of the things this morning, along with more blankets and various pillows. Mercury had grudgingly explained that Kiara had found something wrong with her nest, and they'd ordered her all sorts of nesting material to hopefully fill the void.

"I'm fine," she said, looking around her space. "I have to go. My father will be furious if I don't. He won't listen to you tomorrow if he's furious."

"Does he not understand how heat works?" I asked, crossing my arms over my chest. "You could go into it at any moment. Having you wandering around a high-class restaurant of all fucking places is flat out ridiculous."

"I won't go into heat." She said it with high confidence.

That confidence was immediately undermined by the way she slid off the bed and out of her nest... and whined. A low, involuntary whine that came from deep within her. Kiara didn't want to leave her nest, and she shouldn't have to.

My omega should be able to have a normal heat spent in comfort, and I was furious that she was right.

Noah Connolly wouldn't take kindly to Kiara not listening to his directives, and it would negatively impact our ability to negotiate. It might harm Kiara more in the long run if she didn't come to the restaurant, as uncomfortable as it would be in the short term.

"She can't go," Mercury said.

I hadn't realized he was here. He had his arms crossed over his chest, leaning against the door frame with a fierce scowl.

"I'm going," Kiara insisted again.

Her steps were stilted as she moved away from the nest. She glanced back over her shoulder no less than six times before she got to me where I stood across the room.

"No, you're not," Ambrose said.

Kiara's chest rumbled with a little growl. It wasn't like the sexy, possessive ones she often released. This one was angry, her sapphire blue eyes narrowed into a glare.

"Neither of you can stop me," she said.

Mercury and Ambrose both growled back. Dash hadn't come in here—he was neck deep in hacks as he tried to give us the best possible leverage for tomorrow. After napping in the nest with Kiara last night, he'd locked himself in the office. I imagined he would have the same opinion as his packmates.

"It's unsafe and irrational for you to leave," Mercury said. "Do you really want to leave your perfect nest?"

He softened his tone for the second part, making it a clear bribe. Kiara looked longingly at her nest before shaking her head. "I'm going."

"Your scent is already spiking. If it gets any worse, you could send every alpha in the building into a rut," Ambrose said. "Leighton, tell her she's not going."

It was my turn to growl, every instinct raging at being told what to do. At being told how to handle my own omega.

If I wanted her to stay behind, it was a simple order. The dark bond demanded she listen when I commanded her, and she couldn't resist for long enough to follow me out to the date.

But was that ethical?

It would be to keep her safe. However, I knew she would be furious and I wasn't sure if she would forgive me. This was her own safety. She should have control over it, shouldn't she?

The alpha part of me didn't want her out of her nest—even across the room from it was too far. The rest of me? I knew she had her own free will, and I hadn't dark bonded her so I could take that from her.

"Kiara, do you understand what could happen if you go? If you go into heat while we're out?" I asked.

Her teeth sunk into her bottom lip. She gave a hesitant shake of her head.

"Plenty of alphas will go into a rut around an omega in heat. They'll go crazy trying to get to you. It might cause a riot—it's happened before. I'll try to protect you, but depending on how many alphas are there... It could get messy."

She shifted from foot to foot, hand on her thigh. Her knife holster hadn't been removed. The rest of her clothes had been shed ages ago, leaving her only in my plush robe, but she couldn't bear to part from the weapon. I knew it must be rubbing uncomfortably against her ultra-sensitive skin.

"If I don't go, it could be worse," she whispered. "I won't go into heat. We can go and get the Ashby pack to let us leave early, and I'll be home by the time it hits."

Ambrose and Mercury were stiff and doubtful. Honestly, so was I. Ultimately, it was her choice. Kiara believed she could make it through the night and would rather risk those consequences than the other ones.

"Fine. You'll come," I said.

Mercury growled, but I shut him up with a glare. Ambrose contained himself, not making a sound but creating tight fists at his sides.

"We've got to get you dressed now," I continued. "It's a good thing Dash got you so many fancy outfits. Let's put you in the shower and get you ready."

Worry kept me tense as I stripped Kiara out of her robe and placed her under the cool spray of water. I didn't want to bring her out of this house. I would rather keep my omega safe now and deal with what happened later. If she'd accepted staying home, we would have figured something out.

Since she hadn't, I had to trust in my ability to keep her safe in a hoard of alphas.

When she whispered a quiet, "Thank you," before she got in the shower, I sighed and decided it was maybe worth it to give her this choice. She'd never had it before in her life, and I didn't want to be anything like her father. Not even when it came to this.

FORTY-NINE

KIARA

This restaurant was quieter than the club had been. There were far fewer people milling around, and my feet hadn't faltered on the way through the door.

Maybe it hadn't been a good idea to come here, but I wasn't going to be the reason everything blew up. I absolutely was not.

It was unnerving, though, how alphas turned their heads toward me as I passed, their nostrils flaring. Scents spiked around me and I tried to focus on the one I cared about. Vanilla cream. My alpha, who'd let me decide what I wanted to do.

Although, I was already wondering if she'd been right to want me staying home.

I didn't like the attention.

I pressed myself so close to her side we were almost tripping over each other as we followed the hostess to our table.

This time, the table wasn't very private. It was six chairs instead of a large booth, situated in the centre of the room. I gazed longingly around the edges of the fine dining establishment, wishing we could have a booth again. My scent might be better contained within the half walls.

Cordian rose to greet us. Today, he had dark smears of purple under both his eyes, a sure sign of very little sleep. His hand shook as he reached out to shake Leighton's. I held back my growl, ignoring the twisting in my stomach at the thought of them touching.

I reached out to grab Leighton's after Cordian had released it, though. I rubbed my chin along her palm, making sure she was covered in me and his scent was all gone.

Leighton groaned at the spike of scent, shooting me a narrow-eyed look and helping me settle into my chair.

More eyes were on us, now. Or I was making it up in my head. It was possible I was creating a false reality, imagining attention that wasn't there. Instincts were trying to take over my every movement, and my confidence about not going into heat was waning.

At least the pack had decided it was in their best interests to come.

Dash, Mercury, and Ambrose relaxed at a table on the opposite side of the restaurant. Their eyes were on us—the only attention I wanted from the alphas in this place. None of them were trying to pretend they were anything but interested.

We belonged to them.

That was the energy they were giving off.

If I looked too long at my other alphas, slick pooled in my core. I was drenching this chair enough as it was, so I averted my attention.

I watched the Ashby pack instead. Noel and Hideki were as haggard as their pack lead. They didn't look well. Neither of them was as antagonistic as the last time, either. Each man was... resigned.

It sent a chill up my spine.

I scooted my chair closer to Leighton, ignoring the irritated glance our server sent me.

"Pleasure to see you again Leighton, Kiara," Cordian said after we'd settled, nodding to each of us in turn. "I'm glad you were able to join us this evening."

We didn't have a choice.

My brain to mouth filter was on the fritz, what with my heat sliding closer, but I avoided saying that out loud. Barely.

"Thank you for the invite," Leighton said coolly.

The table lapsed into silence. I tried to stay still. This wasn't the place for my incessant fidgeting. I could hear my father's chastisements on repeat in my head. Then, my brother's taunts.

"Behave like a lady, Kiara. Ladies don't move unless they're told to."

"You could never be a lady. Omegas don't have it in them. Too brainless. Too desperate."

My pack didn't seem to care that I never stopped moving. Dash was the same as me, even. He paced and twitched and his brain went in a thousand different directions. That was why he had so many things he knew how to do.

If I'd had access to more than a hand sewing kit, I might have learned a hundred things too.

We'd see, once I got through this night and Leighton had a talk with my father. If we were safe from him, I would be able to try out everything he'd never let me do. Being safe from my father wasn't the same as being sheltered from Tobias' hatred for me, but Leighton had convinced me we could take it one step at a time.

"The weather has been wonderful lately," Leighton said into the heavy quiet. Only the general buzz of the restaurant was breaking our silence. If we were here to be watched, people would notice none of us were speaking a word. "Not oppressively hot, but a good temperature for a day at the beach."

None of us had been going to the beach. I'd spent a few hours by the rooftop pool, but that was the closest I'd gotten to any body of water. I didn't even know how to swim.

"Maybe one of our future dates will be a beach picnic," Cordian said.

His charisma was flat today compared to the last date we'd been on.

Leighton was noticing it, too. Her unease was growing as mine was. Through my weak bonds, I felt Ambrose and Dash feeling the same.

Something was off, here.

I wanted to go home and bury myself in my nest until the heat hit for real.

"That would be a stellar date for a deserving omega," Leighton said.

Her arm draped across the back of my chair, subtly shifting my seat closer. We were almost pressed together already, but she needed me nearer. I needed to *be* nearer. My hair was rising on the back of my neck, and my nose tickled.

I couldn't tell if it was something to do with the heat, but every inhale made me more uncomfortable.

It became too much far too quickly, but when I pushed my chair back and tried to stand, I was stopped by a hand on my shoulder.

Another inhale, and I recognized why my nose was tingling.

Leighton growled, and the Ashby pack went ghostly pale.

"It's too early for you to head out, little sister."

Tobias' familiar presence was flooding my senses. He was behind me. I trembled in place, remembering the last time I'd seen him. The black van and my knife slicing his arm.

All the times I'd seen him before that.

His cold laughter as he pushed me so hard I split my eyebrow on the table.

The exaggerated noises of delight when he stole my food, leaving me half-starved in the basement.

Him shoving me into the lounge with Jonathan, telling me I'd better behave—or they would keep me in the lounge until I did.

It was impossible for me to swallow because my throat was closed, panic sealing it shut.

I tried to grab onto my bonds.

Leighton was here, furious on my behalf. Dash and Ambrose's bonds were tenuous, threatening to snap. It had been a day or two since I'd claimed them. The bond was only temporary. Mercury didn't even have one, and it was like there was a gaping hole in my mind where he should be, but wasn't.

Tobias pulled a chair over from a neighbouring table, sitting beside me. He kept his disgusting, sweaty hand on my bare shoulder. My skin was hot from my proximity to heat, but his touch made me feel cold and broken.

"Our father suggested I join you tonight. Make sure everyone is behaving, considering what happened the last time," Tobias said casually.

No one else was so nonchalant. Leighton was ready to commit a murder. Cordian and the Ashby pack were stiff and glaring, their hatred for my brother almost as intense as my own. Dash had gotten halfway across the room before Ambrose caught up to him, holding him back.

They were causing a scene. Enough of one that the security guards were heading over to escort them out.

"I doubt this looks good for you," Leighton said through gritted teeth. "You're obviously siblings. Everyone will know she's your sister."

Tobias waved his free hand. "Doesn't matter."

Doesn't matter?

But they were worried about someone else getting to me before they did. Why didn't that matter anymore? I looked frantically at Leighton, trying to quell my panic. The anxiety was making my hormones spike. I was too close to heat to be panicking. This might be too much for my delicate state.

"What do you plan on doing in a public restaurant?" Leighton asked.

"Nothing, of course. We're going to eat, as expected of us. This public venue was to help improve your mother's reputation—I'm not sure having me join your meal is exactly what she had in mind, but we've got extenuating circumstances."

"Extenuating circumstances?" I blurted, finally finding my voice.

Tobias gave me a scathing look, squeezing my shoulder so hard it hurt. "Your mating. Obviously."

"I'm not mating yet."

"You are. Time has run out. Don't delude yourself into thinking you have any choice in the matter."

I spiralled.

My fear increased in intensity so much it spiked my scent. The Ashby pack's pupils dilated and Leighton snarled at them. Cramps grabbed my stomach in a vice grip, so much more intense than they'd been in the lead up.

This was it.

Heat.

I jumped from my seat, and Tobias was too slow to catch me. He might have been stunned from the sudden change in the air. Had he known I was close? He couldn't have, or he wouldn't have risked stressing me out in public.

A rumble of growls rang out from around the restaurant. Betas cowered in their seats at the sudden presence of alpha auras. Omegas clung to their packs, glaring at me with vitriol in their eyes.

I focused on Leighton, who'd gotten to her feet when I had.

She reached for me, gaze darting to the nearest exit. An emergency exit off to the side with a glowing red sign above it.

Our hands had almost clasped when Leighton was pulled back by a sneering woman with a sharp black bob. Her mother. I stared desperately at her hand for a second, before another wave of desperation hit me.

There were so many scents around. So many alphas. Their scents heightened as my arousal did, but while the thought of them was tempting in theory, I knew I would hate it. I needed one of four alphas, and Leighton wasn't easily dragging herself out of her mother's hold.

Tobias had recovered from the shock too, standing from his chair with a scowl. "You couldn't have fucking kept a hold of yourself?" he snapped. "You've gotten yourself into a big mess, Kiara. You're exactly what I always knew you were. A desperate omega."

I couldn't listen, not when I felt like his words were true.

I spun and ran, leaving Leighton behind but wishing I didn't have to. My arms hit the doors and they gave beneath my weight, shoving open and letting me sprint into the waning sunlight of the late afternoon.

My heart was beating so hard I had no idea if I was being followed, but whether I was or wasn't didn't matter. I kept going, my legs pumping in a mad dash away from the brother who'd made my life hell and the pack I never would want.

Away from Leighton, too. That thought made discomfort slice through me and I ran faster, trading the heat cramps for the kind that came from too much physical activity.

I didn't stop until I was sure no one was behind me. People had moved out of my way on the streets, but none had followed. It was only me.

Ducking into an alley, I leaned against the wall and panted. Slick drenched my thighs, and I was a creature of pure need. Need to get off. Need to have an alpha. Need to have a knot. I whined, shoving my fist in my mouth to stifle it.

Here wasn't a good place to draw in an alpha. Anyone could find me, and my body wouldn't be opposed to a stranger even if my mind was. My mind wasn't even completely against it, at this point. Having someone give me a knot would let the pain leech from my limbs.

Half-crazed, I didn't know what I was supposed to do with myself. All I wanted to do was lay down on the ground and rock back and forth. I wanted an alpha to come along and ravish me, but I didn't want just any alpha.

My alpha. I needed my alpha. Any one of the four of them.

This time the whine was too loud to stifle, and I squeezed my eyes shut and prayed.

My alphas had to find me before someone else did.

"Please." The word squeaked out, addressed to whoever was watching over me from above.

"Shh, little omega. You're OK now."

FIFTY

DASH

I found her clutching her stomach in a filthy alley.

It wasn't a proper place for my omega to be under normal circumstances—and heat was not a normal circumstance. Kiara's scent was so heavy and sweet I'd caught it from a block off. Finding her had been ridiculously easy, even though I lost track of her for a minute when she'd made her wild escape from the restaurant.

"Shh, little omega," I soothed. "You're OK now."

She choked on a sob, throwing herself to my chest.

I held in my groan, ignoring the throbbing in my cock. The temptation to rut her against this brick wall was strong, but I wouldn't give in to it. I was a gentleman.

Her hand palmed the bulge in my pants.

Fuck. A gentleman.

Right now I didn't fucking feel like a gentleman. I felt like a feral alpha who needed to claim his omega. My omega needed me, if the little moans from deep in her throat were any indication.

Why had I been the one to follow her? I was the one who was least likely to know what I needed to do.

One hand holding her close, I grabbed my phone with the other. Jabbing at the call button, I waited for it to ring for Mercury. It rang through to voicemail with no response. I cursed, groaning when Kiara sucked on my collarbone.

Ambrose's phone number was next. He didn't answer either.

They'd both stayed behind. I'd been unceremoniously removed from the restaurant—it was why I'd seen Kiara make her escape in the first place. My packmates had still been arguing with the security guards, trying to threaten their way back inside.

With her golden brown hair streaming behind her, there hadn't been time to wait and tell them about our omega's frantic escape.

I'd sprinted to follow.

"Kiara. Heat," I choked out, leaving a message for Ambrose. "In an alley..." I looked around and gave him the name of the pizza place and jewellery stores we were wedged between. "Fuck. Hurry."

My arm hung limp at my side, fingers barely grasping my phone. I should put it in my pocket, but all rational thought was gone. There was only her.

Her tongue on my neck, stroking those marks she'd left on me.

Her hand fumbling for my pants, trying to pull out my cock.

Her tits pressed to my chest.

Her coconut chocolate perfuming up this whole alley, advertising to everyone walking by that she was an omega in heat.

"We can't," I muttered.

I fumbled, shoving my phone in my pocket, and caught her wrist with my final thread of self control.

"Dash," she moaned, trying to pull herself free of me. "I need you. It hurts."

Her desperation pierced my heart. I could feel her hurt

through the bond, and her desperation. It was in her expression—her pupils were so wide you almost couldn't see the blue of her eyes. Her lips were plump, tempting me to kiss. The natural wave in her hair had gone wild, strands everywhere.

"We can't do anything here," I said.

It wasn't a command. It was more like begging. Me begging her to be the rational one here, because I was never the rational one. How was I supposed to be rational today? This was the most taxing situation my self-control had ever been through. I couldn't hold up to her scent for long.

"Need you."

She fisted her hands in my shirt and whined, bucking her hips against mine. I growled, my attention landing on one single drop of sweat rolling down her temple.

It travelled down her cheek and jaw before dripping down into her cleavage.

And that was it.

I was a goner. Her tits were straining against the fabric. My hands followed the path of that sweat, diving into her dress and scooping her breasts out and into full view for me.

My mouth watered as she moaned, arching herself into my touch.

"Dash."

Every whimper of my name was sending me further from what I should be doing. I shouldn't be getting her half naked in an alley, in full view of the road. I shouldn't be undoing my pants, pulling my cock out as she moaned. I shouldn't be sucking her nipple into my mouth and grabbing every part of her I could reach.

"Mine," I growled, sinking my teeth into the side of her breast.

The bite wasn't a mating mark—I wasn't that far gone—but fuck, did I wish it was.

"Yours," she moaned.

Her hands grabbed her skirt, hauling it up around her midsection. She was only wearing a flimsy pair of panties beneath. Thin enough I could rip them off.

So, I did. The fabric tore almost silently, and I balled it up in my hand. It took me a second to find my pocket, and then I tucked the ruined fabric away. Probably. I wasn't paying much attention.

My cock slid along her slick pussy, her desire drenching me. Her leg hitched around my waist, giving me easy access to her. She was so vocal in her desperation I had to bring a hand up to cover her mouth.

Part of me remembered where we were.

That part wasn't big enough to stop me from notching my cock at her entrance.

I locked eyes with Kiara before I pushed inside, wanting one final confirmation that this was what she wanted. Me.

I almost laughed at myself.

Of course she wanted me. She was in heat. In theory, any alpha would do. The idea of her being fucked by another, not in my pack, made me hold her closer. She was *mine*. My omega. One I never thought I would have.

Before I could push inside, her hand caught my chin, claws digging into my jawline. I groaned, letting her hold me in place as she let out a little growl.

"I didn't like that," she said, her lips turning into a frown.

I jerked back, my cock no longer feeling the warmth of her.

She whined and shook her head. "No, not that. I didn't like how you felt. There was…"

Kiara trailed off, making sure I was pressed flush against her again. My throat was tight, because I knew the exact emotion she'd felt from me. This bond didn't allow me to hide anything. It had been the familiar sensation of not being enough.

I didn't feel like enough for her at all.

Burying her face against the crook of my neck, she whined again. "Dash, I need you. But if you... I don't..."

My chest rumbled, a purr coming up without me consciously asking it to. Kiara was in heat, but she wasn't lost to it. My little omega didn't want me to fuck her if there was anything toxic going on in my head, so I needed to get everything out.

"I want you," I murmured. "So fucking badly. I just worry that you don't want me."

Her tongue darted out to lick my neck, her hips moving over my cock which was notched between her legs once again. "I claimed you four times," she mumbled. "And I told Leighton that I wanted you—I wanted all of you during my heat. You're *mine* and you'll still be mine when I'm not feeling like this."

It was the most coherent she'd been since I ran up. Full sentences. Words filled with desperation, yes, but they were sincere. She was pushing a heavy emotion through the flimsy bond at me, too.

Affection.

Love.

My heart swelled almost as big as my cock.

"I love you, little omega," I whispered. "Fuck, I do. I can give you what you need right now."

"Please." Her voice was weak, her flesh hot.

My cock was at her entrance in a second, and I maneuvered her so she was pressed to the brick wall, her hips angled toward me. She was covered in slick and so was I, her scent drowning out all others. That was a feat, in a place like this.

I pushed inside her, not stopping until my knot was rubbing against her entrance and she was crying out, trying to shove down onto it.

I hushed her gently, placing a hand over her mouth. "Not yet. I'm going to fuck you first. Make you come all over my cock."

She couldn't form words, only moans and whines. I wasn't

sure how I was forming words either—my head wanted me to do one thing and one thing only. Knot her. Give my stunning omega what she deserved during heat.

Kiara deserved more than a back alley for her first time having heat sex, but my self control wasn't strong enough to resist her. My pack wasn't here to stop me. And she didn't seem to care. All she wanted was me.

Holding her in a loose grip, I slammed into her repeatedly, grunting as her pussy pulsed and milked my cock. Her breaths came harsh and quick against my hand, the cover doing very little to muffle her sounds. She was loud, like she wanted everyone on this block to know that she had an alpha who was giving her what she needed.

That's how I imagined it, at least.

I was loud too, unable to stop myself from grunting every time she squeezed me tight. When my orgasm was close enough I could taste it, I took my hand off her mouth, grabbed her hand and pushed it to her pussy.

"Touch yourself," I told her. "I want you to come on me."

"Knot?" she asked, strained.

"Yes. After you come."

It took seconds for her to shudder beneath me, a scream wrenching from her throat. I pressed my hand back to her mouth too late. It might have been a better idea to muffle myself, because the way she came for me pushed me over the edge. My cum filled her, dripping out around my cock along with her slick.

With glazed eyes, I watched it for a second. Then, instinct took over and I growled, because my cum wasn't supposed to escape. My knot throbbed with the need to shove inside her and keep all of me trapped there.

I leaned forward, pressing us together as close as we could be. "Can I kiss you this time?" I asked.

She nodded jerkily.

This was a far better way to keep both of us quiet—though it wouldn't change the fact that we were being ridiculously obvious. It was a miracle we hadn't been discovered yet, but I would rip the head off anyone who dared to interrupt this.

Slamming to her in a sloppy kiss, I held her hips in place so I could work my knot inside.

I'd never done this to anyone before.

Betas *could* take knots if they were properly worked up to it. Not everyone wanted to try, though, and it didn't matter to me anyway. After being rejected by our scent match, I'd pretended I didn't even have a knot. No attention was given to it. I never wanted to use it. Not until Kiara.

And I was glad I waited, because I didn't think anything could compare to stuffing my knot inside her pussy. She took it so easily, her walls stretching to accommodate, but as soon as I was securely inside, she fucking clenched. My knot swelled too, both of us happy to be locked together until the heat of this moment faded.

"Dash," she whimpered, finding words long enough to say my name against my lips.

"Kiara," I said her name back, letting the messy kiss lapse so I could look at her.

Her flushed cheeks were stunning, making her sapphire eyes glow in the early evening dimness. She was touching me everywhere she could—her arms around my neck, her breasts to my chest, her thigh around my hip. A sheen of sweat covered her and I wanted to lick the salt from her skin. Part of me was convinced it must taste like coconut chocolate, because there was nothing but her scent surrounding me.

"Rut me."

The quiet plea was enough to have me growling, hoping I didn't go into a fucking rut right now. It wouldn't be polite. Our first heat with her. In an alley. Me going into a feral rut would be out of line, but I could still do as she asked.

I slammed my hips against hers, shoving myself against that spot deep inside her that made her scream. I grabbed her other leg, hoisted her up so she was wrapped around me. Her back against the brick wall kept her secure, along with my arms banded around her. She wouldn't fall, and in this position I had better leverage to give her what she wanted.

We had very little movement with me locked inside. Just enough that I could press my hips forward and the tiniest bit back.

She was desperate for another orgasm, and I was desperate to give her one. I groaned, my cock throbbing from the friction of her around me.

"Love you," I growled again, needing her to know it. Wanting her to give me the same back, even if it was irrational to want that.

Kiara gasped, rubbing her clit and clinging to me. Her eyes were shut, thick lashes fluttering against her pink cheeks.

"I love you too," she admitted.

Maybe it was a coerced confession—she was in heat, not thinking rationally—or maybe it was true. It didn't matter right now. Those words were enough to have me shouting with release, desperate for her to follow me into bliss.

She did, her scream louder than my shout. Too loud for public, but just loud enough to tell me how good of a job I'd done for her.

"Fucking Christ." Mercury's cursing cut through the last of the hazy orgasm.

Kiara whined and reached for him, and I peered over my shoulder. He shook his head, and I knew something was wrong from the panic invading his expression.

If Mercury was panicking, it was fucking bad.

He had his sports car behind him at the mouth of the alley,

Ambrose in the front seat. The back windows were tinted, but you could still see through them.

And it didn't look like there was anyone else in the car.

My blood went from hot to cold in a second. Kiara and I were locked together, but I held her close to me and let her dress drape down to cover her ass. The front was pulled up to cover her breasts again as I made for the car, hoping the lack of passengers was a trick of the light.

I pulled open the back door to an empty leather seat.

"Leighton is gone," Mercury confirmed.

This time, Kiara's scream was for an entirely different reason.

FIFTY-ONE

LEIGHTON

I watched my omega leave the restaurant, a light blanket of relief settling over me. She was gone from this hotbed of pheromones, and these alphas would be able to calm down. I spotted one man try to follow her through the emergency exit, but he was stopped by a security guard.

Despite my mother's fake nails digging into my arm, I was happy.

Tobias was in my sight line too, and knowing he couldn't kidnap my omega was a huge comfort.

I tried to pull myself free of my mother, but she didn't let me go easily. Turning to her, I lifted an eyebrow. "Seriously? We're in public, Mother. This is physical abuse."

She scowled fiercely at me, but didn't release.

That was a surprise.

Now that the omega in heat had left the building, there were eyes on us. She wouldn't usually risk the negative attention.

"What did I fucking say about the Loranger pack?" she hissed.

"They're allowed to go out to a restaurant," I said.

I pulled my arm again, harder this time. My aura strengthened me—an omega like her would never be able to hold me. She left score marks down my flesh, some welling with blood, but I'd freed myself.

My relief had been short-lived, because Kiara was still in danger. If the guys hadn't seen her leave, if they hadn't followed her, she could be stopped by any alpha in the street.

I glanced around the restaurant. None of them were in sight. They must have been removed after the disturbance, but I'd stopped paying attention when Kiara's heat had hit.

An arm draped around my shoulder and I stiffened, Tobias' scent cloying and irritating to my nose. My attempt to shrug him off was stopped. I could do it if I needed to—I was an alpha, and he wasn't. I decided to wait and see what his game was, though.

"I wasn't expecting you tonight, Edith," Tobias said casually.

My mother glared, but there was that same fear and desperation lingering in her expression. Her dealings with the Connolly family were sending her into a spiral. One that was a long time coming, I imagined. It had to have been in the works for a while, if she owed the criminals everything our family owned.

"I needed to make sure my daughter was behaving."

"She was not, it seems."

I growled, hating being treated like a child. My instincts were raging at me to follow Kiara. Through our bond I felt her desire, and I knew it was the accompanying discomfort making her desperate. This may be the moment we needed, though. One more piece of information, and I could put the final nail in Tobias' coffin when I went to talk to his father.

"You should have told us my sister was close to being in heat," Tobias said. "That's part of the deal with the Ashby pack. They should have bonded her by the time she hit her heat."

The Ashby pack were still here. They'd hardly moved. Their

scents spiked when Kiara went into heat, but that was a normal alpha reaction. Not one of them had tried to grab her.

I'd known already, but they definitely hadn't made this deal. They didn't give a fuck about her heat.

"We barely know the Ashby pack," I grit out.

"This is an arranged mating. Were you under the impression that either of you had a choice?" Tobias said.

"My omega will not be spending a heat with a pack she doesn't know and doesn't want."

"She will."

Mother was barely contributing to the conversation anymore. She stood there staring at us. Glaring, really. At me. There was pure hatred in her eyes, the kind no mother should have for their daughter.

I'd always told my brother to get away from her, but I should have too. A long time ago.

A fight broke out on the far side of the restaurant. The lingering heat scent was too much for some of the more sensitive alphas, apparently.

Security guards ran over, and the few people who'd remained finally decided it was time to flee the premises. Our little group stayed still, and a grin spread across Tobias' face.

"My sister is going to spend her heat with whomever I choose. That's the way it's supposed to be," he said quietly. "She may have run before I could catch her—I truly thought she had enough self control to avoid going into heat in the middle of a restaurant—but she's not going to stay gone long."

I growled, the sound not loud enough to draw anyone's attention. The fight on the other side of the room was getting louder, the alphas rowdier.

"I won't let you take her," I said.

He laughed. "I'm not going to take her. There's no finesse in that. She's going to come to me, and she's going to ask for the Ashby pack."

"No, she fucking isn't."

"She is. I know my sister, and I know she's weak. The best way to get her to come to me, is to take what she cares about most."

Our gazes locked. Tobias was thrilled, his pupils dilated. The realization dumped over me like a bucket of frigid water.

Me. What my bondmate cared about most... was me.

I jolted, trying to detach myself from under his arm. My aura pulsed, giving me strength that suddenly didn't matter, because the Ashby pack was there. It wasn't only Tobias holding me. It was three alphas. My best efforts to throw them all off didn't work, and I locked eyes with my mother.

She didn't even look apologetic, her relief obvious as she realized I was not going to get free of the men.

"Thanks for your daughter, Edith," Tobias said condescendingly. "I'll make sure my father shaves some of the debt off your tab since you've been so kind."

"I wouldn't have needed to stop her from leaving if you hadn't shown up," Mother muttered. "And my image is ruined."

One look from Tobias shut her up, and she turned on her heel. Leaving me.

With the man whose arms she'd pushed me into.

I wasn't surprised, but my stomach clenched anyway. A tight ball of betrayal. Blood relations meant nothing to her and I knew that. Yet even I hadn't seen *this* coming. I'd thought she only stopped me because she was furious about the scene we'd all made.

Not because she knew Tobias needed me.

Burying all the things I wanted to say, curses I wanted to throw, and tears I wanted to let fall, I tried one more time to detach myself from the Ashby pack. A hoarse shout left my throat as I moved away, but there was even more chaos now. Another alpha fight. More people leaving.

No one to hear that I was being pushed unceremoniously toward the same emergency exit Kiara had fled from.

I fought until we were in the alley, letting my aura go wild and trying to get them to release me, even for a second. With so many people holding me, it was impossible.

A van was waiting at the mouth of the back alley, guys with guns inside. They pointed them and I slumped, because this was the moment when I'd lost.

I'd never be able to escape with a gunshot wound in my leg, and Tobias didn't need me in one piece to lure Kiara in. He only needed me alive.

I just had to hope that the guys didn't let her try and save me, because she wasn't equipped.

And I would rather die here than have her forced to mate with someone she didn't want.

FIFTY-TWO

KIARA

I didn't want to be in heat anymore.

Dash's cock was lodged inside me in the backseat of their sports car, but I was furious that I'd lost my head and given in to the desire.

He'd been fucking me up against the outside of a building while Leighton had been getting kidnapped.

How fucked up was that?

Dash was holding me close, but his expression was oddly blank. He was unreadable—I tried to gauge how he was feeling through our bond, and that didn't work either. There was nothing from him that I could comprehend.

At least, not now.

Not while slick was sliding down my thighs and desperation was curling my insides. I could hardly focus on anything other than the ache in my core. I wanted his knot to slip out so we could go again, so I could beg Mercury and Ambrose to take me too.

Except, *no*.

This wasn't *right*.

Leighton was supposed to be here, with me. She was supposed to experience all my firsts right beside me, especially my first heat.

We'd pulled into the underground parking at Leighton's apartment building when Dash's knot finally deflated enough to leave me. I let it slide out, our combined release spilling over his thighs. This should have been a comfortable moment where I simply cuddled more against him, but it wasn't.

Of course my brother had ruined this for me, too.

Dash had told me he loved me, and I'd said it back, and now it would be forever marked by the fact that Leighton…

Tears welled in my eyes and I got off Dash's lap, letting my dress fall to cover me. Ambrose had barely stopped the car before I was opening the door and getting out, rushing for the elevator. I stabbed the button, wrapping my arms around myself.

I wanted the perfection of my nest that I'd built with her things.

If I was surrounded by her scent, I could pretend she was still here, and this was still the heat that it should have been. The experience that I'd been hoping it would be, even though I'd known we were still in danger. Stupid. Stupid of me to think that I could have everything I'd ever wanted without consequences.

Ambrose laid a hand down on my shoulder, his chest rumbling in a purr behind me.

I shrugged him off, shying away and hiding against the wall.

The purr stuttered to a stop, and he wasn't good at hiding his reaction through our fading bond. He was hurt.

But I couldn't do that right now. I couldn't be touched. If they touched me, I'd lose myself again. I almost was already, with their scents swirling around me. My stomach clenched in pain, similar to the cramps I'd experienced before the heat hit, except worse.

So much worse.

As they increased in intensity, I wanted to curl up in a ball on this cool concrete.

The elevator arrived and I scurried into it instead.

"Kiara..." Ambrose said softly. "We'll find her. They had her in the van by the time we realized, but we're going to find her. Mercury called Liberty, and if Dash hacks the right traffic cameras... she'll be back in no time. Let me help you, princess. I don't want you to hurt."

Mercury and Dash were in the elevator too, but stayed silent. Dash looked lost—maybe feeling the same about our intimate moment as I had. That it had been ruined even though it was so fucking perfect. Mercury was tapping at the screen of his phone.

"No help," I said, swallowing a lump in my throat. "I'm fine."

"You're in heat. I know you must hurt—"

"Leighton isn't here," I snapped. My cheeks were wet with tears, but a bit of fury rolled through me like a wave, too. All my emotions were out of whack. Omegas weren't meant to deal with this type of stress while they were in heat. "If she's hurting, I can hurt."

I grasped desperately at my bond with her. It was the only thing keeping me sane. I wished I'd left my mark on her like she'd left hers on me—it wasn't necessary, when her bite formed a permanent bond. But my bite would be a reminder to her that I loved her.

She might need the reminder while she was with my brother.

It was a small consolation she wasn't panicked yet, as far as I could tell. She was trying to keep me out of her emotions, but the bond wasn't locked down. I'd know if she completely shut me out.

The elevator opened on our floor and I left it first, reaching the apartment door and tugging on the handle.

Locked.

I sobbed and Ambrose moved me out of the way, shoving his

key in the hole and letting me into the apartment that had quickly become my home.

I made a beeline for my nest, ripping off all the clothing I wore. Only the dress, now. Dash had removed my panties when he knotted me. The dress landed on the floor, ruined from my frantic need to get it off, and I tentatively climbed into my nest.

Leighton's scent was all over it.

But so was everyone else's.

I bit my lip hard enough it bled, looking toward the door of the bedroom. Ambrose was crowding the doorway, silently offering his help once again. I was tempted. *So tempted.*

A cramp wrung my stomach and I cried out, but when he made a move toward me I waved him off.

"I don't want you to fuck me through my heat."

It was a fucking lie.

The biggest lie I'd ever told.

I wanted him desperately. I loved all of them, and this heat was supposed to include them. I'd entertained fantasies of how it would feel to have them all with me in my nest. Curiosity had sparked over whether or not anyone would fuck Leighton—and whether I would be jealous.

That didn't matter now, because it wasn't right to have any help if Leighton wasn't here.

Digging my teeth harder into my lip, I tentatively reached out for one of Ambrose's shirts. What I was about to do... I knew how it would look. And I hoped they understood. I could explain, but I got the sense that wouldn't make it any better right now, not while the wound was fresh.

I clutched Ambrose's shirt in my fist and tossed it from the nest.

Systematically, I went through all the clothes and pillows I'd gathered, removing everything that wasn't Leighton's. The clothes I'd stolen from Mercury. The pillow Dash had used to sleep. All of it was thrown to the floor as far away as I could get it.

Every removal tore a tiny piece of me apart. My hands shook and tears drenched the blankets, but I kept going. Ambrose's horror and pain was a welcome feeling, because it complemented mine. We were both breaking apart.

I didn't stop until every hint of their scent was gone.

It was only me and Leighton, and I curled myself around her pillow. Covered myself in her blanket. I surrounded myself with all of her and none of them.

I bet Ambrose thought I was rejecting them.

I wasn't.

But I couldn't have them in the nest because the temptation was too much. If their scents were here, wrapped around me, I would give in the next time a cramp threatened to take me out. I wanted them to help me, to fix the part of me that needed a knot to heal my aches.

I fucking refused.

This was Leighton's moment too. She had to be here.

I wouldn't have my heat until none of my alphas were missing.

"Do you need anything?" Ambrose asked, his voice choked.

He might have been crying as much as I was, but I didn't want to know. I wouldn't look. I hated hurting my alpha too much to look.

"No."

"We'll be out here if you need anything, prin—" He cleared his throat, started again. "We'll be out here."

I squeezed my eyes shut and palmed Nyla, her holster abrasive against my thigh. Ambrose left, closing the door behind him, and I was grateful. The closed door helped their delicious scents stay far away from me—where they had to be, if I was going to make it through this.

Spring rain and peaches clung to my skin enough as it was.

Hot iron and smoke hung in the doorway.

Old books and cinnamon taunted me, because Mercury might never trust me again. He'd taken so long to open up in the first place, and now I'd kicked all of them out.

Vanilla cream was a far too faint blanket on my nest, but it was the reminder I needed.

If there was no Leighton, there was no heat.

They might not believe me, but it would have been the same if it was anyone else. She may be the only alpha fully bonded to me, but they were all mine and this heat wouldn't be the same if anyone was missing.

"They're going to get her back," I whispered against the pillow, before another debilitating cramp hit me again.

My vision was fuzzy, head spinning. This was the worst pain I'd felt in my life. The injury that gave me my eyebrow scar had nothing on the twist in my stomach. Neither did hunger pains, from all those times Tobias had stolen my food while Father had me in isolation.

The pain in my core might even be worse than the needles stabbing my heart right now, while my alphas were all away from me.

Sobbing, I let the world fade in and out around me. There was no comprehension of time. Only pain. I didn't even hear my alphas moving around outside this room over the pulse of my own discomfort.

But I did hear when my phone chimed on the nightstand.

I sat up halfway and stared at it for a tense minute. It didn't chime again.

Five people had that phone number. My alphas, and Liberty.

I hesitantly grabbed the device, knowing that if it was one of the alphas in this apartment... I would break. If there was some apology lighting up my screen, I would go into the living room and beg for them. I could only be so strong when hormones were playing me like a violin.

Checking it was dangerous for that reason, but I needed to know if it was someone else messaging me.

Like Leighton.

Maybe she was safe after all, and everyone had made a mistake.

I tapped the screen, bringing a hand to my mouth to muffle another sob at the sight of the text.

Leighton: Little sis, if you want your alpha back you're going to have to come home

Another text appeared as I watched the screen.

Leighton: You know what happens if you don't listen

Finally, a picture appeared on the screen. It was Tobias' arm—the cut I'd left on his forearm when he'd first caught me wasn't fully healed, the scabs visible on his flesh. And in his hand... a gun. Matte black metal, his finger on the trigger.

Throwing the phone onto the bed, I tried to scrub the image from my mind as my body threatened to tear me apart from the inside out. Sweat drenched me, my flesh overheated and itchy. I knew the meaning of the picture, but my brain was foggy. I couldn't parse together what I was supposed to do about it.

All I knew was my alpha was in danger.

And since there was no way for my muddled brain to process that, all I could do was scream.

FIFTY-THREE

LEIGHTON

Kiara's sorrow came through the bond, loud and crystal clear. It was strong enough it almost felt like my own, but I wasn't sorrowful. Not yet. There was still a chance I got out of this in one piece—and even if I didn't, Kiara would.

Tobias didn't have her.

My pack wouldn't let him take her.

"It's a shame I couldn't grab my sister while she was at the restaurant," Tobias said casually.

His employees were manhandling me into the Connolly family home. We were going in through a back entrance, secluded and surrounded by bushes. The dark stairway in front of me led straight down.

"This way might be more fun, though." Tobias loved the sound of his own voice. He'd keep talking even if I never responded. I wanted to taunt him, rise to the challenges he was throwing out, but I resisted. "Kiara is going to come running when she realizes what I'll do to you if she doesn't."

She wouldn't.

My bondmate was in heat. She wouldn't be leaving her nest for days, let alone the apartment once they got her back there. I hoped Ambrose was taking care of her. She shouldn't have to be in pain for the first heat she'd ever gone through properly.

"We realized after the first date that she was going to go into heat soon, so the slow courting we promised Edith couldn't happen anymore. That's why I decided to pay a visit."

He smacked a hand down on my shoulder, almost pitching me face-first down the stairs. They'd bound my wrists together in the van, leaving me helpless to stop my fall. I growled low and he laughed.

Tobias was having the time of his life.

He was going to pay for this glee, even if I had to die making it happen.

"Cool down, alpha," he taunted. "You creatures are so fucking feral. I thought the female ones would be a bit better, but apparently you're all animals."

I snarled this time. A couple of his guards jumped, but Tobias didn't. His eyes didn't even widen. He was far too confident in my restraints.

Then again, maybe he should be.

The goddamn Ashby pack was still here, all three of their auras out. An open threat in case I dared try anything. They would be able to contain me quickly.

"See? An animal. She's worse than your pack, Cordian."

The Ashby pack lead was walking in front of me, almost at the bottom of the stairway. He looked back over his shoulder, his eyes steel, and expression flat. Cordian didn't look at me, only at Tobias.

"Maybe we wouldn't be animals if you didn't treat us like them," he said.

He kept going down, turning a corner when he reached the

bottom. He was out of sight for only a moment, and then I was at the end too, being shoved to the side.

"I don't appreciate the sass," Tobias said. More glee infused his tone, though. He enjoyed being challenged, so he could remind himself that he was on top. "I doubt *she* appreciates it either."

The inflection of the word 'she' was... wrong. He wasn't talking about me. Who the hell was he talking about?

Whomever it was, all three of the Ashby pack stiffened at the mention of her. Noel growled softly. Hideki made a choked sound. Cordian was silent, but his aura's flare wasn't only to keep me contained. It was cutting the air with his rage.

"Let's get Leighton settled, shall we?"

Tobias wasn't phased by the tense air.

For a beta, he had far too little care about alpha auras in general. We could take him out easily... if he didn't have threats hanging over us. I imagined there was something he had on the Ashby pack, too.

And it related to the 'her' just mentioned.

The guards shoved me through the basement. It smelled dingy down here, the air dry. Antique furniture covered in a layer of dust lined the walls of what seemed to be an unused rec room. The crown molding was high end, as were the other finishings.

The room I was shoved into was not high end in the slightest.

It was all concrete with a draft coming in through the high, small window. The window was barred like this was a prison—and that's what it seemed to be. Only a mattress laid on the floor of the unfinished room, a tiny dirty bathroom attached. Some dust covered things in here, but not nearly as much.

A growl rumbled from my chest as I realized what this place was.

Kiara was sent here as punishment. To be isolated. I confirmed it when I inhaled, finding her scent was the only one layering this room.

I grit my teeth, resisting the urge to turn around and punch Tobias in the face. It wouldn't do any good. Technically, it was her father who'd put her down here, anyway. Her brother had only made it far worse for her.

When I'd regained my balance from the ungraceful shove, I turned to face the doorway. Tobias was leaning against it casually, looking me up and down.

"I hope you like your new accommodations. You'll be here for a while."

"They're stellar," I said dryly.

"My sister thought so too."

He was trying so hard to get a rise out of me. Damn it, it was working too. My omega had suffered at his hands for years—I'd never forget the terror that washed through her when she realized he might catch up to her again. Or the look on her face in the restaurant when he'd touched her shoulder and made his presence known.

Tobias abandoned the relative safety of the doorway, striding confidently toward me. I stood my ground and tried not to bare my teeth.

When he was close to me, he held out a hand.

"I'm going to need your phone."

My cell was in my small purse, still slung around my neck. The sensation of it seemed to burn me, because I had a bad feeling about what he was going to do. Kiara's number was on that phone.

Tobias laughed. "Oh, yeah. You can't give it to me with your hands bound."

He made a grab for my purse. I let my aura pulse, trying to intimidate him. The sudden intensity of it was far more than I'd ever forced out before.

His eyes widened, fear showing through for a mere second.

Time seemed to freeze there, and I observed his reactions to a female alpha aura threatening him.

First it was that fear, blowing his pupils wide. Then, a tic in his jaw. It was clenching and tightening, his eyes narrowing in irritation—I imagined because he couldn't be what I was. He couldn't have the strength that I had, so he treated alphas like animals to make himself feel better.

Tobias was able to overcome the compelling force of my aura when his rage overtook him.

He reached out to grab the purse, pulling it towards himself and yanking me over with it. I cursed and stumbled, unable to untangle the purse from me and not really wanting to. He couldn't get my phone, because if he texted Kiara instructions I was worried what she could do with them.

My omega wasn't the most rational when it came to the people she loved or the things she wanted.

I couldn't stop him from taking it. He fished it out of my purse and let the small leather bag fall back against me.

"That intimidation tactic doesn't work on me, bitch," Tobias said. He lost his cool, glaring as he backed from the room. "I bet Kiara will be thrilled to hear from you."

The door slammed behind him, multiple locks sliding home. I could barely hear anything from outside this small space, even when I tried to enhance my senses with my aura.

I was alone and bound, in near silence.

All that was left was my bond with Kiara, so I held onto it for dear life and sat down on the mattress, trying to devise a way out of this mess.

FIFTY-FOUR

MERCURY

Kiara's refusal of help was tearing Dash and Ambrose apart. Ambrose, especially. My lover was anxiously watching the door to the bedroom, waiting for the omega to come out.

She wasn't going to.

For once, I understood her better than the others did. Ambrose had said she tossed our things from the nest—he'd taken it as a rejection. I'd taken it as a sign she was perfect for us, after all.

Any doubts I'd had fled into the night when I realized that she was refusing to accept help with her heat.

Because right now wasn't the time. With Leighton gone, fucking her would leave us all a mess. The moment wouldn't be right without the woman who'd brought us all together. We'd have poor memories of it for the rest of our lives.

I didn't want that. Neither did Kiara. Ambrose and Dash didn't either, but they hadn't realized yet that she was doing all of us an immense favour.

Regardless, it was difficult to listen to her sobbing and

screaming out in pain. If she hadn't been the one to put a stop to it, I would have gone to her in an instant to take away her discomfort.

"Let me get this straight." Liberty was on the phone with me, sounds of scuffling in the background. "She's been kidnapped? Like, full kidnapped by Tobias Connolly?"

"That is what I said," I confirmed flatly.

I figured if anyone needed to know immediately that Leighton was missing, it was her best friend. Calling Liberty was a hell of a lot better than calling next of kin, too.

If Marlowe needed to know about this, Liberty could call him. I wasn't about to open that can of worms myself right now. Besides, she was kidnapped, not dead.

We would get her back.

"Well, fuck." Liberty sighed. "I don't know if she would agree, but I'm pretty sure this warrants bringing out the emergency documents. Unless you assholes know how you're going to save her on your own?"

I arched an eyebrow. "We're working on something."

Our pack wasn't exactly the guns blazing type. Dash was friends with people who were, though. The pack lead had locked himself into the office and was neck deep in his contacts, trying to find someone who could either find Leighton or save her. Or both.

I was trying to find a more reasonable solution. Like the police. She had been kidnapped from a public place, after all. Restaurant security cameras should show her not going willingly.

Along with Liberty's snort, my phone pinged with an incoming email from her. "That's not going to be fast enough, but this might be. I'm going to work on some things from my own angle, but you guys can have fun with Soren. He's your best shot."

I stiffened. "Soren?"

I meant to ask more about why he was our best bet, but she

hung up. I was left with the attachment on the email. With a sigh, I clicked it open.

Absolute gibberish was laid out on the screen in front of me.

"Maybe everyone *should* learn to break codes," I muttered.

I hit the button to forward the email to Dash, because as hard as he'd tried to get us all in on the cipher lessons, he was the only one who'd taken them.

He sent me an email back with only a single thumbs up, and I wandered into the living room to wait. Ambrose was there, sitting on the couch with his head in his hands. There was a show playing on the TV, but no one was watching. The volume was turned up loud to tune out some of Kiara's cries.

No TV could stop him from feeling her, though.

Maybe it was best that she'd never claimed me like she'd claimed them. I'm not sure how I would have handled feeling my bondmate in pain. I'd had enough of a hard time being in the pack bond with Dash when he was spiralling—and I loved him like a brother.

Not like a lover.

"Liberty had something," I said, sitting down on the couch beside Ambrose. "It's not legible, so I sent it to Dash, but apparently it involves dealing with Soren."

Ambrose growled low in his throat. "Soren's had his hands in this the whole fucking time, and he hasn't done anything good. Why would he start now?"

"I don't know, but Liberty seemed confident. She's our best bet, unless something else comes through."

"He's a rich asshole."

If we had to see Soren, Ambrose absolutely should not come. I'd never dealt with the eccentric billionaire before, but I knew how he worked. You insulted him, and he would give you nothing.

I scooted closer, putting a hand on Ambrose's back. Rubbing

slow circles, I tried to figure out how to comfort him. I loved Ambrose, but I was a fixer—not the one to go to for emotional comforts. Especially not with this. We may have made up after a year apart, but I was struggling to understand his relationship with Kiara and Leighton.

My own relationships with them were baffling enough.

"So is Dash," I said, trying for a joke. "They can speak each other's languages."

Ambrose barely cracked a smile, but he did pick his head up from his hands and look at me. "I have to stay with her, baby. I can't leave her while she's like this."

"I know."

I wanted to tell Ambrose my theory about Kiara and the nest, but I knew it wouldn't do any good. He'd gain no comfort from it. Not the way I did.

"Dash and I will go when he figures it out."

"And you're staying with me until then."

"I should—"

He cut off any complaint, hauling me onto his lap. "Whatever you're doing to save her, you can do it from right here. I need you."

My heart jumped. It was nice to be needed after a year of distance. Ambrose was right, too. I was only trying to find a way to get the police involved. All my research could be done on my phone.

I stayed in his arms, and he seemed to appreciate my occasional rumbling purrs.

A lot of time passed before Dash came out of the office, but by the grin on his face it may have been worth it. He waved a pile of papers in the air.

"Soren is going to do whatever we fucking say," he proclaimed.

I raised an eyebrow, reaching out for the papers he'd brought. As I skimmed through them, a faint hope began to bubble up.

Dash was right.

We took Dash's orange convertible to Soren's mansion in Citrine Hills. Considering what we'd all heard about the billionaire, we figured he would appreciate the pop of colour more than the grey sports car I drove.

The gate guards hassled us, not letting us pass easily, but when Dash abruptly claimed we were here to threaten Soren's business, they stalled. One call later, and the gate was opening before us, letting us down the lit drive.

This place was extravagant, but I didn't focus on the darkened grounds or the finishings. My mind was on a single track—getting Soren to fix the chaos that he'd put into motion.

By any means necessary.

Including manipulating the billionaire who had been blackmailing Leighton for years.

Soren's assistant was waiting outside on the front steps, wearing a terse expression. She didn't take us inside the mansion, instead gesturing for us to follow her down a path around the back of the house. Grasshoppers chirped in the dark of midnight, and beyond the glow of the pathway lights it was difficult to see.

There was a hedge maze beside Soren's custom-shaped pool, and she navigated it with ease while I did all I could to remember the route. This was a secluded place on the property, hidden from any passing cars on the distant road, especially with the late hour.

She stopped after winding through to the centre of the maze, stepping off to the side to let us pass.

Soren was sitting at a table full of pastries with a creme puff in his hand and a dangerous glint in his blue eyes.

Eyes that we all knew weren't really blue. They were gold, and he was hiding them for our benefit because he thought we didn't know his secret. He was soon going to discover we knew more than that. We knew all his secrets, thanks to Leighton's extensive research.

"Dash Loranger," Soren said cheerily. "I hear you're here to threaten me."

Dash grinned, and his expression was more feral than Soren's. If there was one thing my packmate did not possess, it was subtlety. In the past I'd trailed him around New Oxford to prevent him from showing this side of himself, but for this I was embracing it.

I probably should have embraced it all along. It was who he was.

"Absolutely. You see, Leighton is in a bit of trouble, and you're going to fix it."

Soren's eyebrows rose up, vanishing under messily chopped purple bangs. He popped the creme puff into his mouth and stood. His posture stayed casual, his weight resting mostly on one leg.

"Leighton is my employee, but if she's gotten herself into trouble, that's her problem."

"She's not your employee," I said. His gaze swivelled from Dash to me. "You're blackmailing her. In my opinion, there's a difference."

His eyebrows drew together briefly before he smoothed out his expression again. "I'm doing no such thing."

Dash laughed, crossing the grassy area to snag a pastry from the tower. I followed behind, keeping one eye on our host.

"Look, you're used to going up against people who don't have much money," Dash said. "That's not me. My family's fortune is mine to play with. If you pay someone off to hide the fact that you're gold pack, I'll pay them more to expose the proof that you are. We could both go broke that way."

He tapped his foot, his impatience already showing. The

sooner we got Soren to admit defeat, the sooner we could save Leighton. The man had contacts upon contacts, and plenty of them weren't against getting on the wrong side of the law. Dash knew people, but not the kind of people who could get Leighton out of Tobias Connolly's grasp fast enough for Kiara.

"You want to start a war with me and go broke because of Leighton Winston?" Soren asked.

He had his eyes narrowed on Dash.

"Absolutely. But you could stop it easily. We just need her back from the Connollys in one piece."

"I don't respond to threats."

It was my turn to laugh. From my messenger bag, I grabbed a stack of freshly printed pages full of decoded text. Stepping up to the dessert table, I tossed them down.

"You'll respond to this one," I said. "Did you think Leighton was stupid enough to have nothing on you?"

Soren picked up the papers warily, flipping through the pages.

"Turks and Caicos. Greece. Nepal. Canary Islands." I listed off destinations from the papers he was now holding. "All of your emergency holdings are in those documents. You think you have an escape plan? You think you can vanish somewhere quiet if things go poorly for you? Leighton made sure that you wouldn't be able to live the high life somewhere else. The authorities will be seeing those documents, and then you'll have nowhere to go."

"It's the Cayman Islands, not the Canary Islands," Soren corrected.

He'd put his disguise of nonchalance back on, and I couldn't be certain if it was because we'd broken him down, or because he'd decided he wasn't going to entertain this at all.

I looked at Dash, who shrugged. "I had to decode it quickly, OK? Canary sounded right."

"It doesn't matter. There are multiple copies of this information, Soren, so if you try anything with us right now, it will be leaked."

"Noted."

Dash took another pastry from the table, taking a seat beside where Soren had originally been sitting. "So, what do you say? I really don't give a shit that you're gold pack and creating rogue kids. If you help us out, I'll never breathe a word. I'll even owe you a thank you."

"But nothing else," I added quickly.

Being indebted to Soren was not a comfortable position. He took his owed favours seriously, from what I'd heard.

Soren looked between both of us and the bundle of papers in his hands. I tried not to hold my breath, not wanting to reveal how desperate we truly were—though it may have been obvious. It wasn't every day Soren was threatened, I was sure.

He sat down casually on his original chair, mirroring Dash's relaxed posture. Then, he sighed.

"I could fight your pack on this, and I guarantee I would win," he said.

My chest tightened. I held my tongue, because it didn't sound like he was finished. Surprisingly, Dash stayed quiet too. We both watched Soren, unable to read any thoughts projected on his face.

"But you are not a pack that I want to waste my time with, honestly," he continued.

It should have been an insult, but it deflated the oppressive worry ballooning in my stomach.

"I'd really prefer not to waste my time with you, either," Dash agreed with a grin. "There are so many better things we could do with our billions, don't you think?"

Soren nodded, a small grin curling his lips. "Plenty. Besides, Leighton has been a shockingly good employee considering she was blackmailed into it. The past two years of having her work for me have been very efficient."

He got out his phone, the bright pink case glinting in the lamplight. The keyboard made obnoxiously loud sounds as he typed with his thumbs.

"You said she was taken by the Connollys?" he asked. "I figured she might be."

I growled softly at the second part. "Yes, the Connollys. If you figured that, why did you insist Kiara stay with her?"

"All my employees need a bit of a challenge now and then. Kiara may have been useful, too. She owes me a favour, you know. If I hadn't been golfing that night, she never would have found a safe place to escape to."

Dash's aura shattered the calm night, the air filling with sharp spring rain and a hint of sweet peaches hidden beneath it all. I had more control over my aura—and a weaker aura overall—but fury rolled through me at the thought of Soren having leverage over my omega.

"Kiara owes you nothing," I snapped.

Soren smirked, tapping a few more times on his phone screen.

"Is that part of the deal, then?" he asked. "Leighton owes me nothing, Kiara owes me nothing, and you don't expose my secrets and go to war with me?"

I was about to confirm it, my mouth already open, but Dash beat me to it. "One more thing," he said, reining in his aura. "Marlowe owes you nothing. Neither does his pack. I don't give a fuck if one of his alphas is your son, you don't touch them either."

Our scent match hadn't crossed my mind. I was the one who should have thought of it—Dash hated Marlowe's pack and had since the moment they bonded him. The fact that Dash was adding them to this deal was... more than a little stunning.

"My son and I have our own arrangement," Soren said. "I hide his rogue status, and he occasionally does tasks for me."

"Not anymore."

Soren sighed. "You're demanding, considering I could retract my offer at any moment. What would happen to poor Leighton then?"

I clenched my jaw, half tempted to take back Dash's insistence on keeping our scent match's pack safe. Did they matter to us? Not a fucking bit. Not at all when compared to Leighton and Kiara.

However, Dash needed this. I felt it in the bond, the turmoil swirling in him. The need to close that chapter. Leighton would want it too—she might gut me if she found out we hadn't pushed harder for her brother's safety, after she'd spent so long being manipulated to protect him.

Dash looked at me helplessly.

I crossed my arms over my chest. "We're keeping an astronomical secret for you. Why wouldn't we ask for a fair share? You stay away from Marlowe's pack, including your son. And while you're at it, make sure Edith Winston stays away from them, too. She's got some rather incriminating pictures of him killing someone at an underground fight club."

The tiny widening of Soren's eyes told me he hadn't known that. His lips turned down in a frown, eyes darkening with irritation.

"You drive a hard bargain. You're lucky I don't appreciate other people blackmailing my family members, because I'd be happy to take care of Edith. However, you cannot get all of this for free. It would make me look bad if it got out."

His phone pinged with an incoming message and he read it, nodding to himself.

"I want Leighton," Soren said. He paused long enough for me to panic before snorting a laugh. "As my employee. Her reputation is trashed thanks to the news of the dark bond, but we can rebuild her business together. She's been far too useful to lose."

Committing Leighton to a deal with the devil wasn't the best way to save her, but I liked to think I knew how her brain worked.

If being employed by Soren was the price for her brother's safety, then she would do it.

It was a hell of a lot better than being blackmailed by him.

"You've got yourself a deal," I said, sharing a glance with Dash. His expressive green eyes were pools of relief.

"Perfect," Soren said, standing. "Glad we could come to an understanding. The good news is we know where Leighton is being held—the Connollys don't have an abundance of properties to do their dirty work at. The bad news..."

He grabbed another pastry and took an ungodly amount of time to chew and swallow it. My heart kicked in my chest, unsure if my pack could handle more bad news.

"Your omega is about to be held there with her."

I had to blink a couple of times before I processed what he said. What it meant. Then, panic rushed into the bond—coming directly from Ambrose. Wading through it was like wading through oil, the sticky substance weighing me down.

We'd just negotiated our way into saving Leighton, but somehow...

Kiara was gone.

FIFTY-FIVE

KIARA

The texts taunted me for hours.

I stared at them even when my vision went blurry from the tears. Even as pain like I'd never felt before washed over me. They were burned in my brain before I half-fell out of the nest, my decision made.

I cleaned up in the bathroom, puking when the heat cramps got particularly intense. They were only getting worse the longer I was in heat without relief. Having Dash's knot at the onset may have helped me, but it may have only made me more eager for what I knew I could have, if I'd just give in.

Giving in still wasn't an option.

Tobias wanted me back, and I wouldn't let him hurt my alpha in his efforts to get me.

So I had to go to him—to her.

A quick shower washed away the sweat coating my body, but I was sticky again soon after. The cotton clothes I pulled on were far from comfortable, the normally butter soft fabric scratching my skin.

I briefly debated leaving Nyla behind—Tobias would know I had her, this time. It was impossible to fool him with a hidden knife twice. The idea of leaving this room without my protection stalled my footsteps, though. Unless I left with Nyla, I wouldn't be able to leave at all.

I used my waist holster, tucking it under my clothes.

"She needs me," I murmured, looking at my haggard self in the mirror.

My fatigue was obvious from the smears of purple beneath my eyes and the beginnings of a breakout scattered across my forehead. My neck was a map of purple and green bruises, partially healed but still tender to touch. Leighton's dark bond laid among them, tendrils of the bond leeching like oil across my skin. That's why it was often considered a poisoned bond. It looked like it at first glance, but I only looked at mine with affection.

Placing a hand on my clenching abdomen, I sent a plea up to whoever would listen. I somehow had to get out of this apartment undetected—easier, since I'd heard Dash and Mercury leaving a while ago—and then flee to my parent's mansion without buckling over in the streets.

With the cramps getting worse, it didn't seem likely.

There was also the risk of an alpha catching me out in public, but I couldn't consider it. I had a one-track mind: get to Leighton.

Letting the carpet consume the sound of my footsteps, I slipped on the flats I'd worn to the restaurant. Then I tiptoed to the door, hoping beyond hope that it wouldn't creak.

The hinges stayed silent, but I did not.

Smoke and hot iron washed over me the second I opened the door, wrenching a whine from my throat. Ambrose's scent had been so weak on the clothes, so far away, that I hadn't realized how intensely it would affect me—especially when he was sitting across the hall, watching the bedroom door.

"Do you need anything?" he asked huskily, draping his arm over his crotch to hide the bulge.

My heat scent was hitting him as hard as his scent was hitting me. I looked to the front door off to my right. There was no way I could get to it without him stopping me. He'd wrap me up in his embrace and I'd give in.

I'd be a goner.

Heat made me weak, and I'd beg for him to take the pain away. My stupid hormones would force me to leave thoughts of Leighton behind—at least until the haze cleared. Then I wouldn't be able to stifle the guilt, and my bondmate could be all sorts of hurt.

One hand found Nyla, lifting up my shirt just far enough that Ambrose could see what I was doing. His eyebrows drew together and he stood slowly.

"Kiara? What's wrong?"

My body trembled as I fought with myself. I shouldn't pull this knife on him. I loved him. I loved him as much as I loved Leighton, so I shouldn't get Nyla out and point her at him.

But he was going to stop me.

He loved me too, and he was going to stop me.

For Leighton's sake, I needed to make sure that he didn't.

Tears streaked down my face as I shakily pulled Nyla from her holster. Ambrose watched the movement. I hated the flicker of fear across his features—the same swirling horror I'd caught in the depths of his eyes when he'd had me pinned against the wall by my throat. The blade brought up memories for him, and I hated to be the one to do it.

I couldn't hold it out in front of me. I held it by my side, hoping the threat would be enough.

"I need to go."

Ambrose shook his head. "You're not going anywhere."

I sniffled, wiping my face with the back of my free hand. "Tobias is going to hurt her, Ambrose. He wants me to go to him, so I'm going to go."

He rumbled, the sound sending potent desire straight to my core. My body threatened to curl up into a ball, my grip on the knife tenuous at best.

"Princess, you're not leaving me."

Choking on a sob, I shook my head. The tears could have been from anything at this point—the heat pains, the sense of loss, how much I hated threatening him. All I knew was they wouldn't stop. "No, I am. I—I'll use it. That's why I got it out, b-because I'm not afraid..."

That was such a fucking lie.

I was terrified to use it.

Not because I worried he would react like the last time and get close to killing me. My fear came from how badly it would damage our relationship. He'd forgiven me for the first time—I'd been desperate and misinformed. I'd forgiven him, too.

Would we survive something like that again?

Both literally—the bruises on my neck throbbed in silent warning—and figuratively. He'd never trust me if I did this. Since I purged their scent from my nest, I bet he already thought I favoured Leighton, which wasn't the case. I wanted all my alphas alive, and if Leighton had been standing in my way to get to Ambrose, I would have threatened her too.

No matter how much it hurt.

"Dash and Mercury are finding a way to get her back right now," he soothed.

My stomach twisted with a cramp so intense I screamed, doubling over.

Ambrose rushed to me, his arms around me in a second flat. The knife shook in my weak grip, but I brandished it vaguely toward him. It was hard to see through the new flood of tears.

"Let me go!" I demanded with as much compulsion as I could muster. It was weak. "He's going to hurt her. Don't you love her, too? Let me go!"

"Of course I love her," he growled.

He moved behind me and his arms banded around my middle, keeping me upright through the pain. He was the only reason I was standing. It was a miracle I had Nyla still. I never would have been able to make it across town, even if he hadn't stopped me.

"I love her too fucking much to let you give yourself over. She would be devastated, and what would it help? I know you're not in your right mind now, little omega, but can you tell me how it would help Leighton if you were both imprisoned?"

"Tobias said—"

"I don't give a fuck what your brother said. He's a liar and a cheat."

I bit my tongue, the coppery taste of blood flooding my mouth.

Was I being irrational?

The resounding pulse in my core and unpleasant curl in my stomach told me I was. I wanted Leighton so badly that I'd almost...

"He would have kept us both," I muttered.

"Yes, princess. He would have."

I dropped Nyla, the blade hitting the carpet near silently. For the first time since I'd gotten her, I didn't feel a pulse of emptiness at her distance. Ambrose's presence was safety enough for me, my body sagging back against his.

Gently, he helped me back into the bedroom and onto the bed. I laid limp in my nest, my heart racing as I came down from the adrenaline of my escape attempt. His scent wrapped me in comfort and arousal, and I did my best to focus on the comfort. Still, I whined.

"It hurts," I whimpered.

"I know."

His hand smoothed my sweaty hair back from my face. Another whine scraped my throat. I reached for him, but he pulled back. "You want to wait until we have Leighton back," he said.

A denial was on the tip of my tongue. My body was ready to give in and take his knot, but my head wasn't. I forced the words back, nodding instead. "I couldn't have your scent in the nest."

He closed his eyes for a second, taking a heavy breath. "Of course."

"It's not right if we're not all here."

He nodded, pushing to his full height once again. His dark brown eyes focused on me, so full of affection regardless of my inability to be a normal omega—and my tendency to brandish weapons at him. "I'll just—"

There was a resounding bang that ripped a short scream from my hoarse throat. It sounded like a gunshot—a sound I'd heard frequently enough in my childhood. I scrambled back, holding a pillow to my chest like it would protect me, staring wide-eyed past Ambrose to the door.

Men in familiar black uniforms spilled into the condo, and I realized it hadn't been a gunshot. The bang was the door hitting the wall. Last time, they'd knocked. This time, they'd kicked it in.

My head spun, the stress making my heat aches more pronounced. Each of my temples throbbed with the beginnings of a headache, the noise far too loud for my sensitive heat brain. Footsteps shook the floor, and when I reached for Ambrose he was pulled away by the men in uniform—the police. I patted my holster for Nyla, horror spreading through my veins when I realized she was still on the floor in the doorway. Ten pairs of boots surrounded her now, and I didn't have either of my sources of comfort.

A hand grabbed my arm, the touch too coarse and making me hiss. I jerked back, staring at the person. He was an alpha.

No.

No alpha could touch me right now. Only mine. I held my breath, scrambling to the other side of the bed. It was no use, it was surrounded. Ambrose was being pulled out into the living room, despite his shouting and fighting to get back to me. There were only unfamiliar people. Unfamiliar scents ruining my perfectly crafted nest and disturbing my pocket of Leighton memories.

"Get away from me," I said, glaring at the next person who tried to touch me.

It was a beta this time, his eyes wide. He looked to another man, putting his hands up and backing away slowly.

"She's in heat," one of the men said amidst the chaos.

"Fucking obviously," someone else said, tone dripping with sarcasm.

"We need to bring her in."

"How are we supposed to do that? We should wait for the Omega Safety Division. They know how to deal with shit like this."

"There are reports of this omega being kidnapped away from her bonded alpha. We can't leave her in this place with her possible kidnapper. Let's get her out."

My gaze pinballed from person to person, watching them talk. Most of the alphas had fled the room—my scent would be strong enough to throw them into a rut if they hadn't had one recently. It was betas remaining, none of whom seemed to have a clue what to do with an omega in heat. With me.

But at least there weren't alphas.

I didn't want anyone except *my* alphas, but my body might have other ideas. It was ready to do whatever it needed to do to get rid of this unceasing pain.

Three betas advanced on me all at once.

I screamed, hoping it would deter them. It did for a mere

second, but then they were coming forward again, holding their hands up like they were calming a rabid dog about to attack. I hated their scents invading my space, making it impossible for me to concentrate on anything except my instinctual need to have them *out* of my nest.

"Leave me alone," I begged, shaking my head when one of them got within grabbing range.

He cringed sympathetically. "Miss, we have to take you..."

"I'm not kidnapped. This is my nest, please."

One of the others grabbed my arm while I was focused on his coworker, dragging me unceremoniously from the bed. My vision went red and I thrashed, kicking and punching, and wishing I had Nyla in my hand so I could actually do damage.

They were taking me from my nest.

Where were my alphas?

I *needed* my nest.

If I couldn't have a knot, and they took my nest from me...

All my efforts did nothing, and I was wrestled out of the room. Past Nyla, lying on the floor. It didn't matter how I strained to go back.

They didn't take me into the living room with Ambrose. He was cursing them out, his rage potent in our bond. I was pulled out of the apartment, into the hallway and down to the elevator.

It was a reminder of the last time this had happened.

Last time, I'd stopped and demanded Dash come with me.

This time, they didn't let me stop. I tried to. I pleaded with them to not take me away, my cramps getting worse the farther I got from my nest and my alpha.

None of them said anything as we descended to the parking garage.

A car was waiting for us in front of the elevator doors again, except this time, there wasn't a fake-smiling omega waiting for us.

There was the barrel of a gun. I heard the two soft pops of

silenced gunshots and two bodies hitting the ground with hard thuds. I stared, stunned, at the half-open back window. My brother's eyes met mine from behind the weapon—the one that was now pointed at me.

His blue gaze was empty of empathy, not a second of thought for the two men he'd just killed. I couldn't look away, not even to confirm that the uniformed police officers were dead. Did I want to see them bleeding onto the concrete, anyway? *No.*

"Get her in the car. They'll realize what's going on shortly," Tobias barked.

He kept the gun in the window until the remaining beta officer pulled it open. I yelped, hitting my head as I was shoved in. Then that barrel was pressed against my stomach, cool through the thin layer of my shirt, digging into my body. The beta got in the front passenger seat and the driver zipped away, careening around corners until we hit the street.

The sun was finally rising after a hellish night, but there was nothing glorious about this sunrise or this day.

"You fucking stink," Tobias muttered, holding a handkerchief up to his nose while his other hand held steady on the gun.

I was scared to breathe—his finger was on the trigger, ready to shoot me if I did anything wrong. Yet, the heat was still rolling through me in waves, and before we reached our destination I was curling over in pain, a cry leaving me unbidden.

Tobias snorted, pulling the gun back. It didn't leave my skin for long, the tip of it tracing along the curve of my jaw and pushing some hair back from my face. My tears collected on the black metal.

"If you can't control yourself, there will be consequences," he promised in a low voice.

If the consequences involved unconsciousness, that would be a welcome relief. I could have held back for longer—though I would have eventually given in to the pain and desire—but in a desperate attempt to find emptiness, I let out a whimper.

The gun pulled back and then the barrel snapped against the back of my head, rendering the world to nothing more than a dark abyss.

FIFTY-SIX

AMBROSE

"She's not fucking safe!" I shouted, pulling once again at the cuffs behind my back. "Tell me how you heard she was kidnapped, because the only one who would ever say that is the one who wants to *kidnap* her."

The man in charge sighed, pushing a hand through his grey hair. He was an alpha, and standing up surprisingly well to my flares of aura. He'd been here the last time, too, when Leighton had been arrested. Either he was extremely unlucky to have one of his employees in the Connollys' pocket, or he was the one who got paid by them.

"She's with three of my guys. They're going to the Omega Safety Division where she'll ride out her heat."

I ground my teeth together.

She would never make it there. This was a ploy, and I'd sensed it from the second we'd been interrupted by that first bang.

I was more convinced when they dragged Kiara screaming out of her nest. Everyone knew that was a cruel punishment for an omega in heat. The alphas had said something about her being difficult when they came back into the living room, and I had no doubt she was.

That didn't change how fucked up it was.

Her fury and terror almost made me lose control of my aura, but I didn't want them to knock me out. I needed to be conscious so I could save her when they let me out of these fucking handcuffs.

"I guarantee you, she didn't make it off the property before she was taken," I said, trying to channel Mercury's cold efficiency and keep my voice level.

He sighed again, pressing a button on his radio. "Lucas, give me an update on the transfer of the omega."

The radio crackled, but otherwise stayed silent. The grey-haired alpha's eyebrows furrowed, and he pressed the button again. "Lucas. Report."

I wouldn't be surprised if Lucas was dead, but I wasn't going to articulate my thoughts. It was best to let this guy figure it out on his own.

He gestured with two fingers for a couple of guys to leave the room. I reined in my aura, taking deep, steady breaths. I knew she was gone, but I needed to be as calm as possible when the news was delivered, or I wouldn't be able to handle it.

This situation was already bringing up too many memories.

Hands behind my back—this time it was metal cuffs, the last time it was rope.

Surrounded by standing men, while I was forced to sit.

The utter helplessness of being unable to save the people I love. My mom and dads had died at the pinnacle of that week, at the hands of masked men in black. Like these cops, except their killers never showed their faces.

Kiara couldn't die on my watch.

I already had enough guilt for a lifetime, being the one to survive that night. It was a miracle I had, in the haze of fire and smoke as flesh was sliced from my body. I wouldn't be the sole survivor again. I'd rather die than live through something she didn't.

Tense minutes passed until the radio sputtered to life, a frantic voice on the other end. "Boss, Lucas and Marco are dead. Smith and the omega are missing."

I took a deep breath. Let it out. Watched the alpha cop's face fall, his cold eyes turning to me. He stared at me for a second, hopefully picking up what I was trying to portray. I was calm. Calm enough to release, so I could go and get my goddamn omega back.

"Get a coroner's team here and call it in," he barked down the line before releasing the button on his radio. He turned to me. "Tell me what you know."

My eyebrows rose. "I'm in cuffs, you got my omega kidnapped, and someone on your squad is a narc—Smith can't have been the only one. If you think I'm telling you anything, you're delusional. I'm also not usually the one to utter threats since I have a packmate for that, but today I'm making an exception."

I paused, glancing around at the milling uniformed men. There were about six of them in here, plus the ones who'd left to go check downstairs. And the ones who were dead.

"Everyone in this room is getting fired or demoted. If you've committed a crime, we'll find it. If you're cheating on your spouse, they're going to know about it by the time we're through. No one in my pack will be happy until all of you are ruined, because you're the reason our omega isn't safe with us and is instead being carted around by criminals in the middle of her fucking heat."

My threat settled like a blanket over the room. Even the scuffing of shoes across the floor went silent for a moment as each of these cops realized just how fucked they were.

Then the cop in charge cursed, gesturing to me. "Uncuff him."

"But sir—"

The complaint of one man was cut off by another bringing over the keys. I stood from the couch and turned, breathing out in relief when I once again had use of my hands.

Old memories were receding piece by piece—all the better. I didn't have time for them right now. If my vision was tinged dusky orange, I wouldn't be stable enough to help her. I couldn't risk something like what happened with the stabbing. The closer I was to *that night*, the more likely that was to happen, however accidentally.

"Thank you," I said as politely as possible.

Then, I strode for the front door, sliding on shoes and grabbing Kiara's phone and knife on the way. No one stopped me, and I wasn't sure if it was because of the threats or my aura snapping around me, showing my rage.

I didn't stop until I was in the lobby, free from the gazes of the men who'd fucked up royally.

I opened Kiara's phone, seeing the texts she'd been so upset about. They were listed as from Leighton, but were really from Tobias. They told her to come home, so I had to hope that's where they were.

Mercury sprinted through the glass doors of the building into the lobby, his eyes widening when he saw me. He barrelled into me, grabbing my biceps to steady himself as I planted my feet. "Where is she?" he asked, breathless.

"Gone."

His head dropped to my chest with a curse. He was panting as he tried to catch his breath. I ran my hand across the top of his head, flattening down some of his frizzy burgundy locks.

"Is Soren going to…?"

"Yes. Fuck, yes, but it wasn't supposed to be both of them. He needs time to get things together. Fuck. We were supposed to keep her safe, but I didn't think about Tobias having an inside man in the New Oxford police."

I didn't ask how he knew about the police. Soren was known for having information, so it wouldn't be a shock to hear the details had come from him.

Besides, that wasn't what mattered.

His help was what mattered. If he was going to work around the law to get Leighton and Kiara back to us, then we had a chance.

"Is Dash in the car?" I asked.

Mercury nodded against me. I gently pushed him away, leaning in to brush a soft kiss to his lips.

"Let's go then, baby. I'd rather not be here to get arrested again. We're going to go get ready so we can get our packmates back, OK?"

He nodded again. With the frantic energy of his entrance gone, his posture was slumped. I draped my arm across his shoulders as we walked out into the orange glow of sunrise, colours complementing the car Dash was impatiently waiting in the driver's seat of.

This was the same pack we'd started with—but we were all different now. Changed for the better, because of two women we desperately needed back.

"There's stuff waiting for us at the Dirt with Dash studio," Dash said, slamming his foot on the gas before the back door was fully closed behind us. "We need to get them back. Soren better pull through, because if not…"

He trailed off, but we were all aware.

We were at the point of going in guns blazing, but none of us were especially good with guns.

FIFTY-SEVEN

LEIGHTON

The moment Tobias opened the door, I caught her scent.

Dread seeped into my stomach, sickening me. He didn't let me see her, blocking the door with his body and smirking down at me. I didn't hear a peep from my bondmate. That was concerning. The bond was oddly silent too, and I shivered.

"My little sister didn't know how to control herself on the ride over," Tobias said. "I didn't want to deal with her snivelling omega bullshit, so she's taking a little nap."

My eyes widened and I snarled, jumping up ungracefully from the mattress. With my hands bound in front of me, there was little I could do, but I was slowly undoing the ties. I'd rubbed my wrists raw on the rope, trying to get it to loosen.

"Calm down, she'll be awake soon. We need her for the Ashby pack."

"She'll never belong to the Ashby pack."

She never should have been caught and brought back here at all—what had happened? Ambrose and the guys should have known she would be at risk of running off to find me.

They were smart enough to realize. They should have stopped her.

"She already does, and so do you."

The door pulled closed as he left, all those locks being turned again. This time, however, a small slot in the door was propped open. I hadn't noticed it when I'd first been tossed in here, but it was thin, only wide enough for a plate of food.

Kiara's scent wafted in through it, making me groan. Her heat was affecting how she smelled, the coconut chocolate infinitely more tantalizing than usual.

Tobias had flicked that small hatch open on purpose, knowing I would slowly work myself up higher and higher into a frenzy until I was the animal he claimed I was. He was holding my *omega* captive now, not just me. It took a lot to break my grasp on my more collected nature, but that would do the trick.

I avoided going to the door and looking through that small hole, barely.

If I saw her, I wouldn't be able to be calm. I needed calm. I needed to slowly wrestle my wrists from these stupid bindings, so I had a chance to save her.

For what felt like ages, I inhaled shallow breaths of her scent, trying to forget where we were.

Remember better times.

The times we never had, even. More banter with Dash, comfort with Ambrose, and affection in the form of overprotectiveness from Mercury. A heat without her being in danger and without me getting kidnapped.

I sat in those memories and made up scenarios, confident that I would be able to stay calm.

Until I heard her.

A low groan came from the other room, then some shuffling. The groan morphed into a whine, and when I opened myself up to our bond it was once again full of her. She was panicked and scared, and I tried to push calm through the bond. Manufactured calm, because I wasn't truly feeling it anymore.

"Where's Leighton?" Kiara asked, her voice muffled by the walls separating us.

I gave in and went toward the door, trying to catch a glimpse of her through the tiny gap. People stood in my way. Guards, Tobias, and the Ashby pack all circled where she sat, drawn in by her wakefulness.

"She's in your room, sis. Where else would I have put her?"

My bondmate's fear spiked. She projected it to me through the bond, and it was so strong it soured her scent as well. I growled, drawing attention to me.

Tobias looked over his shoulder, grinning when he saw me peering uselessly through the slim gap.

"Looks like she's ready for the show, too. Cordian, you're up."

Cordian had a blank expression on his face, his movements stiff. He stepped toward where I knew my omega sat, and the shift gave me the tiniest peek at her.

There was blood matting her hair.

I dug my fingernails into my palms, fighting more vigorously to get the restraints off me. It was the first step to getting through this door. To giving Tobias what he deserved.

This was one of very few situations that warranted violence over finesse.

"Tobias, I don't think it's necessary—"

Cordian's complaint was cut off by a short, barked laugh from Tobias.

"Necessary? Of course not. We're not doing it because it's necessary. We're doing it because it's what both these bitches deserve. Dark bond her."

His hand gestured needlessly to Kiara.

I stiffened.

He couldn't dark bond her. She was already bonded to me.

Except, he could. Cordian could give my omega either a dark bond or a normal bond... if I gave him permission to do so. He didn't even need permission from Kiara. She'd already given me permission for the dark bond, so it carried over to anyone I thought worthy of joining our tiny, omega centric pack.

Why did Tobias think I was ever going to do that?

Clamping my mouth shut, I finally felt some give in the restraints. I'd be able to slide my hands free soon.

"A normal bond might be—"

"Are you going to do what you're supposed to, or should I contact the Belisle pack?"

The threat shut Cordian's complaints up. The pack lead stepped up to Kiara. My view was still mostly blocked, only letting me see the side of her head and that bloodied hair. Her whines grew in intensity when Cordian brushed the hair back from her neck, exposing the healing bruises and the bondmark that proclaimed her as mine.

He leaned closer, limbs stiff, a cringe twisting his features. Cordian Ashby was a fucking coward, and when his teeth were inches from my mate's neck, I couldn't sit by and watch it happen.

"Don't you fucking dare," I spat. "I'm never going to accept you into this pack, so there's no point in even trying."

Cordian paused, looking up at Tobias. Kiara's brother spun to me again, looking utterly self-satisfied. He was confident that he'd won.

"Yes, you are," Tobias said.

"No way."

"She's in immense pain," he said with a shrug. "Only going to get worse, too. Omegas aren't meant to go through heat without an alpha or some drug to shut them up. If you accept the bond, she can go in that room with you."

My gaze flitted to Kiara, but I couldn't see her face. Her hair was damp with sweat, and I had the sense of her through the bond. Fear was the prominent emotion. She was terrified of that bond being placed on her neck. Or was she terrified of going through heat alone, with no one but her brother taunting her? The bond was too ambiguous to tell.

I had to guess.

We'd barely known each other for a week. How was I supposed to guess? She'd been willing to bond any pack on the goddamn street when we first met, offering up her neck in exchange for her safety.

This wouldn't be for her safety, though.

She'd be forever bound to her brother if the Ashby pack claimed her.

I hated that I had to make this decision for her, but even if I'd shouted the question, Kiara was in no shape to answer. Every sound that came out of her was a whimper or moan, sounding increasingly more choked each time.

"I'm not letting some random pack dark bond my omega," I hissed.

"Do it, Cordian."

The alpha struck without more hesitation. His teeth sank into Kiara's neck, the attempt at a bond right beside mine. She screamed, the sound echoing around the basement and then bouncing around in my brain.

A bond lit up, a sickly grey glow in my consciousness. It was tenuous, shuddering, not as tangible as the bond I had with Kiara. And it was inquiring. Asking me silently for permission, prodding at me to give an answer immediately, a yes or a no.

For a split second I considered saying yes.

She could be with me through her heat and I could take away the pain. We could deal with the consequences after—killing the Ashby pack would break the bond. I wasn't above doing that to someone who dared to claim what was mine without her permission.

But that would break her more than a painful heat would.

I was confident I was right, as confident as I could be. She wouldn't trust me anymore if I let this pack bond her, and she would have to suffer through the pain of a shattered bond when I killed them.

I shoved the tenuous bond right back at Cordian, the grey glow dissolving into a million pieces with my rejection. That mark on Kiara's neck was just that—a bite mark. One that would heal like any other.

Cordian hissed, pulling back from my omega's neck. He didn't look at me, shifting until he blocked my view of every part of Kiara. "She rejected it," he confirmed to Tobias.

Tobias strolled closer to the door, leaning down to peer at me through the hole. His grin hadn't been dislodged, not even by my defiance. In fact, he looked more gleeful than he had before.

"All the better," he murmured, quiet enough the words were only for me. "She's got a few more days of heat. My sister is only going to be worse off with every hour. And if you still haven't accepted it by the time the heat is over... I'll kill you. Done. No more pesky alpha to get in the way of the bond my sister was always supposed to have."

I didn't say a word. Didn't panic. I couldn't let Kiara know what his plan was, because it would only make this worse.

He stared at me, waiting for something, until his jaw ticked and he scoffed. Standing to his full height, he strolled over to the guards. "Get them ready to move. If this is going to take a while, we should use a different location. Father hates when there's too much screaming in his basement."

I never looked away from Kiara. People moved around her, but my small peep hole didn't give me the right angle to see her. Not while Cordian Ashby blocked most of my view.

She was hauled to her feet amidst heavy footfalls and spoken orders. A keening whine was drawn from her throat as they dragged her toward the exit.

Finally, my wrists came free of the rope.

This was it.

The best chance I would ever have to get us the fuck out of here.

If they were moving us somewhere else, I could fight back. Since my omega was here, I wouldn't go willingly like I had before. I'd strengthen myself with my aura as much as I possibly could, even though my female alpha aura wasn't built for fighting.

I watched through the gap as they cleared out my omega and all the evidence of her existence here, waiting for the moment they opened this stupid fucking door.

Whoever opened it would regret it.

FIFTY-EIGHT

KIARA

The bite from Cordian burned.

It was far worse than Leighton's dark bond.

Maybe it was because I hadn't wanted Cordian's bite, or because my body was overwhelmed with the stress of an unsatisfied heat.

Either way, fire had rushed through my veins when his teeth sank in. I'd choked down a scream, hoping Leighton couldn't tell. I didn't want her to know how much it hurt me, because she might do something rash.

She might have accepted the bond.

The last thing I wanted.

But no. She'd rejected it.

My alpha knew it would break me if she accepted Cordian in, even though most omegas would do anything to escape the heat pain. She'd trusted herself to know what I wanted, despite her instincts screaming at her to take away her omega's discomfort.

The pain was unfathomable, the bite mark throbbing. It was nothing more than a normal bite now that Cordian's attempt at a claim had been rejected. But along with the constant twist in my stomach and the increasing pulse in all my limbs, I couldn't forget it had happened.

I was forced to remember how close I'd come to being bonded to someone I didn't want.

You'd think I wouldn't be terrified of that, after my frantic race to find a bond when I escaped this house the first time.

I was.

Images of faceless alphas danced in my nightmares, their teeth sinking in my flesh. In those horrible dreams, the only faces I could see were my father and brother, because they were the ones in control.

Not me. Not even the potential alphas bonding me by force. Them.

Cordian had to hold me up as the guards led the way up the stairs, away from the basement where a lot of my torment had happened. Wherever we were going would be much worse.

"You're going to be fine," Cordian whispered in my ear.

His hot breath along my flesh made me shiver. My body's need was overtaking my brain's refusal of other alphas, piece by piece. The Ashby pack was looking more tempting every second, and I *hated* it. Especially because of what he'd done.

He hadn't wanted to. His hands had been gentle as he'd moved my hair away, his teeth hesitating for the barest second before delving into my flesh. When Leighton rejected his bond, his eyes had lit up for a second before he schooled his features again.

It wasn't an excuse.

He'd still bitten me, tried to force a bond that would allow him to give me commands like I was a little slave. If I hadn't given Leighton permission to dark bond me, it would be illegal for him to take that bond without my permission.

As it was, who I bonded was ultimately Leighton's choice now.

I trusted her implicitly with that, and she'd known what I would want.

I'd take this pain a thousand times over before I gave in to what Tobias planned for me.

My body was drenched in sweat, shuddering as my muscles quaked. I peered at Cordian out of the corner of my eye. My vision wasn't at one hundred percent either, flecks of colour and light appearing where they shouldn't.

"I will be fine, but you won't," I muttered, hoping Tobias wasn't close enough to hear.

Cordian's eyes widened, but he didn't clap back like I was expecting him to. He bit the inside of his cheek and nodded, hoisting me up another couple steps of the seemingly endless staircase.

"No, I won't," he said.

His quiet acceptance would have intrigued me if I hadn't been awash with my own problems.

I hoped my pack would be here to save me soon. They *were* coming—I had absolute confidence in that. They would never leave Leighton or I to deal with this ourselves, but if they didn't get here soon… we'd be somewhere else. At some random property my family owned, instead of the easily accessible house Tobias never should have taken us to in the first place.

My brother wasn't stupid, but he was cocky. He'd wanted me to be forced to come back to the home I'd run from, and he wanted to force Leighton to see the evidence of his treatment.

Although, that room wasn't the worst of it.

Being half starved and forced into solitude was only the tip of the iceberg. He'd said so many cruel things I couldn't remember half of them. Comments on my weight, my looks, my designation. How I'd never be lovable and never be wanted by anyone.

Tobias was the reason I'd believed some of the things my

father had claimed about the world and about alphas. They couldn't both be so adamant... and still be wrong, could they?

Except, they could.

My family was so fucking wrong about all of it.

All my alphas cared about me, not because I was an omega or despite the fact that I was an omega. My status had nothing to do with it. They loved me because I was me. They didn't even mind the fact that I was violent.

We made it to the top of the stairs.

The sun was shining by now, tinged orange by the remnants of the sunrise. I glanced around, wondering if maybe a neighbour was out and about. No luck. Our neighbours were far enough away that they wouldn't see how I was shaking and almost falling, being forced along by the men holding me. If I shouted they might hear, but Leighton was in the basement and I didn't doubt Tobias would hurt her to discipline me.

How did I ever think going to Tobias willingly was a good idea?

A van and an SUV were parked in our long, secluded driveway, drivers leaning against the front doors. One had a smoke in their hand, casually taking drags as they watched us approach. Cordian led me to the SUV, and I was halfway inside when a sudden bang startled me.

My hearing was extra sensitive. I looked around frantically, trying to determine if it was the banging of a car door or something worse—like a gunshot. Everyone was frozen as I stared, and then someone fell to the ground.

Blood drenched the pavement.

Then the action began.

Shouts rang out, making my head pound. Cordian cursed, trying to push me into the vehicle, but I resisted. I kicked back without thought, uncaring about what part of him I hit, so long as I wasn't forced into the immaculate leather interior.

"For fuck's sake, get in!" he shouted. "You're not safe out here."

I paused, eyebrows drawing together in confusion. Why should he care about me being safe? The cramps picked that moment to cripple me and I doubled over with a moan. Cordian used my distraction to push me into the SUV, slamming the door.

I was alone in the SUV. Cordian hadn't tried to get in himself. I couldn't see him anymore when I sat up, but I wasn't surprised. Not much was visible. My headache was turning into a migraine, the noise far too abrasive when I was already falling apart. People were blobs.

One blob yanked open the driver's door and got in with a slew of curses. His scent tickled me, arousing me, but not enough for me to forget my faculties. He was a beta, thankfully.

A beta who was too focused on the space in front of the car to realize that he wasn't alone in here. He watched people run in front of the SUV, gunshots firing rapidly. I scanned him, seeing two guns at his hip—no… one. My vision was doubled.

I reached out slowly, hand shaking.

I had one chance to pick the right gun, and not the fake one.

Not thinking too hard, I grabbed for the weapon. My fingers touched cool metal and I pulled the gun out. The beta cursed, reaching for me, and I fumbled it. There was a safety… somewhere. I had to flip it off so I could shoot.

If Nyla were here, I could have stabbed him. She wasn't, her holster empty at my waist.

I fiddled with the gun as he tried to get it back, the pads of my fingers finally finding something on the top of it. The safety. I hoped it was the safety. It took me another second to find the trigger, breath catching in my chest.

My body jerked at the kickback.

In the enclosed space of the SUV, the gun going off made my ears ring and head spin. More pain twisted me from the inside out, but I stayed upright, barely. The beta man shouted and brought his hands to his stomach. Blood was gushing from the wound, wetting the leather seats.

I kept the gun shakily trained on him, pushing myself to the side and grabbing the SUV door. It opened and I almost fell out. My feet hit the ground and I swayed, too disoriented to be out here.

There was active shooting happening. I had a gun in my hand, the safety disengaged. I needed to get... somewhere, but I didn't know where. If I ran for the golf course this time, Soren wouldn't find me. My pack wouldn't either. And Leighton... she would still be here. She was downstairs right now.

Someone grabbed my arm and I spun, gun at the ready. My finger had almost pressed the trigger when my vision cleared enough to realize who it was, and I paused. Maybe I shouldn't have had any hesitation, but shooting Cordian felt wrong.

He'd been manipulated like I was.

It didn't make what he'd done right, but he didn't deserve to die.

If I could trust myself to shoot him in the arm or leg, I would have done it. Unfortunately, I was too hazy for anything to be guaranteed. He was doubling in my vision, not as bad as the gun had, but there was a copy of him beside where he stood.

"Let go of me." I slurred the words, but my meaning came through clear.

He dropped me, warily eyeing the gun.

I took a few steps away from the SUV. The beta man had gone quiet. I didn't know if it was because he was unconscious, dead, or biding his time to shoot me in return, but I wasn't going to find out.

"They're here for you," Cordian said, nodding toward the end of the driveway.

I couldn't see what he was nodding at. There were only blobs of colour.

"And Leighton," I whispered, more to myself than him. They were here for her, too.

Cordian's scent drew me forward, my body yearning for relief and a knot, but then a different scent took over. Smoke. It could have been from an actual fire, but I couldn't entertain that possibility. It had to be him. I slumped, peering over my shoulder at the end of the drive.

One figure was coming toward me, faster than the rest of the blobs.

Hot iron and smoke.

I sighed in relief when I caught the other notes of Ambrose's scent. My arm went limp, the gun hanging by my side. Anyone could have come up to me, gotten to me before he did, but I was done. Every piece of me was broken, the pain too much to handle, and I trusted him.

He'd catch me.

"Kiara," he said my name desperately, close enough I could distinguish his features.

The scars on his face and neck—ones he tried so hard to hide. His brown hair hanging in his face, messy and chaotic. He had a gun slung on his back, too. I never thought I'd see Ambrose with a gun. He was a gentle giant.

Then his hands were on me, and I sighed.

My gentle giant.

He took the gun from my hand, finding the safety and shoving it in the waistband of his pants. When I slumped against him, he held me. The cool metal of Nyla's hilt slid across my skin for a second, before he replaced my knife in her holster.

The weight was comforting, but not as much as his presence was. Nyla was how I protected myself—but I didn't need to do that when he was here. My alpha would keep me safe.

I vaguely realized that Cordian was gone, disappearing while my attention had been elsewhere, and I didn't care. I'd decided not to shoot him, but Ambrose might have when he found out what he'd done.

"Fuck, princess," he murmured. "We need to take you home."

"Leighton…" I whimpered her name.

"Dash and Mercury are getting her. She's in the house?"

"Downstairs."

"They've got her, little omega. You're coming with me. Are you OK?"

I shook my head, sweat-drenched hair swaying back and forth. It would be a lie to say I was, but Ambrose could make it better.

Being aroused at a time like this was wildly inappropriate, but my body was begging—and I was about to start begging too. I needed his knot. It would fix everything. He would soothe the pain and tend my wounds.

"I'm going to make it better," Ambrose promised.

He swept me up into his arms as the gunshots decreased. *Because we were winning, right?*

All I could focus on was the warmth of him against me.

My eyes lulled shut as he carried me away, his purr soothing my aches slightly. It was peaceful, even without Leighton by my side yet, because I trusted them.

I knew my pack would bring my alpha home.

FIFTY-NINE

DASH

Ambrose was the one to go and get our omega, but even from a distance she looked wrecked. Her shaking was so intense it was visible as Mercury and I sprinted past, headed for the back door.

We were following the professionals in.

Soren had gathered a team of elite special ops guys—except they weren't government employed, or above board in the slightest. They were fast to get here, though, and efficient as fuck. Almost none of their shots missed against the lackeys Noah Connolly employed to keep him safe.

Some of the team stormed the front of the house, but we followed the guys to the basement.

They'd had a floor plan of the house, despite the rush we'd been in. A petite, blue-eyed omega had laid them out on the floor of the unmarked van we'd arrived in, detailing what was going to happen and when. Everything had gone according to her plans so far.

She said it was most likely they were keeping the captives in the basement, and it seemed she was right. We'd only caught

Kiara outside because they were prepping for a transfer, but Leighton was nowhere to be seen.

I tried to focus on where we were headed, but so much was happening around us that I couldn't. My attention swung to everything and everyone. A body on the concrete. A single bullet in the siding of the house. A glance back at Kiara and Ambrose, halfway to the van by now.

"Dash," Mercury snapped when my feet faltered, and I snapped back to look at him.

He was glaring, and I could have sworn he was about to demand I go back to the van. It would be just like him. The distracted one was most likely to get shot because he wasn't paying attention. I didn't want to have to fight for my right to be here, but I would.

To my surprise, he tilted his head toward the stairway, the hired team pounding their way to the bottom.

"Go first so I can hurry your ass up when you get distracted by a fly."

Not a loving acceptance of my terrible attention span, but I would take it. He trusted me to go down there with him, and that was shocking all on its own.

"I only get distracted by butterflies," I quipped, slipping past him.

He laughed instead of scoffing. Another surprise.

There were gunshots coming from the narrow stairway, but whoever was left down there had to be hemmed in. They had guys upstairs and out in the yard. No one had any escape, and I hoped Tobias was here. We hadn't seen him outside.

When the guns stopped shooting, I'd made it to the bottom of the stairs. I had a joke ready on my tongue, something about sweeping up the competition, but it died when I saw what had caused the ceasefire.

Tobias was down here.

He held a gun to Leighton's head, her hands fisted at her sides with red, raw flesh where she must have been bound.

His lips were curled in a sneer, his body behind Leighton's, using her as a shield. The safety was flicked off the gun, his finger ready on the trigger.

My heart twisted, breaths coming fast as I tried to come to terms with my panic. I'd never felt anything like this in my entire life. There had been dismay when our scent match had rejected us. Guilt to wallow in when I did something stupid that Mercury had to clean up. Fear over Kiara going missing, and regret over being knot deep in her while Leighton was being kidnapped.

Nothing like this.

It was all consuming, a torrent through my veins. The sensation kicked my impulsivity up a notch, but Mercury's hand on my shoulder steadied me.

This would not be another situation he had to clean up because of my mistakes.

I sucked in a deep breath, trying to haul in my aura at the same time. Tobias was glaring at me. The hired guns were throwing me looks too. Using your aura to threaten the man who had a gun to your lover's head was probably unwise.

"What do you want?" I asked, unable to stay completely quiet even though there were professionals who should be handling this.

Tobias laughed. It was a dark, empty sound. Not a hint of warmth. Did he want anything? Or did he only want us to hurt? Killing Leighton would break Kiara—and that might have been his game all along.

So what could we do to stop him, if he was already set on doing it?

I wished Leighton and I were swapped right now, because she would know what to do. I inhaled, realizing her scent was stronger than it should have been in this room full of alphas.

Vanilla cream was everywhere, and so was her aura. More than usual, her aura caressed my senses.

Was that on purpose, or because of the stressful situation?

My eyes met hers and I tried to figure it out, knowing that if I got it wrong, she would be dead.

"You're going to let me walk out the front door of this house and get into my car," Tobias said, shaking Leighton in his grip.

She grit her teeth, scowling fiercely. Staring back at me, she tried to speak without words. This was exactly the kind of thing I was no good at. I could impulsively decide that I knew what she meant... only to be extremely wrong.

But I thought I knew what she meant.

Tobias was a beta.

Betas were susceptible to an alpha bark, to a degree. It didn't affect them like it did omegas, but it could give her the split second of hesitation she needed to get free.

It was fucking risky, though. You could train to resist an alpha bark—and I bet Tobias had done plenty of that training. He had an inferiority complex, so I doubted he would leave himself open to being manipulated by alphas.

The female alpha aura was different, which was the only reason I thought this might, maybe, work. It was impossible to train against the gentle compulsion of a female aura. With Leighton's aura combined with mine, it might be enough to stun him.

Like I said, risky.

I glanced back at Mercury, finding him glaring. At Leighton, not Tobias. He was picking up the same vibes I was. He had the same idea, but Mercury was too protective to risk it. My aura was stronger, anyway. If anyone's bark would work, it was mine.

"And what are you going to do with Leighton when you get in that car?" I asked Tobias, buying time.

He was shifting from foot to foot, sweat dripping from his brow.

"I'm going to toss her ass out the moving vehicle once I'm on the road," he spat.

That wasn't instilling any confidence in me.

I locked eyes with Leighton one more time, trying desperately to see some kind of sign or confirmation. She couldn't give one, because if Tobias caught on, it wouldn't work.

"No," I said, taking the risk no one else would, and throwing the full weight of my aura behind my words. "You're going to let her the fuck go."

Tobias flinched.

Mercury cursed, jumping into action.

But *Leighton* was ready.

She ducked, and Tobias—caught between my bark and Leighton's will—was too slow.

The gun went off, missing her and blasting a hole through an old dresser that laid against the wall. Leighton grabbed Tobias' wrist and twisted, the matte metal falling to the ground before Mercury reached her. Half of Soren's hired hands were pinning Tobias to the ground before my packmate got there, but all I could do was stare.

My pulse was pounding, the sound of blood rushing filling my ears. The panic was back, but this time it was almost... happy panic? Did that exist?

I watched as Leighton and Mercury embraced, their lips slamming together for a quick kiss. I was incapable of moving as she came over to me, placing her hands on both of my cheeks with a grin.

"Thank fuck you were here," she said. "Mercury never would have done it."

Then she kissed me too, and it unfroze me. I wrapped my arms around her, squeezing until she gasped for air against my lips. She tasted a bit like blood—from a bitten lip or tongue, I imagined—but mainly she tasted like I'd always expected her to. Like fucking heaven.

I kept her against me until Mercury forced us apart, pointing down at Tobias.

I couldn't help but laugh. They had him bound like a pig to the slaughter. Arms and legs both tied together. They hadn't bothered to gag him, and he was cursing.

"We've got about three minutes until this place is swarmed with cops," the guy in charge said. I vaguely remembered his name being Bastian. "What do you want done with this one?"

His question was directed to Leighton. She tipped her head to the side, grabbing the gun I wore at my waist. If she killed Tobias, I didn't think anyone in the world would be upset by it.

Instead, she aimed haphazardly and shot him in the lower leg. Then in the shoulder. Two quick gunshots that made me cringe from the noise and proximity. Tobias screamed, throwing curses and rolling around on the ground pathetically.

"Not going to kill him?" Mercury asked, almost disappointed.

"There's something satisfying about knowing he'll have to live with this failure," Leighton said. She addressed the next question to Bastian. "What happened to Noah Connolly?"

"Soren wants him," the man said with a shrug.

"Tell him to sell his son off for an alliance, because his daughter isn't fucking available. I'm sure there's some pack that wants to bite in a beta asshole."

"Noted. If we're leaving this kid, let's get the fuck out of here."

I walked past Tobias without looking at him again. Honestly, the blood kind of freaked me out, considering how much of it there was. He might die despite Leighton sparing him, but that was no longer our problem.

Placing my hand on the small of Leighton's back, I stayed

close to her as we ascended. Mercury did the same. "Kiara's safe, right?" Leighton confirmed. "She feels... pleased."

My bond with her barely pulsed anymore, fading as time passed without me biting her in return. I felt a hint of pleasure, though, and knew Ambrose was already taking good care of her. She'd been in rough shape when we'd wandered past.

"Ambrose has her," Mercury confirmed.

"Perfect. Let's get her home, because she deserves a better heat than the one she's gotten," Leighton said.

A flash of arousal rushed through me, and I pressed closer to Leighton once again. With my nose buried in her hair, we made our way off the property before the cops arrived.

SIXTY

LEIGHTON

Kiara was safe.

Her distress had already decreased in the time it took me to get away from Tobias. My omega was letting Ambrose help her now, because she trusted the pack to get me back safe.

And they had.

Trying to escape from that room may not have been my best plan—but how was I supposed to know that help was coming? Was upstairs already? Their timing could have been fucking better.

I'd managed to live through it because of these two men.

Dash hadn't let go of me for a second, not as we sprinted across the vast lawn to the back of the van and definitely not as we hopped in to find Kiara in Ambrose's arms, his knot filling her up.

"Leighton," Kiara mumbled. Her eyes were glassy, hips squirming on Ambrose. She inhaled sharply, then snapped her gaze to mine with far more clarity. A little whine left her, and she reached for me with one hand while the other grasped Ambrose's shirt. "I love you."

"I love you too, little omega," I murmured, winding our fingers together. I knelt behind her, my chest to her back. After being forced apart, I was as desperate for the touch as she was. "We're going to take you home, OK?"

Dash's presence was at my back. Mercury moved further into the van, one hand trying to discreetly cover his mouth and nose. One woman sat up front, driving—I would have been furious at her presence while my omega was in heat, but she was an omega herself. It wasn't exactly acceptable, but I wasn't going to fly into a rage.

"No," Kiara said, shaking her head. "Can we go somewhere else?"

I frowned. Ambrose pulled her closer to his chest and buried his face against her shoulder. One of his arms came to wrap around me, bundling all three of us together.

"They dragged her out of her nest," he explained, growling. "The fucking cops came—they got a tip that we kidnapped her. She was dragged out screaming before she was taken by Tobias in the parkade."

I squeezed her hand, wrapping my free arm around her torso. It was a challenge to avoid a growl and start purring instead. It came out as kind of an angry purr. What kind of law enforcement officer dragged an omega from their nest while they were in heat?

One who was in Tobias' pocket, obviously.

But what higher up fucking allowed that?

"You three have an apartment, right?" I asked, looking at the pack. They nodded. "We'll go there. Someone can pick up some of her unsoiled nest materials later. Once she's... settled."

More like taken care of. She needed a lot more than one knot to satisfy her after so long under stress and without sex. I didn't have my knot strap-on, so the guys would have to take the first round.

Although, there was always fisting. I'd heard that for a sapphic pair, it worked almost as well as a knot.

"I can pick them up right away," Mercury offered after giving their address to the omega getaway driver.

Kiara whined and he looked at her with his eyebrows drawn together. The man was befuddled—funny, for someone who was normally so smart. Apparently, Kiara bringing his clothes into the nest wasn't enough to inform him that our omega also wanted *him* there.

"Did you want something specific, little omega?" Mercury asked hesitantly.

She whined louder, squirming on Ambrose's lap. They'd gone a round by the time we'd gotten into the car, but by the choked moan Ambrose let out, they were going for another before his knot deflated.

"You're not *leaving,*" she said, accompanied by a soft, puppy-like growl.

"But you need your nest—"

"I need your knot. And *you.*"

Mercury's cheeks went a bit pink. Dash huffed a laugh, pressing his chest to my side and resting his chin on my shoulder.

"I shouldn't. There's not really consent during a heat, and we never really…"

"She gave consent," I said. "Kiara told me before her heat that she wanted all three of you to help her through it."

"No way." Mercury shook his head. "Why would she want me? All I've done is be rude to her about Ambrose."

"Kiara," I said, infusing my tone with the kind of command she was incapable of refusing. "Tell Mercury what you told me a few days ago."

She whined, grinding down on Ambrose's knot as he slowly

rutted into her. His face was buried against her, grunts and groans coming from him, but she was staring with hooded eyes at Mercury.

"I want all of you for my heat. Even you. All of you, and you're not going to fetch me my things from my old nest. You're going to make me a new nest."

Ambrose's hand worked its way between them, finding her clit easily. She shuddered and cried out, her nails digging into my hand and her body falling back against me. I held her up, fondling her breasts.

"I want another knot," she begged.

Dash groaned, his lips coming down on my shoulder. "Where would you put another knot, little omega?"

"My ass."

She wasn't shy—not now. Kiara didn't seem to have a care in the world for the intensity of what she was asking for, or our one-woman audience in the front seat.

"You think you'd like that?" he asked.

"I loved when Leighton played with it."

She gasped, claws digging into Ambrose's shoulder. He didn't seem to mind, moaning from the pleasure. They were drawing closer to another peak, this one lazier than their first frantic one would have been.

"I can play with it again, dove," I murmured. "Get you all nice and stretched out to take Dash's knot in your ass. Mercury can knot your pussy at the same time."

My omega was past the point of speaking, but her moan and a heightened flash of arousal through the bond told me she liked it.

"Maybe you can suck Ambrose's cock while you're at it."

Dash's voice was a low purr at my ear when he spoke. "And what will you be doing, while we fuck your omega?"

I grinned, turning my head so we were face to face. His eyes flashed with heat, spring rain and peaches spiking—though

Kiara's coconut chocolate was always stronger. He cast a glance down at my lips.

"Watching. To make sure you all do it right."

I swallowed down his husky groan, tasting him more thoroughly than I had down in the basement. Kiara's scream shook the van—or maybe that was a pothole. Either way, she came hard, body bowing as Ambrose growled and filled her once again with his release.

I lazily kissed Dash until Ambrose slid his cock out of her, then left the bratty alpha with a glazed expression, wanting me. Gathering Kiara into my arms, I held her to my chest.

"I want another knot," she whimpered.

"Does it hurt anywhere, dove?"

She shrugged, wincing. "Not because of the heat."

"In that case, we're going to wait. I want you showered so that head wound doesn't get infected. What did he do to you?"

"Hit me in the head with his gun," Kiara said, biting her lip.

Maybe I should have killed him. It may have made her more comfortable, knowing that asshole was no longer on the same planet as her. When she was out of heat, I could ask.

There was always the option to take back my kindness. Liberty was a whizz at cleaning up anything. I was sure that extended to bodies.

"I was glad he did, because everything hurt so bad."

Kiara's quiet admittance had me bundling her closer, cursing the morning traffic that was making the trek across town longer than it needed to be. We rocked back and forth until the van came to a stop, then I got her dressed again. She was dishevelled and bloody, and her scent would draw attention if we happened to run into anyone, but clothed was good.

The guys tossed their weapons down in the van, looking somewhat presentable for polite company.

"Thanks for the ride," I tossed at the young, petite omega in the front seat.

She gave me a single nod, waiting until we were at the front doors before pulling calmly away from the curb.

There were people in the building lobby, but with the guys surrounding Kiara, no one looked too hard. They could smell an omega in heat, and no one wanted to get on the bad side of her alphas.

In the elevator we were alone, and whenever it stopped on another floor, Ambrose stood in the doorway and shook his head. Then, we were in their apartment. The place was oddly... empty, but I didn't have a chance to assess it.

Ambrose bundled Kiara and I into a bathroom, closing the door behind us.

"Both of you in the shower," he commanded.

I lifted an eyebrow, even as the order sent a shiver down my spine. He turned pleading brown eyes on me, adding a soft, "Please."

My response was to undo the zipper on my dress, sliding it down my body until it pooled on the floor. Kiara groaned, reaching out to touch me but stopping when I pinned her with a look. She was undressed in seconds, clothes discarded and her knife placed lovingly on the counter in its holster.

I took off my panties, then stepped under the warm spray Ambrose had gotten ready for us.

"I need you to clean and bandage that bite mark on her neck," Ambrose said. "If it's visible..."

He trailed off. I knew what he was getting at. If I didn't already have a bondmark on her neck, I'd be tempted to bite her to make sure no one else could. The other alpha seemed to be struggling with similar impulses.

Not that I thought Kiara would be upset by a bite from him, but she'd been through a lot this heat. It might be best to keep the good memories away from the bad. Give her a chance to process almost being bonded against her will, too.

"Come here, dove," I murmured, holding my arms out for Kiara.

She stepped into them, sighing when the torrent hit her. It washed away some of the evidence, blood-tinged water circling the drain. Her slick flesh slid against mine, and I was wet in more ways than one.

When Ambrose handed me a bottle of shampoo, I squirted some into my hand. The scentless shampoo sudsed up her hair, getting rid of all the blood in it. She hissed when the soap hit her injury, but I soothed her with a soft purr.

I washed the rest of her, Ambrose handing me products as I went. She went still when I paid special attention to the attempted claiming, whimpering. Her whimpers were for a different reason altogether when I moved soapy hands down to her breasts, playing with them gently.

"Leighton, I want a knot," she murmured when I was almost done cleaning her up. "I'm scared it's going to hurt again if I wait too long."

I kissed her cheek, nodding. "All your alphas are going to fill you up, don't worry. I'm going to dry your hair and bandage you up, and then we'll be set for however long you need."

"Forever. I need forever."

I laughed, but she wasn't kidding. The possessive omega was too intense to kid about forever.

Ambrose left the room for me to bandage her injuries. It was hard for me to do—and I was already bonded to her for life, plus as a female alpha my instincts were slightly less potent than his. I couldn't imagine what he'd wanted to do to the alpha who bit Kiara.

I wanted to kill Cordian. Forced to do it or not, he was a fucking coward.

"Thank you," Kiara murmured when I finished up.

The scent of her was thick in the air of this small room, her slick a puddle on the side of the tub where she sat. I ran my hands down her sides, over the faint bruises on her hips where Ambrose had grabbed her during sex, and along her outer thighs. She was stunning, her pale skin flushed with heat.

"Can I have a taste of you before I've got to share?" I asked.

She yelped when I spread her legs, bracing her hands on the edge of the tub. "Do you not want to share?" she asked.

I chuckled, gathering some of her slick on my fingers and bringing them to my mouth. "I'll share you, but only with them. I'm just a little used to having you all to myself."

She moaned, losing her grip on the edge of the tub and threatening to fall backward. I caught her around the waist, helping her keep her balance. It brought us close together, my breath mixing with hers.

"Dash stole another first while you were gone," she whispered.

Our lips brushed. "Oh?"

"He was the first person to fuck me while I was in heat."

"When was that, dove?"

"In an alley, after I ran out of the restaurant."

I should be furious he'd been so reckless, but it was very Dash. He'd lost control of himself. I was coming to love that about him —especially since his recklessness had just saved my life.

"And who was the second?" I asked.

Kiara's gaze flicked away. "Ambrose, in the van."

My eyebrows drew together. "They didn't help you through the heat overnight, while you were at home?"

"I didn't let them. It wouldn't have been right without you."

No wonder she'd been in such bad shape when Tobias brought her in. That was an eternity's worth of time to go without a knot for an omega in heat.

"Dove..."

"I hurt Ambrose's feelings by tossing all their things out of the nest, but I couldn't have their stuff and not them. My resolve would have broken."

Sighing, I brushed my fingers through her damp hair. I could tell her to never do something like that again, but I would never let anything like this happen to her again. All I could do now was make up for the sex she'd lost out on.

"We can talk about it later. Right now, we've got to make sure you're satisfied."

Kiara flushed and I kissed her, making sure she was nice and ready for the knot she would get once we left this bathroom.

SIXTY-ONE

MERCURY

"You're pacing more than me. Not a good sign," Dash commented from the bed.

We were in Ambrose's room—it had the biggest bed, and an attached bathroom. The place was incredibly familiar from our time as a couple. Nothing had changed in the year we hadn't been seeing each other.

The only thing that was changing was right now.

It was about to become Kiara's nest.

And I felt wildly out of place.

"I should go get some of her nesting things from Leighton's apartment," I muttered.

Dash snorted. "She might stab you for disobeying her when you come back. Isn't that something you used to worry about?"

"Fuck off," I said. "The nest is important to an omega. This one isn't proper."

It didn't have the layers of pillows and blankets her original nest had. We'd tried our best to gather everything in the house, but we didn't have much. Plus, the stuffed animals had been the most integral part of the nest and we didn't have a single one of those. Kiara had been distraught at the state of her nest before we'd gotten them.

I couldn't handle the idea that she might be upset. Not after what she'd been through.

Avoiding her heat was a good idea, too. I wasn't sure where we stood.

"I think she made it clear she's past the nesting stage and onto the knotting stage. She wants your dick, Merc. Not soft shit."

"Don't be so goddamn crude."

"If you stop being in denial, I'll stop being crude. Maybe. I'm not making any promises."

Growling, I undid my hair from its braids and let it hang loose around my shoulders. Dash had already taken the liberty of getting naked, lying back on Ambrose's bed like he owned it. He was ready to knot the pretty omega, but I wasn't.

She'd barely wanted me when she wasn't in heat, right? Did it count if we built bridges while she was nesting? Wasn't that just pre-heat, when she was still excessively emotional?

I cursed, halfway out of the room when Ambrose stopped me.

One arm wrapped around my waist, the other lifting my chin. He gazed down at me with concern, but when I inhaled all I smelled was Kiara. That tantalizing heat scent was everywhere. I couldn't escape from it, could never make myself think straight.

I tried to pull back from Ambrose, but he didn't let me. His arm held fast, drawing me closer until my chest was pressed against his.

"Do you really not want to fuck her, baby?" he asked.

"That's not the problem," I said, a little strained. "She just... There's no reason for her to have asked for me."

"You think she's going to regret it when she's not in heat."

Ambrose's matter of fact statement summed up all my feelings in much simpler words than I could have come up with. I shakily nodded, not wanting to vocally admit it, but willing to accept when he said it.

"She won't," Ambrose said, his confidence unflappable.

"How do you know?" I demanded.

Kiara had said she wanted me. On a fundamental level, I was aware of that. The dark bond compelled her to tell the truth, so she hadn't lied about wanting me with her. And why would she? It wasn't like she was forced to have me by having my pack.

I was being so goddamn stupid about this.

I just couldn't let myself have her if she was going to regret it.

Ambrose brushed his lips against mine. "She was nervous to tell you, baby. That's the only reason she didn't. Our omega didn't want you to feel pressured into being with her. There isn't a single piece of her that thinks she might have regrets."

"That's…"

I trailed off, my complaints dying on my tongue. She'd been similarly shy when we'd been dealing with her nesting issues.

Fuck. Kiara was pushy at first glance, but really was too shy to admit anything unless she knew what the response was going to be. I was the most unreadable member of my pack, and I hadn't exactly been kind to her.

She didn't know that I'd decided she was ours, and I would never let any other pack have her. The little omega thought I was unsure, and because of that, I thought she was unsure.

We were dancing around each other.

"I'll say it a million times if you need to hear it, baby. She's not going to regret fucking you when her heat is done. Kiara wants you as much as she wants us."

"And she wants us a lot," Dash chimed in, reminding me of his somewhat annoying background presence. "She was begging me to rut her, Merc."

Kiara's short, pleased scream from the bathroom cut off any

further reservations. Leighton was making her come, but soon she would be in here. Naked. All that gorgeous skin on display. Way more than just the peek I'd gotten when she'd sat on my lap in the living room, her robe splaying open.

"You get her pussy first," Ambrose murmured. "It's going to change your goddamn life."

"She already has." I had to admit it. It was time.

Dash laughed, and when I glanced over he had his hand on his cock, stroking it. None of us had gone soft since getting in that damn van, not when Kiara was perfuming up every space we entered.

Ambrose went over to the bed and lounged beside Dash, pushing our packmate out of the middle of the space. My lover was casually shirtless, no longer bothered with the idea of hiding his scars around the people in this apartment. It was a huge step for him.

I stood by the door, bouncing from foot to foot and trying not to pace—Dash would call me out on it again, the asshole.

Kiara moaned a few more times, loud enough to be heard through the walls, and then... footsteps. They were quick slaps against the hardwood, bringing her down the hall until she turned the corner into Ambrose's room.

Naked.

Fucking hell.

I'd known she was going to be naked, but there was something about seeing her without a stitch of clothing that bowled me over. Her skin was flushed from her cheeks down to her chest. There were bruises and cuts all over her—some that made me furious, others that sparked interest. Like those faint bruises on her hips. They had to be from Ambrose.

Her tits were heavy with pert nipples, and I bet they were extra sensitive during her heat. At the apex of her thighs, a patch of honey brown hair teased me by hiding the pretty pink flesh I would find there.

Coconut and chocolate blasted me with her arousal, and I was stepping up to her before I realized I'd moved. My hands came down on her sides, sliding across her ample hips and down her thighs, then back up to cup her breasts.

She moaned softly but didn't reach out to touch me. Her hands stayed balled into fists at her sides. Her lips were parted, glistening and swollen from her kisses with Leighton, and her stunning blue eyes were glazed over.

"You don't have to," she said. The words came out strained, like it hurt her to say them. "I know I said on the way here—"

I smashed my lips to hers, cutting her off. She tasted sweet. Leighton was on her lips, along with a hint of what I imagined her pussy would taste like. An image flashed through my mind of what they must have been doing in that bathroom—the female alpha alternating between kissing her pussy and her mouth.

Kiara whimpered and melted against me. Her hands came up to claw at my clothing. I should have done what Ambrose and Dash had done. Stripped, or half stripped. It just felt too fucking presumptuous.

I pulled back from the kiss to do it then instead, getting down to my boxer briefs. Kiara's small hands never left my skin, touching me anywhere she could reach.

"That was all the restraint I had," she murmured. "Now you have to knot me."

It was hard to believe I'd ever considered not taking her. Wrapping my arms around her, I walked her back toward the bed, pushing her to sit on the edge. Her slick was dripping on the floor, and I could see in her expression that all rational thought was gone.

It was impressive she'd lasted this long.

"I've always wanted to knot you, princess," I said, picking up

Ambrose's name for her. It was fitting. She deserved to be treated like one after the hell she'd lived through. "Just didn't know if you wanted it."

"I want."

She grabbed the waistband of my boxer briefs and tugged them down. My cock sprung up to slap my stomach, and I groaned when she wrapped her fist around it.

The brush of her skin against mine was almost enough to send me prematurely over the edge.

Kiara didn't stroke my cock, though. She used that grip to try and manoeuvre me to where she wanted me.

And she wanted my cock deep in her pussy.

Chuckling softly, I grabbed her wrist and removed her hand. "On your back on the bed," I said. My underwear slid down to the floor and I stepped out of them.

She looked longingly at my length, knot swollen and ready for her at the base. Then she scooted backward on the bed until she ended up between Ambrose's legs. She jolted, surprised by her new position since she hadn't been watching where she was going.

My lover smiled down at her, wrapping his hands around her thighs and spreading her legs.

I groaned, crawling onto the bed with my gaze fixed on her. It was so fucking perfect. She was so wet I couldn't help but swipe my tongue across her for a taste.

She whimpered, hands clutching Ambrose's arms. "I want your cock," she begged.

It was damn near impossible not to give her what she wanted.

I lined myself up with her entrance, mixing my precum with her slick. Before I pushed inside, I paused, looking at Ambrose with a small frown. "Is she on birth control? Should I get a condom?"

There were some somewhere in this house, and we didn't want to risk getting our hyperfertile little omega pregnant.

"She's on it," Ambrose grunted. "And even if she wasn't, have you ever heard of an omega being satisfied with *condoms* during heat? Baby, she'd probably claw it off your dick."

He leaned in closer to Kiara, whispering in her ear. "You want your alphas to fill you up and breed you, right princess?"

Her head bobbed, a keening sound coming up from her throat. These reactions she was having to us... I hadn't realized omegas could make sounds like this, but it was threatening to make me feral. I didn't often have ruts, but she was going to push me into one before her heat was up.

It was a foregone conclusion.

"Fuck her," Ambrose commanded.

I was helpless to refuse, and I didn't want to. My cock slid home, her pussy soaking me with slick. My eyes threatened to close from the intensity of the pleasure already building at the base of my spine, but I forced them to stay open.

I needed to watch the heave of her chest as she panted, the way her eyes rolled back when I was seated all the way in her. And I loved catching Ambrose's eyes, their intense orbs urging me on, demanding I fuck our omega.

"She doesn't need you to wait for her to adjust," Leighton purred from behind me. "Kiara can take it."

I shivered. She pressed her body to mine, her teeth nipping at the back of my neck. We still had some kinks to work out—I didn't know where I stood with Leighton. Apparently, I stood in a good enough place to have her tits brushing against my back and her hands exploring my torso.

Pulling out until just the tip was in Kiara, I waited until she choked out a, "Please!"

Then I slammed in again, fucking her hard and fast the way Leighton had told me to. I got a thrill out of doing what she wanted, the same as I did when it was Ambrose ordering me around.

Leighton stayed behind me, touching me where she could and making sure she didn't get in the way of me fucking our omega. Having her hands on me sent me to the edge that much faster, and when Kiara's pussy tightened around my cock, an orgasm rocking her, I cursed.

My cock spilled in her, each pulse of her pussy milking more out of me. When my come started dripping out of her, I grit my teeth.

That wasn't supposed to be let out.

It was my job to fill her up better than that.

My knot throbbed and I grabbed her thighs, my hands beside Ambrose's. Kiara let out a warbled moan when her cunt stretched around my knot, practically sucking it inside. Then it expanded just enough to lock us together, and her body fucking shook. It was an instant orgasm for her, every part of her trembling as she cried out.

"She takes my knot so fucking good," I groaned, leaning my head back.

Leighton was right there, smirking and stroking my wild hair. Her lips brushed mine and I was caught between wanting more, and wanting to slam my hips against Kiara's until I'd filled her up again. Properly, this time. Not a drop of my cum escaping until she was good and bred.

"Are you going to rut her, or can I knot her ass?" Dash asked.

I narrowed my eyes at my cocky packmate. He was watching hungrily, but he hadn't touched anyone but himself.

"There's going to be plenty of time to knot her ass," Leighton said dryly. "She's in heat for a while longer. Give Mercury a minute."

Kiara reached out to grab me, pulling me down so we were chest to chest and proving that she wasn't done with me just yet.

She whimpered when I shifted my hips the tiny bit that I could, rubbing a spot inside her that made her back arch.

I vaguely realized that Leighton moved away, going over to Dash, but my attention was mostly focused on my omega.

Her lips connected to mine, and I groaned, letting her kiss me absolutely senseless.

SIXTY-TWO

KIARA

Mercury wasn't mine.

Yet.

I'd brought him in for a kiss to try and convince my irrational heat brain that it was fine. He cared for me. His affection was enough. His knot was enough.

All the kiss did was bring me closer to his neck. His burgundy hair hung in the way, blocking my view of skin that *should* bear my mark. But it didn't. Because he was the one person in this room that wasn't connected to me in some way, and that was so fucking wrong.

His hips pressed against my thighs, shifting his knot inside me as much as he could. It had me moaning into his mouth, but the sense of wrongness didn't dissipate.

It only grew.

He was inside me, but I couldn't feel him.

Not like I could feel Leighton. Not even like I could feel Ambrose and Dash, our bonds fading rapidly.

"Bond me." My insistence came out on a desperate whine.

Mercury pulled back from the kiss, his eyes wide. His cock throbbed so intensely I felt it pulsing against my inner walls. "Princess..."

"I need you. I can't feel you."

My lips turned into a pout and Mercury hissed, glancing behind me at Ambrose. My other alpha's large body bracketed me on either side, my back to his chest and his cock leaking and rubbing against me.

"We can't claim you like this," Ambrose said, nipping at my ear.

"Why?" I drew out the word, wrapping my legs around Mercury to tug him closer.

"You know why."

In the back of my mind, I did. This heat was marred with so many traumatic memories, I would hate to look back on it as containing both the worst and the best moments of my life. The bonding should be saved for when I wouldn't have to remember this as being frantic, the aftermath of a barrage of pain and a bite I never wanted.

My hand lifted to cover Cordian's bite mark—bandaged and hidden from my alphas for the time being, though they knew it was there.

Mercury growled, the sound vibrating all the way down to his cock.

"I'm yours, little omega," he said.

With a second of hesitation, he brushed his hair back from his neck, exposing unmarked skin. My mouth watered, looking at my opportunity to form the bond I was desperate for in this intimate moment. My rational brain screamed at me to pause, to make sure Mercury really wanted it—I still wasn't convinced he did. He'd spent so long hating me because of what I did to Ambrose.

My rational brain's scream was quiet as a little mouse.

I grabbed him by the back of the neck and drew him close. My teeth sank into him, opening up that weaker type of bond I was becoming familiar with.

His emotions crashed in, adding to the cacophony from everyone else. I didn't know how to shut them out. Didn't want to, either. I wanted their existence in my head all the time, forever.

Mercury lost his grip on calm, letting out a strangled groan. I slid back on the bed as his hips smashed against me, pummelling a spot in my pussy that made me see stars. I whimpered, holding him close and sucking on his neck beside where my mark now laid.

His old books and cinnamon scent heightened until it was the only one I could smell, drowning out all my other alphas. Vaguely, I realized that was because he'd gone into a rut. My bite had put him into one. Me, driving my alpha wild with lust.

"More," I begged, holding on for dear life as he took me.

He didn't say anything else. No sweet nothings, no calling me princess. There was nothing but grunts, groans, growls, and the slapping of flesh on flesh. He held me tight and close, and I lost track of how many times my body clenched and released around his cock. How many times my vision went white and I screamed with pleasure.

I only came back to myself when Mercury groaned, flopping onto his back and taking me with him. It removed my sweat-slicked body from Ambrose, who I realized had been touching us both through the haze of rut and heat.

Part of me wondered if I should be satisfied—Mercury had knotted me for an indeterminable amount of time. Hours? I didn't know.

What I did know was that it wasn't enough. My core ached, but not because it couldn't take anymore. I wanted so much fucking more.

Turning my head, I whimpered when I saw Dash between Leighton's thighs, his tongue swirling her clit. He looked dazed, almost as much as I was. I had to wonder if he'd been doing that the whole time I'd been with Mercury.

"Alpha," I whispered, locking eyes with Leighton.

My alpha grinned, her cheeks flushed from the pleasure. I was a little jealous of Dash for getting to touch her, but I knew I would get the chance soon.

Leighton's hand wound through Dash's hair, pulling him away from her pussy.

"Looks like she's ready for you to knot her ass," she murmured.

Dash perked up, his cock red and leaking as it stood out from his body. "You should prep her for me, sweetheart. I think she misses you."

Rolling her eyes, Leighton pushed him out of the way and moved to kneel behind me, my ass on display for her. She massaged each cheek, patting them gently. When I whimpered, she gave me what I wanted.

Mercury's cock was still lodged inside me, even as the man panted, unmoving beneath me. I was full of so much of *him* that I wasn't sure anything would fit in my ass—but I wanted it to.

Leighton gathered my slick from where Mercury and I were joined, making both of us groan. Then she slid her fingers up, pressing one slowly into my ass.

The fit was definitely tight, but somehow immensely better than even the time I'd been sitting on her face. My moan was so loud it drowned out all other noises. I'd been trying to peer back at Leighton, watch her do this to me, but I couldn't. All I could do was slump on Mercury's chest and feel her ministrations.

Her single finger worked its way in and out until it didn't feel tight anymore, and then she added a second. A third, after that. A fourth. Then something thick pressed at my ass, making Mercury choke.

If it felt this tight for me, I couldn't imagine how much it was squeezing the life out of his cock. The thick heat pressing at my asshole could have been a knot—but wasn't. Ambrose and Dash were watching from the sidelines with wide, hungry eyes.

"What are you putting in me?" I asked, pushing back on it even without an answer.

Leighton chuckled, working it in a tiny bit at a time. "Usually I would have toys to knot you with, dove, but today all I've got is this."

I wanted to ask what this is, but it dawned on my muddled brain that she'd never really taken her fingers out... just added more.

Oh, fuck.

She was putting her *whole hand* inside my ass.

"Good girl. You can take it," Leighton purred.

She pushed her hand into me a little deeper, the stretch growing so intense I wasn't sure I could take it, no matter what she told me. It was borderline painful. I didn't know how her hand was supposed to fit, or how a knot was supposed to fit while Mercury was still knotting me.

Then she slid an inch further and the pressure lessened. My entrance clenched around what I imagined was her wrist, the bulk of her fist inside of me.

Leighton purred in pleasure, moving her fist around. Pleasure tightened my insides, but this sensation was so foreign and unfamiliar, I didn't feel the oncoming release of an orgasm. My hand pressed between Mercury and I, searching for my clit, but he caught my wrist before I could find it. His nimble finger twirled around that sensitive bud instead.

"Come for me, then you can get Dash to fuck your ass," Leighton commanded.

I whined, squirming, though it was almost impossible for me to move. It was a slow build to orgasm with all the small movements, but when I hit the peak...

I screamed, every part of me shaking violently. Leighton groaned, removing her hand from my ass before I'd finished with the long, drawn out orgasm.

Dash replaced her, his slick length sliding home.

This level of movement was an entirely different feeling.

He didn't wait for me to recover from coming, simply starting to slam into me with a series of grunts and groans. Dash was eager. He'd been waiting the entire time Mercury was rutting me, drenched in my scent the whole time. Now, I was drenched in his. All of theirs, all over me.

I couldn't speak, only whimpering and crying out. Mercury kept rubbing my clit, coming out of his post-orgasm daze enough to pump his hips. His knot had yet to go down, keeping us connected—and I preferred it that way. If I could have all my alphas at once, that would be the absolute best case scenario.

Out of the corner of my eyes I saw that Ambrose and Leighton were tangled together, sweat shining on Ambrose's shoulders and back as he drove into her. My alpha was covering her mouth to muffle her moans.

"Fuck, Kiara," Dash hissed.

He leaned over, chest pressed against my back as he drove into my ass in long strokes. His hands grabbed my breasts, squeezing and rubbing them.

"I want to fuck her tits so bad," Mercury said in a choked tone.

"We're more alike than you fucking think, then," Dash groaned. "Because I've wanted to do that since the second I saw her. Almost as much as I wanted to knot her."

I whined, trying fruitlessly to shove my hips back and take his knot by force. I couldn't, Mercury's cock holding me in place.

"You want that, little omega? My knot?"

I nodded, pleasure tears beading in my eyes.

His thick knot pressed against my entrance, and again it was almost too much. I cried out as he pushed further in, squeezing my eyes shut, but then it was back to pure pleasure again. He swelled in me, curses falling from his lips as he came.

Then he began to grind against me, chasing me toward yet another peak.

And I was so eager to get there.

SIXTY-THREE

LEIGHTON

The guys lost themselves in Kiara's heat. She was insatiable for days, barely letting us leave—even if one or three of the others were there with her still. We were dead tired and I was sore in places I hadn't known existed by the time she was calming down.

My omega would be in heat for a day or two longer, but we were close to breaking it. She was sleeping again, too. For the first few days, she hadn't slept. It had been constant fucking, and we'd only slept in snippets of stolen time.

Mercury had finally gone over to my apartment, gathering up some of Kiara's nesting items now that she was beginning to get cuddly again. He strode through the door with a couple of stuffed animals in hand, blankets draped over his shoulders.

"They got their scent all over everything," he said with a low growl, placing the unmarred items down on the couch.

I was sitting on the couch with a laptop on my thighs and a snack on the coffee table. Ambrose and Dash were passing Kiara back and forth for cuddles and lazy knotting until she inevitably took another nap.

"If I never see another cop, it'll be too fucking soon," I replied.

"We'll see them again when we take them all to court. Their scents were on things they never should have fucking touched."

It was nice to see Mercury so protective over Kiara.

Less nice when he avoided eye contact with me, stalking toward their kitchen.

"Come here," I demanded.

He froze in place, his back to me.

"Unless you don't think we should clear the air?" I asked.

His shoulders slumped and he turned on his heel, his lips turned down in a scowl. "There's no air to clear."

"Oh, so we're not going to talk about how Ambrose and I have been fucking for years? Or the way you came in your pants last week at my apartment?"

Mercury's little growl was nothing short of cute. He stormed over to the couch, sitting as far away as he could get. Kiara's rescued nesting items created a barrier between us.

"I knew that Ambrose was seeing someone. That wasn't a secret," he stated abruptly. "We were never exclusive. I could have been seeing someone else too."

He didn't mention our moment last week. With the armchair. I wanted a repeat, but I wasn't sure if he did.

"I'm not saying that he was cheating on you. I know he wasn't. I was more wanting to ask how you feel about it being... me."

There were a few things standing in the way of us being a perfect pack. One, was any lingering negative feelings between Mercury and I. I owed it to Kiara to try and get this out of the way, whether or not it resulted in me also banging Mercury. He'd accepted my omega. That was enough for a basis of a happy pack, as long as we didn't hate each other.

I ignored the twinge of discomfort that brought.

Mercury was more like me than any of the others. Secluding

himself to protect his pack. It was harder to break his shell. I had some of the same coping mechanisms.

Maybe that made us the least compatible as romantic partners, but I wanted to at least try.

He intrigued me.

Not just in a sexual sense, but that too. I'd absolutely been imagining what it would be like to fuck him and Ambrose at the same time.

"I was furious," Mercury said. "Because I thought Ambrose seeing you would hurt Dash. As it turned out, I was wrong, and now we have a pack. So that's irrelevant."

He tried to stand, but one look from me stopped him.

Ambrose must have so much fun with him. He listened without me even having to speak.

Sexual thoughts really need to leave during this conversation.

"You were furious for Dash, but how did you feel for yourself?"

His jaw clenched, expression cooling into the facade he wore so well in public. Uncaring and frigid, only there to problem solve for other people. Never himself.

Maybe Ambrose should have been the one to have this conversation.

Except asking him would be the coward's way out. You're not a coward anymore.

"Tell me, or we're going to dance around this conversation a million times until you're ready to. We can't be in a pack together with whatever this is," I waved a hand vaguely, "between us. It might stress our omega out."

Or me. It could stress me out, too. I'd touched him during the heat, but those had been different circumstances. Was I allowed casual affection with him in general? Would these scenarios in my head get to be played out, or was that not an option?

"I was jealous of you," Mercury said after a long pause. "It felt like he cared more about you than me, because he continued a relationship with you in secret while allowing me to end ours. I'm well aware it was my own damn fault for being so pushy when he didn't want to end things with me. Ambrose and I have talked about it. It's in the past."

"Are you jealous of me now?"

"What part of *'it's in the past'* wasn't clear to you?"

My eyebrow lifted and I growled softly. "It didn't necessarily sound like it was in the past, and I'd like to fuck both you and Ambrose without that tension lingering."

His aura flared, sharp cinnamon filling the air. Mercury was quick to get himself under control, but his scent lingered. The cool expression cracked, his teeth sinking into his bottom lip.

"Look, I'm dealing with it," he muttered. "It's hard to... reconcile. The fact that I'm jealous of you having the last year with Ambrose, while also being wildly attracted to you."

I tried to keep my arousal under control. He'd said it was hard —which equated to not ready. That's what I thought, at least. There was no need for me to push. Mercury had accepted that Kiara wanted him, meaning we would be in a pack together soon. Packs were forever. We had forever to figure this out.

"You can fuck me if you think that would help you reconcile," I said.

Those words were not what I'd thought about saying. Mercury looked me up and down, though, clearly tempted.

"Not sure if fucking you would have the desired effect," he said.

I shrugged, turning back to my laptop. The screen had gone dark during our conversation, but if I didn't want to get pushy, I knew I had to go back to work. There was a twinge of disappointment, which I did everything I could to quell.

"You fucking me, on the other hand..."

Mercury trailed off and my gaze snapped to him. His eyes were hooded, a faint flush to his cheeks. His burgundy hair hadn't been in any tight braids since the heat started—they would only get ruffled and fall out, so he'd taken to keeping it down. Chaotic waves around his shoulders.

Slowly, I closed my laptop. It ended up on the coffee table, and I stood, walking past the blankets and stuffed animals to sit directly beside him. Our thighs pressed together, his heat leeching into me. We were all running a little hot. Kiara was giving us plenty of physical activity.

"So, you're saying you have no desire to be dominant over me?" I asked, cocking my head to the side.

He snorted softly. "No. It's just hard to submit when I have that lingering envy."

"You don't have to submit," I said. "Sex doesn't have to be a power exchange between us."

Did *I* want him on his knees for me? Yes.

I once again reminded myself that we had forever. This pack was going to be my forever, same as Kiara was. We could work up to that.

"There's already been a power exchange," he said. His voice was going husky. "Like you said. When I came for you."

He admitted it was *for me*.

My thighs clenched, core tightening with desire. Mercury was a different kind of sub than Dash was. He had to be handled with care, not roughly tossed around.

Hesitantly, I threw my leg over his lap, waiting for him to stiffen. He didn't. His hands came down to my hips, long fingers meeting my bare skin. I was only wearing one of Ambrose's t-shirts. With Kiara's heat raging, the less clothing we all wore, the better.

I settled my weight on his thighs, the expensive fabric of his slacks soft against me. My arms draped over his shoulders and I leaned close enough to nip his bottom lip. He groaned, his day-old stubble brushing my cheek. He'd tidied himself up during a lull in Kiara's neediness, but hadn't bothered to do it again before he went out.

"If you came for me then," I murmured, "are you going to do it again?"

"Fuck, yes," he hissed.

His hips bucked, the bulge in his pants rubbing against me. When I leaned back his lips chased mine and I let them. We connected in a searing kiss.

The only time we'd kissed before had been when I'd lived through Tobias having a gun on me. We'd both been so giddy, high on the emotions, that we hadn't had a chance to process it. The kiss had barely felt real.

This one was real. He parted his lips, begging me to plunge my tongue past them. I tasted him, inhaling deep breaths of cinnamon and old books. His hands slid up under the thin fabric of my shirt, cupping my tits in his palms as he groaned.

Mercury was wearing too much clothing for me to deal with. A button up shirt and slacks. I grabbed the expensive fabric, ripping it open so aggressively buttons flew onto the couch beside us. My hands explored his slim chest, gently pinching his nipples.

He hissed, but pushed into the touch.

I played with him, kissing messily until his hips were bucking uncontrollably against me. Then my hands went down, undoing the button and zipper of his slacks. It was easy to slide his cock out of the confines of the fabric. The head was wet with precum and I gathered it on my palm, stroking him.

With a moan he broke from the kiss, glittering brown eyes glancing down at his cock. He watched, transfixed, as I jerked him off, tension tightening his muscles.

I lifted myself from where I sat on his upper thighs, using my free hand to tilt his chin up with me.

"You're going to make me come before I fuck you," I said.

He nodded, tongue flicking out to lick his lips.

I moved forward a tiny bit, rubbing his tip against my folds. My pussy didn't get as slick as Kiara's, but I was more than wet enough to take him right now. Mercury groaned, wrapping his arms around me.

"You want me to fuck you?" he asked.

Laughing, I shook my head. It was easy to line him up with my entrance, sliding down to take his length. I moaned, because he was the perfect length for this position. It wouldn't take much to get off.

"No," I said, resting my arms on his shoulders. "I'm going to use your cock to get off. Because pegging you is going to be more about your pleasure. I don't have the right harness here to come while fucking you."

"Why didn't you tell me to pick it up?" he asked with a groan. His hands were splayed out on my back as I ground down on him. "I was just at your apartment."

I rolled my eyes.

Until approximately ten minutes ago, it would have been real awkward for me to ask him to pick up a strap on harness for me.

"Next time," I murmured.

Using his shoulders as leverage, I pulled myself up off his cock before slamming down to take it again. He grunted and I moaned, letting my eyes slide closed.

"Do you want me to do anything?" Mercury asked.

He was the perfect sub, for sure. I smiled. Most people would have assumed I wanted their help—their fingers would be my clit already.

I really didn't need that.

"No. Stay still and think about how it's going to feel to have me pegging you, baby."

The endearment was what Ambrose called him, but it felt right for me to use it too. He didn't complain, and I found the perfect rhythm to give me what I wanted.

SIXTY-FOUR

MERCURY

She was heaven.

Having her pussy clenching down on my length as she used me for her pleasure was a special kind of arousing. This wasn't about me—she didn't even want me to do anything. All I could do was enjoy her and hold off the orgasm tingling the base of my spine.

Leighton's cheeks were flushed from exertion, her hips speeding up as she grew closer to her peak. The freckles across her skin gave her face a softness it wouldn't otherwise have. It was especially obvious right now, with her eyes closed and her lashes splayed out across her cheeks.

Her vanilla cream scent was claiming me as hers, but the shirt she wore had hints of hot iron and smoke. She was Ambrose's too, and I belonged to both of them.

I groaned as she sped up her movements and she opened her eyes. The stunning green orbs locked with mine, her lips parted as she panted.

"Don't come," she murmured.

I shook my head. "Not going to."

That was the other reason I wasn't touching her. She'd told me she didn't need it, but I wouldn't have been able to hold back my own release if she'd asked me to help get her off with more than just my cock.

"Good boy."

"Christ," I mumbled, dropping my head back against the couch.

Ambrose's voice was always a rumble when he praised me, but hers was a purr. It tickled my senses, and I had a moment where I wondered if I was going to be able to keep my word.

Then her pussy clenched on my length, her body shuddering. She was quiet through her release, only letting out a small sigh of pleasure. Leighton let her breathing level as she slowed to a stop. Her fingers grabbed my chin, moving my head up so I looked at her.

"I bet you would love it if I used my lock on you, wouldn't you?"

My eyes widened.

Why had that never crossed my mind? Female alphas had a lock. Usually it was used to please omegas, like a male alpha knot did. But the lock was versatile.

"Please," I said, glancing down at her pale thighs spread across mine.

"Another time," she said, smirking. "I haven't done it much. I tried using it on Ambrose once, but he didn't enjoy the experience."

Her hips lifted and my cock was released from her cunt. Cool air hit me and I groaned, almost wishing I'd been allowed to come in her.

Almost, because I knew what was coming was even better.

The t-shirt fell to cover her down to mid thigh, and she padded away from the couch. I watched her, transfixed by the sway of her hips, until she'd vanished around a corner. There were things she needed for the next part.

But without her present, I was far more likely to lose myself in my own head.

Was this a good idea?

I'd been jealous of her for years. It didn't matter that my relationship with Ambrose was open—a part of me had despised that he wanted more than just me. Dating had never gone well when I'd done it, so I'd stopped a long time ago.

Those negative feelings couldn't easily go away.

Could they?

Was putting that behind me as simple as getting pegged?

Fuck.

I wanted it to be that quick of a turnaround. We shared an omega now. We'd be in the same pack, once Kiara was ready to be bonded.

And I'd never been willing to admit it, with our scent match being her brother...

But Leighton intrigued me. I put on the cold, impersonal facade whenever I saw her because I didn't know what my expression would do if I let it relax. I might have smiled when she told some asshole off, or let my eyes grow hooded when she gave an order.

I couldn't be trusted around her.

Brushing a hand through my hair, I fought the urge to get up and pace. She hadn't told me to stay here—but it was implied. The desire to be good was almost outweighed by the need to work off some nervous energy. Then she reappeared.

"Were you ever jealous of me?" I asked.

I scanned her after I spoke, swallowing the lump in my throat.

Ambrose's shirt covered her, but now there was a tent in the fabric where the fake cock poked it. She clutched a bottle of lube in her hand.

"Not really," she said. "Not about your relationship with Ambrose, anyway."

"About something else, though?"

She came to stand in front of me, and I looked up to meet her eyes. "You had a pack. I thought I never would." Leighton shrugged. "I think I was a bit too deep in denial to realize that I wanted a pack, though."

That somehow made me feel better. She wasn't perfect. Well, she was in most ways. Leighton was everything an alpha was supposed to be—according to society. The only thing she wasn't, was male. But anyone who held her gender against her didn't deserve to be in her presence.

But she'd been in denial like I was, and that humanized her more than anything else could.

"Do you still want to do this?" she asked.

I nodded quickly. "Please."

She smirked. "Good. Ambrose has implied that the best way to make you stop overthinking is to fuck you senseless."

It was.

Maybe getting pegged was going to help me gain some clarity.

Leighton lifted the shirt by the hem, drawing it over her head and discarding it onto the floor. I groaned, trailing my gaze down her torso to her hips. A black leather harness rested against her flawless skin. Attached to the harness was a dildo in the same nude tone as her skin. It was long and thick, but slightly smaller than Ambrose's cock, so I knew I could take it.

There was no knot at the base, though. It was a typical beta cock.

"Why isn't there a knot?" I asked. "I thought you got the toys to use on Kiara."

"I got this one for you. Open your mouth."

I didn't have time to process her statement, because my jaw dropped open at the order. A moment later room temperature silicone touched my tongue. I peered up at her and she pushed her hips forward, driving the toy into my mouth until I gagged on it.

"Is there anything you want me to do to you, baby?"

The pet name sent a thrill through me. She didn't let me answer right away, choking me with the dildo again.

Spit dripped out of the corner of my mouth when she removed the cock, but Leighton shook her head at my attempt to wipe it off.

"Sensory deprivation," I murmured. "Usually getting blindfolded is my favourite, but today maybe something else."

Today I wanted to see her. I wouldn't be able to escape the knowledge that it was her fucking me if I was watching her body flex on every thrust. That was how I'd get my clarity.

"Got it. Take all your clothes off for me."

I stood from the couch, coming chest to chest with her. I sucked in a breath of vanilla cream, feeling my cock twitch, and then shrugged off my ruined shirt. My pants went next, boxer briefs along with them.

Leighton bent over to grab the shirt, running the soft fabric between her fingers. "Bend over the couch."

My heart kicked, but I did it. The position was vulnerable, everything on display for her. It had been a long time since I'd done that for someone new. My hands braced on the back of the couch, and my cock was leaking onto the cushion where I'd just been sitting.

The dildo pressed to the crease of my ass as Leighton leaned over me. She held my shirt suspended between both of her hands. I opened my mouth without being told, and a moment later it was full of the fabric. She tied the ends of the shirt around the back of my head, leaving me gagged.

"Tap me if that's not OK."

I kept my hands where they were. She purred and moved back. I looked over my shoulder, watching as she dripped clear lube onto her fingers. More onto the dildo. Even more onto me, the cold liquid making me shy away when it hit my hole.

The pad of her finger pressed against me and I groaned, no longer concerned with the temperature. I wanted her to own me, and I wanted the release I'd been denied when she made herself come on my cock.

She was gentle and slow, working a single finger in and searching around until she found my prostate. I bucked and she purred, rubbing it until my cock was weeping.

"You're really responsive," she murmured.

I couldn't speak, all my sounds muffled by the shirt. My body was speaking for me, though.

It was impossible to stay still when she was teasing me.

Leighton gave me another finger, this one giving me a faint stretch. She didn't keep teasing me long before she gave me a third, and then she pulled herself away.

I whined. A glance back over my shoulder confirmed she was stroking the dildo, spreading the lube from base to tip. She stepped forward, her clean hand grabbing my hip while the other led the fake cock to my hole.

"Is it going to take you long to come like this?" she asked.

I shook my head. My cock ached already, the orgasm just out of reach. Getting fucked was hands down the quickest way to get me off. I couldn't stop myself from coming once I'd been filled up.

"Perfect. You're going to come when I tell you to."

I failed to nod properly, because the tip speared me. I was loud despite the gag, which was growing increasingly wet with spit. She eased the cock into me, slow and steady, as my hands clutched the back of the couch.

When her thighs were against mine, she paused. "Look at that. Good boy."

Every time she gave me that praise, I nearly fucking came.

This time was no different. I groaned, fighting back the pleasure.

She pulled out, slamming back against me hard. Choking, I lost my grip on the couch and pitched forward. Leighton caught me, her arm banded around my chest. She turned us, then maneuvered me to kneel on the couch. My head hit the cushions, ass in the air with her behind me.

"There. More comfortable for you, so you don't need to think about how to stand."

Her words were vaguely teasing, but not in a cruel way. She seemed pleased that I'd epically failed at staying upright.

And she went hard after getting me in the new position.

I was a mess as she fucked me, my body sliding against the couch cushions. Tears beaded in the corners of my eyes from the effort of holding back my orgasm, because my body was already desperate for one. I wasn't even able to beg, but I would have. If the shirt hadn't been preventing me from doing anything more than mumbling, I would have pleaded for permission to come.

Leighton knew it, too.

She was pleased by my neediness, which you could see from the glint in her eyes. It was hard to take my eyes off her, though I had to strain my neck to see her behind me.

"Are you ready to come?" she asked.

I nodded, fingers digging into a nearby pillow almost hard enough to tear a hole in it.

She didn't give me what I wanted right away, letting my impatience rise for a minute longer before her purr washed over me. "Come for me, baby."

The orgasm released instantly. The only thing holding it back had been her commands, and without the barrier...

I sobbed against the gag, slamming my hips back onto her strap-on in a desperate attempt to extend the pleasure. My cock jerked, making a mess on the couch beneath me. Leighton kept fucking me until the pleasure turned to oversensitivity and I pulled away, letting out a little whine.

She undid the gag first, and I groaned huskily. "Did that help you reconcile?" she asked.

I licked my dry lips, moaning when she pulled out the dildo and left me empty. My brain wasn't firing on enough levels to answer that question.

"Maybe," I mumbled.

Leighton ran a hand down my back. "Be right back." Her soft footsteps padded away. Water ran, and she was back quickly.

A cool, wet glass was pressed against my cheek and I hissed. "Sit up and drink some water," she commanded.

I did as I was told, grabbing a blanket from the pile of Kiara's nesting material to drape across my lap. The other alpha didn't have the same impulse to cover up, standing in front of me fully nude.

When I'd gulped down a few sips of water, she asked me again. "Did it help?"

Her expression was more open than I'd ever seen it. Maybe a little nervous, even.

She wanted us to be good. No more tension.

"It definitely separated our relationship with each other from our relationships with Ambrose," I said, resisting the urge to glance away from her. "So... yeah. It helped a lot."

Leighton smiled, sitting down on the couch beside me. We were close to each other. Almost a snuggle, but not quite. I wasn't sure if we were at cuddle territory—or if that would even be something we did. Steps were being made, though.

She grabbed the remote, flipping on the TV. "Relax for a bit," she commanded. "We're going to have to switch onto Kiara duty soon, and I don't want you exhausted."

I almost complained, insisting on doing dishes or something. It's what I would have done before. But I didn't. I leaned back into the couch and downed the rest of my water, letting my mind take a moment to be a little quieter than normal.

SIXTY-FIVE

AMBROSE

"You're so good for me, princess," I murmured, raining kisses down on Kiara's body.

I started at her ankle, going up one leg, down the other, and across her entire torso. She whined softly, squirming beneath me, but didn't grab me and demand more. Her movements were lazy, her body tired.

Her heat was almost over. It would break soon, and her skin would cool down to a normal temperature again.

Then, we'd be able to have the difficult conversations.

Like about how long it would be before I could claim her, because I didn't want her walking around without my mark for long. Especially not as her bandaged neck taunted me with what had almost happened.

She'd almost belonged to someone else. Not my pack, but someone else entirely.

"Can you fuck me, Ambrose?" she mumbled, her lips parting on a yawn.

I purred, reaching down to stroke my cock. I was always hard for her, the scent of coconut and chocolate heavy around us. She was far too complementary to Leighton. It drove me goddamn insane.

"Come here if you want it," I said. "I don't want to fuck a half-asleep little omega."

Laying down on my back, I patted my thighs. She grumbled softly but mounted me, her pussy sinking down on my length as she sighed softly. This would be a lazy fuck, but that's what she needed right now. One more to break the heat.

All of us alphas were dead tired—and that should have been an easy heat. Omega heats varied in intensity depending on how many alphas they had bonded to them. Kiara only had one alpha, unless her biology had counted the bondmarks she'd left on my pack.

I was intrigued to see how her next heat would go.

Holding her hips, I fucked up into her as she bounced on my lap. Her hands landed on my arms, nails digging in and threatening to leave more scratch marks. They were the kind of marks I enjoyed receiving from her.

It was good that she was now keeping her knife to herself.

"Harder," Kiara breathed.

"Ask properly, princess."

Her breath hitched. Even as she got closer to orgasm, her scent was fading. The heat was officially broken, so it wasn't unfair of me to ask this of her. She had the faculties to do what I wanted.

"Sir, please fuck me harder."

"Good girl."

My grip on her tightened, helping her bounce as I slammed up into her. On each thrust my knot teased her entrance, but didn't slip past. She came apart on my cock within minutes, trembling and curling over as she groaned through her orgasm. Hers triggered mine, my release weak after so many within the past few days.

"You don't need my knot, right princess?" I asked.

She shook her head, slumping onto my chest with a moan and another yawn. I gently moved her off me, kissing her forehead. By the time I'd untangled my limbs from hers, she was fast asleep.

"We need to discuss what happened," I said, leaning casually against the kitchen counter.

My pack had been in here when I'd arrived, eating takeout.

"Did you break her heat?" Leighton asked.

I nodded. "She's going to be asleep for a while. I've been solely focused on her through the whole heat, but I know you and Mercury have been working through the aftermath of what happened. Neither of you can control yourselves."

Mercury looked mildly told off, but Leighton was completely unconcerned with the accusation.

"There wasn't much I could do without leaving the apartment, but Liberty has been keeping tabs," she said. "Tobias was taken to the hospital and the gunshot wounds didn't kill him. Noah Connolly has been seen back at his estate—the police questioned him heavily after Soren released him back into the world. We haven't been able to figure out what Soren wanted from him."

"What about your mother?"

Leighton's expression shuttered for a second. She'd given us bits and pieces of detail in between heat with Kiara. We knew her mother had sold her out for a chance to clear some debt.

"Seems to be living her life as normal. I've got plans for her. Might as well utilize Soren, since I'm going to be working for him."

She raised an accusatory eyebrow at Dash and Mercury. Dash grinned. "He's actually kind of fun, when he's not blackmailing you. Besides, your reputation is in shambles. That billionaire asshat is probably your best chance at building yourself back up."

He paused, tossing a fry into his mouth and swallowing. "Not that you have to work. I can be your sugar daddy, Leighton."

She growled, shaking her head. "I do *not* need you to support me."

"Not saying you do, sweetheart. But I've got enough money that you could just lounge around all day, waiting for me to get home from work…"

His teasing was making her green eyes flash. Dash was poking a bear, and he knew it. He was angling for another spanking from her, and if I was gauging this correctly, he wouldn't have to wait long.

I cleared my throat. "That's off topic. Is Kiara safe? Her brother is still alive. Father, too. What's stopping them from coming for her now? And your mother could still release the information about your brother's alpha."

I didn't particularly care about the last bit, but I knew Leighton would.

Leighton sighed. "Soren. As usual, everything revolves around him. I bet he's expecting me to report for work soon, so it might be time to settle everything up with him. Make sure we're all on the same page."

"Do you need me to come with you to see him?"

She waved me off, straightening her posture. She was wearing my clothes, and somehow looked incredibly professional regardless. "I can handle him. I'm going to have to. He might be angry about the info I collected on his safe havens, but he might also be impressed. Only one way to find out."

The idea of her going there alone didn't sit right with me, but I held back my complaints. Leighton wasn't a fragile omega like Kiara, a woman who needed to be protected and knew nothing of the world. She was an alpha, and I had to treat her like one.

Even though I wanted to wrap her up and keep her as my doll, so she couldn't be hurt.

"Let me drive you to your apartment, at least," I offered.

She gave me a small smile of agreement, then sent Mercury and Dash to the bedroom, so they could be there for Kiara when she woke up.

SIXTY-SIX

LEIGHTON

They let me right through the gate at Soren's estate. Guards didn't need to speak with me—they saw my car and the gate opened, an extended baton waving me through.

Soren's assistant Lyra didn't even wait in the foyer of his home. I had to wander through the place until I found him in his conservatory, laid out on a lounge chair. It was the middle of the day and the sun was beating down, humidity making my hair frizz.

"Your omega's heat ended, I take it?" Soren asked, peering at me out of the corner of his eye but not getting up.

He wasn't wearing the contacts today. His gold eyes were on display.

"It has," I confirmed.

I gave a nod to Soren's bodyguard—he was one of Soren's sons and knew my brother and his pack. We weren't well acquainted, but had run across each other before. Both in Soren's employ and at my brother's many social events. I thought his name was Wilder.

"You're ready to start work for me, then?"

Shaking my head, I strode over to a bench and sat down. Ambrose had dropped me off at my apartment, and I'd worn the red suit I had specifically for meetings with Soren.

I'd also stopped on the way here and gotten him an exotic fish. Maybe not the extravagant gift he'd demanded from me when I'd insulted him, but the man did enjoy pretty fish. I'd left it at the desk in the foyer, knowing Lyra would be back soon to put it in a tank.

I was doing my utmost to butter him up.

"We have to discuss the terms," I said.

"Your new pack dealt with terms," Soren said, chuckling.

"They're not the ones that have to live with them. I don't want much."

With a sigh, Soren sat up. Wilder handed him a blended beverage with a little umbrella and twirly straw, and he sipped it casually, watching me. He always did things like that. Staring and watching until the person he was trying to intimidate gave in.

I wasn't easily intimidated. He should know that by now.

Crossing one leg over the other, I lounged back on the bench.

"Tell me what you want, Leigh-Leigh, and I'll see if I can make it work."

"I want to know what you brought Noah Connolly in for."

"Well, I can't give you all my secrets. Next."

"I want you to make sure Tobias never gets near Kiara again."

"What do I look like to you? A bodyguard?" Soren rolled his eyes. "Ask me for something I can actually make a reality."

He could make all of my requests reality, and he *would* by the time I walked out of here. I gave him my final request. "Buy out my mother's debt to the Connolly family. I want her indebted to you, instead."

Soren laughed, standing from the lounge and twirling in the maxi skirt he wore. "Oh, see? Now *that,* I can do. It's already done. I don't appreciate when people blackmail the people I'm blackmailing. I'm a little selfish. Your mother is mine—and that's a piece of your other request. It's one of the things I spoke to dear Noah about while he was on his visit. She's not going to breathe a word about my son or his... condition. I, however, still might."

His eyes glinted in the sunlight, the gold seeming to glow. It made me uncomfortable to be sitting while he stood, but I considered it a power move to stay on this bench.

"You're not blackmailing me anymore, Soren. I found every single one of your little hideaways. I'm sure you've changed them up by now, given yourself some new escape plans. I'll find them too, and considering I'm now a member of a pack as rich as you —" I didn't want to flash Dash's money around, but I would make an exception for Soren. "—I'm a real danger to you."

Wilder didn't often react to things. He was impassive by necessity. At my words, though, his lips quirked up for a split second, eyes softening.

"Are you threatening me?" Soren asked.

His casual air dropped, arms crossing over his chest.

"Yes. I'm aware it's not your favourite, but I'm going to choose protecting myself and my pack over making you comfortable," I said.

Reaching into my small purse, I slid out a card from the side pocket. It had a picture of the fish I'd gotten him on it, along with a short description. I handed it to Wilder, who turned it over once before passing it to his boss.

"I got you a fish. Peace offering. If we can make this work, I'll head back to the specialized pet store and bring you another one. I was having trouble deciding between a freshwater stingray and a dinosaur bichir, but I figured the stingray went better with your current tank aesthetic."

He held the description card between two fingers, raising an eyebrow.

"Wilder, call Lyra and ask if there's really a stingray," he demanded.

Wilder got out his phone, calling the secretary.

"You need a permit to keep advanced tropical fish like freshwater stingrays in New Oxford," Soren said, narrowing his eyes at me. "They shouldn't have let you walk out with one."

I smirked. "I'm extremely convincing. That's why you want to hire me."

It only took a minute to confirm that Lyra was getting Soren's new stingray settled in his tank.

"The worker said he was a good breeding male. We all know how much you enjoy breeding," I said.

Wilder covered his mouth with his hand, shoulders shaking with silent laughter. Soren had more children than any other omega in the city, guaranteed. And far more than any gold pack omega had—considering it was extremely illegal for them to have children at all.

Soren sat back down on his lounge chair, letting the info card rest on the small table beside him. He hummed softly, looking me up and down again.

"I really do despise being threatened, almost as much as I adore being pampered. If you were anyone else, I'd have you killed."

A brief thrill of fear rushed through me. He could do it. There was an illicit side of his business, and it wasn't without violence.

"Since I'm me, and not anyone else, what do you plan on doing?"

"You're hired."

"I only accept if you accept my terms."

He laughed. "I just threatened to kill you, and you're still trying to drive a hard bargain?"

"They're my terms."

"How are you the same woman who let herself get blackmailed for two years?" Soren mused. "Fine. Noah Connolly is part of a larger plan. He's not overly important, but is indeed a fun tool to bend to my will. We only discussed the new terms of him doing business."

If I cared more, I could push for what the larger plan was. But it may be better if I didn't know. My life would be more peaceful that way—and with an omega in the picture now, peaceful sounded good.

"And Tobias? You're going to keep him away from his sister?"

"I have it on good authority that Tobias has already been shipped off—bullet holes and all—to be bitten into a West Coast pack. It was the only alliance Noah could get by selling off his useless son. A mostly useless alliance, really, but he wanted Tobias out of his hair as much as you do. If he ever ends up back in town, you'll be the first to know. I seriously doubt it, though. His new pack is going to keep him... busy."

Soren grinned. What he meant by 'busy' was another thing I would rather not know.

"Your mother's debt is already mine, so there's nothing to do there. If you'd like, you can be Edith's point of contact. I was going to have Lyra manage her, but if you'd rather have the job..."

"I would love to."

It was probably the only time I'd ever find absolute glee in talking to the woman.

"Perfect. We can discuss other duties at a later date. I'd like your little assistant on my payroll too, but I suppose she would have to come willingly, wouldn't she?" He sighed. "Ask her for me, would you? I've got to rush off to a rather important meeting, but this has been an exhilarating start to my day."

The hours he slept were a mystery to me, because this was far from what I'd consider a start of the day.

He got up in a swirl of colourful fabric, his sandals slapping against the paving stones as he strode toward the conservatory exit. Wilder gave me a small nod and followed behind, not seeming too concerned for Soren's safety in this place.

I stretched as I got up from the bench, nursing sore muscles from so many days of heat. My steps were leisurely as I left Soren's residence, giving Lyra a wave when I passed her beside the giant fish tanks. In my car, parked in his vast cul-de-sac driveway, I made a call.

"This is Edith Winston," she said in a clipped tone.

I grinned. "Mother."

She didn't reply, the only sound her breathing. I wasn't sure what she was going to do next. In her eyes, I'd ruined her life. It didn't matter that she'd tried to sell me off to a crime family to pay off a fraction of the debt she'd wracked up. The fact that I hadn't gone along with it, made it my fault.

"You're an ungrateful—"

Exactly as I'd expected. I cut her off.

"Shut up. I'm not calling as your daughter, so maybe I should have called you Edith. I'm calling as your boss."

"Excuse me?"

"You owe millions of dollars—not to the Connollys, but to Soren Rosania. I'm in his employ, and he's given me the absolute pleasure of being in charge of you."

"There is no—"

"Did you not understand what I meant when I told you to stop speaking?" I asked. My smile was growing wider every second. I was grinning like a goddamn fool in my car. "We'll be speaking regularly, because I get to tell you everything you have to do. I tell you which high society soirées to attend. Which people to talk to. Which gossip to fish for. When to stay home, and when to go out. So, kind of like what you've been doing to me for the past two years of my life. Except for you, this is the rest of your life."

She was breathing heavily. I would have killed to see the expression on her face—but I did plan on *seeing* her as little as humanly possible. We could keep our conversations to phone calls.

"Call Lyra. Ask her who's your boss now, and she'll tell you the same thing. Then, the next time I call, you're going to answer the phone. Day or night. Any hour."

I wanted to ask her if she understood, to force her to say yes. I wasn't keen on dealing with her vitriol, though.

So I hung up.

For the first time, I hung up on her instead of her hanging up on me.

That alone might be worth being Soren's errand girl for a while.

I turned my keys to start the engine and pulled off the curb, and the smile lasted for the rest of the damn day.

SIXTY-SEVEN

KIARA

"I've never done this before," I admitted softly.

Dash's arms came around me, his breath brushing my ear. "Don't worry, little omega. I can help you."

His touch was warm against me, and he grabbed a couple of items from the dining room table in front of us. Mercury snorted from the sidelines, and I glanced over to see him rolling his eyes.

"If Dash can learn it, so can you," Mercury stated. "All he did was binge watch sewing videos online. He'd never touched a sewing needle before we got this delivered. You've spent plenty of time hand sewing, haven't you princess?"

I bit my lip, flushing. Having Mercury calling me 'princess' still felt fake, but he hadn't grown distant with me. My heat had ended days ago, and he was being as affectionate as ever. Not as overtly as Dash, obviously, but in his own ways.

"Yes. It was one of the only things Father let me do. Sewing and playing piano. And I hated piano."

"The machine will be easy, then."

Dash hummed his agreement, his chest rumbling with a purr.

I relaxed back against him, watching his hands work to thread the machine.

I'd been constantly tired since my heat ended, enough that Mercury had been trying to insist I see a doctor. Leighton had—thankfully—shut the idea down. She claimed it was fine for me to take a while to recover, considering my heat had been traumatic.

There was a phantom clench of my stomach, an echo of the pain that had felt like it was eating me from the inside.

My mates both stiffened, my flash of fear not hidden from the bonds. Especially when my bondmarks were fresh on them, claiming all the alphas as mine and refreshing the temporary bonds.

"Maybe she should go back to the nest," Mercury said tightly. "This might be too much."

His arms were crossed over his chest and he scowled at Dash.

Dash had been the one to pull me from the nest, but only because I wanted to. When I was awake, all I could do in there was fidget. There wasn't anything to occupy my hands or time.

"I'm fine," I reassured. "But I could maybe use a snack?"

Mercury had vanished to the kitchen in seconds, and Dash nipped teasingly at my ear. "You know how to work him, don't you princess?" he murmured.

"I have no idea what you're talking about," I said, smiling.

We worked through the functions of the machine—which could do so much more than I could with my hands and some needles. They were right that it was easy to comprehend when I knew the basics of the stitches. By the time I'd finished the apples and peanut butter Mercury had chopped for me, I was ready to bring my dream garments to life.

Leighton and Ambrose came home, laden down with bags of things from Leighton's apartment, before I could lose myself in the project.

I had no desire to go back to that apartment myself.

The thought made me a little sick, actually.

All I could associate with my original nest was how I'd been dragged from it. How from then on, my pain had only gotten worse.

From being struck unconscious by the gun, to the searing dark bond attempt by Cordian...

Shuddering, I hopped off my chair.

No one had told me anything about what happened either, but I was about ready to start threatening violence for answers. They were my alphas, but I'd escaped my family on my own and I had a right to know if they were on their way to take me back.

I gave Leighton a chaste kiss in greeting.

"Did they treat you good while I was gone?" Leighton asked, a quirk to her lips as she looked at the sewing machine and beginnings of my project. "This is the most I've seen you do in a while."

"They did," I said, stepping back. "And it is. Which means I'm ready for you all to tell me what happened to my brother and father."

All movement stopped so abruptly it was like time froze.

Mercury was horrified that I'd asked. Ambrose's expression was unreadable, while Dash smirked, knowing it was only a matter of time before I asked. Leighton sighed, looking me up and down.

Maybe I should have waited until I had put on proper clothes, as opposed to fluffy pajamas with Nyla's holster strapped to my hips.

Then again, I couldn't see myself wanting real clothes for a few more days, and I wanted answers now.

"It was taken care of," Mercury said. "That's all you need to know."

I pinned him with a glare and he had the good sense to look away.

"Would you be comfortable only knowing that, Mercy?" I demanded.

He had no answer.

That's what I thought.

"Are you going to tell me, or do I have to find out on my own?"

"We'll tell you, dove. We're not doing it in the front entrance, though. Go sit on the couch."

She injected a bit of command into her words, enough to get my feet moving before she let it drop. Leighton wasn't hesitant to use the dark bond, and maybe I should be scared of that. I wasn't. I liked having her use it, because it was a constant reminder that she was confident she knew what I wanted. My alpha was certain she would only ever command me to do what I wanted to do.

I brought my knees to my chest on the middle couch cushion, and Dash was quick to plaster himself to my side. The rest of the pack trailed in slower, Mercury arguing with Leighton in hushed tones.

"I shot your brother twice," Leighton said, sitting on the coffee table in front of me.

While my satisfied grin might have put some people off, my mates didn't mind that I was a fan of violence.

"So, is he...?"

Did I want him dead? I couldn't decide. He couldn't hurt me anymore if Leighton had shot him in the head, but why did he deserve a quick death when he never would have given that to me?

"Not dead," Leighton said.

I tried to place how I felt about that. Not relieved. I'd cared about him when we were children, but he'd stopped feeling like family a long time ago.

"Where is he, if he's not dead?" I asked.

Maybe it was better for him to be dead. I couldn't have him

near me, his threats constantly hanging over my head. He would never stop.

"Across the country, bonded to a pack."

"The alphas aren't the nicest, from what we've found," Ambrose added.

Across the country? I had no concept of how far that was. What length of flight was it? How long would it take to drive? Could he easily come back?

I bit my lip, trying to stifle my fear over the possibilities—his new alpha pack could be as unkind as he was, and bring him back to take me.

Mercury growled, always the most attuned to how I felt since I'd claimed him.

"He's never coming back here," he muttered. "The pack controls him. He was sold to them, like your family was trying to sell you."

"But won't they want to keep him happy?"

Dash snorted, pulling me closer to him. The skin to skin contact soothed me. "Tobias doesn't have as much power as he seems to, little omega. The pack who bit him in is as feral as he claimed all alphas were. They don't give a fuck about a beta's feelings."

I hadn't thought there were packs like that.

With everything my father and brother had made up, I'd assumed that was one of the things.

"Oh. He can't come back, then?"

"Never, dove," Leighton confirmed. "And your father isn't going to touch you, either. He's controlled by Soren now."

My original saviour. Another man with an agenda, but at least his agenda had worked in my favour, and still was.

I curled into Dash, nibbling my bottom lip.

"What about the Ashby pack?"

That got growls from all my alphas.

The bite mark on my neck was healing well, but tingled from time to time as a reminder. I'd had to keep it covered because my mates couldn't look at it without rage spiking through the bond.

I didn't fear the Ashby pack, though. I feared what they'd done, but not them.

"They haven't seen any consequences," Leighton said through gritted teeth. "They all left the house before the police arrived. Did you want anything to happen to them, dove? After what they did to you…"

My head was shaking before I'd decided. "No. They were coerced into it. I think they're being punished enough."

"We couldn't find any evidence of how they were blackmailed," Mercury said. "It's possible they did it by choice."

No. Cordian's expression had been too full of regret, and far too relieved when Leighton turned down the bond. Something forced them. I'd had the chance to shoot Cordian outside the family home, and I hadn't taken it. My brain had been muddled, but it had been a choice I'd made as consciously as possible.

There was no need to take it back now.

"I don't want to ever see them again," I said. I couldn't count on my ability to keep Nyla in her sheath if I did. "They can live their lives, though."

None of my alphas were especially pleased with that decision, and I determined it wasn't me who was having trouble with this conversation. It was them.

Hypocrites.

Faking a yawn, I stretched my arms overhead and glanced toward the sewing machine. "I think I'll come back to that later. Can we leave it out?"

I pursed my lips in a pout, and everyone was quick to agree. Then Ambrose swept me up in his arms and carried me back to my nest. There was an extra layer of comfort blanketing me now, with the knowledge that I was truly safe.

My alphas had kept me safe.

They'd take care of me until the end of time, and they were the ones I'd chosen—and who'd somehow chosen me right back.

EPILOGUE 1

LEIGHTON

About a week later

Marlowe had arrived first to the small downtown cafe. It was one of many we cycled through for our monthly meetings, and there was already a croissant sandwich waiting on a plate for me, along with a coffee. He was halfway through a pastry, with a second lined up and ready in front of him.

"You're alone today," I commented.

He spun to face me, beaming. My brother was up from his chair before I could sit down, wrapping his arms around me.

"I'm allowed to go places alone," he said, his voice muffled against my shoulder.

I rolled my eyes. No, he wasn't. I was willing to bet one of his pack members was across the street watching his every move through the large glass front windows. He had some very overprotective alphas.

Returning the hug, I detached him from me and took my seat.

The coffee was still hot, the way I liked it. His blended drink was half gone, and I bet he'd order another before we were done catching up. We had a lot to catch up on, after all.

I'd gone and gotten myself an omega and a pack since the last time we had one of these meetings.

Not to mention almost dying, but I wasn't going to let Lowe in on how close of a call that had been.

"How's everything with the pack?" I asked casually.

Marlowe scoffed, running a hand through his fluffy black hair. He had green eyes that matched mine—they ran in the family—and a face full of freckles. More than I had. "We're not here to talk about me."

"We always talk about you," I countered.

"That's because you never have anything interesting to say. Until recently, you had no life," Marlowe said.

It may have sounded like a harsh comment, but he said it good-naturedly. And it was true. My life before Kiara was governed by Soren and my mother. I should probably tell Marlowe about our mother's years of blackmailing me, but it would only make him feel guilty for no reason. I know he would have done the same for me or a member of my pack.

"Now you have a life and a pack. Is Dash happy?" Lowe's tone turned worried, his teeth sinking into his bottom lip.

My only remaining bone to pick with Dash was that he'd made Marlowe feel guilty for so long. I'd mainly forgiven him for it, and I knew Marlowe would never have a bad word to say about anyone in the Loranger pack.

Trust my brother to worry so deeply about the man he'd unintentionally broken.

"Dash will be happier when it's all official," I said. "But he is thrilled."

Marlowe perked up. "Official? Have you not all bonded yet?"

I shook my head. "Kiara went through a lot when she was

kidnapped by her brother. We had to wait for her heat to break, and she's been recovering since then."

Her neck bruises were almost entirely gone, the would-be bondmark from Cordian scabbed over and fading more every day. She was extra tired, the same way she'd been before her heat, and spent most of the days and nights sleeping. Only time would tell if that happened every heat, or was only because of the stress associated with this one.

"You're going to, right?"

"You're nosy," I complained. He pouted at that. "Yes. We're going to."

"And then the scent match will dissolve." Marlowe sounded thrilled by the prospect. "The Loranger pack's scent match to me, I mean."

It would dissolve. Any time you changed the composition of a pack, there was a chance of a scent match dissolving, but this was a big change. They would be joining my pack—an omega-centric pack that was based around Kiara.

Plus, there was the fact that I was Marlowe's blood relative. I couldn't be scent matched to my brother. The universe, gods, or whoever governed scent match magic were smart enough to realize that was fucked up.

If the Loranger pack stayed scent matched to him after bonding Kiara, it would be a freak accident.

"It better, because that would be weird," I said.

"And when the match is dissolved, I'll be like… a normal person to them!" he exclaimed. "We can all have dinner and it won't be awkward and your omega won't hate me."

I wasn't as confident it would be like flipping a switch, but I wasn't about to rain on my brother's parade. They'd had to deal with a lot of emotions around his rejection—primarily feeling unworthy, especially Dash. Mercury a little bit, too. It wasn't Lowe's fault, but it was hard to just turn that off.

The first dinner was going to be awkward as fuck. We'd make it through, though. They were my pack, and Lowe was family. It wouldn't be good if they couldn't at least be civil.

"My omega won't hate you regardless," I said. "You have your own pack and no interest in the Loranger pack."

Marlowe snorted, grabbing his drink and taking a big sip through the straw. "Usually, you're the one lecturing me, but you have a lot to learn, big sis."

I raised an eyebrow.

"It doesn't work like that," he said simply. "If I was scent matched to her pack, Kiara would hate me on principle. She might anyway, because of the history."

"You and your pack literally met your scent match mate and you love her," I said.

"Yeah, but I joined the pack before we met her, so she's my scent match too."

Part of me was confused, but then I remembered the way Kiara had pettily scent marked my whole apartment after I'd fucked Ambrose that first night. She was a possessive omega and didn't like to share. Marlowe had always been more of a share-er, and he had a point about the scent match logistics.

"Point taken. I'll tell Kiara to be on her best behaviour," I said.

I didn't tell my brother that I might have to give her a command to not stab him. She still kept Nyla with her at all times, and with her colourful weapons history... Better safe than sorry?

He laughed like I was joking. "She just needs to be herself. Everyone is going to love her."

Well... I can see her clashing heavily with Denzel, my least favourite of Marlowe's alphas.

But I'm going to keep that to myself.

We moved on to more casual topics for a while. Small talk about life stuff. Marlowe was going to a new yoga studio and was curious to know if Kiara would come. He knew yoga wasn't exactly my thing. No one in his pack was a huge fan either. Kiara was one of his last hopes. He beamed when I told him I would pass on the invitation, even though I said not to hold his breath.

As we were wrapping up and Marlowe was sucking down his second blended coffee beverage, I cleared my throat and tried not to avoid eye contact when I brought up the elephant in the room.

"You're not upset that I'm with your scent match pack, are you? I don't want a people-pleasing answer, Lowe. Your real feelings only."

He tipped his head to the side, hair falling into his face. The dark curls were just a touch too long, ready for a trim. He took a second to think, fiddling with the edge of his plate.

"I'm not upset," he said. "I was a little... worried, when I first found out. You know I need people to like me, and I was horrified that my sister's pack might hate me. I always said I'd win your pack over if you ever decided to join one, but it wasn't that simple with the Loranger pack."

There was a lot of baggage, that was for sure. These concerns were right on brand for Marlowe.

"Are you still worried?"

"Yeah, but there's no way Dash can hate me *more* than he did before, right? I was persona non grata for the Loranger pack. They were furious when my pack went to them for help during the fiasco earlier this year."

Fiasco was one way to put it. Not the word I would have used, but whatever.

"I think Dash believes you owe him a favour for how he helped out that time."

Marlowe perked up, grinning. "I'm happy to deliver! I can bake a birthday cake? Wedding cake? I've always wanted to do a wedding cake."

Snorting, I shook my head. "We're not having a wedding. Not

that kind of pack. I'll let him know you're offering up baked goods, though. He might take you up on it."

"Perfect," he said, smiling. "I guess I should let you go. Lock down your pack, and all that."

There would be no locking down tonight. Kiara had been asleep when I left the apartment, and historically speaking she would remain asleep until dinnertime. She was sleeping a little less every day.

"Your pack is getting antsy too," I commented, tilting my head toward the glass cafe windows.

Denzel leaned against a pole outside the building, holding his phone but looking right at us. Marlowe pouted, making a shooing motion with his hand. All his mate did was put his back to a different part of the pole, facing the cafe door instead of us.

"He's getting better," Marlowe defended, affection clear in his tone.

"He is," I agreed, giving the asshat more grace than I usually would.

As it turned out, packs were about compromise.

Marlowe compromised by letting his alphas follow him around occasionally. I compromised by letting Kiara stab a person on occasion.

At my statement about Denzel, Marlowe's eyes widened in surprise, but he shook it off fast—in true Marlowe fashion. Standing from our seats, he politely took our dirty plates over to the counter, dropping them off and leading me outside. We stopped outside of the cafe doors for a hug, and he squeezed me extra tight.

"I'm really glad you've found someone, Leigh."

He worried for me. I knew that. All I did was work, which wasn't healthy for anyone—especially not when I was blackmailed into it.

"Thank you," I murmured, making sure his alpha couldn't hear. "For caring. We both know our parents never did."

Marlowe laughed, pulling back with a glint in his eye. "Hey, speaking of, I hear Mother got kicked off all her event boards. There are tons of rumours about it. Would you happen to know anything?"

I grinned, shaking my head. A secretive smile passed between us. "No, but what a shame for her."

"Yes, an absolute shame."

He laughed again, waving over his shoulder as he went to link arms with Denzel, who gave me a shallow nod.

I finally kind of understood why Marlowe loved that asshole. Sometimes, when you love someone, you can work together and get past anything.

EPILOGUE 2

KIARA

About a week after that

"We can't live here," I said.

My alphas turned to me, eyebrows raised. Dash was only grinning, his form lounging back in a recliner.

"What do you mean, dove?" Leighton asked.

The guys' apartment had been suitable while I was in heat—I'd been too out of it to notice—and in the time while I was recovering. Now that I was up and walking around, I kept noticing things that irked me.

There were too many... angles. Leighton's place had too many angles too, but they'd been softer and more manageable. I also hadn't had as much time to notice them. I had nothing but time, now. Plus, all the rooms were too big and dark. They didn't have as many windows as Leighton did.

The caveat was that I couldn't go back to Leighton's apartment, either. I'd tried, but hadn't made it past the elevator before I had Nyla clenched in my fist, my body shaking.

All I could remember from there was how I'd been dragged from my nest when I should have been safe. It was a shame the one incident was overshadowing all the good memories. I bet it would fade eventually, but it was so fresh.

"I don't like it," I said simply.

They would probably tell me to figure out how to fix it. We could add some lighter colours, maybe, to make it better. My father never would have entertained anything like this, so there was something freeing about being able to voice my opinion when I knew I wouldn't be completely belittled for it.

"What don't you like?" Dash asked, patting his thighs.

I nibbled on my bottom lip, going over and depositing myself in his lap. His arms wrapped around me immediately, stroking me in places that made me blush. Leighton growled softly, possessively. It wasn't anything I was concerned about. It kind of seemed like a kink between the two alphas. Who could have me more?

"Angles," I said. "And it's dark. The rooms aren't the right size. There's something off about it."

Mercury got out his phone, a serious expression on his face. Ambrose's lips quirked in a smile. His hand was resting on Leighton's thigh, fingers squeezing occasionally. It made her blush, and it made me want to prove I could pleasure her better.

I totally did not have any lingering jealousy about Ambrose having her first.

At all.

At least, not any that my pack could see. I was very good at hiding it.

"If you don't like these angles, what angles would you prefer?" Dash asked.

I shrugged. "Um... I'm not sure. These just feel wrong."

"I've got a few showings booked for different houses to see if you can figure out which angles seem right," Mercury said, looking up from his phone.

My eyes widened. That was like... half a minute. Were they seriously going to move because I didn't like this apartment? I couldn't even put into normal words why I didn't like it. I was running purely on vibes.

"Are we... moving, then?" I squeaked.

"Did you not just say that you want to?" Mercury asked.

"Well, yes, but—"

"Then we're moving."

I swung my gaze to Leighton, pleading for an explanation on why they were so accepting. This was their home. They'd lived here for years.

Leighton shrugged, grinning. "This place doesn't have enough rooms, anyway. Some packs are comfortable with sharing spaces, but I'm a fan of privacy. We need enough rooms for each of us, plus a proper nest for you. We're a couple rooms short here."

Dash grabbed my chin, turning my face to give me a soft kiss. "None of us are attached to this apartment, little omega. This place was from a time when we thought we wouldn't have an omega. Or a fourth pack member."

It still felt a little wrong that they would drop everything so easily to please me, but it may be my upbringing talking. My family never cared about my feelings at all. To have people that did... was odd.

"We're not bonded yet, and you're still going to uproot yourselves?" I asked.

"Are you having second thoughts about having us claim you?" Mercury asked. "I was under the impression it was a sure thing."

My eyes widened and I frantically shook my head. Mercury's pinched expression softened into a tentative smile. I couldn't feel what he felt—my bond with him was too weak at the moment. It was a pain trying to constantly refresh my claim, as much as I loved giving the bites.

"You're our omega, princess," Ambrose said. "Bond or no bond. We'll find a house that you love."

I blinked rapidly, shoving back tears. My emotions were still swinging back and forth, a lingering aftereffect of my heat. Or maybe the trauma.

Leighton wanted me to go to therapy, but I wasn't completely comfortable leaving the apartment yet. I had to unlearn my father's fucked up perceptions of the world, and there were plenty of things I knew nothing about. I'd been watching a lot of TV and episodes of Dash's show.

I think he liked me watching the Dirt with Dash backlog. He was incredibly flirty with some of his guests, and whenever I got through a particularly intense episode, I ran to scent mark him.

And do other things to claim him.

"I want the bond, then," I announced.

Three auras flared all at once. Leighton purred so loud I could hear it from here, and Dash's cock went hard against my ass. Bonding didn't *have* to mean sex, but there was no reason not to—and people said the claiming was especially intense if done at the peak of pleasure.

"Are you saying now, little omega?" Dash murmured. "Because I heard now, and I'm about to remove every single piece of clothing you're wearing."

I was in tight leggings and a loose-fitting t-shirt—one that belonged to Ambrose. Reaching down, I grabbed the hem of the shirt. It was off me in a second, and Dash was burying his face in my cleavage. I'd gone braless today.

"Fuck," he groaned. "You're so fucking perfect, Kiara."

My body hummed in response, sending tingles and slick between my legs. More hands landed on me and my leggings were worked down over my ass and thighs. The position was awkward, with Dash in the recliner, but eventually I was in his lap, straddling him in only a pair of panties.

He'd undone his pants and shoved them down just far enough to expose his cock. It was already leaking, despite having barely been touched.

All my alphas scents were in the air, but only Leighton stayed close. She'd been the one to help me get undressed, and now she was leaning in, her tongue stroking over the dark bond on my neck. I shivered, the darkened skin extra sensitive compared to the rest of my body.

Then Dash dragged me forward and kissed me frantically, our lips smashing together. I moaned against him, rubbing my clit along his cock a few times before lifting my hips. I reached down to position his cock properly against me, but Leighton beat me to it. She shoved my panties to the side, the material digging into my skin. His tip was pressed to my entrance, and I sank down with a long moan.

Leighton's hand snuck between Dash and I, touching me as I bounced on his length.

His grunts and groans were music, his cock thick and long inside me. I wasn't patient, though, and moved back from the kiss quickly, baring my neck.

"Claim me," I murmured.

Dash groaned, leaning in to kiss along my shoulder and neck. His lips trailed over Leighton's bond, but when he kissed the spot Cordian had bitten me, I froze.

My knees locked, a whine leaving me as I recalled the fiery pain the other alpha's bite had left. I tried to block it out. I'd been trying for weeks. As much as I didn't fear the Ashby pack, I was still terrified of what they'd done.

Of someone trying to do it again.

"Don't dark bond me." The words came out as a pleading whisper.

Dash let out a shaky breath, growls coming from my other alphas. "I would fucking never. You get a normal bond. There's no reason for me to give you a dark bond, little omega, because I don't want to control you."

Heat surrounded me from all sides, the others crowding around the recliner. My mates touched me gently where they could, and the situation was so different than it had been with Cordian that I relaxed.

Cordian had touched me as little as he could. He didn't want the bond anymore than I had. This was vastly different. I was desperate for a permanent bond with my pack. I just hadn't realized it would be this difficult.

Tilting my head, I offered him the other side of my neck. I didn't want his bite where Cordian's had been. The scabs were mostly gone now, but if Dash bit me there I would remember what the other bite had looked like forever.

Dash trailed the tip of his finger across my neck, sliding strands of hair out of the way. "You want me here?" he asked.

"Yes."

"We don't have to do this now," Leighton said.

I shook my head. "No. They're mine. I want it to be permanent."

She opened up our bond, showing me her worry and affection for me. I did the same, giving her a stark look at my fear. The only thing stronger than it was determination.

Her finger started stroking my clit again and I let out a little whimper. My workload was severely diminished this time, because all my alpha's hands helped me bounce on Dash's cock.

He kissed and licked at the spot I'd offered him, groaning and waiting until both of us were on the precipice of orgasm. Then, his teeth sank in.

Leighton accepted him instantly, letting his pack become part of ours.

This bond was so much stronger than the ones I'd had with him before. He wasn't a faint presence in the distance. Dash was inside me, his feelings melding with mine. Our auras swirled together, and for a moment my world was only spring rain and peaches.

Then the bubble burst and I cried out, my back arching as I came.

MERCURY

Kiara had never looked more gorgeous than she did with two marks on her neck. Leighton's dark bond was black and leeching across her skin, while Dash's was normal, a simple bite mark. They contrasted, but our omega wore them both with pride.

She was going to wear mine with pride too, but I had a more private location in mind.

"I'm taking her next," I said, helping her get off Dash and the recliner.

Her limbs were jelly, each movement a struggle. I hadn't given her a chance to recover from her release, but my cock was aching and I desperately needed her to be mine.

Ambrose didn't complain about me taking her, so I led her over to the couch and laid her down on her back. Her eyes were glazed, Dash's cum dripping from her cunt. My packmate was still panting where he sat, looking stunned.

Taking off all my clothes, I placed one knee on the couch, my other foot planted on the floor. I didn't wait for her to ask for it before plunging my cock all the way inside her. Her pussy hugged me, sucking me deep and trying to hold me hostage.

I groaned, and Ambrose's body blanketed mine from behind.

"You're not usually so eager, baby," he murmured. "I expected you to do a thousand calculations about how and where you wanted to bond her."

Shaking my head, I hissed when his finger slid down the crack of my ass, wet with spit. I wasn't going to last long if he did that, and I might prefer it that way this time. I wanted to bond her while I came. And I wanted to bond her as soon as humanly possible.

"Already done," I grunted. "All the calculations. All I want is to fucking have her, and I want my mark..." I ran a hand up her torso before squeezing one breast. "Right here."

Kiara's eyelids fluttered, her legs trying to pull me closer.

"Do you want that, princess?" Ambrose asked. "His mark there?"

She moaned, grabbing me around the shoulders and pulling me down to kiss her. It left Ambrose with unfettered access to my ass. He took advantage, pushing his finger inside me.

"You didn't answer," I said against Kiara's lips. "Ambrose likes when you answer his questions. Or did you want him to punish you, little omega?"

Her sapphire eyes sparkled, teeth nipping at my bottom lip.

"I want you to claim me," she said. "Wherever you want."

Unlike Dash, I didn't need to put my bondmark on her neck. My fingers tweaked her nipple and I started to fuck her. It pushed me back and forth between Ambrose's finger and her pussy. With how keyed up I was, it wasn't going to be long before I came.

Her cunt clenched and pulsed around my length every time I pinched her nipple, so I hoped that meant she was close too.

Keeping up the pace of my thrusts, I detached from the kiss and trailed my lips down her neck. I paused to kiss Dash's bite mark and Leighton's, then carried on. Down her chest, between her breasts and around until I had soft flesh between my teeth.

She moaned, her fingers tugging on my braids and making a mess of my hair.

I took it as the confirmation I needed that she wanted this. Me. For life.

My teeth sank in.

Dash claiming her had brought our pack into hers, a bond already living between us. This was different. What was muted before now exploded into colour, her coconut chocolate scent filling my space until I could smell nothing else.

I groaned, burying my cock inside her to match my teeth, the sensation of her so strong it tipped me over the edge. She cried out below me, clutching me for dear life.

"Mercy," she whimpered. "Oh, fuck."

That silly nickname made me melt for her, my forehead dropping to rest against her sweat damp skin.

Ambrose didn't steal her away from me, nor did he stop fucking my ass with his finger. Not even when Leighton gave Kiara a bottle of water and the omega sat halfway up to chug the liquid down.

He had other plans for bonding Kiara, and I imagined they involved me.

AMBROSE

I'd been waiting impatiently to have all three of my lovers together, and I didn't want to bond Kiara in any situation other than this one.

Dash was going to watch, but I didn't really care. My packmate was a voyeur and an exhibitionist, but harmless. And quiet. While he watched was about the only time he was ever quiet, probably because he didn't want to risk being unceremoniously kicked out of the vicinity.

"Doll, can you get me the bag from my bedroom?" I asked Leighton.

Spitting on my fingers, I slid another one into Mercury's ass. He was limp beneath me, but I knew him. My lover would perk back up momentarily, and he loved some over stimulation.

Leighton took the empty water bottle from our omega and nodded. Everyone knew where this was going except Kiara. She probably had an inkling, but I hadn't gone into the depths of my kinks with her yet. I kept fucking Mercury's ass with my fingers until he was grunting, pushing his hips back to meet me. Leighton dumped the bag on the coffee table, open.

"Get some rope," I commanded.

She complied, handing me a black piece of silky soft rope. Mercury preemptively put his hands behind his back, his cheek resting on Kiara's stomach, and I chuckled. "So eager, but you're not getting tied right now."

It had been ages since he'd had my ropes biting into his skin, and I knew he missed it. We'd been too tired to do anything together other than sloppy kisses and affectionate hand jobs for the past few weeks.

"We've got to shuffle around a bit, baby."

Mercury groaned in complaint, but sat up when I patted his ass. I got off the couch and grabbed Kiara, pulling her in for a kiss. Then I pointed at the couch. "On your back, doll."

Leighton lifted an eyebrow. "What do you have in mind?"

"Kiara's going to lay on top of you, and Mercury is going to spend some time between both of your legs while he gets fucked," I said. "Is that too much of me telling you what to do with your omega?"

She shivered, shaking her head. "Not today."

Noted. My little doll was in a submissive mood today. I might have to take care of her solo, later.

She stripped down without me asking, laying herself out on

the couch. Dash groaned from the recliner. His cock was in his hand and he was lazily jerking himself off as he watched. Leighton pinned him with a look and he flushed.

"Get on top of your alpha, Kiara," I ordered.

"How are you going to bond me like this?" she asked.

Her hesitation slipped away when I gave her a single push. She spread her thighs on either side of Leighton's hips, and their pussies looked so delicious together I was shocked I hadn't done this before.

"Mercury, between their legs."

My lover settled himself on the couch, tongue stroking down Kiara's pussy before he tasted Leighton with a husky groan. His ass was up, ready for me. I had to do one more thing first.

"Hands, doll."

Leighton presented me her hands, wrists pressed together. I bound them with the rope, forcing them to stay together. She could hold Kiara around the neck, but had limited movement otherwise. Just how I liked her, and how she liked it in return.

Kiara whined, shaking her hips back and forth in a silent plea for more of Mercury's tongue. I chuckled, walking down the couch again so I was behind Mercury.

As a test, I leaned forward over him, my hips pressed to his and my cock in the crease of his ass. He groaned. I shoved him a little more, forcing his face to be buried in Leighton's pussy, but it was perfect.

My lips pressed against the curve of Kiara's ass, my hand slid down and traced her inner thigh. Then my lips followed the path of my hand, before I nipped the perfect spot. "That's where my bondmark is going to go," I murmured.

She peered back over her shoulder, shimmying closer to my mouth. I laughed and shook my head, moving back and letting Mercury pull back enough to breathe. His entire face was wet with Leighton's juices, and he was dazed.

But he definitely didn't have a problem with me pushing him against her and folding over him to reach our omega.

I snagged a bottle of lube from my bag of supplies, drenching my hand in it. Some slicked my cock, while the rest made Mercury's hole shine and eased the push of my fingers inside him.

I had so much to watch as I prepped him, I couldn't blame Dash for his voyeur tendencies. Kiara and Leighton were lip locked, both moaning as Mercury sloppily kissed their pussies. He had a finger plunged into each of them, his weight propped up on one elbow.

Mercury's ass sucked down my fingers, and he didn't need much prep. When three were sliding in and out with ease, I notched my cock against his rim.

He cursed, pushing back.

"Ask me, baby."

His cheeks went pink, vulnerable for a second. This was the first time he'd been like this in front of the rest of the pack. I knew he subbed for Leighton, but their dynamic was different than this.

"Fuck me. Please, Sir."

I purred, pushing my cock an inch into him.

"Good boy."

I used that sole inch to fuck him for a minute, popping it in and out of him. At his frustrated groan, I paused.

"Need something?"

He curled his finger inside Kiara and she moaned, her legs trembling. It was an attempt to distract me, and it honestly almost worked. I smacked Mercury's ass, grabbing his hip. He groaned.

"Fuck me deep, Sir. Properly. Fuck."

My cock slid inside him in one smooth stroke. Mercury's choked moan was the loudest thing in the room. It seared into my brain, his sounds complementing Leighton and Kiara's so fucking well. I could have listened to it for hours, but my cock was already threatening release. Watching Kiara get bonded by my packmates had me more keyed up than I thought.

"Make them come for me, baby," I said.

"Yes, Sir."

He got back to work, but his movements were messy as I fucked him. He forgot to switch back and forth, focusing on Leighton and only fingering Kiara. Her hand came down to touch herself, making up for the lost tongue, and I found I loved that all the more.

We were a train of pleasure, and I hoped none of us were going to last long because I sure fucking wasn't.

I reached one hand around to wrap around Mercury's leaking cock, and my lover choked. His teeth grazed Leighton's clit and she shivered, arching up into the touch.

I was so close I could taste it, but I wanted a bond with my omega before this pleasure burst from the base of my spine.

Shoving Mercury forward, his groan was muffled against Leighton. I bent over him, my tongue gathering up Kiara's slick from where it had dripped down her thighs.

Without warning, I bit her.

Her short scream of pleasure was lost in the chaos of our bond strengthening and her emotions overwhelming me. It was too much for my cock to handle, my movements stopping abruptly as I spilled inside Mercury. I couldn't tell which way was up, let alone whether or not anyone else came.

Only when my head stopped spinning did I register that everyone else was panting in the aftermath too. I dropped my grip on Mercury's cock, his cum all over my hand. Leighton was still kissing Kiara, but lazily.

And Kiara had my mark on her inner thigh, right where I wanted it. Easy to see every time I fucked her or pleasured her in any way.

"You know, people love Broadway shows, but I think that was the greatest show of all time."

Dash's comment broke the satisfied silence, but I barely had enough energy for a half-hearted glare and a laugh. I rained kisses on Kiara's thighs until we were all cramping from the position, and then I cleaned my packmates up.

EPILOGUE 3

LEIGHTON

Having a pack, officially, was surprisingly daunting.

I'd never thought about it seriously before. What it would mean for me. Even since bonding Kiara, I'd mainly been thinking about the pack bond being a benefit to her...

But it was one hell of a benefit to me, too.

I wasn't alone in my head, anymore. I could be. After the initial stumbling blocks with Kiara, I'd discovered how to keep my feelings to myself and keep her out when I wanted to. The Loranger pack was very... open, though. It was hard to block them all out when they seemed to want me to feel their excitement.

"What's one thing you want to do to explore New Oxford?" Dash asked Kiara.

His head was resting on her chest. I was tucked against her other side, with Ambrose beside me and Mercury beside him. The couch had left us all a little sore, so we'd moved into the makeshift nest, with a bed that wasn't really big enough.

"There isn't just one thing," Kiara said, shrugging. "There's lots."

"We should start tomorrow," Dash said.

She nibbled on her bottom lip, her nerves obvious in the bond. All of us could feel it with this new pack connection, and Dash was quick to soothe her. "Or another day. Tomorrow might be best spent consummating the bond a few more times."

I laughed, and so did she. Dash's suggestion got an eye roll out of the other two.

"I should probably go to therapy like Leighton suggested," Kiara admitted softly. "I thought... it would get better. You know? Since Tobias isn't here anymore, and my father can't take me back. But I feel so anxious at the thought of going out and being with normal people. I could say something horribly wrong."

"You're not going to," I said.

"I stabbed Ambrose because I thought it was common to dark bond omegas who were dangerous. I still have to carry around a knife everywhere I go. There are so many things I could do wrong."

"Nyla is more a friend than a knife, at this point."

My attempt to lighten her mood worked.

She raised an eyebrow at me. "As if it's normal to be friends with a knife."

I grinned. "You don't have to be normal to be out in the world, dove. There aren't many normal people, anyway. I can get you an appointment with the therapist, though. He likes to see his patients in person for the first time, but after that you can do video appointments if you'd prefer."

Hesitantly, she nodded. Her head slumped back onto the bed, her arms reaching to each side even though they weren't long enough to touch all of us.

"I love you all," she whispered.

My lips laid a kiss on her skin in response.

I loved this pack more fiercely than I'd thought I could ever love another human being.

I'd spent so much time forcing myself to be alone—half because I was scared of the consequences of love, and half because I didn't know if I was capable of it. I could have ended up like my mother, only able to care about herself and her status.

As it turned out, I wasn't like that at all.

There just wasn't the right time or the right group of people until now.

Since I'd found this pack and this omega, there wasn't a second of any day I would spend lonely again. None of us would be the lonely creatures we were before, and that—more than anything else—gave me a warm feeling in my chest.

"Love you too, dove," I murmured. "I love you all."

The pack goes house hunting! Sign up to my newsletter for weekly bonus content drops starting ~Aug 22/2023.

Want more Marlowe? His pack's story is Pack of Lies!

WHAT'S NEXT IN THE POISONVERSE?

MY NEXT POISONVERSE

Want more from me in the PoisonVerse?

There will be! I'm just not sure yet what I'm writing next, so there's no preorder. Keep an eye on my email newsletter or Facebook group (Olivia Lewin Readers) for updates!

SWEETHEART: A POISONVERSE BULLY DUET

WHAT'S NEXT IN THE POISONVERSE?

What's next in the PoisonVerse? Marie is coming in hot with a bully duet! You can preorder now for a release date of September 8, 2023.

THE POISONVERSE

Havoc Killed Her Alpha - *Marie Mackay*
Forget Me Knot - *Marie Mackay*
Pack of Lies - *Olivia Lewin*
Ruined Alphas - *Amy Nova*
Lonely Alpha - *Olivia Lewin*
Sweetheart Part 1 & 2 - *Marie Mackay*
Shaken Knot Stirred - *Amy Nova*
Novellas and Shorts:

WHAT'S NEXT IN THE POISONVERSE?

His Gold Pack Omega - *Miyo Hunter*
Something Knotty, Something Blue - *Lilith K Duat*

AUTHOR'S NOTE

Y'all, I'm the worst at author's notes.

I always forget to write them, and if I do… I forget who I have to thank. Because there are SO MANY people!!!

This book wouldn't exist without the alpha readers - you are always there to call me out when something doesn't *quite* make sense.

Oh, and my author besties who catch the worst ideas before they even make it onto the page.

And my normal life besties, who always go along with my crazy ideas, like deciding I was just going to become an author.

And the omegaverse community as a whole, because they've welcomed me with open arms. I didn't know there was a whole community behind it at first, but I'm learning, and it's wonderful.

There are so many more people to thank, but we'll leave it at that. You are all the best for reading this book and supporting my work, and I hope you loved Leighton, Kiara, and the guys as much as I do!

Come bug me in my Facebook group if you want to keep up date on all my new works, including my past and current projects in PNR omegaverse and fantasy monster romance <3

ALSO BY OLIVIA LEWIN

FRAYED SERIES

Frayed Trust

Dangerous Heat

Forged Bonds

Spinoff:

In Mated Bliss

HADLEY HOUSE SERIES

Hadley House

Hallowed Convict

POISONVERSE

Pack of Lies

Lonely Alpha

DUSKVERSE

Knot Me Kill Me

ABOUT THE AUTHOR

Olivia Lewin is a Canadian West Coast cat mom who loves all things sex, love, and magic. She spends half her time writing smutty scenes that make her go back and question her own sanity, and the other half of her time reading books with spice.

She can be reached by email at olivia@lewinauthor.com. Whether it's to point out a pesky typo or let her know what you want to see in her next book, she'd love to hear from you!

Or, you can come hang out in her Facebook group (she spends a lot of time interacting there!)

Printed in Poland
by Amazon Fulfillment
Poland Sp. z o.o., Wrocław